PRAISE FO

The Belle of Belgr

"Shiveringly gothic . . . Watching Julia blossom away from prying eyes is almost as satisfying as seeing Jasper Blunt pine for her from nearly the first page. . . . For best effect, save this one for a windy night when trees scrape against the windowpanes."

—*The New York Times Book Review*

"Mimi Matthews never disappoints, with richly drawn characters and couples whose individual shortcomings become strengths, when paired together. In this "Beauty and the Beast" retelling, we get to root for two underdogs who get to rewrite their own stories."

—#1 *New York Times* bestselling author Jodi Picoult

"*The Belle of Belgrave Square* is such tremendous good fun: a heroine with a big horse, an even bigger novel-reading habit, and a hidden anxiety; a hero with a crumbling estate, a trio of wary children, and a literary secret—what's not to love? Mimi Matthews paints Victorian England with vivid humor, and her Belles of London is set to go on for at least a few more much-anticipated installments. Julian Fellowes fans will rejoice!"

—*New York Times* bestselling author Kate Quinn

"Mimi Matthews just doesn't miss. *The Belle of Belgrave Square* is exquisite, a romance that delivers the perfect balance of passion, tension, and tender moments."

—*USA Today* bestselling author Evie Dunmore

"This story unfolds like a rose blooming, growing more and more beautiful as each delicate layer is revealed. A tender, luminous romance. I loved it more and more with every chapter!"

—*USA Today* bestselling author Caroline Linden

"Absolutely enthralling: an endearing, novel-reading heroine who's in dire danger; a swoonworthy war hero with a scandalous past; and secrets, lots of secrets. Mimi Matthews's *The Belle of Belgrave Square* is a thrilling, emotion-packed read from start to finish. I loved it!"

—*USA Today* bestselling author Syrie James

"Combines deception, risk, and a resourceful heroine to create an intoxicating, suspenseful romance. Highly recommended."

—*Library Journal* (starred review)

"A grand cross-class romance, a twisty mystery, and emotional internal struggles combine to excellent effect. . . . Fans and new readers alike will root for this well-earned love story."

—*Publishers Weekly* (starred review)

PRAISE FOR
The Siren of Sussex

"What I love about Mimi Matthews is that in the crowded field of historical romance, she always finds new and interesting slants for her plots and characters. That, along with her wonderful writing and meticulous research, makes every book she puts out a rare treat to enjoy and savor. Highly recommended!"

—*New York Times* bestselling author Kate Pearce

"Unflinching, tender, and moving, the delicately crafted *The Siren of Sussex* might just be my favorite work from Mimi Matthews; it certainly is one of my favorite historical romance reads this year."

—*USA Today* bestselling author Evie Dunmore

"Lush, seductive, original—*The Siren of Sussex* drew me in from the first page and wove its magic. A fresh, vibrant, brilliant Victorian romance, making it an unforgettable read."

—*New York Times* bestselling author Jane Porter

"A moving love story and a vivid re-creation of Victorian life, *The Siren of Sussex* by Mimi Matthews is a treat of a book for the historical romance lover." —Award-winning author Anna Campbell

"Impeccably researched, brimming with passion and chemistry, and a loving tribute to Victorian fashion and horsemanship, *The Siren of Sussex* is a page-turning, powerful, and endearing love story about two people rising above the pressures of society to follow their hearts. A five-star fantastic read!"

—*USA Today* bestselling author Syrie James

"A tender and swoonworthy interracial, cross-class romance in Victorian London . . . Readers will delight in this paean to women's fashion and horseback riding." —*Publishers Weekly* (starred review)

"An exquisite historical romance that is so captivating I had to force myself not to gallop through it at breakneck speed, wanting to savor the author's obvious care and delicate attention to detail. . . . A must-read for lovers of historical fiction."

—Meg Tilly, author of *The Runaway Heiress*

"The best book I've read in a long time: gorgeously written, thoughtfully considered, swoonily romantic, and unafraid to examine issues of class, race, and gender."

—National bestselling author Olivia Dade

"Readers have learned to expect absorbing dramas from Mimi Matthews, and her latest—in which a strong and intelligent woman finds a way to save her family's fortunes while following her own heart—is no exception. Any reader who has ever loved horses, high fashion, and brooding protagonists will fall hard for *The Siren of Sussex.* I savored it to the final page."

—Stephanie Barron, author of *That Churchill Woman*

Also by Mimi Matthews

BELLES OF LONDON NOVELS

The Siren of Sussex
The Belle of Belgrave Square

The Lily of Ludgate Hill

MIMI MATTHEWS

BERKLEY ROMANCE
New York

BERKLEY ROMANCE
Published by Berkley
An imprint of Penguin Random House LLC
penguinrandomhouse.com

Library of Congress Cataloging-in-Publication Data

Names: Matthews, Mimi, author.
Title: The lily of Ludgate Hill / Mimi Matthews.
Description: First Edition. | New York: Berkley Romance, 2024. | Series: Belles of London
Identifiers: LCCN 2023016606 | ISBN 9780593337189 (trade paperback) |
ISBN 9780593337196 (ebook)
Subjects: LCGFT: Romance fiction. | Novels.
Classification: LCC PS3613.A8493 L55 2024 | DDC 813/.6—dc23/eng/20230414
LC record available at https://lccn.loc.gov/2023016606

First Edition: January 2024

Printed in the United States of America
1st Printing

Book design by Daniel Brount

For my mother, Vickie,
a fierce friend, a formidable ally, and a continuous inspiration

The plant was raised from seeds sent by Major Madden some five or six years ago; but it has only now for the first time blossomed. . . .

—*The Botanical Magazine* on the giant Himalayan lily, 1852

The Lily of Ludgate Hill

One

London, England
June 1862

Lady Anne Deveril flattered herself that she had many outstanding qualities. Chief among them was her willingness to do anything for a friend. And Julia Wychwood was her best friend in the whole world. She had been thus ever since the pair of them had endured a first season together; two unwilling wallflowers—one in unrelieved black and one in overflounced blue—left to languish, unadmired, at the back of every fashionable ball, society musicale, and amateur theatrical on offer.

One disappointing season had followed another in rapid succession. Three altogether. It had only served to strengthen the bond Anne and Julia shared. No longer wallflowers, they were comrades-in-arms. Fellow horsewomen. Sisters.

Yes, for Julia, Anne would do anything, even face the devil himself.

Tucking her folded copy of the *Spiritualist Herald* morc firmly under her arm, she marched up the freshly swept stone steps of the Earl of March's stately town house in Arlington Street and firmly applied the brass knocker to the painted door.

Lord March was no devil, but he was currently housing one.

The door was promptly opened by a young footman.

"Good morning," Anne said briskly. "Be so good as to inform his lordship that Lady Anne Deveril is here to see him."

The footman didn't question her identity. Indeed, he appeared to recognize her. And why not? She was herself an earl's daughter, and one of some notoriety thanks to the conduct of her famously eccentric mother. A widowed countess couldn't garb herself entirely in black for years on end, traipsing about the city to consort with crystal gazers and mediums, without drawing some degree of attention to herself. Anne had long accepted that she must bear some guilt by association.

"Yes, my lady." The footman stepped back for her to enter. "If you would care to wait in the library, I shall see if his lordship is at home."

Of course he was at home; in his greenhouse, no doubt. Anne had little intention of actually seeing the man. She nevertheless permitted the footman to show her into the earl's spacious library while he trotted off to find his elderly master.

The twin fragrances of pipe smoke and parchment met her nose. Lemon polish, too, though there was no sign that the maids had done any recent tidying up. The library was a place of spectacular clutter.

Bookcases lined three of the walls; leather-bound volumes on botany, agriculture, and natural history were pulled out at all angles as if an absent-minded researcher had wandered from shelf to shelf withdrawing tomes at random only to change his mind midway through extracting them.

The fourth wall was entirely covered in framed sketches of flowers and greenery. Some images were produced in pencil and others in delicately rendered watercolor. They were—along with the teetering stacks of botanical journals and drooping maps that spilled over the sides of the earl's carved mahogany desk—evidence of his prevailing passion.

Lord March's love of exotic plants was legendary. He'd spent much of his life traveling the globe, from the wilds of America to the highest peaks of the Himalayas, bringing back rare seeds to nurture into bloom.

A distracted fellow at the best of times, but a kind one, too, as far as Anne recalled. It had been a long time since she'd darkened his doorstep. A lifetime, it felt like.

She tugged restlessly at her black kid-leather gloves as she paced the worn carpet in front of the library's cavernous marble fireplace. She'd never excelled at waiting for unpleasantness to arrive.

Fortunately, she didn't have to wait long.

"Hello, old thing." A familiar deep voice sounded from the library door.

Anne spun around, her traitorous heart giving an involuntary leap in her breast.

Mr. Felix Hartford stood in the entryway, one shoulder propped against the doorframe. Lord only knew how long he'd been observing her.

She stiffened. After all these years, he still had the power to discompose her. Drat him. But she wouldn't permit her emotions to be thrown into chaos by his attractive face and figure. What cared she for his commanding height? His square-chiseled jaw? For the devilish glint in his sky-blue eyes?

And devil he was. The very one she'd come here to see.

"Hartford," she said. Her chin ticked up a notch in challenge. It was a reflex. There was no occasion on which they'd met during the course of the past several years that they hadn't engaged in verbal battle.

This time, however, he made no attempt to engage her.

He was dressed in plaid trousers and a loose-fitting black sack coat worn open to reveal the dark waistcoat beneath. A casual ensemble, made more so by the state of him. His clothes were vaguely rumpled, and so was his seal-brown hair. It fell over his brow, desperately in need of an application of pomade.

There was an air of arrested preoccupation about him, as if he'd just returned from somewhere or was on his way to somewhere. As if he hadn't realized she was in the library and had come upon her quite by chance.

An unnatural silence stretched between them, void of their typical barb-filled banter.

Greetings dispensed with, Anne found herself at an unaccountable loss. More surprising still, so did Hartford.

He remained frozen on the threshold, his usually humorous expression turned to stone on his handsome face.

At length, he managed a smile. "I knew one day you'd walk through my door again. It only took you"—withdrawing his pocket watch from his waistcoat, he cast it a brief glance, brows lifting as if in astonishment at the time—"seven years to do it."

She huffed. "It hasn't been seven years."

"Six and a half, then."

Six years and five months, more like.

It had been early December of 1855, during the Earl of March's holiday party. She'd been just shy of seventeen; young and naive and not formally out yet. Hartford had kissed her under a sprig of mistletoe in the gaslit servants' hallway outside the kitchens.

And he'd proposed to her.

But Anne refused to think of the past. Never mind that, living in London, reminders of it were daily shoved under her nose. "You're not going to be difficult, are you?" she asked.

"That depends." He strolled into the room. "To what do I owe your visit?"

"Presumptuous, as always," she said. "For all you know, I'm here to see your grandfather."

Hartford was the only child of the Earl of March's second son—the late (and much lamented) moralist Everett Hartford. Anne well remembered the man. He'd been as strait-laced and starchy as a vicar. Rather ironic, really, given his son's reputation for recklessness and irreverence.

"My grandfather is in his greenhouse," Hartford said, "elbow-deep in chicken manure. If it's him you've come to speak with, you're in for a long wait."

She suppressed a grimace. There was no need for him to be crass. "Really, Hartford."

"Really, my lady." He advanced into the room slowly, his genial expression doing little to mask the fact that he was a great towering male bearing down on her. "Why have you come?"

Anne held her ground. She wasn't afraid of him. "I've come to ask a favor of you."

His mouth curled up at one corner. "Better and better." He gestured to a stuffed settee upholstered in Gobelins tapestry. "Pray sit down."

She nimbly sidestepped him to sink down on the cushioned seat. The skirts of her black carriage gown brushed his leg as she passed, silk bombazine sliding against fine wool in an audible caress of expensive fabric.

Her pulse thrummed in her throat.

She daren't look at him, instead focusing on the business at hand with renewed vigor. Withdrawing her copy of the *Spiritualist Herald* from beneath her arm, she smoothed the wrinkled pages out onto her lap.

He remained standing by the fireplace. "What do you have there?"

"First things first." She forced her gaze to meet his. "You've doubtless heard of Captain Blunt's abduction of Miss Wychwood?"

His brow creased. "Abduction? That's quite a charge."

"Do you dispute it?"

"I haven't enough of the facts to do so. Still—"

"Allow me to enlighten you." She sat rigidly on the settee, the dire facts of her friend's unfortunate situation putting steel in her spine. "Captain Blunt, an ex-soldier of dubious fame, has spirited away a vulnerable heiress and married her against the advice of her friends and her family, possibly against her own will. If that's not a crime—"

"He's a war hero," Hartford said, as if that excused everything.

"He's a villain," Anne countered. "He stole her from her sickbed. Did you know that? Quite literally carried her away from her parents' house in Belgrave Square and conveyed her to his haunted estate in the wilds of Yorkshire, just like some rogue in a penny novel."

"Miss Wychwood's circumstances were far from ideal. And I'm a little acquainted with Blunt. Granted, he's somewhat rough around the edges, but she had no objection to him, not on the few occasions I saw them together. Given that, your conclusions are hasty at best."

"I don't require you to validate them. Miss Wychwood is *my* friend, not yours. It's my duty to see that she's all right. I won't rest until I can assure myself of the fact."

A shadow of irritation ghosted over his usually humorous countenance.

Anne had observed the expression before. "You don't approve of my friends."

"As ever, you presume to read my mind."

"I'm not reading your mind. I'm reading your face. And anyway, it doesn't matter. I don't care what you think of my friends."

Hartford's jaw tightened imperceptibly. "Shall I tell you what I think?" He didn't wait for her to answer. "You use your friends as a shield."

She scoffed. "I most certainly don't."

"You travel with them in a pack—a pack that grows with every passing season."

She opened her mouth to object, but Hartford plowed on, unconcerned with her protestations.

"First there was only Miss Wychwood," he said. "Then there was Miss Hobhouse. And now Miss Maltravers." His smile turned wry. "The Four Horsewomen."

"Yes, yes, it's quite diverting, I'm sure." *To someone with a pea brain*, she added silently.

Four Horsewomen indeed.

Though Anne supposed it was preferable to the tired epithet he'd previously used. Until Miss Maltravers had arrived in London, Hartford had been calling Anne and her friends the three Furies.

"Not diverting," he said. "Merely interesting. I wonder why you need their protection."

Her chin went up another notch. "I'm here, aren't I? Unescorted. Unprotected."

She hadn't had much choice in the matter.

Julia was somewhere in Yorkshire, a prisoner of the evil Captain Blunt. Evelyn Maltravers was in Sussex awaiting the arrival of her beau, Mr. Malik. And Stella Hobhouse—dear Stella!—was presently cloistered with her dour clergyman brother in George's Street. Newly returned from accompanying him to an ecumenical conference in Exeter, she'd been tasked with transcribing his mountain of notes.

Not that Stella would have understood Anne's reasons for calling at the Earl of March's residence. When it came to Felix Hartford, Anne preferred to hold her secrets close. Nothing good could come of sharing them, not even with her dearest friends.

"Unwise of you," Hartford said. "You should have at least brought a maid."

"To visit an aged family friend? Your grandfather is no threat to my reputation. That's why I asked for him."

"In hopes that I'd show up eventually?"

"You always do where I'm concerned." The words were tantamount to an accusation. Anne's stomach trembled a little to say them aloud.

His smile faded. "What do you want of me, my lady?"

"What I want," she said, "is for you to write something very particular in the next column you publish in the *Spiritualist Herald*."

He stilled. A look of uncommon alertness flickered at the back of his eyes. "I don't have a column in the *Spiritualist Herald*."

"Nonsense," she said. "Of course you do. You have columns in several publications. The *Spiritualist Herald*, the *Weekly Heliosphere*, *Glendale's Botanical Bi-Monthly*. I could go on."

"You're mistaken."

"I'm not. You're Mr. Drinkwater, aren't you? And Mr. Bilgewater, and Mr. Tidewater. You know, you really should diversify your pseudonyms—*and* your turn of phrase. It's recognizable to anyone who knows you."

His gaze sharpened, holding hers with an air of unmistakable challenge. "And you know me, do you?"

"Regrettably," she said, "I do."

It took a great deal to shake Hart's good-humored equanimity. He prided himself on his ability to see the absurd in every situation. No matter if it hurt him. No matter if it broke his heart.

But today was no ordinary day.

He'd been up since before dawn broke, attending to yet another remnant of his late father's distasteful legacy. An unknown legacy as far as society was aware. Hart wished he might have been spared the knowledge of it as well.

There had been no chance of that.

His own mother had unloaded the burden onto his shoulders, confessing every sordid detail from her deathbed nine years ago. Hart had been only twenty at the time, poorly equipped to face the reality his mother's dying words had wrought.

Lack of readiness hadn't alleviated his responsibilities.

His father had left him scant money or property. Only a small sum in the three percents and a remote, ramshackle estate in Somersetshire that cost more in repairs than it ever generated in income. But what Everett Hartford's legacy lacked in material concerns it had more than made up for in hidden scandal.

Hart had begun to view his father's secret life as the many-headed Hydra of mythology. Nothing was ever fully resolved. Just when he'd lopped off one of the sea serpent's poisonous heads, two more grew in its place. He was tired of it and, after this morning's events, quite tempted to wash his hands of the business once and for all.

And now this.

Her.

Lady Anne Deveril was the last person he wanted to see at the moment. And, rather paradoxically, the person his heart most yearned to speak with.

But not about his family's past.

And not about *her* family's, either. It was a past her mother seemed to cling to with increasing determination. Anne clung to it, too, in her way, a willing victim to Lady Arundell's obsession with the dead.

As usual, she was clad in lusterless black bombazine. An aggravating sight, though her mourning gown was one of impeccable cut. It molded to her delicate frame, the tightly fitted bodice, with its long row of dainty jet buttons, emphasizing her narrow waist and the lush curve of her bosom. Full skirts swelled over her hips in a voluminous sweep of fabric that made the most sensuous sound, rustling over her layers of petticoats and crinoline, when she moved.

He felt it as much as heard it, tickling his senses and thrumming in his blood.

Thank heaven she'd agreed to sit.

A seated Lady Anne was far easier to deal with than an Anne in motion. And she was almost always in motion, whether striding about in her mother's wake or galloping down Rotten Row in company with her bluestocking friends. Mounted Amazons, all—and just as formidable.

He chose his next words with care. "Whatever it is you think you know—"

"What I know," she said in the lemon-tart tones of a British schoolmistress, "is that you never met a frivolity you didn't like. These columns you write are another of your childish diversions, clearly. I'm not here to judge."

"No?"

"I'm here to make use of you." She tapped one kid-gloved finger on the cover of the printed journal on her lap. "All you need do is say something of a spiritualist nature about this house of Blunt's in Yorkshire."

"Is that all?"

"Yes."

"And what am I to say?" He paused, adding, "If I *am* this Drinkwater fellow you claim."

She was, unsurprisingly, prepared with an answer. "There's no need to reinvent the wheel. Blunt's estate is already rumored to be haunted. You need merely expound on the fact with an emphasis on immediacy. You might say, 'The veil between worlds is closing soon' and that 'all practitioners of a serious bent should journey north to take advantage of it.' I'll do the rest."

His mouth quirked briefly. She was so assured of her plan. So all-fired determined. It was one of the things he used to admire most about her, this unwavering confidence she had in herself. "Have it all worked out, do you?"

"Naturally." She moved to rise. "All that's required is for you to do your part. I'll do the rest."

"Manage your mother?" His amusement at the situation flickered out as quickly as it had arisen, extinguished by half a decade of bitterness. "Forgive me if I take leave to doubt your capabilities on that score."

She fixed him with a withering look as she stood, brown eyes sparkling with flecks of gold, like strong spirits ignited by fire.

It brought to mind the game of snapdragon they'd played six and a half years ago, here in this very house, at a Christmas party hosted by his grandfather before he and Hart had left on their 1856 expedition to India. Brandy-soaked raisins and nuts had been set aflame on a silver plate. The young people in attendance had taken turns snatching the sweet treats from the fire.

Anne had been fearless, of course. Heedless of being burned.

And she *had* been burned.

Hartford had caught hold of her scorched fingers a split second after the flames had singed them. He'd drawn her away from the game, taking her down to the kitchens so that Cook could soothe Anne's burns with cold butter from the larder.

It was as they were leaving the kitchens that it had happened.

The two of them, alone in the servants' hallway, the light from a gas wall sconce shimmering in the threads of Anne's fair hair. Like spun gold it had been, swept back in a glittering net. He'd felt the silken strands with his fingers as he'd tipped her face to kiss her under the mistletoe. Her voluptuous mouth had trembled beneath his. He'd trembled, too.

"I've been wanting to do that all night," he'd said, rather unsteadily.

There was no use pretending. They both remembered it. And not only that kiss, but everything that had come after it.

Would that he could forget!

"You may say what you like," she said, "so long as you do what I ask of you."

He leaned back against the mantelpiece, folding his arms. "Why should I exert myself?"

"*Why?*" she echoed, her temper visibly rising. "For novelty, if for no other reason. Lord knows you've done nothing honorable or responsible in your life."

His temper briefly flared to match hers, the harsh scrape of suppressed resentment deepening his voice. "You know nothing of my responsibilities."

"I know that you live only to find amusement for yourself. Is it too much to hope that you might, for once, do something useful? Something that might help another person besides yourself?"

"Help you, you mean."

"It's not helping me. It's helping Miss Wychwood. Whatever you may think of me, she's done nothing to earn your hatred. She's a sweet and gentle soul who might even now be in the utmost peril. If you—"

"I don't hate you," he said gruffly.

She broke off. "I beg your pardon?"

"I said that I don't hate you. I've never hated you."

"Well . . ." A rare expression of vulnerability stole over her face. She masked it instantly, bending her head as she smoothed her gloves. "In that case, you won't mind doing what I ask."

"Would that it were so simple."

"It's not difficult, surely. I can write the column myself if necessary. All you need do is see that it's published as soon as possible."

"Writing it isn't the difficult part."

She gave him a suspicious look. "Then what?"

"I told you. I'm reluctant to exert myself."

"Hartford—"

"I see little incentive to do so." He managed a thin smile. "As you so rightly pointed out, I'm a selfish ne'er-do-well who thinks only of myself."

"I didn't—"

"Now," he said, "if there was something in it for me . . ."

The last vestige of Anne's self-restraint crumbled in spectacular fashion. Her countenance hardened to marble, and her hands dropped to clench at her sides, crumpling the pages of the *Spiritualist Herald* in her fist. She bore down on him like one of the mythical Furies he'd so often accused her of being. "Why, you arrogant, blackmailing rogue!"

His heartbeat quickened as she approached. Anne in a rage was a thrilling sight to behold. "It's not blackmail," he said. "It's an exchange. Something you want for something I want."

"And just what *do* you want?"

The idea struck him all at once—a lightning flash of genius. Or possibly madness. Tomorrow he'd likely regret the raw honesty of his words, but in this moment they seemed right. They *felt* right.

"I want you," he said.

She stopped mid-stride. Her mouth fell open. "*Me?*"

"You," he said. "And not like this. Not here in London, dressed in black, like some wraith at a funeral feast. I want you in Hampshire. And I want you in color. Red, preferably."

She looked appalled by the suggestion. "I am *not* wearing red. Besides, what on earth is in Hampshire?" Understanding darkened her gaze. "You can't mean Sutton Park?"

Sutton Park was the seat of the earldom of March. Hartford descendants had been living there for centuries. Hart's grandfather hadn't been the best custodian of the place during his tenure as earl. He preferred traveling the globe to languishing in the English countryside looking after his estates. Still, the great house occasionally served a purpose.

"Grandfather's hosting a house party for the holidays. Gentlemen naturalists, mostly. A few tradesmen, too, I believe. Perfumers and the like. He plans to give them some of his newest strain of roses."

Her eyes locked with his. "You're talking about a Christmas party."

Another Christmas party, she might have said.

"So what if I am?" he asked. "Is Miss Wychwood not worth the sacrifice?"

"My friends are worth anything," she retorted.

"Then you know what you must do."

Anne glowered. Folding her arms, she paced the length of the room, skirts twitching as she walked. She looked rather magnificent.

"There'll be other ladies there," he offered helpfully. "I expect my aunt will have a whole contingent of eligible young misses to throw at my head. Perhaps you can help me choose one?"

She shot him a sour glance.

"It's high time I married. A fellow wouldn't want to end his days gathering dust on the shelf."

He was pushing his luck, and he knew it. Nettling her past all bearing. It had become a habit in his dealings with Anne. Anything to get a reaction from her. To rouse her from this infuriating role she'd chosen for herself as a mute, obedient, unquestioning shadow to her overbearing mother.

An angry Anne was preferable to one that was fading to nothing before his eyes. Slipping further away with every passing season.

Though why he should care anymore, he didn't know.

"You could bring your horse," he offered. "Spend the whole week riding if you like."

"My mother would never permit me to go away for so long without her chaperonage."

"Then bring her with you, by all means."

Her brows lowered in a scowl. "So long as I don't wear black?"

He shrugged. "A small price to pay."

Her skirts swished about her legs as she paced back to the fireplace. "December is a long way away. A great deal could happen between now and then."

"It could," he conceded. "Regardless, if I do as you ask—if I write this drivel to persuade your mother to travel to Yorkshire—I'd expect you to hold up your side of the agreement, no matter what the intervening months might bring."

Anne came to a halt in front of him, her elegant features set with a sudden resolve. It was the look of a lady willing to endure the bitterest of medicines in order to effect a cure. "Very well," she said at last. "You have yourself a bargain."

Two

Anne returned home as though the hounds of hell were behind her, snapping their demonic teeth at the wheels of the Arundell carriage all the way from Arlington Street back to Grosvenor Square. *I have made a deal with the devil*, she thought grimly.

Pray God it would be worth it.

"It will be," she muttered to herself as Horbury, the family's aged butler, admitted her into the marble-tiled entry hall.

If she could just get to Yorkshire. If she could just assure herself that Julia was free from danger. It didn't matter how steep the price of the bargain. For her friend, Anne was willing to pay anything.

"Your mother has been asking after you, my lady," Horbury said, taking Anne's bonnet and gloves. "She awaits you in her chamber."

Anne failed to stifle a wince. She'd hoped her mother might still be asleep. Except for when riding her beloved horse, Saffron, Anne was rarely permitted to venture out alone. Mama preferred to keep her close. To control her every behavior.

Many in society wrongly presumed this to be a manner of bullying. Another sign of Lady Arundell's notoriously domineering personality.

It wasn't the case at all.

As if Anne would permit herself to be so diminished!

The fact was, Mama wanted to protect her. She believed, however wrongheadedly, that every moment Anne was out of her control was a moment fraught with risk. She'd have preserved Anne in aspic if she could.

"Has she been up long?" Anne asked.

"Half an hour," Horbury said. "The maid's just taken up her tray with the morning post."

Anne sighed. Smoothing her skirts, she ascended the stairs to the second floor.

Mama always breakfasted in her room. It was a privilege denied to her unwed daughter. Only married ladies were allowed to linger in their beds in the morning. Anne suspected it had something to do with the belief that married women must be tired out from the amorous activities of the night before. A scandalous notion, really, if one took the time to think about it.

She rapped softly at her mother's door before entering.

The heavy draperies of Mama's four-poster bed were drawn back to reveal her sitting up against a plump pile of feather pillows. A striking dark-haired woman, with a slight double chin and a formidable bosom, she was a lady whom the society pages frequently referred to as a force to be reckoned with.

Anne couldn't disagree with their assessment. Even situated in bed, wearing a ruffled white cambric wrapper and lace-trimmed India muslin morning cap, her mother managed to look like an empress. Catherine the Great, perhaps.

"Anne," she said. "At last." A breakfast tray was arrayed over her lap, steam swirling from the spout of a porcelain teapot. Her usual morning meal of two hard-boiled eggs and a single piece of bone-dry toast remained on the tray uneaten as she perused her correspondence.

There was no sugar bowl or jam pot in evidence. There never was. Mama believed sweets were ruinous to a lady's teeth and figure. Indeed, in their household, the prohibition of sugary substances was tantamount to settled law. It was a law Anne abided by herself on occasion, but only as a show of solidarity when in company with her mother. She loved sweets too much to disavow them completely.

"Where have you been?" Mama asked.

Anne made no effort to conjure a falsehood. There was no point in doing so. Her mother could easily find her out. "I called on Lord March in Arlington Street."

Mama flashed her a sharp look. "The Earl of March? At this hour?"

Anne crossed the room to her mother's bed. "I had the uncanny notion that I had better do so. It's been too long since we've seen him."

Mama didn't argue with the explanation. To her, so often guided by signs and symbols, an uncanny notion was as persuasive a reason as any to call on a person. "Had a dream, did you?" she asked with a knowing frown. "Sensed he was ill or otherwise on his last legs?"

"Something like that."

"And was he?"

"Was he what?"

"Ill?"

"I don't believe so." Anne absently straightened the edge of her mother's embroidered coverlet. "I didn't see him. He was busy working in his greenhouse."

"Naturally he was. He rarely receives in the mornings. Had you consulted me, I could have told you so and spared you a fruitless journey." Mama returned to perusing her letters.

"Horbury said you wished to see me?" Anne reminded her.

"Ah yes." Mama riffled through the already opened envelopes on the side of her tray. She withdrew a letter from one of them. "This came with the early post," she said, passing the single sheet of expensive stationery to Anne. "What do you make of it?"

"Who is it from?"

"The Earl of Arundell."

Anne blanched. "*Papa?*"

"Not your father, girl. It's from the new earl. That second cousin of yours, Joshua Deveril. He's signed it at any rate, though I have no doubt it was the pup's mother who dictated this piece of impertinence." Mama waved her hand. "Read it."

Anne's gaze dropped to the letter—if it could be called such. It contained no more than a few brief lines penned in a cramped but elegant hand.

My Dear Lady,

Having lately returned from a short tour of Europe, it is my fervent ambition to settle in London. Though it has so far pleased me to allow you to remain in Grosvenor Square, I am keen to assume my duties as earl and to take my proper place in society—and in my home.

My mother will accompany me to town on the fifth of August. I look forward to meeting you to discuss arrangements for your future comfort.

I am, your most obedient,
Arundell

Anne slowly lowered the page, the beginnings of a knot forming in her stomach. She wasn't prone to nervousness or anxiety. Not typically. But if Joshua was in earnest, the situation warranted worry. "He means to come to London? To evict us from our home?"

"So he threatens." Mama extended her hand for the letter.

Anne returned it, amazed by her mother's air of unconcern. "What do you intend to do about it?"

"Precisely nothing." Mama tossed the letter to the side of her tray. She selected another envelope from the small stack of correspondence remaining, breaking open its seal with a mother-of-pearl letter opener. "The impudent creature hasn't bestirred himself in six years. I see no reason to believe he would do so now."

Anne wasn't as confident as her mother.

If Joshua hadn't bestirred himself in the past, it was owing purely to his minority. On inheriting the title, he'd been too young to come to town. Instead, he and his odious mother—a grasping individual with little claim to birth or fashionable connection—had taken up residence at Cherry Hill, the family seat in Shropshire.

As if that hadn't been enough of a blow.

Anne had been born at Cherry Hill and had spent most of her youth there. An idyllic girlhood by any measure.

Of course, it had been.

She was the product of a noted love match. A cherished only child raised by parents who were singularly devoted to each other.

Yes, Mama and Papa had been wondrously happy. Anne had been happy, too, until Papa had taken ill. A weakness of the heart, the local doctor had called it.

Mama had had no faith in the man's diagnosis.

Under her direction, they'd brought Papa to London, situating him in their town house in Grosvenor Square—one of the many lavish properties belonging to the earldom. In London, Papa could be close to the finest physicians in the country. He could receive the best treatment.

And there had been countless treatments, one after the other. Everything the medical men recommended, regardless of invasiveness or expense. It had all been endured by Papa—and by Anne and her mother—in the earnest belief that he would eventually regain his strength. That he would soon get well.

He hadn't done.

His condition had only worsened with time, leaving him so weak he was eventually confined to his sickbed.

Anne had refused to give up on him. It had seemed unthinkable that Papa's heart, which had been bigger and more generous than anyone's, should ultimately be his undoing. To the last, she'd been confident he would recover. He'd still had good days on occasion. Lucid days when she could sit with him and talk with him. She'd been waiting for one of them so she might seek his counsel on the subject of Hartford's proposal.

She never got the chance.

Less than two days after the Earl of March's Christmas party, Papa had died in his sleep.

The Earldom of Arundell, and everything that came with it, had passed to Joshua. Not only Cherry Hill and their town house in Grosvenor Square, but all of the family wealth and properties. Even Papa's name. Joshua *was* Arundell now.

If not for Mama's jointure—a generous sum Papa had set by for her on their marriage—Anne and her mother would be all but destitute. Neither of them could rely on Joshua's uncertain generosity. Since ascending to the title, he'd offered them no support at all.

"We can't judge his future actions by what he's done in the past," Anne said. "He was just a boy when Papa died."

"He's still a boy."

"Indeed, he isn't. He must be at least one-and-twenty. If he and his mother demand we vacate the premises, what are we to—"

"*Precisely nothing*," Mama repeated in a voice of implacable calm. "Had we anything to concern ourselves with on that score, Dmitri would have warned me of it."

Anne's lips compressed.

Dmitri was the name of Mama's familiar spirit, an imaginary entity that communicated with her alone. Such creatures were a fashionable affectation in the spiritualist world. Anne loathed the very mention of him, not least because his otherworldly pronouncements (which all too frequently aligned with Mama's opinions) spelled the end to any argument.

"Dmitri isn't infallible," Anne said.

Mama refused to entertain the possibility. "His understanding can't be disputed. He sees things we do not. It's the nature of his existence beyond the veil." She perused her next letter, the threatening missive from the new Earl of Arundell seemingly forgotten. "How vexing," she muttered. "Fielding advises me not to call on him this week. He's taken ill and fears he might be contagious."

Mr. Harris Fielding was an eccentric elderly bachelor residing in Russell Square. A devoted spiritualist and collector of antiquities, he was one of Mama's closest friends in town. He was also Evelyn Maltravers's uncle.

Anne glanced at his letter with immediate concern. "I trust it isn't anything serious?"

"A putrid throat," Mama said. "No doubt he contracted it during our journey to the West Midlands."

Mr. Fielding had recently accompanied Anne and her mother on a brief trip to Birmingham. Evelyn had gone with them. Stella had been away from London at the time as well, in Exeter with her brother. Only Julia had remained in town. She'd been all alone, without the protection of her friends. It was then Captain Blunt had chosen to strike.

Anne felt herself partially to blame. If she'd been here, Julia might even now be safe from harm. "How unfortunate," she said.

"Exceedingly unfortunate. We were to attend Mrs. Frazil's lecture on the planchette this Thursday in Fitzroy Square."

Anne refrained from remarking on the questionable value of such an event. She'd long ago learned that the busier her mother kept herself with her spiritualist endeavors, her social engagements, and the charity school she sponsored in Wimbledon, the less time she had to sink into black despair.

It seemed a fair exchange to Anne's mind.

When it came to it, she was as protective of her mother's health and happiness as her mother was of her. It wasn't in Anne's nature to be otherwise. She'd do anything—sacrifice anything—to keep those she loved from coming to grief.

"No matter." Mama cast the letter aside. She poured herself a cup of strong Assam tea, her preferred drink of a morning. "You and I shall attend. It will take your mind off this business with your little friend."

Anne bristled at the description. "My *little friend* may even now be in the utmost danger. If we could but travel to Yorkshire and see for ourselves—"

"Impossible," Mama said. "I've an entire week of engagements penned in my diary. I won't alter my schedule because of some foolish girl's ill-advised elopement. My commitment to the spiritualist cause must always come first."

What about my commitments? Anne wanted to ask. But she didn't say anything. She bit her tongue, just as she always did in these situations.

She made it a rule never to argue with her mother. Never to challenge her or to throw their relationship into turmoil. Better to be quiet and strategic. To get what she wanted by other means.

And she hoped she would, if everything with Hartford's ridiculous column went according to plan.

Nevertheless . . .

She couldn't shake the feeling that she'd miscalculated somehow by involving her old adversary.

He wanted her in Hampshire.

He wanted her in red.

December was many months away, it was true. But it would be here eventually, and she'd be obliged to honor their cursed agreement, regardless of the danger to her reputation, her conscience, perhaps even her heart.

Located on the outskirts of fashionable London, the Neales' modest little house was situated in a respectable but otherwise undistinguished neighborhood, in an equally undistinguished street, not far from the Battersea crucible manufactory in which Hart was a silent partner. A fitting location, given that most of his earnings from that venture went directly into the Neales' pockets.

Hart stood at the parlor window, hands clasped at his back.

This was the second morning in a row he'd been summoned here. He was hard-pressed to maintain his good humor. Indeed, lately it seemed a herculean task—keeping up his smile, keeping up appearances, stopping himself from simply saying to hell with it all.

He had the unsettling premonition that someday, possibly quite soon, he was going to lose his composure in spectacular fashion.

God help whoever was with him when it happened.

"How can I make it plainer, sir?" Mrs. Neale asked from her wingback chair near the fire. Her black hair was arranged in a youthful style, the matron's cap on her head her only concession to age. "We require more than the scraps you've been content to feed us on these nine years. We're not church mice to exist in such conditions."

"Mother," her daughter Ethel said under her breath. At seventeen, she was the second eldest of the Neale children. She sat, along with her fifteen-year-old younger sister, on a chintz sofa across from her mother.

"Why shouldn't I demand more?" Mrs. Neale asked. "It's mine by rights. You were the children of your father's heart. He wouldn't wish you to starve in the streets."

Hart resisted the urge to point out that his late father, the Honorable Everett Hartford, had made his wishes abundantly plain. On his death, neither his mistress nor the three children he'd sired on her had been provided for in his will.

It wasn't until nearly a year later that Hart had learned of their existence—a parting gift from his embittered dying mother.

"She was my lady's maid," she'd said between the rattling coughs that had shaken her frame. "My own servant!"

Hart had listened to the whole of the story, and then—much to his mother's dismay—he'd laughed. It had been an odd, hollow sound, devoid of his usual humor, but a laugh nonetheless. The truth of his father's betrayal was quite comical, really, in a pathetic sort of way.

But there was nothing humorous about the possibility of Hart's grandfather finding out. Immersed as he was in all things botanical, the Earl of March still had a care for his good name. Not only for his own sake, but for the sake of his heir, Hart's uncle, Viscount Brookdale.

Brookdale was one of the leaders of the opposition party in Her Majesty's government. A staunch conservative with aspirations to higher office, he wouldn't take kindly to his political career being scuttled by a family scandal.

Hart was doing his damnedest to prevent one.

He paid Mrs. Neale a handsome allowance out of his own pocket. Made extra funds available to her in times of trouble. He even called on her when needed, though his visits were necessarily restricted to the early morning hours, when he was less likely to be observed.

"It's as I always say," Mrs. Neale railed on. "We wouldn't have half the worries we do if Marcus had the means to live like a gentleman. Now he's home again, you can't expect him to continue going without."

Marcus was Mrs. Neale's oldest child and only son. A boy of nineteen, he'd spent most of the past nine years at a boarding school in Plymouth. Since returning, he had become a perpetual strain on his mother's purse—and on Hart's.

Only yesterday morning, but a few short hours before Lady Anne had come calling in Arlington Street, Hart had stood in this very parlor, constrained to sort out the extensive gambling debts Marcus had racked up at various gaming establishments around town.

"Is that why you've summoned me back?" Hart asked. "It's been a mere twenty-four hours since last I was here. Surely, Marcus isn't in trouble again already?"

Mrs. Neale looked away briefly. "This isn't about Marcus," she grumbled. "It's about us getting our due."

Hart doubted she'd called him here merely to demand an increase in funds. But he wouldn't force the subject. He had other obligations to attend to today, the most pressing being his business with Anne.

Fulfilling his side of the bargain he'd made with her wasn't going to be easy. He had less than a week until the next edition of the *Spiritualist Herald* went to print. And despite what Anne believed, Hart didn't make a habit of penning baseless drivel merely to amuse himself.

That is, he *did* write to amuse himself, but he took care—especially in his column for the *Herald*—that even his most outlandish assertions were built around verifiable truths. It was discovering that truth that often proved difficult.

He'd have to hunt down the source of the rumors about Captain Blunt's estate in Yorkshire. The house's haunted reputation must have originated from somewhere. A grisly murder, perhaps, or a spectral sighting on the grounds.

It was that which occupied Hart's mind at the moment, not Marcus's latest scrape.

"The quarterly allowance I give you is more than sufficient to your needs," he said.

"Allowance?" Mrs. Neale puffed up like an offended grouse. "Is that what you call it?"

"A *generous* allowance," Hart said.

Generous enough to keep them clothed, shod, and fed, and to employ a cook-housekeeper and a manservant. Hart wasn't stingy by any means. Neither was he needlessly extravagant. He couldn't afford to be. He had no large inheritance of his own. What money he had, he made himself.

Yet another secret Hart kept to protect his family.

The mere suggestion that any of their members had prospered from trade would be enough to send shock waves through the ranks. It wouldn't matter how successful he was, nor how valuable the Parfit Plumbago Crucible Company was becoming to the British Empire.

Plumbago, also known as graphite or black lead, was an essential component of their crucibles. When mixed with clay, it created a groundbreaking vessel that could melt metals faster than any others on the market, resulting in a savings in both fuel and labor across a range of industries, not least of which was the railway.

If things continued to go according to plan, Hart and his partners stood to become very rich indeed.

But Hart wasn't rich yet.

Mrs. Neale gestured at her daughters. "Ethel and Ermintrude haven't had a new frock made in months. And what about my son? A young man should be allowed to set up his stable. I don't mind being denied a carriage, but Marcus is the grandson of an earl!"

"An illegitimate grandson," Hart said mildly. "It would be folly for him—or any of you—to aspire to exist in a sphere that will offer you no welcome."

Hart had no wish to be needlessly cruel. The fact was, despite the sordid origins of their connection, he felt a certain responsibility for his half brother and half sisters. He'd be delinquent in that responsibility if he didn't apprise them of the social limitations imposed by their birth.

"Is that so?" Mrs. Neale rose from her chair in high dudgeon. "We shall see what the rest of the world has to say about your tightfistedness. If they were to learn how Everett felt about me, about all of his children . . . why, I might become as respected a figure as Lady Hamilton was in her day."

Hart moved from the window with a beleaguered sigh. It was far too early in the day for threats against the earldom. "My father was no Admiral Nelson, madam. He was a staunch moralist. If society learned of your existence, he'd widely, and deservedly, be reviled as a hypocrite."

Mrs. Neale's face mottled with the dual emotions of embarrassment and indignation. "The nerve of you! To come here, as sanctimonious as a curate. You, who would have us hide in the shadows, depriving my beloved's own precious children of an extra crust of bread—"

"Mother, please," Ethel begged.

"I won't have it; do you hear me?" Mrs. Neale raged on, deaf to her daughter's pleas. "You may show yourself the door, sir. I won't be insulted in my own home!"

Hart threw a look of brotherly sympathy in Ethel's direction. There was nothing more that could be said. Not once her mother had worked herself into a state. Sketching a bow, he promptly took his leave.

There had rarely been a visit where Mrs. Neale hadn't thrown him out in a fit of temper, conveniently forgetting that it was he who paid her rent.

Nine years ago, Hart had found her conduct alarming. Now, it was merely tiresome.

Collecting his hat and driving gloves from the hall table, he exited the house.

What he needed was a holiday. A few weeks away from London, somewhere he could be free from the suffocating responsibilities of managing his father's secrets.

If not for his promise to help Anne, Hart would have been tempted to depart this very day.

He settled his tall beaver hat back on his head. His curricle awaited him in the street, his matched team of chestnut mares—Kestrel and Damselfly—stamping with impatience. The local lad Hart had paid to hold them was still at his post, gripping Kestrel's bridle with youthful determination.

"All right?" Hart inquired as he took charge.

"Good as gold, guv," the boy replied.

Hart flipped him a silver thruppence.

The boy caught it with a grin before darting off down the street.

Hart vaulted into his curricle. He was just gathering up the reins when the door of the Neales' house opened and Ethel rushed out after him.

"Hartford?"

Hart dutifully waited for his half sister. Though he resented the situation, he held no animosity for the girl. On the contrary, she seemed the only sensible one of the bunch.

She came to stand by the curricle, a patterned shawl drawn around her narrow shoulders. "I beg forgiveness for my mother."

"Freely given," Hart said amicably. "But I must hold firm on the subject of increasing her funds."

"I fear you don't understand. It's my brother, you see. He had an additional gaming debt he failed to disclose to you yesterday. He only admitted it to us last night. The sum is enormous. I despair of how—" She broke off, catching sight of one of their neighbors staring at them out of an open window. Her face fell. "I'm making matters worse by speaking to you in the street."

Hart's mouth curved in a resigned smile. "Come along, then."

Ethel's eyes went round. "With you? Now?"

"I'll take you for a turn about the park. We'll have a bit more privacy." He extended his hand.

It was the early hours of the morning, and Battersea was far from the purview of fashionable London society. Even if he was observed driving his sister, there was minimal chance it would cause any talk.

Ethel allowed him to assist her up onto the seat of his curricle.

When she was safely beside him, Hart gave his horses the office to start, speaking to them as cordially as if they were old friends—which they were. "Walk on, Kestrel. Walk on, Damselfly."

Ethel gave him a curious look. "What strange names for a pair of horses. Did you choose them?"

"No," he said. "It was a friend of mine."

The bittersweet recollection made his smile dim. The memory of her—of Anne—standing up on the wooden slats of the paddock fence at Sutton Park, arms folded on the top rail as she watched the yearling fillies at play. He'd stood at her side, his attention drawn to her as much as to the horses, losing his heart to her so gradually, he hadn't realized it was gone until she'd captured it completely, making it hers for all time.

He suspected that a piece of it would always be hers, whether he liked it or not.

With an effort, Hart brought his attention back to the present, and to the very different young lady who was now at his side. He sprang his horses into a trot as they left the Neales' secluded neighborhood to enter the busy street.

"Very well," he said, steeling himself for the worst. "Tell me how much Marcus owes this time."

Three

Anne intercepted Horbury as he crossed the hall with the morning post. It had been a week since she'd called on Hartford. Seven days spent in endless anticipation, waiting for the results of that wretched visit to manifest.

She hadn't been idle in the interim. Between fretting over Joshua's impending arrival and worrying about Julia's safety, Anne had been conducting her own investigations into Captain Blunt's background. This very afternoon—providing she could manage to slip away for an hour—she intended to visit the offices of the *London Courant*. Surely a newspaper would have something in their archives to shine a light on the true character of Julia's new husband.

To what end, Anne didn't know. A divorce for Julia was impossible. The scandal would be too great to bear. An annulment, on the other hand . . .

Anne reined in her galloping thoughts.

So much hinged on what she'd find in Yorkshire. And getting there wholly depended on Hartford's dratted column.

"Has it come?" she asked.

"It has, my lady." Horbury passed her the latest edition of the *Spiritualist Herald*.

Anne's pulse quickened as she took it. "Pray don't mention its arrival to my mother. I'll bring it to her myself the moment I've finished with it."

"As you wish." Horbury's face was void of expression. He'd been their butler since Anne was a child and knew the value of discretion. "Will there be anything else, my lady?"

"That's all, Horbury, thank you." Anne bestowed him with a grateful smile before hurrying to the library, where she could read Hartford's latest column in peace.

Unlike the Earl of March's library, with its whirlwind of clutter, the Earl of Arundell's library was a sanctuary. It remained just as it had been in Anne's father's time—dark, masculine, and rich with the lingering remnants of expensive pipe tobacco. On entering, she always felt as though Papa's protective arms were wrapping around her, gathering her close and keeping her safe.

Shutting the door behind her, she took a seat on the library's leather-upholstered sofa. The heavy curtains were drawn back from the windows, the morning sun illuminating walls lined with impeccably organized mahogany bookcases and floors covered in thick red-and-gold Aubusson carpets. It was more than sufficient light to read by.

She flipped through the pages of the *Spiritualist Herald* until, heart hammering, her eyes lit on the distinctive border of stars and flourishes that surrounded Hartford's column.

THE EARTHLY MUSINGS OF MR. DRINKWATER

Saturn is a powerful and malignant planet. When it is ascendant, great care must be observed in undertaking journeys. This month, however, the mighty Saturn has vouchsafed a rare gift to those who venture forth. Its aspect with Mercury and Venus, unique in the calendar of our short lives, has briefly thinned the veil between worlds in those sites of spiritualist significance in the northern counties. Among them, Edgemoor

House (or Goldfinch Hall as it is called by some) is certain to be of interest. Executions committed during the Civil War have left an indelible psychic stain on the premises, sparking century-old tales of ghostly perambulations.

No good has yet been derived from ignoring our mutual history. Injustices from the past cry out for acknowledgment. Those of my esteemed readers who summon the strength to confront these restless spirits will find themselves amply rewarded. Do you, dearest friend, have the courage? If so, make haste to Yorkshire before the first of August lest you lose the opportunity forever.

Anne's cheeks heated. She was nettled just as she always was by Hartford's turn of phrase. Injustices from the past indeed. But he'd done as she'd asked him to do. All that was left was to share the column with Mama.

And with Stella.

Anne's conscience twinged as she exited the library. She hadn't yet confided in Stella about her visit to Arlington Street. In truth, Anne rarely discussed Hartford with her friends at all, except for declaring that she disliked him excessively. Sharing her reasons for approaching him would only open a Pandora's box of personal mortification.

She was too proud to admit that she'd recognized Hartford's voice in Mr. Drinkwater's writing. That she'd begun to read his column regularly, and that, when she'd seen a similarly worded column in the *Weekly Heliosphere*, written by one Mr. Bilgewater of all people, she'd suspected Hartford was behind that as well.

Her suspicions had set her hunting for more of his anonymous work—and finding it, too, much to her disappointment.

Hartford had always been of a frivolous turn of mind. Everything done for his own amusement, never caring about the consequences, only about satisfying his warped sense of humor.

He was laughing at all of them. Making fun of spiritualists, novel readers, horticulturalists, and temperance adherents with short columns penned in publications all over the city. Even his pseudonyms were satirical. Drinkwater, Bilgewater, and the like. Ridiculous.

And now this. Allusions to their "mutual history."

As she ascended the stairs to her mother's room, Anne couldn't help but wonder if he was laughing at her, too.

It might have been six and a half years since Lady Anne had last darkened his grandfather's doorstep, but Hart hadn't shown the same iron-willed forbearance in relation to Anne's residence in Grosvenor Square. He often attended parties and other events there, ignoring the fact that such gatherings generally involved mediums, crystal gazers, and various other crackbrained performers of dubious merit.

In the past, Hart hadn't minded enduring the trappings of spiritualism so long as he had a chance to remain on the fringes of Anne's life. In recent months, however, the idea of ending his days as Anne's hapless hanger-on held increasingly less appeal.

Not that those qualms had stopped him from calling today.

He consoled himself that it was curiosity and not lack of self-restraint that had brought him to Grosvenor Square this morning. He'd written what Anne had bid him to write, and his publisher had seen to it that it was printed in the very next edition of the bimonthly *Spiritualist Herald*. Hart had expected news of Lady Arundell's departure for Yorkshire would soon follow.

It hadn't.

Nearly a week after the publication of his column, the countess and her daughter were still in London.

Curious, to be sure.

He followed the Arundells' grizzled butler up the curving marble staircase and into their green-and-gold-silk-papered drawing room.

"Mr. Felix Hartford, my lady," the butler droned.

Hart paused on the threshold as he was announced, his gaze

sweeping over the lavishly furnished room. Disappointment swiftly followed. There was no sign of Anne. Only her mother was present.

Her *formidable* mother.

Seated on a tufted green velvet sofa, garbed in her usual black crepe, Lady Arundell was as stately as the figurehead of a ship. "Hartford," she said in tones that might have emanated from Queen Victoria herself. "To what do we owe the pleasure?"

"My lady." He bowed before entering. "Need there be a reason?"

She snapped open her black lace fan, motioning with it for him to sit. "You're returning my daughter's courtesy, I gather."

He sank down in a chair across from her, his ready smile masking a reflexive surge of irritation. Of course Anne had told her about her visit to Arlington Street. Anne kept no secrets from her mother.

Or rather, she wasn't in the habit of doing so. Not these past six years, anyway.

But something had changed of late.

Hart had felt it sizzling and sparking in the air when Anne had called on him.

It was this business with Miss Wychwood. Anne's worry over her fragile friend had managed to do the impossible. It had reignited Anne's guttering sense of independence—a flame that had been all but extinguished after the death of her father.

Desperation made for powerful fuel.

And she must be desperate to have enlisted Hart in her scheme.

"It was good of her to call on my grandfather," he said.

"A fool's errand," Lady Arundell replied. "She tells me she didn't see him."

"Grandfather spends most mornings in his greenhouse. He rarely receives visitors anymore. He means no discourtesy by it."

"No offense was taken," she said. "Our families are friends of old. We needn't stand on ceremony."

It was true. The acquaintance between the Hartford and Deveril families was one of long standing. It had begun with Lady Arundell and Hart's mother, Eloise. The two of them had been away at school together as girls, prompting a bond of friendship that had lasted for the remainder of his mother's life. On her death, that bond had splintered. And then, when Lord Arundell had died, it had seemed to fracture completely.

"I hope we still are, ma'am," he said. "Friends, that is."

Lady Arundell gave him an assessing look. "I expect you're pining for the closeness of the old days, when your mother would stay with us at Cherry Hill. You can't have been more than fourteen at the time. And Anne—she was but a child of eight, still in the nursery. What pleasure you took in teasing and tormenting her."

His mouth tugged into a grin. "Anne was a very teasable girl."

A singular one, too, especially as she'd grown older. Unlike other young ladies of their set, she hadn't hesitated to tease him back.

"Is she at home?" he asked.

"Where else should she be?" her ladyship wondered. "She's gone to fetch my writing box. I've a mind to dictate a letter."

"I see." It took an effort to preserve his smile.

So, she'd made Anne her secretary as well as her companion. What next? Her nurse?

"I'd thought the two of you might be preparing for your journey north," he said.

Lady Arundell blinked. "Journey? What journey?"

"Forgive me. I believed you to be a reader of the *Spiritualist Herald*."

Her ladyship's face lit with comprehension. "Mr. Drinkwater's column! A fascinating turn of events. To think that the veil should be at its thinnest between the worlds for only a month's time—and only in that particular part of the country."

Fascinating, indeed.

Hart had made a considerable effort in constructing the story. He'd even gone so far as to comb through old issues of the *Herald*, looking for some grain of fact on which to build his fiction.

He'd been lucky to find it.

"Goldfinch Hall has a history, it seems," he said. "Something to do with the executions of Royalists that took place there during the seventeenth century."

Lady Arundell leaned forward eagerly in her seat. "A great injustice, Mr. Drinkwater calls it."

"I daresay it must seem so to those who lost their lives. Spirits have no comprehension of politics."

She nodded. "It would explain the house's reputation. It's long been rumored to be haunted."

Hart was as familiar with the rumors as all the rest of society. Captain Blunt's scandalous behavior didn't help matters. A dangerous-looking individual, with a battle-scarred face and a permanent sneer, he was said to reside in his haunted Yorkshire estate with several of his illegitimate children. Indeed, the facts of the man's life might have been lifted straight from the pages of one of the ridiculous sensation romances Hart often reviewed for the *Weekly Heliosphere*.

No wonder Miss Wychwood had been taken with the man.

"It appears the rumors are true," Hart replied gravely. "Goldfinch Hall is a house of great spiritualist significance."

"Mr. Drinkwater has called it such," Lady Arundell said.

"Then you can understand the importance of the news in his column. To refrain from going to North Yorkshire at this particular moment would be to miss a rare psychic opportunity."

"Yes, yes." Her ladyship wafted her fan with increasing agitation. "A great pity. But it can't be helped. As I reminded Anne only this morning—Ah. Here she is."

Anne stood in the doorway, a large rosewood writing box cradled in her arms. Her cheeks were flushed from exertion.

Hart was at once on his feet, all thoughts of the idiocy of the situation forgotten. He crossed the room to assist her, his blood warming just as it always did whenever he was in her presence.

"Permit me," he said, reaching for the box.

She held fast to it for a moment before relinquishing it into his charge. A strand of hair, the color of golden wheat, had worked free from its coil of plaits to curl about her face. She looked adorably flustered—a rarity. Anne wasn't often out of countenance.

"What are *you* doing here?" she demanded under her breath.

"Satisfying my curiosity," he whispered back. "What else?"

Lady Arundell's booming voice put an end to their murmured exchange. "Do sit down, both of you."

Hart gestured for Anne to precede him. She strode past with a flick of black silk skirts, her tresses shimmering in the sun that streamed through the tall, damask-draped drawing room windows.

He followed her, his smile broadening in spite of himself.

Lady Arundell pointed her fan in the direction of the chair next to Hart's. Anne obediently sat down, arranging her full skirts all about her.

"Where would you like your writing box, ma'am?" Hart asked.

"On the malachite table," her ladyship said.

He placed it where she directed, all the while aware of Anne's sherry-brown gaze burning a hole in his back.

"I was just informing Hartford how disappointed we are that we must miss the opportunity of convening with the spirits in Yorkshire," Lady Arundell said.

"Yes, very disappointed," Anne agreed tightly.

Hart looked between Anne and her mother, puzzled, as he resumed his seat. Tension rarely existed between them. Not that he'd observed these half a dozen years and more. "Is there something that prevents you going?"

"We cannot travel such a distance unescorted," Lady Arundell said.

"You've just returned from a lengthy journey," Hart pointed out.

Lady Arundell and Anne had lately visited Birmingham in company with Miss Maltravers and her uncle, Harris Fielding. They'd gone to investigate the authenticity of a child medium reported to have made contact with the recently deceased Prince Consort.

A ridiculous enterprise, which Hart could only assume had achieved nothing more than exposing Anne to an even greater array of charlatans and their all-too-willing victims.

"We were accompanied by Mr. Fielding," Lady Arundell said with a touch of irritation. "His presence is beyond reproach."

The solution seemed obvious enough to Hart. "Perhaps Mr. Fielding might be persuaded to accompany you again?"

Lady Arundell gave an impatient snap of her fan. "If only he could! Alas, he's suffering the remnants of an indisposition and isn't sufficiently recovered to leave his rooms."

Hart glanced at Anne. Her hands were clasped tight in her lap. "A footman, then," he said. "Many ladies journey in the company of trusted servants. It's perfectly unobjectionable."

Lady Arundell waved the suggestion away before Hart had finished uttering it. "On no account. A lady can't visit a site of spiritualist significance without a gentleman to attend her. Think of the dangers. No, no. We must accept the impossibility of the venture. A great pity, as I said."

"It *is* a great pity." Anne's words were edged with palpable frustration. "For if we had gone to Goldfinch Hall, I could have seen Miss Wychwood. I could have assured myself of her health and happiness."

"Miss Wychwood again?" Lady Arundell cast her fan aside in a flare of temper. "The tiresome girl! Will I have no peace now she's wed?"

"*I* can have no peace," Anne said. "I can't rest until I know she's all right." There were shadows under her eyes. A weariness to her features Hart hadn't seen before.

His chest tightened on a rush of familiar emotion. It was this blasted urge to come to her rescue. To make the way smooth for her, no matter how she might balk at his assistance. He felt it springing to life in him whenever Anne, or anyone dear to her, was in distress.

It was his own personal curse. One that was all tangled up with his sense of lingering resentment at the choices she'd made.

The woman had elected a life as her mother's shadow over a life with him! It was worse than disappointing. It was downright insulting. Any self-respecting man would have washed his hands of her long ago.

But Hart's self-respect was of little concern to him at the moment.

By God but it was intolerable to see her looking so worn down and defeated. This wasn't Anne. Not the Anne he knew. He wanted her to be herself again.

The desire spurred him into action.

"All you lack is a proper escort?" he asked.

"A gentleman," Lady Arundell reiterated.

Hart's shoulders set with reckless determination. "If that's the case . . ."

Don't say it, his conscience warned. *Don't you dare say it.* But what man ever prospered by listening to his conscience in circumstances such as these?

"I'm pleased to volunteer my own services," he said.

Anne's head jerked up. "*You!*"

"*You?*" Lady Arundell queried at the same time. Her eyes brightened at the possibility.

"Me," he said. "Am I not a gentleman?"

Anne made a choked noise.

Hart's mouth ticked up at one corner.

"A tempting offer," Lady Arundell said. "But you're a young man," she added magnanimously. "Not a man of Fielding's age. And Yorkshire is no small distance. It would be an imposition."

"Not in the least." Hart met Anne's stunned gaze. "This is an occasion not to be missed. I'd be a fool to stay away."

"You were intending to travel to Yorkshire yourself?" Lady Arundell asked.

"I was. Or rather, I am." Hart vowed to atone for the falsehood at some point in future. "If you would entrust yourselves to my care, I'd be happy to see to the arrangements."

"That's very generous of you," Lady Arundell said. "Is it not, Anne?"

Anne made no reply. She was still staring at him, eyes wide with both amazement and something very like horror.

"As I say," her ladyship went on, warming to the idea, "we don't like to be an imposition, but I suppose, if you're already making the journey, we might avail ourselves of your escort."

"It would be my honor, ma'am," Hart said. "We are, after all, old family friends."

Four

"Mr. *Hartford is accompanying you to Yorkshire?"* Stella's silver-blue eyes were round with amazement behind the silk gauze veil of her riding hat.

Expertly perched in a well-worn sidesaddle, she sat atop her high-strung mare, Locket, looking every inch the accomplished equestrienne. Her new riding habit only aided the picture. Recently designed by Evelyn's beau, up-and-coming dressmaker Ahmad Malik, the mazarine-dyed wool had been masterfully tailored, every dart and seam placed to accentuate Stella's charms.

And Stella had abundant charms.

She also had one arguably ruinous feature—hair that had gone completely gray at the age of sixteen. The unfortunate color was presently concealed in a closely woven silk net.

"I can't believe it," she said.

"Nor can I," Anne said. A gentle breeze ruffled the short veil of her own hat. It was a temperate summer day, the sun shining brilliantly in the sky above Hyde Park's Rotten Row.

Anne felt none of its warmth.

Since Hartford's visit yesterday, she'd been in a near constant state of apprehension.

With a subtle press of her leg, she guided Saffron out of the way of a gentleman trotting by them on a flashy bay. Saffron responded to her slightest movement, the ease of their communication honed over more than a decade of partnership.

The pale golden stallion, with his striking flaxen mane and tail, had been Anne's trusted mount since she was a girl. Her father had bought him for her at the sales in Shrewsbury, a gift on the occasion of her eleventh birthday.

It had been as much a surprise to Mama as it had been to Anne.

"A stallion, my love?" Mama had questioned. "But Anne is just a child!"

"Anne is a horsewoman," Papa had replied, his words ringing with unassailable confidence. "She must have a horse to suit her skill."

At the time, Anne had doubted whether she was ready for such a glorious animal, but the passing years had proved her fears to be ill founded. Nearly eighteen now, Saffron had matured into her perfect partner.

Beside her, Stella skillfully maneuvered her own mount. "What could have compelled Mr. Hartford to make such an offer?"

"The same thing that always compels him," Anne replied sourly. "The unholy pleasure he takes in tormenting me. The odious man!"

"Odious he may be," Stella said. "But his escort is better than nothing."

Anne conceded the point. "I suppose you're right. This way, at least, I can get to Yorkshire."

Another rider approached on their left. Lord somebody or other, freshly up from the country. Anne recalled having been introduced to him at one of Mama's parties.

"Good afternoon, Miss Hobhouse. My lady." He touched the brim of his hat as he passed, his gaze lingering on Anne's bosom longer than was decent.

Anne acknowledged him with a frosty inclination of her head.

He wasn't the first gentleman to stare.

Like Stella, Anne wore a habit of Mr. Malik's design—a figure-flattering ensemble of black Venetian cloth. But Anne wasn't wearing the fashionable creation in order to cut a dash in the Row. She wore it to help Evelyn.

Before Mr. Malik could marry, he first had to make a success of his business. To do that, he needed his designs to be seen. It was why Anne and Stella had gone to him, commissioning not only their new riding habits but the gowns they'd worn to a recent ball at Cremorne Gardens.

Anne hadn't realized solid black garments could be made to look so stylish and seductive. She hesitated to imagine what Mr. Malik might achieve with the color red.

"Thank heaven for Mr. Drinkwater's column," Stella said, resuming their conversation. "What a stroke of luck that he should write about Captain Blunt's estate!"

Anne stared straight ahead as they rode, guilt gnawing at her already precarious spirits.

She still hadn't told Stella the whole of it. She doubted she ever would. It was embarrassing, frankly. What sort of mature lady still recognized the ironically written flourishes of a gentleman she'd kissed in her youth? A ninny, that was who.

"Do you suppose it's true?" Stella asked. "About the veil between worlds being at its thinnest in North Yorkshire this month?"

"It's nonsense," Anne said. "All of it. But I can't complain, so long as it helps me achieve my ends."

"I pray you won't be too late."

"I'm already too late. Blunt abducted Julia weeks ago."

"He *married* her weeks ago," Stella said. "We don't yet know that he abducted her. And after what you discovered at the newspaper—"

"What I *didn't* discover," Anne corrected her. There had been no reports of Captain Blunt's rumored cruelties in the archives of the

London Courant. All she'd unearthed was a glowing account of his heroism. "The article I found was full of praise, not censure."

"I suppose the article might be wrong," Stella allowed. "According to my brother, one can't believe the press any more than one can believe fashionable tittle-tattle."

Anne gave her friend a speaking glance.

Stella's older brother was a petty despot whose views on most subjects were positively medieval. Though he permitted his sister to take part in the London season (a stipulation of her late father's will), he hobbled her success at every turn.

"I have no good cause to doubt the newspaper's accounting," Anne said. "Much as I might wish to."

"Did you procure a copy of it for Julia?"

"I did, though I daresay it will provide little comfort. Captain Blunt is still nine-tenths a mystery to us."

"We know he was a hero," Stella said. "And Julia does love a hero."

"Heroes in novels, perhaps. As for Blunt, may I remind you that the last time he approached her, she nearly swooned into a faint."

"She nearly swoons when *any* gentleman approaches her."

"Precisely," Anne said. "Do you truly believe she left with him willingly?"

Stella furrowed her brow. "No, but neither can I readily believe her a victim. Julia is stronger than she seems. Only look how she handles Cossack. Not every young lady could manage such an oversized mount."

"We all of us are stronger when we're on horseback," Anne said. It's how the four of them had become friends. "That doesn't mean we could fend off a man of Captain Blunt's great size. I couldn't even manage to outwit Hartford. And if I can't prevail over him, there's little hope for Julia's having prevailed over Blunt."

"Mr. Hartford and Captain Blunt are two very dissimilar gentlemen," Stella said. "In my experience, it's the humorous ones who often pose the greatest danger."

Anne's mouth opened in question only to snap shut again at the sight of a familiar blond figure riding toward them at a trot on a graceful little mare.

It was the Viscountess Heatherton.

Anne's face wiped clean of expression, her demeanor becoming as cool as that of the viscountess herself.

Lady Heatherton was a prominent figure in London society owing to her marriage to a much older viscount. Renowned for her beauty, and notorious for her vicious and vindictive nature, she'd taken a deep dislike to Anne and her friends, even going so far as to instigate a confrontation with Evelyn and Mr. Malik during the ball at Cremorne Gardens.

If not for the intervention of Anne's mother, the encounter might have escalated into a full-blown scene.

Anne had counseled her friends to avoid the woman ever since.

"Lady Anne," the viscountess said coldly, inclining her head as she approached.

"Lady Heatherton." Anne returned the stiff salute.

Nose in the air, her ladyship rode on, trotting past Stella without a look or a word of acknowledgment.

The cut direct.

Anne stiffened with outrage on her friend's behalf. Stella may only be the sister of a clergyman, but she was still a gentlewoman and therefore worthy of notice.

"Dreadful woman!" Anne said the moment Lady Heatherton was out of earshot.

Stella had paled at the insult, but she quickly rallied. "Oh, never mind it. I won't let her ruin my ride."

"Nor should you," Anne said.

The two of them urged their horses on.

"What did you mean before?" Anne asked. "About humorous gentlemen being dangerous?"

"They *are* dangerous," Stella said. "They lure you in with their jokes and their banter, as if they're no more threatening than a teasing uncle or an affectionate brother—then they strike. Meanwhile the sinister-looking ones are usually far less menacing than they appear. It's that way in nature, too, isn't it? With snakes and other lethal beasts?"

Anne knew little about the nature of snakes and, admittedly, even less about the nature of men. "Are you saying that Hartford is more of a threat to me than Blunt is to Julia? *Hartford?* A gentleman who would as soon laugh at me as touch me?"

"Well, dear," Stella replied candidly, "I do think you might be a little more on your guard with the fellow. Though you may have known him in his youth, and though he may tease you, he isn't a boy any longer. He's a man. An *unmarried* man."

"I know he's unmarried, the swine. He had the audacity to mention it to me recently."

"To you? When?"

"In my hearing," Anne answered vaguely. "Something about his aunt being keen to matchmake for him."

"He *is* highly eligible," Stella said. "I've often wondered why he's remained unattached. For a time, I even suspected, given the attention he pays you—"

"Hartford has no intention of making me one of his conquests. I doubt he even thinks of me that way."

"Oh, I know that *now*," Stella said.

Anne's hands tightened reflexively on her reins. Saffron tossed his head, prompting her to loosen her contact. "What does *that* mean?"

"I'm only agreeing with you."

"Quite readily, it seems. Am I such an antidote?"

Stella gave a soft laugh. "You know very well you aren't. You're easily the most beautiful of all of us."

Anne was duly chastened. "I wasn't fishing for a compliment."

Stella smiled. "I'm merely speaking the truth."

"It isn't true," Anne said, "as you're well aware."

The most beautiful of all of them was Stella herself. Even her gray hair managed to be alluring, though most in society were disposed to view it as a fatal flaw.

But Anne refused to catalog her friends according to their physical attributes. It was a fruitless exercise. Each of them had traits to be envied.

Evelyn was bold and determined, with the athletic ability to make her Andalusian stallion perform airs above the ground.

Julia was a sweet and gentle soul, as happy with her nose buried in a novel as she was cantering down Rotten Row.

And Stella was tender and grave, an excellent listener, and the best rider among them, despite never appearing to exert an ounce of effort.

"There's no point in our arguing about it," Stella said. "The simple fact is your beauty is neither here nor there for a man in Mr. Hartford's position."

"What position is that?"

Stella cast her a conspiratorial glance. "I believe his heart is otherwise engaged."

Anne came to immediate attention. "What have you heard?"

"It's not what I've heard, but what I've seen." Stella hesitated a fraction of a second before admitting, "I saw him in the park two weeks ago, in the early hours of the morning."

Anne frowned. "Here? In Rotten Row?"

"Not here. It was in Battersea Park."

"Battersea Park!" That was all the way across the river.

A space opened up ahead of them, and Stella nudged Locket into a lofty, ground-covering trot. Anne kept pace on Saffron. Their two grooms followed after them at a respectful distance, never permitting either of the ladies to slip out of their sight.

"I was accompanying my brother on a visit to the old aunt of one of his parishioners," Stella explained. "She's been gravely ill with leg ulcers. It was as we were leaving, traveling down the Prince of Wales Road, that I saw Mr. Hartford entering the park. I recognized him straightaway."

"What was he doing?" Anne asked. "Not riding, I assume."

Hartford wasn't a keen rider. He preferred to drive his curricle—something he did with aggravating aplomb, featheredging corners and galloping his matched team of fiery chestnut mares up and down outrageously steep hills.

He'd trained the two mares himself and had never once let anyone else drive them, not even his groom. They were that sensitive and unpredictable.

Kestrel and Damselfly, they were called.

Anne knew the pair well. She'd given them their names as fillies and still felt a certain fondness for them.

Not so much for their owner.

"He was driving his curricle," Stella said. Her gloved hands remained steady on her reins as she brought Locket back down to a walk.

With a subtle shift in her weight, Anne signaled to Saffron that he, too, must adjust his gait from a trot to a walk. "Is that all?"

Stella lowered her voice. "He was with someone. A *lady*."

Anne's stomach tensed. "Who?"

"No one of our acquaintance. Indeed, I've never seen her before. But she was gazing up at him as if she admired him greatly."

A needle of jealousy pricked at Anne's heart. She despised herself for the emotion. And she doubly despised herself for asking, "What did she look like?"

"Young," Stella said. "Eighteen or nineteen, I'd guess, with raven hair and a fair complexion. Quite lovely, really."

Some of the blood drained from Anne's face. She felt an unaccountable ache in her midsection.

Stella glanced at her. Her gaze turned speculative behind her veil. "But not as lovely as you are. It's as I told you. Everyone says—"

"What people say is that I'm an eccentric harridan," Anne replied crossly. "And they're not half-wrong."

Stella's eyes softened with sympathy. "You're not a milk-and-water miss, I grant you. Who would wish to be? The life of an eccentric is far more interesting."

Anne's heart rejected the compliment, even as she acknowledged it was kindly meant. What joy was there in eccentricity when Hartford—the devil!—was secretly courting some pretty young lady?

A *very* young lady.

A lady in her first bloom, in fact, no more than nineteen.

It was an age that put Anne's antiquated years in the shade. At nearly three-and-twenty, with two failed seasons behind her and a third underway, she stood on the threshold of spinsterhood.

She shouldn't care. And she told herself she didn't. Hartford didn't belong to her. He never had, save for a brief moment six years and five months ago. She'd long accepted that that part of her life was over. She nevertheless felt an alarming pang in her breast.

It wasn't her heart. It was something worse. It was her spirit. The very essence of her, crying out at the injustice of it all as surely as those fictional Royalists in Hartford's ridiculous column.

She'd already lost so much. She couldn't lose Julia, too.

"I wish I were *more* eccentric," Anne declared, rousing her spirits to the cause. "I might have traveled to Yorkshire weeks ago and saved Julia from her fate."

"Thank goodness you didn't," Stella said. "Your reputation would have been in tatters." Locket pranced nervously beneath her. Stella stroked the mare's neck, soothing her with her touch. "When do you leave?"

"Tomorrow. Hartford is collecting us at half past nine. He's procured tickets on the train to York. We're to lodge at inns along the way."

"Which means you'll be in company with him for days."

"No more than absolutely necessary," Anne said.

But she knew that even a day would be too long. Even an hour. Especially now that Hartford was courting another.

How will I bear it? How will I endure?

Her shoulders threatened to sag. She held them in place through sheer strength of will. "Shall we gallop?" she asked.

Stella beamed. "Oh yes, let's. A good gallop always sets things to rights."

Five

"Where are you off to in such a rush, lad?" the Earl of March inquired from outside the door to his library. His rumpled white hair and soil-stained clothing attested to a morning spent mucking about in his greenhouse.

Hart descended the stairs, his hat and gloves in hand. "A brief errand," he said. He offered no explanation.

His grandfather didn't ask for one.

A gentle and exceedingly absent-minded old gentleman, he was forever consumed by thoughts on matters botanical. It would never occur to him that his grandson could be up to anything ill-advised. The earl's descendants were, to his mind, as noble as the plants he tended with such devoted care. To learn that Hart was on his way to a meeting at a Battersea crucible manufactory of all places, to discuss something as coarse as the influx of capital needed to extend plumbago-mining operations, would crush him.

"Why?" Hart stepped down into the hall. "Do you have need of me today?"

"Those Himalayan lilies of mine are doing poorly. I'd like your opinion on them."

Hart gave him an interested look. The *Cardiocrinum giganteum* seeds were among the many specimens he and his grandfather had brought back from their 1856 expedition to India.

Giant Himalayan lilies were still a rare sight in England, not least because it took them as long as six years or more to come into bloom. They had first been exhibited at the Royal Horticultural Society show in 1853 by the botanist Thomas Lobb. Competition to collect and cultivate the notoriously difficult flower had been fierce ever since.

"I thought they were thriving," Hart said.

"The leaves have turned a concerning shade of brown." Grandfather wandered back into his library. "You can have a look at them after luncheon. Brookdale and his wife are coming, along with Mariah. You'll join us, of course."

Hart suppressed a surge of annoyance. "Of course."

He didn't get along well with his uncle, nor with his uncle's paragon of a wife. As for his cousin, Mariah—a silly sort of girl in her first season, with little of wit or conversation about her—she wasn't really his cousin at all. She was the child of Lady Brookdale's first marriage to a wealthy Berkshire squire by the name of Spriggs.

If it were up to him, Hart would rather have attended to his business. But (he reminded himself as he dashed off a note of apology to his associates at the crucible factory) family must always come first. It was Grandfather's only law. He expected his children and grandchildren to abide by it.

During luncheon, Grandfather sat at the head of the polished mahogany table in the dining room, looking over his family with pride.

The five of them talked of the veriest commonplace until they had finished eating and the servants came to clear away the remains of the soup, cold chicken, cheese, and fruit that had been served.

At the first opportunity, Brookdale sent a wordless signal to his wife to withdraw.

Aunt Esther was a dignified woman, with a countenance almost as severe as that of her husband. Widowed in her youth, she'd married Brookdale some ten years ago, giving birth to three sons in quick succession, all of whom were still in the nursery.

She stood along with her daughter. "Mariah and I will leave you to your politics."

Mariah followed her mother, her head bent in obedience.

After the ladies had gone, a liveried footman brought in a decanter of sherry, along with three small glasses and a crystal ashtray. The latter was silently placed beside Hart's uncle.

Brookdale waved the footman away, and then, after lighting a cigar, set to explaining the cause for his visit. "The Earl of Denham's heir called in Mount Street yesterday. He's offered for Mariah."

"Viscount Storridge?" Grandfather exhibited uncharacteristic interest. "Isn't his younger brother—"

"In trade," Brookdale said. "That isn't all. There have been unsettling rumors about Denham himself."

"Also in trade?" Hart asked wryly as he poured himself a glass of sherry.

Brookdale's brows sank with disapproval. He was a humorless man, nearing his fiftieth year, with dark hair and even darker eyes. A neatly trimmed black beard and side-whiskers framed his face, giving him the look of a respected statesman.

Hart supposed he was one.

Uncle Brookie, as Hart had taken to calling him as a boy, had had a long and distinguished career in politics. First elected to Parliament when he was three-and-twenty, he was known for his devotion to traditional institutions—marriage included. Indeed, so spotless and chaste was his reputation that he was often heard to proudly proclaim that smoking was his only vice.

"Do you find my stepdaughter's marital prospects a source of amusement, Felix?" he asked.

"I find everything a source of amusement," Hart said.

How else to view it? He was in trade himself, though not in a public-facing manner. The fact of it would still be enough, if revealed, to send his uncle into an apoplexy.

And if that didn't kill him—*and* his career—the revelations about Mrs. Neale surely would.

"Your father would be disappointed in your levity," Brookdale said. "As am I." He puffed at his cigar. "You'll soon be a liability if you don't mend your ways."

"What about Denham?" Grandfather pressed on. "It's not trade, I trust?"

"Not that I've discovered. But the man keeps a mistress in Clarges Street. There are rumors he's fathered a child on her."

Hart nearly choked on his sherry.

"This is no laughing matter!" Brookdale snapped. "Such lasciviousness—such vice—it cannot be tolerated."

"No, indeed," Grandfather said. "I liken it to rot."

"Quite right," Brookdale said. "Her Majesty would agree."

Hart looked between the two of them. "Let me understand. Lord Storridge has proposed to Mariah, but since his brother has dabbled in trade and his father keeps a mistress—"

"And a bastard, potentially," Brookdale said.

"What about Storridge himself?" Hart asked. "Does Mariah object to him?"

"Mariah has some damned fool notion to marry for love. I suspect she has her heart set on another young man. She won't say who he is, but her mother will get it out of her, on that you may depend." Brookdale took another long draw of his cigar. "Pity Storridge isn't up to the mark. Mariah might have been persuaded to accept him."

Hart set down his glass. His uncle's intractability irritated him to no small degree, not least because Storridge's situation seemed to mirror Hart's own. "Is Storridge somehow morally compromised by his father's behavior? By his brother's?"

"Obviously," Brookdale said. "As in nature, so, too, in the human family. Isn't that right, Father? A rot in one branch must corrupt the entirety of the plant."

"Must guard against rot," Grandfather agreed. "Best to cut it away at first sighting."

"I intend to," Brookdale said. "Young Storridge may marry some other girl. I'll not be connected to such a family."

"I begin to wonder what might be worse," Hart murmured. "Trade or adultery."

Brookdale flipped the ashes of his cigar into the ashtray with unusual force. "Sometimes I wonder as well. I wonder how a man like my brother could have sired a son with no understanding of the duty that's owed this family. If you spent as much time in solemn reflection as you did in indulging in abject tomfoolery—"

"I've not been up to much in the way of tomfoolery in recent years," Hart said. Not publicly, anyway. Only a few curricle races and the occasional good-natured wager.

It was nothing to the stunts he'd pulled in his youth.

Then, he hadn't had much thought for risking his neck—or for looking foolish. If something had appealed to his sense of amusement or adventure, he'd embarked on it without any care for how dangerous it might be, from drunken tightrope walking at Cremorne Gardens to an ill-advised dare at university that had had him swimming the River Cam naked in the dead of winter. He'd nearly perished from pneumonia as a result of the latter, a fact not easily forgotten by his family.

"I've heard differently," Brookdale retorted. "Your father would never have lowered himself to engage in—"

"Everett was a decent and honorable man," Grandfather said, cutting off his eldest son. "The memory of his piety gives me much comfort in my old age. As does Felix's presence. I'll not have you censoring his good humor. A garden would be a dreary place without a touch of brightness."

Hart's mouth hitched in spite of himself.

Brookdale wasn't so easily routed. "Speaking of brightness," he said, leveling his ruthless politician's gaze at Hart, "when do you intend to marry?"

"An excellent question," Grandfather said.

Hart's smile faltered. "Eventually," he replied. "When I've a mind to it."

"Lady Grantley tells my wife that Lady Anne Deveril called here several weeks ago," Brookdale said. "Is that true?"

Lady Grantley was a neighborhood busybody who spent much of the day at her drawing room window, peering out into the street through what must be the most powerful pair of opera glasses in Christendom.

Hart might have known she would have observed Anne's arrival. "What of it?" he asked.

"One hopes you haven't renewed your interest in her," Brookdale said.

Hart's fingers stilled on the stem of his sherry glass. "You object to her?"

Brookdale raised his cigar back to his lips. "Anyone must do so."

"Is that a fact?" As always, Hart kept a tight rein on his emotions. "And yet, the last I was aware, Lady Arundell was still considered one of the most prominent women in fashionable society."

"I don't speak to fashion. My concerns relate to her eccentricity. This business with the occult. One has to ask oneself—"

"It's harmless nonsense," Hart said.

"It's against God," Brookdale returned. "Not good for popular opinion. A grieving widow would have done better to turn to the church."

"The Queen herself is rumored to have shown an interest in spiritualism," Hart reminded him. "If it's good enough for her—"

"Lady Arundell is not yet on level with Her Majesty, my boy,"

Brookdale said. "She risks making herself ridiculous. As for her daughter—"

"Take care," Hart warned him.

Brookdale's eyes gleamed. "Hit a nerve, did I?"

"Leave him be, Brookie," Grandfather said. "I wed later in life and was none the worse for it. We can't all be as fortunate as you were in your choice."

Brookdale's expression was smug. "One hopes Felix will find someone equally worthy." He resumed smoking. "It's a shame you didn't marry Miss Sterling when you had the chance. She'd have made you an excellent wife."

Miss Sterling's name provoked a twinge of conscience in Hart's breast.

He well remembered her from his younger days. She'd been an extraordinarily elegant young lady, the belle of every ball she attended. It was a fact that hadn't gone unnoticed by Anne. Many a time, Hart had observed her looking at Miss Sterling with something like envy.

In the end, Hart had used that knowledge against Anne, targeting her weakness in a despicable fashion. He wasn't proud of himself for it.

"I hear she's wed now with five children of her own," Brookdale continued. "Bad luck, though my wife assures me there are other promising candidates for you to choose from this season. She intends to introduce you to some of them at the Ketterings' ball on Thursday."

Hart finished his sherry. "I won't be here this Thursday."

"You have a prior engagement?" Grandfather asked.

"I do," Hart said. "I'm leaving London in the morning. I don't expect I'll be back before Friday."

"Leaving for where, pray?" Brookdale asked.

Hart didn't hesitate. "I'm escorting Lady Arundell and her daughter to Yorkshire."

His grandfather and uncle burst into speech simultaneously—one curious, the other appalled.

"Yorkshire?" Grandfather repeated. "What's in Yorkshire?"

"Lady Arundell!" Brookdale said. "Then you *do* have intentions toward her daughter."

"I have no intentions whatsoever," Hart said. "They simply required an escort to call on Captain Blunt and his new bride. As I was at liberty, I offered myself for the role."

The reference to Captain Blunt's notorious elopement did little to reassure Hart's uncle.

"Scandal upon scandal," Brookdale muttered. "What do you imagine can be gained by involving yourself in this affair?"

"I don't know," Hart admitted.

But he was very interested to find out.

Six

Dressed in a black silk carriage gown, her hair neatly arranged in a braided chignon, Anne sat alone in the breakfast room in Grosvenor Square, nibbling on a piece of dry toast. It was a quarter to nine. Her maid had already packed her bags. All that remained was for Mama to finish readying herself and for Hartford to come and collect them.

Anne had been girding herself for battle since she awoke.

According to Stella, a journey undertaken in Hartford's company was more hazardous to Anne's well-being than anything Julia had yet endured. Anne was resolved to keep her wits about her. To stay on her guard every minute she was in Hartford's company. A momentary lapse could result in catastrophe. She might say something she shouldn't. *Do* something she shouldn't.

Lord knew Hartford could be devilishly provoking.

Horbury entered the breakfast room on silent feet. "The post, my lady." He proffered two letters to her on a silver salver.

Anne examined the direction on the back of the envelopes while the aged butler took the liberty of freshening her tea.

Her heart jumped into her throat.

Good gracious!

They were both from Julia—one sent mere days ahead of the other—and both hopelessly delayed.

"Why has it taken me so long to receive these?" Anne wondered. "They were sent above a fortnight ago from—" She squinted at the blurry postal stamp. "Hardholme, North Yorkshire, wherever that might be."

"If I may be so bold, my lady." Horbury returned the teapot to the table. "These remote village outposts are by no means as efficient with the post as we're accustomed to in town."

"No, indeed. Not if this is any indication." Anne cast him a grateful glance as she tore open the first missive. "Thank you, Horbury. That will be all."

Horbury withdrew.

Alone once more, Anne unfolded the pages of Julia's first letter and began to read.

My dearest Anne,

By now you will have heard of my elopement with Captain Blunt. Pray do not be alarmed. Things aren't at all how they appear. The truth of the matter is that not long after you departed London, my situation became untenable. Nay, unsafe. My mother summoned Dr. Cordingley to bleed me, and the vile man insisted on performing two consecutive bloodlettings. I was quite fearful for my life.

Later that day, Captain Blunt called on me. I know you will not credit it, but he's a good and honorable man. He's been exceedingly kind to me in your absence, coming to my rescue on more than one occasion. To see him in my darkest hour was tantamount to a sign from God. He sat beside me, so solemn, so gentle. It was then I took my fate into my hands and (please don't be shocked, dearest) I proposed to him.

Anne broke off with a startled exclamation: "Oh, Julia! What have you done?"

Ladies didn't propose to gentlemen, not even from their deathbeds.

It was the sort of thing that might happen in the pages of one of Julia's romance novels, never in real life.

Anne resumed reading, feeling half a dozen conflicting emotions at once.

My parents will have no doubt given a different account of events. I beg you not to believe them. Trust that I know my own mind, and more importantly, my own heart. If you could but see me now, you would recognize the truth of what I say.

Each successive word only served to further drive home the wrongheadedness of Anne's current course of action. Indeed, the only complaint Julia had about her new home in Yorkshire was in relation to the profound lack of staff. Without a lady's maid to attend her, she had no one to sponge and press her gowns. A minor inconvenience in comparison to what Anne had suspected.

But Anne had been wrong, it seemed. Wholly and catastrophically wrong.

If she was in any doubt of that fact, Julia's second letter made matters even plainer. It was a veritable catalog of rosebuds, moonbeams, and glowing romantic sentiment.

I didn't believe happiness could be possible outside the pages of one of my novels, but if it exists in this world, I have found it here with Captain Blunt in Yorkshire.

By the time Anne finished reading, the reality of her friend's situation was abundantly clear.

Julia hadn't been abducted. On the contrary. It sounded as though, left alone during Anne's brief journey to Birmingham, Julia may very well have fallen in love.

"Good God," Anne muttered to herself. "What madness have I set in motion?"

Shooting up from the table, she dashed out of the breakfast room and up the stairs to her mother's bedchamber.

Mama was at her elaborate rose silk-draped dressing table. Her French lady's maid, Hortense, stood behind her, putting the finishing touches on Mama's coiffure.

"We don't have to go," Anne said breathlessly.

Mama gave her a distracted glance in the gilded looking glass. "What's that?"

Anne pressed a hand to her corseted midriff, imposing control over herself. "Miss Wychwood is in no danger." *But* I *might be*, she added silently, *if I'm subjected to Hartford's company for any length of time.*

"Of course the girl's in no danger. The harm has already been done to her reputation. All that's left is for her to make the best of her reckless decision."

"That's not what I meant." Anne stepped closer. The skirts of her carriage gown bunched up against the curved side of her mother's dressing table. "I meant that we needn't travel to Yorkshire."

Her mother's lips thinned. "If this is a jest, your timing leaves much to be desired."

"It's no jest, Mama. We can remain in London."

"Nonsense. According to Mr. Drinkwater's column, our visit to Blunt's estate is of the utmost urgency."

Anne made an effort to moderate her tone. She wasn't going to fall into a panic. She'd made this mess, and she could unmake it, too. "Mr. Drinkwater isn't the authority you might think him. Only consider the small circulation of the *Spiritualist Herald*. Scarcely anyone reads it."

"Quite right. It's an exclusive publication."

"A publication that no one takes seriously. We needn't disturb ourselves merely because one man makes a ridiculous claim."

"Ridiculous?" Mama shot her an exasperated look. "Really, Anne. This is not to be borne. Only a week ago you were lauding Drinkwater to the skies."

"Yes, I know, but on reflection—"

"Enough of this nonsense. We leave within the hour, and I still have my toilette to complete." Mama addressed her maid: "More pins, Hortense. I don't wish to have to repair my hair during this journey any more than necessary."

Hortense obediently reached for a handful of metal hairpins from an opaque green jar on the dressing table. In doing so, her fingers jostled the jar, causing something to fall from behind it with a soft clink of glass.

The hidden object rolled into view, revealing itself to be a stoppered vial half-filled with a reddish-brown liquid.

Hortense promptly righted the vial, tucking it back out of sight.

But it was too late. Anne had seen it.

She stared for a long moment at the place where the vial had fallen, and then, slowly, she raised her gaze to that of her mother's maid.

Hortense's face was dutifully blank. A lady's maid was something very like a priest. A keeper of her mistress's secrets. Even if those secrets were deadly.

"Leave us," Anne said curtly.

With a bob of her head, Hortense withdrew.

Mama turned on Anne. "What on earth has got into you, my girl? I won't have you ordering my servants about."

Anne retrieved the vial from its place behind the jar. She held it between her fingers much as one might hold the neck of a venomous snake. "Where did you get this?"

Mama went still. "You go too far, Anne."

"Where?" Anne demanded. "Did Hortense acquire it for you? By God, if she's been supplying you with this poison, I swear I'll—"

Mama swept the vial from Anne's fingers. "Hortense has nothing to do with it. I acquired the laudanum myself."

"*Why?*" Anguish crept into Anne's voice. She couldn't go through this again. Not after the agonies she'd already suffered in the aftermath of Papa's death. Mama had been so lost then. So broken. No one in society would ever know the extent of it.

But Anne could never forget.

When Papa had died, her mother had crumbled all to pieces. She'd refused to eat or even to speak. Indeed, she'd seemed to give up on life entirely. For a long while, she'd remained confined to her bed, dosing herself with laudanum to numb her pain, the curtains drawn shut and her chamber all in darkness.

Anne had never felt such desolation—such *fear*—as she had then. She had already lost her father. She'd been terrified of losing her mother, too.

"You promised—"

"I've had difficulty sleeping," Mama said defensively. "What would you have me do? Lie awake for hours on end, driving myself mad?"

"You should have sent for me."

"At two and three in the morning? Night after night?"

"Yes!"

"Don't be silly. It was only a few drops of an evening. Just to get me through until Fielding is well again. I've come to rely on him so." Mama returned the vial of laudanum to her dressing table. "You don't know what it's like to be a woman alone."

"You're not alone," Anne said. "You have me."

"And I thank God for it," Mama said. "Your presence is a comfort. But it isn't the same as having a gentleman in one's life. In Fielding's absence, this journey with Hartford will do me a world of good."

Anne stiffened. Surely her company was as agreeable as Mr. Fielding's. Or Hartford's, for heaven's sake!

But Mama was from a different generation. Married at a young age, she had valued the guidance and companionship of her husband above all things. It was no slight against Anne. It was the way of the world. No daughter, not even a cherished one, could ever be as prized as a husband or son.

Anne didn't agree with the attitude—she didn't *like* it—but there it was. Nothing could be served by pretending it was otherwise.

She covered her mother's hand with her own. Compassionate understanding overshadowed any lesser emotions. "Have these feelings only returned since Mr. Fielding's absence?"

Mama squeezed Anne's fingers. "Foolish girl. You speak as though the feelings had ever left."

"What about Dmitri?" Anne hated to mention the creature's name, but she'd long ago learned to encourage her mother to seek solace where she could. "Has his presence provided no comfort?"

"Dmitri has fallen silent of late."

"Oh, Mama," Anne murmured.

Mama's face briefly sagged under the weight of her bereavement. She collected herself immediately. "There is no solace from any quarter. I'm not naive enough to expect any. No one can comprehend what I suffer in these moments. No one, save perhaps Her Majesty. The magnitude of her recent loss is something equal to mine."

Prince Albert had died six months ago, leaving the Queen, and many others in society, immobilized under a crushing weight of grief. But Anne didn't expect Queen Victoria to give way to that emotion. Her Majesty was resilient. She would surely be herself again when a year or two of formal mourning had passed.

Unlike Anne's mother.

When she'd finally emerged from her rooms, eyes swollen from tears and her complexion dulled from laudanum, the widowed Countess of Arundell had embraced her grief with the whole of her being. She'd enmeshed it into her very bones, casting herself and all those around her into a perpetual season of black-clothed sorrow.

Anne had well understood the inclination.

Papa had been their rock. Their North Star. When she and her mother had lost him, they'd lost the very ground on which they stood. They'd been in free fall ever since, reaching out for anything that might give them purchase.

Mama had grabbed hold of ghosts, desperate to find meaning in the world that lay beyond the grave. And Anne . . . she supposed she'd grabbed hold of her mother.

Had it been right to do so? Would it have perhaps been better to let her go?

Anne wouldn't allow herself to entertain the thought. Never mind that Mama was more interested in the spirit realm now than in the world of the living. After Prince Albert's death, it seemed many in London were disposed to feel the same.

"I daresay that's what's triggered this melancholy," Anne said. "The loss of the Prince Consort will have reminded you of those early days after we lost Papa."

"A dark time." Mama patted Anne's hand before releasing it. "Best not to speak of it. We have more pressing matters to attend to. Hartford will be here at any moment. I trust you have no further objections to our departure?"

"No, indeed," Anne said, resigning herself to her fate. "If this journey will rally your spirits, then of course we must go."

Seven

Hart regarded Anne from his seat across from her in their first-class railway carriage as the train rattled relentlessly toward York. There was a strained atmosphere between her and her mother. A different variety of tension from what he'd observed when he'd last called on them in Grosvenor Square. Something less near the surface.

Strange, that.

He couldn't quite put his finger on it.

Lady Arundell herself appeared to be in good spirits. Comfortably ensconced in their private compartment, with its varnished wood-paneled walls and richly upholstered seats, she was engrossed in the pages of one of her spiritualist journals—an astrological almanac, by the look of it.

Anne, meanwhile, was still and silent. She often was in the presence of her mother, as if the strength of Lady Arundell's domineering personality had cast her daughter permanently into the shadows. But this was something else. Anne wasn't only silent, she was withdrawn.

With no reading material to occupy her, she'd spent the first two hours of their journey north staring out the window at the passing scenery, her thoughts plainly elsewhere. She'd only once ventured a glance in his direction, and then solely to scowl at his choice of apparel.

Hart had felt that disapproving sherry-brown look all the way to his soul. He'd drunk up every second of it, the way a desert-bound wanderer might gulp a glass of water. The result had been much the same. He was still parched and wanting, wholly unsated.

Anne frequently had that effect on him.

Outside, the sound of groaning gears and grinding metal announced their approach to Derby Station.

He straightened his blue-and-green-plaid waistcoat as the train decreased its speed. Made in wool twill, it matched the pattern of his plaid coat and trousers. A rather dashing ensemble, he thought, despite the disdain his valet, Bishop, held for it. The long-suffering fellow was currently consigned to a lower-class carriage at the back of the train with the ladies' maids.

"We can get out briefly," Hart said. "It will give us a chance to stretch our legs."

Lady Arundell looked up from her journal, oblivious to the noise of the slowing train. "I'm quite comfortable as I am."

Hart could well believe it. He'd paid handsomely for their fare, and a king's ransom on top of it in order to ensure they weren't obliged to share their compartment with any strangers.

"We won't have another stop of this length until we change trains at York," he said. "If you're feeling at all restless—"

"You go ahead," Lady Arundell cut him off, returning to her reading. "And you, Anne. I don't require you keeping guard over me."

Anne compressed her lips, visibly displeased with her mother's directive. But when the train pulled into the station, announcing its arrival with a shrill whistle, she rose along with Hart to disembark.

He offered her his arm as they stepped down from the first-class carriage.

She grudgingly took it. "You look an absolute peacock."

Hart grinned. He frequently wore loud colors and patterns in the presence of Anne and her mother. Someone among them must, particularly on this occasion. If he'd submitted to wearing a black suit, as Bishop had suggested, the three of them would look no better than a trio of mourners on their way to a Yorkshire funeral.

"And what does that make you, my fair Fury?" Hart asked, guiding her through the crowd of passengers waiting to board. It was a noisy, chaotic scene, with porters shouting and travelers rushing in every direction through the billowing smoke that swirled about the platform.

"A black crow, I don't wonder," Anne answered frankly. She had never hesitated to voice plain truths, even if they pricked her vanity.

Hart liked her all the better for it.

"A raven, surely," he said. "A noble and intelligent bird."

"Whereas a peacock—"

"Not as intelligent, to be sure." He dropped his head to hers, sinking his voice to murmur in her ear. "But attractive to have around, you must admit."

A smile quivered on Anne's lips. She mastered it before it could fully appear. "Why must you always be so—"

"Cheerful? Felix means happiness. Or don't you recall your Latin?"

"I gather you've taken up your Christian name as a personal challenge."

"Perhaps I have," he said. As a boy, it had certainly been aspirational. "I suppose you disapprove of good cheer, just as you do of peacocks?"

"Don't be absurd," she said. "And I have good reason to think ill of peacocks. We had them at Cherry Hill when I was a girl. They screeched awfully. It was the most alarming sound."

"I remember." Hart tucked her black-gloved hand more firmly in the crook of his arm. "Shall we walk to the bookseller's?"

"If you like."

Hart turned them in the direction of the bookstand. The small counter with its background of shelves was just visible halfway down the platform.

Anne's skirts brushed his leg as they walked. A trace of her perfume drifted to his nose, stirring his blood and bringing his senses to attention. It was the same scent she'd worn in her youth—a bewitching blend of vanilla and rose, at once exotic and lushly sweet. The fragrance conjured vivid memories of the past.

He hadn't been this close to her in a long while. He'd forgotten how natural it felt. How perfectly and wonderfully right.

They fit each other. They always had. Though not so much in size. He was well over six feet tall, and she . . . markedly less so. But she was no frail damsel, for all that. She was brisk and vigorous. A bastion of strength.

That strength had appeared to lessen over the years. Her mother had taken it from her. But a diminished Anne Deveril was still more vital—more deliciously formidable—than any lady of Hart's acquaintance.

He savored every second in her company.

"You might enjoy something to read," he said. "It would be preferable to staring out the window for the whole of our journey."

"I've no wish to read," she said. "I have a great deal on my mind."

"So I gather." He paused. "Tell me, sweetheart. Did you and your mother have a quarrel?"

She gave him a sharp look.

It was answer enough.

"Well, well," he murmured. "Will wonders never cease?"

Anne's brow darkened with annoyance. "Must you be such a know-all?"

"I know nothing. I'm a man who exists only for my own amusement—or so someone recently told me. I do, however, take the occasional interest in matters outside the pleasurable. You among them."

"How flattering."

Hart studied her face. The weariness was still there, present in the smudges under her eyes and the rare hint of gray in her alabaster complexion. It did nothing to mar her beauty. She was, and always would be, the dazzling golden girl of his youth.

"You may as well tell me what's happened," he said. "I'll only plague you until I find out."

She gave an irritated huff. "Very well. If you must know, Miss Wychwood isn't in any danger after all. I received a letter from her this morning informing me that she's married Captain Blunt of her own free will. Which means there's no reason on God's green earth for us to be making this infernal journey."

Hart failed to suppress a shout of laughter.

A fashionable woman passing by, in company with her children and servants, gave him a look of well-bred contempt. Outward shows of emotion were viewed as being lower class and therefore undesirable. Hart was well aware of the prejudice. It had no effect on his good humor.

Anne, however, was mortified.

And furious.

"Of all the—" She attempted to free her arm. "If you're going to bray like a jackass—"

Hart covered her gloved hand with his. "Forgive me. It was a reflex."

"The reflex of an insensitive—"

"A jackass, as you've established. Come. Don't make a scene."

"*Me?* I'm not the one laughing at another's misfortune on a busy railway platform."

"What misfortune?" Hart gently settled her hand back in place. "You still get to see your friend. There must be some utility in that. And, as an added bonus, you get to spend a few days in my company. How long did you say it's been? Six and a half years?"

"You know exactly how long it's been," she said. "Must you always be teasing me?"

"You'd prefer to talk seriously?"

She looked away from him, turning her face to stare out at the platform. Her expression turned pensive. "I wouldn't know where to begin."

Hart felt a nameless stab of regret. This was his fault, this lost look on her face. Anne may have rejected him six and a half years ago, but he hadn't been blameless in what came after. He'd been surly. Unsympathetic. He'd wanted her so damned much. At the time, not having her had been a blow from which he feared he might never recover.

And perhaps he hadn't.

His voice deepened with genuine sincerity. "I'm not always of a mind to tease you, Anne," he said. "I'd like to speak seriously, too. If you're willing."

"To what end?" she asked. "You've moved on with your life, clearly."

Hart's brows notched in a frown. "What is *that* supposed to mean?"

"You said yourself that you're in the market for a bride."

"I never—" He stopped himself, recalling his provoking words to her when she'd called on him in Arlington Street. "That was only my feeble attempt at—"

"What you failed to mention is that you were already courting someone."

"What?"

"Don't deny it. You were seen with her in Battersea Park, driving her in your curricle. A great beauty, by all accounts."

Later, Hart would replay the scene in his mind, excoriating himself for his stupendous insensitivity. But in the moment, thinking of Ethel Neale and the melodramatic circumstances she'd been relating as he'd driven her in the park, he couldn't help but utter another laugh.

It was the exact wrong thing to do.

Jerking free of his arm, Anne spun on her heel and stalked back toward the first-class carriage in a furious swish of black silk.

Hart strode after her through the smoke, immediately contrite. "Anne, wait."

"Don't speak to me again," she said.

He dared a half smile. "Ever?"

She glared back at him, cheeks flushed with something like embarrassment. "Never," she said. "Not unless you first manage to grow up."

On arriving in York, Anne's mother announced her intention of stopping for the night. They'd originally planned to pass the first night of their journey further north, in Malton, but exhaustion had set in, and Mama could not be budged.

Hartford found them a respectable inn near the station and secured a set of rooms. Three altogether. Mama preferred to have her own chamber, which she shared with Hortense.

Anne was relegated to the adjoining room—a small closet-like space just big enough for her and her own French maid, Jeanette. There, Anne stripped off her dusty, perspiration-damp carriage gown and indulged in a thorough wash.

Railway travel was a dirty business. She didn't know which was worse, the smoke or the soot. It settled on one's clothes and in one's hair. Appalling stuff.

By the time she'd washed, changed, and repaired her hair, it was nearing eight o'clock. Hartford sent word that he'd procured them a private parlor.

Anne had no reason to doubt his capabilities. He'd been annoyingly efficient in looking after them. She didn't like to admit it. She was still fuming over how he'd laughed at her.

Her cheeks burned to recall it.

That he should still have the power to vex her so! As if she were a girl of sixteen and not a woman grown.

She hadn't spoken a word to him since they'd reboarded the train at Derby. To his credit, he'd refrained from nettling her. If she didn't know better, she'd almost suspect he was feeling guilty.

But no.

Anne wasn't going to fall into the trap of feeling sorry for the devil.

The moment she finished her toilette, she went to her mother's room. She knocked softly on the connecting door before entering. "Mama?"

"Come," her mother said.

Anne came to a halt at the end of the brass bed.

Mama was propped up in it, a tray across her lap, midway through eating her dinner. "I've had a tray sent up," she said, quite unnecessarily.

Anne drew closer. "I thought we were dining downstairs?"

"The journey has overtaxed me. I must rest."

"Then I'll retire early as well."

Her mother waved the suggestion away. "By no means. You'll dine with Hartford. One of us must do so."

Anne's muscles went rigid. "Mama, I really don't think—"

"Apologize for my absence. Tell him I expect to resume our journey bright and early tomorrow. He won't find me lagging." Mama gave Anne a bracing look as she cut her meat. "Come, my girl. Surely you can be civil to the gentleman for an hour or two."

"In a private parlor?" Anne was incredulous.

"Don't be missish. He was practically a brother to you when you were a girl. I've no fear he'll behave indecorously. He's long past the age of tugging your plaits or putting frogs down your pinafore. The worst you might expect is some well-intentioned quizzing."

Anne wondered that Mama could be so blind where Hartford was concerned. Then again, she knew nothing of his proposal, or of Anne's refusal of that offer.

It was Papa who had had a keen eye in that regard. That was why

Anne had been so anxious to speak to him on the subject before he'd died.

"Hartford isn't my brother," she said. "He's a—"

"Really, Anne." Mama lowered her fork. "Must you question me at every turn? You were never so disobliging before you started spending time with those horse-mad friends of yours. I begin to suspect they've had a bad influence on you." She jerked her head toward the door, her patience at an end. "Off with you."

Anne swallowed any further objection. What would be the point of it? Mama's word was law, and Anne would be a thankless daughter indeed if she chose this moment—when her mother was feeling a resurgence of grief—to engage her in an argument over something as trifling as a dinner.

Though it didn't feel that trifling to Anne, truth be told.

She exited the chamber in sullen silence.

It was one thing to endure Hartford's company in the presence of her mother, but quite another to be alone with the man.

Anne recalled again how he'd laughed at her.

Oh, but she despised him!

Eight

Downstairs, Hartford awaited Anne in the front hall of the inn. Like her, he had washed and changed. His dark hair was combed into meticulous order, his square-chiseled jaw freshly shaven. No longer in plaid, he was now garbed in striped trousers and an outrageous mulberry-colored velvet coat.

Anne briefly closed her eyes. What crime had she committed in her life that she was to be punished thus?

Hartford smiled at her look of martyrdom. "An improvement, I thought," he said, straightening his coat. Shocking as it was, the garment was impeccably tailored, setting off his aggravatingly broad shoulders to magnificent effect. "Don't you like velvet?"

She refused to be goaded. "My opinions are of little matter."

Still smiling, he searched over her head. "Where is the countess?"

Anne hated to answer him. She knew how gleefully he'd react to her predicament. "My mother's fatigued from our journey," she said stiffly. "She begs you would excuse her, and promises to be fit to travel first thing in the morning."

Hartford's response wasn't at all what Anne was expecting.

He didn't laugh or smirk or make a sarcastic remark. He merely looked at her—silently, solemnly—a sudden thoughtfulness in his gaze. "So," he said at last, "you and I are to dine alone?"

"It seems so." Gathering her dignity, Anne brushed past him, determined to make the best of things.

He gently caught hold of her upper arm. "Our private parlor is this way."

Anne felt the press of his fingers around her silk-bombazine-encased arm as intimately as if he'd touched her bare skin.

Butterflies took wing in her stomach. She couldn't think why.

Perhaps it was because she was in a strange mood, worrying about Mama, Cousin Joshua, and even still about Julia. Or perhaps it was because they were in a strange place, in imminent expectation of being alone.

Whatever it was, Anne refused to succumb to the sensation.

Lifting her chin, she allowed him to guide her to the private parlor he'd reserved for them.

It was a tidy room, warmed by a recently laid fire. Two servingmen were setting hot dishes of roast chicken and boiled vegetables on the table, along with a bottle of wine.

Hartford pulled out a chair for her. "I apologize for the austerity of the meal. I ordered it with your mother in mind."

Utterly bland, he might have said.

Mama's proclivities for plain dining were well-known. She didn't only condemn sugar, she disapproved of rich sauces and excessive seasonings as well. It was paramount to her to keep control of her diet.

"I shan't complain," Anne said as she sat down. Her place had already been set. So had two others at the old wooden table.

Hartford instructed the servingmen to clear the third setting away. They hastily complied and then bustled out of the room with a great deal of bowing, scraping, and mutterings of "yer ladyship" and "yer honor."

Anne was accustomed to such behavior. Whenever she traveled with her mother, the innkeepers along the way made a horrid fuss.

Hartford took a seat across from her at the table. "Do you mind that?" he asked. "The genuflecting?"

"I hardly notice it." She spread her napkin over her lap. "I'm surprised you do."

"You forget, I'm only a mister."

"You're the grandson of an earl, even if you're not titled yourself."

"The distinction means little to a publican." Hartford poured her a glass of wine. "In any event, I'd rather my pedigree not enter a room before I do. I've found it best to be judged on my own merit." His mouth quirked. "Or lack of it."

Anne held up her hand for him to stop filling her glass. "Are you implying that I rest on my honorific?"

"I don't know, my lady. Do you?"

"I certainly don't." She picked up her knife and fork. "And don't pretend for a moment that you're on terms of equality with an innkeeper. You may not have a *lord* or a *sir* in front of your name, but you're still a gentleman of breeding. Anyone can see."

"You admit it, then?" He filled his own glass. "To think, all this time, I was convinced you thought me a rogue."

"What *you* are is predictable. Not five minutes in my company and you're already seeking to provoke me."

"I don't wish to provoke you." His blue eyes twinkled. "But I do like to see a flash of your old fire now and then."

Anne cut into a piece of her roast chicken. "You'll see the back of me if you don't cease your needling. You're lucky I'm even speaking to you after how you behaved at Derby."

No sooner had she uttered the words than she regretted them.

They were a reminder not only of Hartford's ill-timed laughter, but of the conversation that had preceded it. A conversation about the beautiful young lady he was courting.

Anne could have kicked herself for resurrecting the subject.

The smile died out of Hartford's eyes. For a taut moment, it seemed as though he might say something serious. But the words never came. Turning his attention to his plate of food, he lapsed into brooding silence.

Anne fell equally quiet as she ate.

For a long while, the only sounds in the room were the clink of cutlery, the fire snapping and crackling in the hearth, and the soft glug of wine as Hartford wordlessly refilled their glasses.

Anne found herself drinking far more than she was accustomed to. Not only because of the unnatural silence but also because of the precarious emotions that simmered beneath it. Tension fairly vibrated in the air. It was so thick between them, she could scarcely manage to swallow her roast chicken.

Oh, why hadn't she insisted on dining in her room? If she had, this entire awkward dinner could have been avoided.

Just when she felt she could bear it no longer, Hartford put down his fork and fixed her with a troubled frown.

"Anne," he began gravely. "About that young lady in Battersea—"

"Don't," she said.

"You don't even know what I'm going to say."

"I do. And you needn't." Setting down her own knife and fork, she boldly met his eyes. There was no room for faintheartedness. It was she who had introduced the subject, fool that she was, and she who must put it to rest. "I should never have brought it up in the first place. It's no business of mine whom you're courting."

"That's the crux of the matter, old thing," Hartford said. "I'm not courting that girl."

Anne looked at him in blank confusion.

And then, all at once, understanding came.

A wash of heat swept up her throat. *Good Lord.* It had been his mistress.

Hartford kept a mistress.

Inexplicable feelings of hurt and betrayal constricted her chest, squeezing at her heart and lungs until she could scarcely breathe.

Stupid, stupid. What right had she to be hurt? She had no claim on him.

Besides, she wasn't naive. Many gentlemen kept mistresses.

Beautiful, experienced women with whom they shared kisses and other intimacies. It was surely no worse than Hartford courting a girl.

And yet, somehow, it wounded Anne even deeper.

Hartford wasn't just with the young lady in Battersea Park out of a sense of duty—a familial obligation to marry and set up his nursery. He was with her because he fancied her. Because he *wanted* her.

In all this time, Anne had never once dared to consider that Hartford might be bestowing his tender affections on someone else.

"Her name is Ethel Neale," he said. "She's my—"

Anne winced. "Pray don't continue—"

"Sister."

"I don't want to—" Anne belatedly registered the word he'd used to describe the woman. It wasn't the one she'd been expecting. "I'm sorry. *What* did you say?"

Hartford set his jaw. "She's my sister. My half sister."

Anne stared at him, dumbstruck. It took her a full five seconds to find her voice. "But . . . you don't have a sister. Or a half sister for that matter. Not that I ever knew."

"No one knew about it, save my parents." Hartford's eyes were absent their usual humor. "My mother confessed it to me before she died. I've kept the secret ever since, for my family's sake. It's imperative I continue to do so. I'm only telling you now because . . . I won't have you believing something about me that isn't true. I'm not courting Miss Neale." He paused, adding, "And she's not my mistress."

Anne blushed fiercely. "I never thought—"

"You did," he said. "I saw it on your face."

She bit off a tart reply. By heaven, she hated when he was right.

"Do you know who her father is?" she asked.

Hartford's mouth curved in a shadow of a smile. It was edged with unmistakable bitterness. "She's not my mother's child, Anne. She's my father's."

"Your father!" Anne drew back in astonishment. "But he was—"

"Yes, I know. A paragon of morality."

"And all this time, he had a natural child?"

"Three of them."

"*Three?*" Anne's mouth nearly dropped open. "I don't believe it."

"Believe it. He kept a mistress for over a decade. A former lady's maid of my mother's."

"Gracious," Anne murmured under her breath. His mother's own lady's maid! Was nothing sacred?

"She's a brash sort of woman," Hartford went on, "though I suppose she has her charms. Together they had a son and two daughters—Marcus, Ethel, and Ermintrude. I've been subsidizing their upkeep since I turned twenty."

"Your father left no provision for them?"

"Not a penny."

"That doesn't sound like him."

Hartford gave her a sardonic look.

She stifled a grimace. "No, of course, you're right. None of this sounds like your father. Not the man we knew."

The late Everett Hartford had been a pattern card of propriety. An honorable and somewhat severe gentleman who, through his selectively charitable acts and sternly penned tracts on the corrupting influence of immorality among the working classes, had earned the respect of the crown, the church, and the majority of the fashionable public.

Naturally, he hadn't been perfect. He'd been an indifferent sort of father to Hartford. Cold, distant, and seemingly unfeeling. Anne had frequently observed it as a girl. There had been no warmth toward his son in word or deed. It was a fact she'd often lamented on Hartford's behalf. He'd been such a happy, mischievous boy. Rather like an enthusiastic puppy eager for any scrap of paternal praise or encouragement.

His father's coldness had hurt him.

Even so . . .

There had been nothing in Everett Hartford's outward character to indicate he was capable of such hypocrisy.

On the contrary, Hartford's parents had both seemed to be somber and responsible individuals. Twin pillars of the community who had, by some strange happenstance, produced a roguish son with a reputation for taking nothing seriously.

But it wasn't so, was it? Not if what Hartford said was true.

He'd been the responsible one all along, protecting his family's reputation at a cost to his own peace of mind—and to his own pocketbook.

"How can you afford them?" Anne couldn't stop herself from asking. "Your inheritance isn't enough to—"

"Quite," Hartford said tersely. "Luckily, I have other sources of income."

"Not your writing."

He gave a humorless laugh. "You say that with such conviction."

"Because you're not a writer," Anne said.

She meant no insult by it. It was merely a fact. Anyone could see from the columns he wrote in the *Spiritualist Herald*, the *Weekly Heliosphere*, and even the *Botanical Bi-Monthly* that Hartford wasn't serious about his work.

At least, anyone who knew him could see that.

He'd never been of a literary bent. As a younger man his passion had been for action. From hair-raising curricle races and bloody boxing matches to extravagant dares that had him climbing into steam-powered vehicles or participating in bloodcurdling balloon ascents. If he wasn't involved in a hazardous prank, he was participating in a reckless wager. All of it for his own juvenile diversion, regardless of risk.

"I never claimed to be one," he said. "It's just a hobby of mine. One of many I undertake to amuse myself."

Anne finished her wine. She didn't like to be reminded of Hartford's penchant for frivolity. "I hesitate to ask what the others are."

"*Are* you asking?"

It was none of her affair. Nevertheless . . .

"I suppose I am," she said.

"If you must know, I enjoy investing in novel patents."

Her brows lifted in question.

He grudgingly explained. "A reengineered independent feed pump for a locomotive engine. A newly improved wringing and mangling machine that will save women time in their washing. And—more recently—a patent for a horseless road vehicle, formulated in the vein of Mr. Trevithick's invention. Not the most economical of devices as yet, but—"

"You're jesting."

"Not at all."

Anne didn't know what to say.

Hartford had been an admirer of the late inventor Richard Trevithick for as long as she could remember. He'd once lent her a book on the subject. Anne had read it, besotted as she was, observing that Mr. Trevithick's steam-powered road inventions had resulted in more catastrophes than successes.

Her opinions had done nothing to curb Hartford's enthusiasm.

"I support the patents of several promising inventors," he informed her. "I suppose you disapprove of that, as well."

"I don't disapprove," she said. "I only wonder how such speculative investments can be enough to maintain your father's mistress and three children."

"They aren't. I have other, more reliable sources of income. Common, you might say. And thank God for them. If I didn't, I'd have no means of settling Marcus Neale's debts." He downed the remainder of his wine, returning his empty glass to the table. "That's what Miss Neale and I were discussing while driving in Hyde Park, by the way—the two thousand pounds her brother owes."

Anne inhaled sharply. "*Two thousand pounds?* How on earth—"

"Did I not mention? Since returning from boarding school this spring, my half brother's developed a fondness for gambling. If I don't satisfy his debts, his mother threatens to expose the whole of my father's perfidy to the world. She has some notion that she'll be greeted as a romantic figure in the mold of Emma Hamilton."

"Good Lord."

"Yes, it's quite a comical dilemma. I'm half-tempted to let Mrs. Neale do her worst."

Anne shook her head in disbelief. "Your grandfather truly has no idea?"

"None. Nor my uncle. They can't know, much as I'd like to let Mrs. Neale enlighten them. If my father's sins were to become public, it would cause a scandal that would reach from Arlington Street all the way to Westminster. Brookdale could say goodbye to his career in politics." Hartford's smile turned wry. "No, my dear Fury. I'm afraid it's only been me for the last nine years—useless as you think I am—standing between my family and utter reputational ruination. I'm sure there's a Dutch parable in there somewhere."

Reluctant compassion stirred within Anne's breast. "Oh, Hart," she said softly.

An odd emotion crossed over his face. It was impossible to read.

She belatedly realized that she'd called him by the affectionate nickname she'd used when they were children. The same one she'd whispered when he'd kissed her so long ago.

"Oh, Hart," she'd breathed, one hand lifting to curve around the strong column of his neck.

He'd held her so masterfully in his arms. So confident and self-assured. And yet, he hadn't been. Not entirely. Indeed, it was the first and only time she'd ever felt him tremble.

Her insides quivered at the memory.

Was he remembering it, too?

But he must be to be looking at her so intently.

"I don't want your sympathy," he said, his voice gone rough. "If you're going to address me that way, let it be because you—"

The door to the private parlor opened before he could finish.

Hartford's jaw tightened as the innkeeper entered, accompanied by the same two servingmen who had set out their dinner. He held a tray bearing a small iced cake and another bottle of wine.

"My lady. My good sir." He bowed low. "I trust your meal was satisfactory. Can I tempt you with our Madeira cake? We've a reputation for it in these parts. I took the privilege of setting this one aside for you."

"Some cake would be excellent," Hartford said, anticipating Anne's refusal. "And leave the bottle, if you please."

"Very good, sir." The innkeeper set out the cake and wine as the servingmen cleared away the remains of dinner. When they'd finished, the three of them bowed themselves out of the room, closing the door behind them.

Anne glared at Hartford. Whatever he'd been about to say had been lost in the moment, overshadowed by the interruption, and by his exasperating high-handedness. "You know how my mother feels about sweets."

"Your mother isn't here," he said. "Or hadn't you noticed?"

Her frown deepened. She'd noticed all right. Being alone with Hartford this evening had put her through seven kinds of hell.

The worst of it was that she'd almost let her guard down. On hearing his tale, she'd felt the urge to help him. To *comfort* him.

He refilled her glass for the third time. "Is this on your mother's forbidden list, too?"

Anne was vaguely alarmed to realize how much she'd drunk this evening. At home, she usually had no more than a small half glass of French red with dinner. But this vintage—nowhere near as fine as she was accustomed to—seemed both more palatable and more potent. The more she drank, the looser her tongue.

"On the contrary," she said. "She considers wine to be healthful."

"Convenient."

"My mother makes her own rules. Every lady should do so."

Hartford returned the bottle to the table. "For themselves, perhaps. Not for others."

Anne opened her mouth to respond, only to clamp it shut again. Drink or no drink, she wouldn't allow him to resurrect this old argument. The last time they'd spoken on the subject, it had created a chasm between them that hadn't been breached in years.

He didn't help things by teasing her so incessantly—reminding her always of her choice to remain with her mother rather than marry him. A few weeks ago, he'd even involved one of her friends in their quarrel, sending a message to Anne through Evelyn, of all people.

"He said I'm to tell you that no plant can flourish in the shadow of another. Whatever that means," Evelyn had relayed.

Anne bristled to think of it.

One would almost suspect that he wanted them to fight again. That he wanted the chasm to become not only unbreachable but fatal to them both.

"Perhaps we should send some up to your mother?" he suggested as he cut the cake.

Her pulse jumped at the very idea. "On no account."

"You're right. This is a pleasure we should keep to ourselves." He placed a large slice of cake on a plate. It was thick with heavy icing.

Her mouth watered. The cake *did* look delicious. And it wasn't as though she always adhered to Mama's restrictions. When in company with her friends, Anne often indulged in a sugary treat or two. They were one of her few weaknesses.

Felix Hartford was another.

He pushed the plate to her from across the distance. "Come," he said, as silkily as a devil sent to tempt her. "Have a bite of something sweet."

"I shouldn't."

"You should. It will leaven the moment. It *is* your turn, after all."

She regarded him warily. "My turn for what?"

Hartford smiled. "To tell me one of your deep, dark secrets, of course."

Nine

Anne scoffed, but there was no mistaking the pink tinge in her cheeks. It stood out in stark contrast to the paleness of her complexion and the relentless black of her clothing.

She was wearing another bombazine mourning gown. A different one from the gown she'd worn on the train, but equally severe in its construction. The sight of it was as provoking to Hart as a red flag in front of a bull.

He cut himself an obscenely large piece of cake. "Isn't that how it works? A secret of yours for a secret of mine? It seems only fair after everything I've confessed."

She gave him a repressive look. "You weren't obliged to confess anything to me."

"Wasn't I?" His confession might not have been an obligation, but it had certainly been an imperative.

It was his curse again. This damnable urge to alleviate her pain, no matter the cost to himself—or to anyone else.

And it *was* pain he'd seen on her face when she'd mentioned his having been observed driving a young lady in the park. She'd been troubled to think he was courting someone. More troubled still to imagine he might be keeping a mistress.

Troubled. Hurt.

Jealous.

Hart had felt her reaction to his core. It had encouraged him to hope as he hadn't hoped in a very long while.

By God, but she *did* care for him after all. Not only in some reluctant fashion, but in a distinctly proprietary sense.

It was the same way he cared for her.

Lord only knew how he'd respond if their situations were reversed. If it were Anne who had been driving in the park in company with some mysterious gentleman.

If that day ever came, Hart hoped she wouldn't leave him to twist in the wind. That she'd tell him the truth—however painful it might be—and put him out of his misery as swiftly as possible.

"No, you were not," she said. "It was your own decision to tell me about your father's . . . about Mrs. Neale and her children."

Hart still couldn't quite believe that he had. His father's scandalous secret was just that. A secret. One that Hart had intended to take to his grave. At the same time . . .

He'd wanted to tell Anne everything. Not just today, but every day since he'd learned the truth of it.

It was nostalgia, that's what it was. An impulse from the past; a time when he'd been accustomed to confiding in her as a friend. In his weakest moments, Hart desperately wanted that friendship back. The privilege of her advice. The reassurance of her commiseration and comfort.

And not only that.

He wanted all the rest of it, too.

"I trust the secret of what's going on between you and your mother won't be anywhere near as damning as what I've confessed," he said. "Here." He nudged her glass of wine closer to her. "Have another drink. Gather your courage and tell me."

"It isn't a matter of courage." She paused for the space of several heartbeats before raising her glass and downing a large swallow. She set it back down with a decided clink. "And it isn't a deep dark secret. It's no secret at all."

Hart tucked into his cake. "I'm waiting."

She folded her hands in her lap, leaving her own slice of cake untouched in front of her. "My cousin Joshua has written. He says he'll be coming in August to take up residence in Grosvenor Square."

"With you and your mother?"

"I doubt that. He's bringing his own mother with him. Mama would never countenance sharing the house with such a person, even if that's what my cousin has in mind. Which it isn't. I expect he means us to move out."

Hart's expression sobered. If what she said was true, it was indeed serious. "What will you do?"

"Nothing, very likely. My mother is disposed to think it all a hum. She doesn't believe he'll come to London."

"Do you?"

"I don't know. Probably. That is, he must come eventually, mustn't he? He has the title and a seat in the Lords. He's not the type to languish in the country now he's reached his majority."

Hart knew what the new earl's arrival could mean to her happiness and security. "I'm sorry, Anne. I'd no idea this was hanging over your head."

"I confess, I've had more pressing matters to trouble me. Miss Wychwood and . . ."

"And?"

A guarded look came into her eyes. "Why do you concern yourself with my troubles? After everything that's passed between us—"

"Yes," he said. "Precisely that. You and I have a history together. It's the reason you came to me in the first place. The very reason I'm here. I'll *always* care what happens to you, Anne. The truth is . . . I wouldn't know how to stop."

Anne found herself at a loss. Not because she was surprised. She wasn't blind to Hartford's interest in her.

If it could be called interest.

It seemed at times to be fueled as much by anger as it was by any residual feelings from the past.

She supposed it was the same variety of interest she took in him. A bitter, aching sort of furious regret.

No. His interest didn't surprise her. It was that he should give voice to it.

The two of them never spoke of the past. Indeed, they rarely spoke at all except to bicker and quarrel.

Anne had the depressing premonition that if they ever talked about it—*really* talked about it—the whole episode would finally be done with. And she wasn't sure she wanted that, much as Hartford vexed her.

Their interlude had been the sole bit of romance in her life. She was accustomed to keeping the memory close, preserving it much in the way an aged spinster might keep a dried-out piece of wedding cake under her pillow. It was the faded dream of a happily-ever-after. The hope an old maid cherished when all other hope was gone.

Anne hated herself for clinging to it.

"Perhaps it's time to let all of that go," she said. "We can't keep holding on to the past."

"Let go of the past?" He directed an ironic glance at her black gown. "Are you really in any position to make that suggestion?"

A rare glimmer of self-consciousness went through her. It wasn't pleasant to be judged and found wanting. Not by him.

Her chin lifted a fraction. "You've never understood my position."

"No," he said. "Happily, I haven't."

"You never *tried* to understand." She couldn't keep the accusation from her voice. "If you had made the smallest effort to see things from my point of view—"

"What's to understand? You've all but climbed atop a funeral pyre with your mother. In five years' time, I wouldn't be surprised to hear that you'd actually done so." He shoveled another forkful of cake into his mouth. "The only unanswered question is how anyone with your spirit could be so weak as to give up on life altogether."

"*Weak?*" she repeated.

"Do you think I'd obey my grandfather if he told me to entomb myself alive? That I'd be so cowardly as to give up the one person I—"

"*Cowardly?*" she echoed with growing outrage.

It was the same thing he'd said when they'd argued the last time.

That, and worse.

"You know nothing of my choices," she said.

Hartford's fork clattered to the table. His eyes gleamed with a strange light. "I know *everything* about them. I've been living with your choices for six and a half bloody years."

"I never asked you—"

"You didn't have to ask." He sat back in his chair. "My God, Anne. What do you take me for? Did you think I would forget?"

It was the worst thing he could have said.

Indeed, her heart contracted so hard it was a physical pain in her chest. Even after all these years, the memory of that final argument was still too raw. Too tender. In other circumstances, she could never bring herself to speak of it. But tonight . . .

Three glasses of wine had emboldened her.

"You *told* me you would forget," she reminded him. "You said it would be easy. That I was nothing very special. Just a weak, cowardly little wallflower whom no one liked very much in the first place. You said—"

Hartford's jaw clenched. "I *know* what I said."

"You said you only proposed because you felt sorry for me. That you'd already found someone else. Someone better. Diana Sterling, I believe it was."

"I was angry. I said a lot of stupid things."

"*Cruel* things."

His gaze held hers, unrepentant. "As I recall, I didn't have a monopoly on cruelty."

Anne looked back at him steadily, no sorrier than he was.

She might have been cruel to him—to be sure, she *had* been cruel. She'd also been young, grieving, and provoked beyond all bearing.

"What does any of it matter now?" she asked. "We neither of us may have forgotten, but there's no point in reviewing it. I suggest we end this conversation. That we finish our meal—"

"I've already finished mine." He crumpled his napkin and angrily tossed it onto the table. "What about you? Aren't you going to eat that?"

Anne's gaze fell to her cake. Though she looked at it with longing, she made no move to pick up her fork.

Her hesitation only served to stoke Hartford's temper.

"It's right in front of you," he said. "All you have to do is reach out and take it." His harsh words were edged with unmistakable meaning. "It's not going to wait forever."

An alarming burning sensation prickled at the back of Anne's eyes.

She'd drank too much. Said too much.

And she couldn't eat her piece of cake now, much as she'd like to. He'd ruined it. Turned it into something different. It was no longer Madeira cake. It was everything else. All the things she'd given up. Romance. Marriage. *Him*.

"Oh, must you complicate everything?" she asked in a burst of frustration. "As if I don't have enough to—"

A knock sounded at the door, arresting her speech.

"My lady?" Hortense entered without invitation. She bobbed a curtsy. "Begging your pardon, but I've a message from her ladyship."

Hartford's black mood vanished behind his perpetual smile of wry amusement. "Of course you do," he said. "What is it? Pray, don't keep us in suspense."

Anne ignored him, such that she was able.

It didn't prevent a stray fact from registering at the back of her brain.

She comprehended, in that moment, that Felix Hartford wore his good humor the way a knight might wear a suit of armor. It was both sword and shield to him. An iron-forged mask that concealed untold emotion beneath.

An unnerving realization.

She was in no fit state to make sense of it.

"Go ahead, Hortense," she said.

"Lady Arundell says I'm to remind you that you have an early start in the morning," Hortense said.

"Yes, indeed," Anne said. Rising from her chair, she forced herself to meet Hartford's eyes. "Dinner has been most entertaining, sir, but it's past time I retired. I shall bid you good evening."

Hartford stood. For an instant, it seemed his mask might slip. But it didn't, not by so much as an inch. He bowed to her as she and Hortense withdrew.

It wasn't until Anne was safely back in her own small chamber that she realized her hands were shaking quite out of control.

Ten

The following morning, Hart escorted the ladies back to the railway station and onto the train to Malton.

He had a devil of a headache.

After Anne had departed the private dining parlor last evening, he'd remained there alone until the fire died, finishing not only her slice of cake but the entire bottle of wine.

If Anne was feeling any of the effects of her own drinking, she showed no sign of it. Hart nevertheless found himself being careful with her. More careful, perhaps, than he'd ever been before.

"You told me you would forget. That I was nothing very special. Just a weak, cowardly little wallflower whom no one liked very much in the first place. You said that you only proposed because you felt sorry for me."

The words had haunted him all night. *His* words, spoken in hurt and anger, thrown back at him after all these years.

She'd remembered them. Every syllable of every cruelty he'd uttered.

Of course she had.

Hart remembered, too. Not only his cruelties, but all the ones she'd flung at him first. Punishing, razor-sharp words that had flayed him open to the bone.

He'd been freshly returned from a year spent in the Himalayas. Still a lad in many respects, though recently obliged to grow up. Since the death of his parents, and the revelations that had come after, the very foundation of Hart's life had seemed to crumble beneath his feet. There had been nothing solid any longer. Nothing true.

Only Anne.

On returning to England, he'd anticipated she would be out of mourning. That she'd, at last, be ready to marry him and start their life together. He could well recall the tightness in his chest as he'd ascended the stone steps to knock at the front door of her house in Grosvenor Square.

His entire happiness had hinged on having her.

But Anne hadn't greeted him with the same anticipation. And she hadn't been out of mourning. She'd still been clothed in black, her countenance pale and rigid with resolve.

"You don't understand," she'd said. "I'm needed at home."

Hart had known then that he was never going to have her.

The realization had robbed him of every last vestige of warmth. It had turned his hopes to ash in his throat, leaving him cold with disappointment and—he was ashamed to admit—anger.

"For how much longer?" he'd asked.

"I don't know. Another year, I suspect."

"You must be joking," Hart had said. He'd already waited too long. He'd had no choice. The rules of mourning were clear on the length of time a child must mourn their parent. Hart had borne it because he'd had to. But no longer. "I'll not wait another minute."

"Hart, please try to—"

"Your mourning period is over. We've no need to delay. We can marry directly and leave this unhappy place once and for all."

"I can't leave London," she'd said.

"You can. You and I must be done with our families. We must go away from here and start anew. It's the only way forward for either of us."

She'd shaken her head. "I can't. Not yet. Not in good conscience."

"Can't or won't?" Desperation had lent a sneering harshness to his words.

"Both," she'd said. "If I must choose between my duty to my mother and my feelings for you—"

"Yes," Hart had shot back. "The choice shouldn't be difficult."

He hadn't considered the repercussions of such a callous ultimatum. He'd been too angry. Too bitter at having been deprived of her for so long. She'd asked him to go away—to leave her to her grief. And he had. Was it so unreasonable for him to demand her undivided devotion on his return?

At the time, he'd thought not.

"If you understood what I've endured," she'd replied, "what I'm still enduring, you'd never ask that of me. Things haven't been easy in your absence. My mother requires—"

"Your mother requires," he'd repeated scathingly. "A convenient excuse."

Anne's sherry eyes had glittered with a brief flash of outrage. It had been made more noticeable by the dull aura of gloom that hung about every other part of her. "It's not an excuse. If you knew a thing about duty or obligation—"

"Which I don't, clearly."

"No, you don't," she'd said, goaded. "You have no comprehension of what it means to sacrifice yourself for the ones you love."

Hart's face had hardened into an implacable mask. "You're right on that score. I'm not going to make a needless sacrifice of myself for anyone."

"But that's what love is," Anne had replied with all the arrogant wisdom of youth. "Don't you know that? Or has this all been a game to you? A careless kiss under the mistletoe? An equally careless proposal?"

"A foolish kiss," he'd bit out. "And an ill-advised proposal. Both of which I sorely regret."

She had been standing by the drawing room window, her posture stiff with dignity. "You're not alone in your regret," she'd said. "Fortunately, we neither of us need suffer for it."

"I'm already suffering for it," he'd replied ungenerously.

"Then allow me to put an end to your misery." She had turned to face him, twin spots of color burning in her cheeks. "I release you from our engagement."

Hart had recoiled as if she'd slapped him. It had rather felt as though she had.

Anne had continued without mercy. "I expect you'll soon forget your foolishness. You never did keep to anything for long."

His face had paled.

And just like that, all the injustices he'd had to deal with, all of the hurt and betrayal and loss, had welled up within him, manifesting in an icy-hearted cruelty he'd never have believed himself capable of until that moment.

"On that score, madam, I have no doubt," he had said. "I suspect this affair will be easy to forget, now I'm sober and viewing you in the cold light of day."

It had been her turn to recoil. "Are you implying you only proposed to me because you'd been drinking?"

Hart had felt sick to his stomach, fully understanding that he was setting fire to the bridge between them. But that hadn't stopped him. He'd been too angry. Too bloody hurt.

"Why else?" he'd asked. "Too much wassail, I don't wonder. As I recall, it was flowing freely that night."

"You hardly touched it!"

"I had plenty," he'd said in a snarl. "I was muddled enough to think myself in love with you. I couldn't see then that you were nothing very special. Just a weak, cowardly little wallflower whom no one ever liked very much in the first place."

Her mouth had fallen open with shock. "Weak?" she'd repeated in growing anger. "Cowardly?"

Hart had walked to the fireplace then, where he'd stopped, giving her his back. A queer coldness had sunk into his veins. "I only kept to our agreement because I felt sorry for you. The truth is, I've been looking for a way out of it so I might court someone better. Miss Sterling comes to mind. She's long expressed her interest in me."

"She may have you," Anne had said in tones of vibrating fury, "with my blessing. I wish her joy of such a useless, empty-headed nothing of a gentleman. You will soon let her down, just as you do with everyone who knows you."

She'd never seen his face as she'd uttered those fateful words. She'd never known how they'd affected him.

Hart had just stood there, absorbing the blows, and then he'd straightened, bowed, and, with a few muttered words, strode from the room.

A useless, empty-headed nothing of a gentleman.

If only Anne had known how those words would follow him down the years, like a curse uttered by some beautiful avenging Fury.

It hadn't taken him long to regret everything he'd said to her. To realize his ultimatum had been a critical mistake.

By then it had been too late.

She sat across from him now, black clad and expressionless, in the shadow of her formidable mother.

Hart felt the old urge to nettle her. Anything to rekindle the spark in her eyes. To bring her back to life. But he couldn't do it. Not after last night. Not when he'd seen her trembling as she'd exited the parlor.

The sight had shaken him as nothing else ever could.

"Malton is the last rail stop on the road to Blunt's estate," he said. "The rest of the journey will have to be made by hired coach."

Anne gave a faint wince at the prospect. She discreetly raised a hand to massage her temple.

So her head was aching, too.

The fact inspired Hart's immediate sympathy. "We can take rooms there if you prefer, and resume our journey in the morning."

Lady Arundell glanced up from her astrological almanac, her silver-filigree lorgnette poised in her hand. "Nonsense. We'll proceed by coach directly. According to my calculations, we should be in the village outside the Hall by early afternoon. What was it called again?"

"Hardholme," Anne said in a colorless voice.

Hart looked at her with concern, even as he addressed her mother. "It's a remote and wild sort of place, ma'am. The accommodations there aren't likely to be very luxurious."

"This isn't a pleasure trip," Lady Arundell said. "We're here on spiritualist business. Fielding and the others will expect me to report my findings without delay."

"You intend us to call on Blunt today?" Hart asked.

"Naturally," her ladyship said. "The weather is fine, and we're all fit to the task. We have no good reason to wait."

No good reason?

Hart felt a surge of irritation at Lady Arundell's selfishness. Couldn't she see that her daughter was poorly?

"We might do Captain Blunt the courtesy of sending a note first," he suggested.

It would give Anne the remainder of the afternoon to rest. And it would give Captain Blunt fair warning. Hart didn't know the fellow particularly well, but Blunt didn't seem like the sort of man who would appreciate a trio of unannounced visitors.

"Quite unnecessary," Lady Arundell said. "This is wild country, as you say. We've no need to be so formal. And we've no need to suspend our errand by so much as a second."

"I'd like to stop," Anne surprised Hart by saying.

Lady Arundell's brows elevated. "What on earth for, child?"

"I must purchase a wedding gift for Julia."

"In Malton?" Lady Arundell sounded appalled. "What sort of gift can one buy in such a place?"

"A book," Anne replied. "There must be a shop somewhere near the station."

"I'll find one for you," Hart offered.

Anne's gaze briefly touched his. "I would be grateful."

He inclined his head to her.

"Very well," Lady Arundell said. "So long as it doesn't take you above ten minutes." Raising her lorgnette to her eyes, she resumed reading her almanac.

Anne turned her attention back to the window as the train rolled onward.

The rattle of wheels on the track was accompanied by the steady chug of escaping steam. It was a relaxing sound, generally, but not so much when one was suffering the aftereffects of strong drink. Anne flinched at every hiss and clatter.

Hart withdrew a small notepad and pencil from the interior pocket of his coat and jotted a short note. Folding the paper in half, he stood and rang for the train attendant.

Lady Arundell glanced up. "Is anything amiss?"

"Nothing at all," Hart said smoothly, resuming his seat. "Only a message for my valet."

The attendant answered the summons directly and Hart gave him the note.

Nothing more was said on the subject until they arrived at the station in Malton. There, Hart's valet, Bishop, sought him out on the platform.

A wiry fair-haired man in his middle fifties, Bishop was as competent as he was discreet. He handed Hart an engraved silver flask. "Just as you requested, sir."

"Excellent." Hart tucked the flask into his suit pocket. He moved to join Anne and her mother, who were conferring with their own servants. As he approached, Lady Arundell and her maid departed for the ladies' retiring room.

Anne remained behind. She was standing, arms folded, at the end of the platform. The glare of the midmorning sun cast a shadow over her face.

Her maid hovered nearby, seeing to the luggage.

"My mother requires ten minutes to refresh herself," Anne said.

Hart scanned her face. "Of course. Do you—"

"I'm fine."

A strong wind gusted over the platform, stirring up a profusion of dust and grit.

Hart angled himself in front of Anne, instinctively shielding her from the worst of it. "Forgive me, but you don't look it."

Her countenance hardened. "I don't recall asking your opinion."

"It was an observation, not an insult." He produced the flask. "Here," he said, offering it to her. "This is for you."

She took it, frowning. "What am I supposed to do with it?"

"Drink it," he said. "It's Bishop's remedy for too much wine. God only knows what he puts in it. If he should ever confess it to me, I'll patent the stuff and make my fortune."

Her frown faded. "How did you know—"

"Call it fellow feeling," he said. "Now drink up before your mother gets back. We still have that bookshop to find."

Anne unscrewed the cap and slowly brought the flask to her lips.

She had a lush mouth, petal soft and wickedly voluptuous, with lips the exact color of the flowering pink meadowsweet that covered the grounds of his grandfather's Hampshire estate.

Hart couldn't look at those lips without remembering the way they'd felt under his.

"I find it's better to down it in one go," he said helpfully.

For once, she obeyed him, tossing back the contents of the flask with a grimacing swallow.

"Good Lord," she choked. "It tastes vile."

"Bitter medicine is usually the most effective, I find." He took the empty flask back from her, returning it to his pocket. "You should feel the benefit of it within the hour."

"Have you already had some?" she asked. "You mentioned fellow feeling. I daresay your head aches as much as mine."

"More so, I imagine." At the moment, it felt as if an energetic blacksmith was using Hart's cranium for an anvil. "I shall consider it a just punishment for having upset you last night."

Her brows knit. "Hartford—"

"Don't trouble yourself over it, old thing. I expect I'll hurt you again. It seems what we do, you and I. Hurt each other."

The wind whipped at her fashionable bonnet, causing the dyed black feathers to curl along the alabaster curve of her cheek. She brushed them away with a slim, black-gloved hand.

"I suppose we must talk about it someday," she said. "Properly talk about it. There's no other way to put it to rest." Her bosom rose and fell on a sigh. "It seems foolish, really. It was over so long ago."

Hart's eyes narrowed.

Over?

Is that what she thought?

He moved closer to her, blocking out the wind and the glare, filling her vision, and his own, until it felt as if there were no one on the remote northern platform but the two of them.

"It's not over," he said. "But we will have that talk; you may depend on it."

Eleven

Anne cast another look out the window of the hired coach. There was still no sign of civilization, only an endless stretch of desolate moorland as far as the eye could see. She dropped the faded velvet curtain back into place.

Her head was no longer throbbing, thank goodness. And it was all owing to Hartford. Or rather, his valet. She couldn't have made it this far otherwise. The three of them had been traveling for hours, the poorly sprung coach shuddering and shaking as it bounced over every jut in the road.

On arriving in Hardholme that morning, they had remained only long enough to deposit their servants and luggage at the village inn—a dilapidated establishment with a painted sign above the door proclaiming it as the Red Lion. Mama couldn't be persuaded to linger. The closer they came to Captain Blunt's haunted estate, the more animated she became.

Anne was glad of it, though her own weariness threatened to overtake her.

It didn't help that Hartford kept throwing concerned glances in her direction.

He was seated across from her in the coach, looking rakishly handsome—and thoroughly frivolous—in his plaid three-piece suit.

But he wasn't, was he? Frivolous, that is.

Indeed, he claimed to have business in London that required him back in town by Friday.

Anne wondered what sort of business that might be.

"I have other, more reliable sources of income," he'd told her. "Common, you might say."

Common.

She supposed he meant trade. It was the only thing people of their class would consider to be common. But what manner of trade? She wanted to ask him. She wanted to know. At the same time, she was conscious of a desire to keep as far away from him as possible.

It's not over.

He'd told her that, too.

And he wasn't wrong.

She wasn't so silly as to deny it to herself. There had been something between them for years. Animosity, she'd thought. But that didn't account for how she'd felt when she believed he was courting someone else.

Rather than clarifying the matter, their argument last night had only served to confuse her feelings. His subsequent kindness to her had confused her even further.

Since leaving York, he'd been all that was solicitous, not only helping to cure her sore head but refraining from teasing her, too. He'd even found her a bookshop in Malton and escorted her there, waiting patiently while she purchased a copy of *Beeton's Book of Household Management* and had it wrapped as a gift for Julia.

"Not much longer," he said. "According to the coachman, it should be just around the next turning."

"I can sense its proximity," Mama said. "There's a certain vibration in the air. Can you not feel it, Anne?"

Anne pointedly avoided Hartford's gaze. She could, indeed, feel something, though she doubted whether it had anything to do with the restless spirits of murdered Royalists. "I don't know, Mama," she said. "Possibly."

Her mother pulled back the curtain on her side of the coach. As they approached the bend in the road, a pair of tall metal gates appeared in the distance, sagging open on their hinges.

"The original iron, I'd wager," Mama murmured. "Extraordinary."

Anne folded her hands in her lap. She reminded herself of Julia's letters. They'd been filled with happiness and joy. Ominous though the gates may appear, what lay beyond them must surely be nothing short of paradise.

It wasn't.

"Well," Hartford observed as Goldfinch Hall came into view, "one can understand why Blunt desired to marry an heiress."

Anne's spirits threatened to sink as she took in the derelict grandeur of the hall.

Made of severely weathered granite, it possessed a questionable roof, a sagging tower, and a crumbling facade covered in a wild tangle of thorny roses. It was a wholly gothic sight, but there was nothing of romance about it, only neglect and decay.

Could Julia truly be happy here? Could anyone?

The carriage rolled to a halt in front of the moss-covered stone front steps.

In that same moment, the doors of the house opened, and Julia emerged on Captain Blunt's arm. He was looming over her, battle-scarred and scowling, looking for all the world like a fearsome dragon guarding his treasure.

But Julia didn't appear afraid of him, not by any stretch of the imagination. Standing tall at her new husband's side, she was not only unharmed but positively radiant.

Anne's flagging spirits soared.

She didn't wait for the footman's assistance. Unlatching the door herself, she climbed out of the carriage and marched straight up the front steps.

"Anne!" Julia ran to meet her.

Anne enfolded her friend in a powerful embrace, conscious all the while of her mother and Hartford alighting from the carriage behind her. "Forgive me," she murmured. "There was no other way."

An hour later, after many cups of tea in the drawing room, and several abridged explanations of how each of them had come to be there, Anne was finally able to get Julia alone.

The two of them sat side by side in the shade of a vine-covered arbor at the edge of the house's overgrown garden. There, Anne gave Julia her book, along with a promise to lend her Jeanette's services on the morrow.

"She's at the inn now, making things comfortable in our rooms," Anne said. "But I shall bring her when we visit tomorrow, and she'll clean and press all your gowns for you."

Julia's eyes shimmered with tears of gratitude. Since eloping with the captain, her laundry woes had been her only source of unhappiness. "Thank you," she said, embracing Anne again.

"It's my second wedding gift to you," Anne said when they broke apart. "And this is the third." Reaching into the black velvet reticule that hung at her wrist, she extracted a copy of the newspaper article she'd found in the *London Courant*. "I confess, I went in search of it with the intention of exposing Captain Blunt as a villain. Now I know you have feelings for the man, I'm relieved I didn't succeed."

"What is it?" Julia asked.

"The most thorough report I could find on what happened all those years ago in the Crimea." Anne smiled. "You needn't look so anxious. The report says he was a hero. Here, take it. Read it for yourself."

Julia took the clipping. As she read it, the bloom slowly faded from her cheeks.

Anne was instantly attentive. "What's wrong, my dear? I thought the news would hearten you."

"It's nothing." Julia blinked rapidly. "I mean, it does." She thrust the newspaper article back at Anne. "I'm sorry. I'm quite overcome. It's all the excitement of your visit, I expect."

"Is that all?" Anne searched her face. "I believed you happy here, but if I suspected for a moment—"

"I *am* happy. Only . . ." Julia bit her lip. Her expression turned rueful. "I wonder how well a lady can ever know a man?"

Anne frowned. She'd been asking herself the same question since her dinner with Hartford.

Seeing him in those charged moments, absent his usual humor. Realizing it was some manner of protective armor. That underneath he was an entirely different person. Vulnerable, weary. A gentleman burdened by his responsibilities.

A gentleman simmering with unresolved feelings for her.

Perhaps she'd been wrong about him. Perhaps—just perhaps, mind—she didn't know him anywhere near as well as she'd thought she did.

A troubling notion. It had been eating away at Anne all day.

"I don't know," she said honestly. "Very well, I hope, if she's married to him."

"Marriage doesn't make one privy to all a husband's secrets," Julia informed her. "I've learned that of late."

"No? If ever I marry, I should demand to know everything."

Julia's mouth tilted in a faint smile. "I thought you didn't wish to marry."

"I don't," Anne said.

It's what she'd always told her friends, anyway. And it was largely true. Though she took part in the season, it had never been out of a particular desire to marry. It was a diversion, merely.

What else was one to do when one resided in London nearly all the year round?

Since Papa's death, Mama needed a constant whirl of activity to distract her from her grief. Anne had long accustomed herself to accompanying her, less in the guise of an eligible young miss than that of a spinster companion.

"Marriage isn't as bad as you might fear," Julia said.

"Isn't it?" Anne smiled. "I can't imagine I'll ever attempt it."

"Why not?"

"Because I find most gentlemen lacking in some regard or another. And there's none of them who would think *me* a prize. I'm too opinionated by half."

Julia took Anne's hand, holding it tightly. "What you are is the best friend anyone could ever hope for. To come here as you did . . . it was excessively heroic."

Anne squeezed Julia's hand in return. "I'd move heaven and earth for you, you know that."

"I do know it. I wish I might do the same for you."

"Why? I'm in no danger. My situation is the same as it ever was."

"Exactly," Julia said earnestly.

Anne laughed. "Don't be ridiculous. I'm quite content with my life."

"I would that you were more than content. I would that you were wildly and deliriously happy. If Mr. Hartford might make you so—"

"Hartford? Really, Julia."

"Why not? I've always suspected he was secretly fond of you. He never misses an opportunity to do you a service."

"Rubbish."

"It's true. When you were away in Birmingham, Lord Gresham importuned me in the garden at the Claverings' ball. Captain Blunt came to my aid, of course. But so did Mr. Hartford. It was he who hauled Gresham away and forced him into a cab. I've no doubt he was acting for your benefit, because he knows me to be your friend. He must care for you."

Anne gave her friend a look of mock severity. "How have you managed to turn the subject? I was meant to be consoling you."

"I don't need consoling, only your companionship." Julia stood, drawing Anne up with her. "Let's walk to the barn. You must see the kittens before you go."

It was one of the first things she'd mentioned on Anne's arrival, the wild moor cat who had given birth in their barn. Julia had wanted pets all of her life. She was a great lover of animals, though until now, her affections had been confined to her horse.

"Is Cossack there?" Anne asked as the two of them crossed the grounds. Julia's great black gelding had accompanied her on her flight from London. Anne assumed he was somewhere nearby.

"Not in the old stable block, no," Julia said. "He's in a paddock on the other side of the house. We can visit him, too, if you like. Unless your mother will be wanting you back?"

Mama had remained behind with Hartford. She was intent on questioning Captain Blunt and his aged steward about the house's history.

Anne almost felt sorry for the three men.

Almost.

"Not at all," she said. "Mama has the gentlemen to entertain her. She has no need of me."

On returning to the Red Lion, Hart bid the ladies good evening and retired to his room until dinner.

Unsurprisingly, they hadn't been invited to dine at the hall. Hart doubted whether Blunt employed a cook. Only one thing was certain, the man was grateful to see the back of them. He was plainly in love with his wife, and she with him. He wanted no one else in this world.

Hart rather envied the pair of them. He wondered if Anne felt the same.

There had been no chance to ask her.

Lady Arundell had commanded the whole of the conversation on the carriage ride back to Hardholme. Despite the lack of ghosts evident at the hall, she was convinced she'd felt a certain presence.

Hart had had his fill of it, frankly. He could only take Anne's mother in small doses at the best of times. She was an overbearing lady, more enamored of her own opinions than she was of anything her daughter might think or feel.

He couldn't help but blame her for separating him from Anne.

Lady Arundell might not have known of his proposal to her daughter, but she'd caused the death of his hopes as surely as if she'd forbidden the banns. If not for her, Anne might have accepted him.

They might even now be married and living at Barton Court, the unassuming Somersetshire estate Hart had inherited from his father. Perhaps they'd have children. Perhaps they'd be happy.

Instead, in the aftermath of Anne's rejection, Hart had taken his small inheritance and, rather than using it to subsidize a growing family, had sunk it all into the small-scale production of a newly patented variety of crucible.

A daring gamble.

As business decisions went, it had been the making of him. The new crucibles were soon heavily in demand, resulting in the Parfit Plumbago Crucible Company earning Hart a greater income than anything he could have realized as a country squire idly tending his lands in Somersetshire.

It was rather ironic, really. Though Hart had no wife or children of his own, his money, nevertheless, went to maintain a family. His *father's* family. A thankless business. One that was proving to be a greater burden on Hart's purse than anything he'd yet encountered in the realm of trade.

Removing his hat and gloves, he entered his chamber on the second floor of the inn. Bishop awaited him there. In Hart's absence, the valet had managed to make the room minimally habitable.

"A wire came for you, sir." Bishop gave it to Hart as he divested him of his things. "A boy brought it round from the telegraph office at three."

Hart opened the message, his brow creasing with apprehension. He'd told only two people he would be staying in the small village in North Yorkshire: his grandfather and his uncle.

The wire was from neither of them.

TELEGRAPHIC DISPATCH

MR. FELIX HARTFORD

HARDHOLME STATION, NORTH YORKSHIRE

FUNDS INSUFFICIENT TO COVER DEBT. REQUIRE IMMEDIATE ASSISTANCE. IF NONE FORTHCOMING OBLIGED TO SEEK HELP FROM MARCH OR BROOKDALE. UTMOST URGENCY.

—MARCUS NEALE

A muscle ticked in Hart's cheek as he lowered the telegram.

Only two weeks ago, he'd given Marcus two thousand pounds to cover his latest gambling debt. It was no small sum. Especially as it came on the heels of three other payments Hart had made to cover Marcus's losses. When added to the money Ethel had entreated on her brother's behalf, it was six thousand pounds altogether, a greater amount than the annual salary Hart drew from the crucible company. A greater amount, even, than his annual earnings from Barton Court.

Hart was beginning to feel as though he was bleeding money from a cut artery.

Meanwhile, Marcus showed no sign of reforming his habits. If anything, he was getting worse.

And now this. More threats.

Specific threats.

Not to mention the obvious question: How the devil had he discovered where Hart was? Had he bribed Hart's servants? Or his grandfather's?

The audacity of the lad!

Crumpling the telegram in his fist, Hart retrieved his hat from Bishop and strode back out the door.

Twelve

That evening, Anne dined in her mother's room. It was cowardly of her, she knew. But Mama insisted on having a tray brought up, and Anne couldn't bring herself to dine alone with Hartford again.

This time, Mama didn't press her.

"Hartford was right," she said. "This inn is a far cry from our accommodations in York. It's best you avoid the dining room. The locals are a raucous bunch. I'll not have you exposed to their ribaldry."

A muffled shout of masculine laughter permeated up through the floor, giving weight to Mama's words. The taproom was directly below them. It was the only place in the village that served strong drink and, therefore, quite popular of an evening.

"I don't fancy your being exposed to it, either," Anne said as she finished her small portion of steak-and-kidney pie.

Mama gave an eloquent snort. "At my age? I have nothing to fear from the common people, my girl. In fact, they have much to teach us. Were you older—and a trifle less fetching—I'd encourage you to observe them at close quarters."

"To what purpose?"

Mama dabbed at her lips with her napkin. "It occurs to me that my investigations into the spirit realm are hampered by our location in Mayfair. If we're ever to make progress, we require intercourse with a wider section of society."

Anne choked on her pie. She downed a hasty swallow of watered wine to clear her throat. "I'm sorry, what did you say?"

"To live among them. To include them in our daily lives. I shall consult Fielding on the subject when we return to London."

Anne lowered her glass. "What's brought this on?"

"A great deal of thought," Mama answered.

A flicker of suspicion sharpened Anne's gaze. "It hasn't anything to do with Cousin Joshua's letter?"

"Don't be foolish."

"What else am I to think? You've never broached the subject of moving house before. Not since we were obliged to leave Cherry Hill."

Mama's expression tightened at the reminder. It had been a dark day when Joshua and his mother had taken over the family seat in Shropshire.

"These are wholly different circumstances," she said. "Ones that have nothing to do with that wretched boy and everything to do with the world beyond the veil. You can't have failed to notice that all the truly gifted practitioners are from the lower orders. Zadkiel, Mrs. Frazil, even the boy medium in Birmingham. It wouldn't hurt us to mingle with such people more freely."

"And to mingle with them, we must live among them?"

"I've not settled on anything yet," her mother said. "It's only a notion I have." She stabbed at the final morsel of her steak-and-kidney pie with her fork. "We shall see how it develops."

Anne drew her dyed black cashmere shawl tighter around her shoulders.

Their makeshift table was situated beneath the bedchamber's only window. It had been warm enough when they sat down to dine, but the temperature had since cooled. A draft filtered in through the rotted window casement, fluttering the moth-eaten curtains.

But it wasn't the evening air that prompted a chill in Anne's veins.

"All things considered," she said, "I would rather stay in Mayfair."

"You have nothing to compare it to, save Shropshire," her mother replied. "Once we're established, you'll soon see I'm right. There's a great wealth of psychic energy in the British Isles. We've scarcely penetrated the surface of it. Only think of what's to come."

Anne wasn't sure she could handle what was to come, not if it involved a further descent into eccentricity. It was difficult enough bearing the strain of their notoriety in Mayfair, settled among people who had known them for ages. To start again somewhere else was a daunting proposition.

"What about my friends?" she asked. "What about yours? Everyone we know is in Mayfair. Surely, with a few economies, your jointure will stretch to our securing another house there?"

"Don't quarrel with me, Anne. I need you to enter into my feelings. You know I require distraction. In times such as these, it's all that sustains me. I cannot bear the quiet. My thoughts prey on me so."

Anne exhaled a weary breath. "I know they do. I just fear that you may be responding to the threat of Joshua's arrival in an extreme manner."

"Joshua's arrival," Mama repeated with disdain. "I take leave to doubt he'll come. But these are bleak times, my dear, make no mistake. We must explore new avenues or risk sinking altogether."

Anne didn't like the look on her mother's face. There were shadows in her eyes. A certain remote and all-too-familiar quality, as though she were looking backward instead of forward.

That look didn't bode well for either of them.

"You must do what you think is best, of course," Anne said.

It seemed to satisfy her mother.

Anne herself wasn't so easily placated. She spent the remainder of their meal absorbed in morose ruminations, imagining six dozen different futures, each of them worse than her present course of existence.

Mama's own sinking spirits didn't help matters. When she'd finished her last sip of wine, she announced in prophetic tones, "Sleep won't come easily tonight. I shall have to resort to a few drops of laudanum."

Anne had anticipated something of the sort. Her mother's words nevertheless settled like a lead weight in her chest. "Is that wholly necessary?"

"If I'm to have any peace it is." Mama stood. "Summon Hortense, if you please. She will see to me."

Anne rose from her seat. "*I'll* see to you."

For a moment, it seemed her mother would refuse. But she uttered no objection. With a terse nod, she withdrew to her bed.

Anne followed her. She helped her mother change into her nightclothes, and then, when she was at last tucked up in bed, Anne retrieved the vial of laudanum from Hortense.

The lady's maid wasn't a danger in and of herself. She was only an obedient servant—a woman who would do Mama's bidding, regardless of the harm it might cause.

But Anne's relationship with her mother wasn't one of master and servant, despite what anyone else might believe. Anne was her mother's equal. She would never obey a command that might inadvertently lead to harm.

Sitting down on the edge of the mattress, Anne measured out a small dose of laudanum, just as she'd done so many times in those early months after Papa's death.

Mama swallowed it down as obediently as a child. "Things will be brighter soon," she promised, her eyes growing heavy. "We'll have much to occupy us in the weeks ahead."

Anne turned down the lamp. "Yes, Mama," she said quietly.

She knew when she was beaten.

If her mother required diversion, and if she needed to tell herself they were leaving Grosvenor Square for some other reason than that the new earl was arriving to displace them, Anne wasn't going to be the one to force her to face reality. What purpose could it possibly serve except to send Mama back to that same dark place she'd sunk to after Papa died?

Anne would rather almost anything than witness that again.

She remained until her mother drifted to sleep. Only then, satisfied that Mama was settled for the night, did Anne depart for her own room. It was located a floor above, up a cramped flight of rickety stairs.

As she was ascending, a deep voice sounded behind her, arresting her step.

"Off to bed already?" Hartford inquired.

Anne reluctantly turned to face him. She was in no mood to spar.

He stood several steps below her, half-shadowed in the light that drifted up from the taproom. His hair was rumpled, his usually clean-shaven jaw darkened with evening stubble. It lent him a sinister air, as if he were a dangerous rogue she'd encountered unaware.

Her heartbeat quickened. "Where else?"

"It's barely eleven," he said.

"What does that signify? In case you hadn't noticed, we're at a ramshackle inn in the middle of nowhere. There's little to do after dark other than drink or sleep, and I have no desire for the former."

He climbed up a step. "Come for a walk with me."

She took an immediate step backward. "At this hour?"

"There's a full moon, and a secluded sort of wilderness on the other side of the stable yard. I can think of no better way to spend an evening."

"No doubt you can think of better company."

"Not at the moment." He was uncommonly solemn. "I want to be with you."

Anne's stomach gave a disconcerting flip-flop. He sounded so serious. So unlike himself.

She studied his face in the dim light. As always, he looked infuriatingly handsome. He also looked tired, frustrated, and desperately in need of a friend.

Compassion for him temporarily conquered her defenses. "Very well. But we mustn't go far."

"Not if you don't wish to." He moved out of her way, gesturing for her to precede him down. "After you."

Drawing her cashmere shawl more firmly about her, Anne descended the stairs. The passage was dreadfully narrow. Their arms brushed, and her skirts bunched against his leg with a rustling sound as she passed him.

For a perilous instant, they were close enough that she could hear the ragged intake of his breath and smell the faint fragrances of whiskey and tobacco, and the lingering scent of his cologne.

Her pulse thrummed.

She was grateful for the noise from below. It grew louder with every step, preventing any thought of further conversation.

Mama had been right to call the patrons raucous. They were deep in their cups.

As Anne stepped down into the passage, one of them—a burly fellow of middle years—staggered out from the taproom and straight into her path, blocking her way.

His bloodshot gaze dropped to her bosom. A lascivious grin spread over his face. "Well, aren't *you* a plump-breasted little partridge."

Before Anne could do anything more than recoil at the fellow's impudence, Hartford strode in front of her and, in one seemingly effortless movement, hauled the man up by his neckcloth.

"I beg your pardon," he said in a voice of lethal calm. "Were you addressing someone?"

The man emitted a blistering oath as he struggled to free himself.

Hartford's fingers only twisted the neckcloth tighter, lifting the fellow straight up onto the scuffed toes of his boots. "I'm sorry. I couldn't hear you."

The man choked and sputtered. His face turned a distressing shade of red.

Alarmed, Anne set her hand on Hartford's sleeve. "Do release the fellow. You'll strangle him otherwise."

"I'll release him," Hartford said, "if he can manage to keep a civil tongue in his head."

"Didn't mean—" the man wheezed. "Didn't know she was your—"

"You know now," Hartford said ominously. With that, he loosened his grip, allowing the man's boots to come back to the floor.

The man's hand flew to his throat. Muttering his apologies, he beat a hasty retreat back to the taproom.

Anne scarcely noticed his departure.

She stared at Hartford in the lamplight. Her heart hammered painfully hard, not because of the insult, but because of the way he'd reacted to it.

His defense of her had been as proprietary as it was uncalled for. It had nevertheless fired her blood. She wasn't so blind she couldn't recognize the fact. Her body had turned traitor. So had her heart, much to her annoyance.

"Was that wholly necessary?" she asked.

"You'd rather I let the blackguard insult you?"

Her chin lifted a fraction. "I beg your pardon. You seem to have mistaken me for a swooning damsel."

"Hardly."

"Then why did you find it necessary to fly to my rescue? Do you imagine he's the first ineloquent lout to remark on my bosom? I daresay he meant it as a compliment."

A dangerous expression came over Hartford's face. He looked, for a moment, as if he wished the drunkard back again so he could resume choking the fellow. "The next time one of them does so," he said tightly, "you will kindly inform me of it."

"Whatever would I do that for?" she wondered. "And why should you care in the first place? You're not my father or my brother to be taking up arms in defense of my honor."

"No," he said, looming over her. "I'm not your father or your brother, thank God. Most days I question whether I'm even your friend. But make no mistake, my lady, if anyone—and I do mean *anyone*—should dare insult you or threaten you harm, I will defend you until my dying breath."

Thirteen

Hart thrust his hands into his pockets as he crossed the empty stable yard at Anne's side. He'd all but declared himself to her, offering her his undying devotion—or, at the very minimum, his lifelong protection—and in response . . .

She'd buttoned up completely.

Indeed, she'd been unnervingly quiet since they departed the inn. So had he, come to that. He couldn't help it. He was still stewing over what she'd said earlier.

Do you imagine he's the first ineloquent lout to remark on my bosom?

As a girl, Anne had been self-conscious of her figure. She had a delicate frame, making her curves all the more noticeable. They were still noticeable, even when they were bound up tight in a modest black silk bodice that fastened all the way to her throat.

Hart was, admittedly, a little possessive of those curves, just as he was of the lady they belonged to. The fact that any man would have the temerity to remark on them made his blood boil.

Yet, Anne had alluded to those impudent remarks, not with the blushing self-consciousness of her youth, but with the matter-of-factness of a world-weary spinster. She hadn't needed his protection. She hadn't even seemed to want it.

It had struck him in that moment how little he knew her anymore.

A sobering realization. One of many he'd had today.

He cast her a brooding look as they entered the stretch of trees that adjoined the inn. Her arms were folded at her waist, a cashmere shawl—dyed black to match her mourning gown—wrapped firmly around her.

"I believe," he said finally, "that you and I have been alone more these past two days than we have these six years entire."

"I believe you're right," she replied.

The moon was at its fullest tonight, bright enough to bathe the whole of the outdoors in its soft, silvery glow. It illuminated Anne's face and glistened in her hair, rendering her more beautiful than on any occasion in recent memory.

A lump formed in Hart's throat. "I'm amazed you accepted my invitation."

"I shouldn't have," she said. "We might be observed by anyone out here."

"Observed doing what?"

She flashed him a reproving glance.

His mouth hitched. Even now, it was impossible not to tease her. "There's no one about, in any case. Anyone who hasn't already retired for the night is in the taproom, too drunk to see straight." He paused, his smile dimming. "Why *did* you accept my invitation?"

"You seemed in need of company," she said frankly.

He gave a short laugh. "True enough."

A blanket of stars twinkled in the night sky, in greater number than any Hart had lately observed in the coal-smoke-clouded skies of London. In company with the moonlight, they lent a magical quality to the little stretch of trees and cow pasture beyond the inn. He was reluctant to spoil it by talking about his troubles.

"How did you find Mrs. Blunt?" he asked instead.

"Mrs. Blunt," she repeated as if trying the name out for size. "I shall have to get used to calling her that, though it does seem strange, I confess."

"There's nothing strange about a wife taking a husband's name."

"Not to you, perhaps. A man gives up nothing in the bargain. While a woman must give up her name, her home, her family. She must leave everything behind and commit her life to another. It doesn't seem fair, does it?"

Hart felt a prickle of irritation to hear Anne speak disparagingly of marriage. "Mrs. Blunt didn't appear unhappy in her choice."

"No. She was quite content, I believe. A little altered, but I suppose that's to be expected."

"Has seeing her put your worries to rest?"

"No, indeed. I always worry about my friends." Her eyes met his, a trace of irony in their sherry depths. "While we're on the subject, do you plan on telling me what it is that has you looking so grim this evening?"

He gave her a fleeting smile. "Am I to take from that question that you consider me a friend?"

She shrugged one shoulder. "A curious acquaintance, at the very least."

Hart hesitated all of fifteen seconds before making the decision to confide in her again.

Anne may be headstrong, intractable, and infuriating, but she was loyal to the bone. Despite their muddled past, he still valued her discretion.

Besides, he'd already trusted her with the worst of it during their ill-fated dinner in York. There was no reason to hold back now.

As they continued along the path, the delicate fragrance of wild heather whispering over the moonlit moors, he told her about Marcus's telegram.

And he told her how he'd responded to it.

"I wired his mother," he said. "I warned her that if Marcus makes any attempts to approach my grandfather or my uncle, my financial support for the Neale family will cease immediately."

Anne's brows lifted a fraction.

Hart perceived the infinitesimal movement as surely as a reprimand. "You disapprove?"

"Your half sisters have done nothing to merit losing your support, have they?"

"I've no real intention of leaving them destitute," he said.

"Then why—"

"Because I've tried everything else—reason, kindness, appeals to their better natures. Money is all Marcus and his mother seem to understand. I've no sooner paid off one debt than two more spring up in its place."

"The Hydra," Anne murmured.

Hart felt a spark of satisfaction. She'd always shared his fondness for mythology. "Precisely," he said.

She paused to consider. "As I recall, the Hydra had one immortal head. It was how Hercules eventually prevailed over it. Perhaps you need only find that one weakness in your half brother—"

"His weakness is money. If I cut that off—"

"He'll have nothing left to lose. Then he really will go to your grandfather."

"I've only threatened the lad. With luck, it will be enough to scare him back onto the straight and narrow."

"You haven't just threatened him," Anne said with a touch of impatience. "You've threatened his family. Lord only knows what someone might do if their mother's well-being is put at risk."

His brow contracted in a scowl. The last thing he wanted at the moment was to be reminded of her mother. "Do you have a better solution?"

"It seems simple enough to me," she said. "Let him tell your grandfather and your uncle."

Hart came to an abrupt halt beneath the gnarled branches of an old oak tree. They curved overhead, reaching out a staggering distance from the tree's massive trunk. "Have you taken leave of your senses?" he asked.

Anne stopped to face him. "On the contrary. I'm exceedingly sensible. And this is the only sensible course, given the limitations of your purse. You can't keep paying your half brother's way forever, not if he's taken a likeness to the gaming tables. He'll soon bankrupt you, and then tell your grandfather anyway. Isn't it better to have it all out in the open and be done with it?"

He stared at her numbly. He'd wanted her counsel on this matter for a lifetime, it seemed. And *this* is the advice she was giving him? The one thing he could never do?

She took a step closer, her brown eyes glittering with gold flecks in the moonlight. "And you've mixed up your myths, as usual," she said in her lemon-tart schoolmistress voice. "It's not the Hydra. It's the Augean stables. A filthy secret that must be washed clean. And nothing cleanses more effectively than sunlight."

He felt the sudden urge to laugh. The Augean stables. Good God. "You're suggesting I reveal it not just to my relations but to the whole of society."

"Why not? It would do you a wealth of good."

"Me, perhaps, but not my grandfather. Not my uncle."

Anne responded to his concerns with maddening practicality. "They're grown men, not children. Let them bear their share of the burden."

"The burden is mine. He was *my* father."

"He was also your grandfather's son and your uncle's younger brother. Surely, they must take some responsibility for his sins?"

Hart shook his head. "No." He took a step back from her. "It's impossible."

She closed the distance. "Why impossible?"

"Because . . ." He gritted his teeth against the truth. It came anyway, an admission he hadn't yet made to another living soul. One he'd barely acknowledged to himself. "If the world knew of my father's secret family, what would it say about his legitimate one? What would it say about me?"

"You were a child."

"I was old enough to be a disappointment to him. His first child with Mrs. Neale was born when I was but ten years old. What does it say that my father had already given up on me?"

A look of vague disquiet passed over Anne's face. "Is that what you believe?"

"What else?"

"I should think it obvious."

He regarded her in stubborn silence. He didn't want her practicality, or her good sense. What he required was something else altogether. He didn't know quite what it was, but he despaired of ever getting it from her.

She sighed. "My dearest boy, your father didn't give up on you. He gave in to temptation. All that piety and moralism, and underneath he was as fallible as any mortal. There's nothing more to it than that."

My dearest boy.

She hadn't called him that in ages.

Hart's chest tightened, his heart latching on to the old endearment so ferociously, he scarcely registered the words that followed.

"Are you listening to me?" she asked. "There's no point in your excoriating yourself over the business. Nor in bearing the shame of it. Your father succumbed to his weaknesses, that's all. He's not the first gentleman to do so."

The statement brought Hart back to attention.

"You speak with some authority on the subject," he said.

Her shawl slid down, unheeded, over one shoulder, revealing the lusterless fabric of her black gown. "I know what I see about me," she said. "Gentlemen married to perfectly lovely ladies, yet those gentlemen are still rumored to keep mistresses. It's not a secret."

"Not all men are so inconstant."

"No, indeed. My father was true to my mother during his lifetime."

Hart's voice deepened. "I wasn't speaking about your father."

Fourteen

Anne's gaze locked with his. A charge of electricity seemed to pass between them. It was coupled with a palpable ache of unrequited longing. She was struck by the overwhelming urge to walk straight into his arms.

But a lady hadn't the luxury of giving in to her romantic urges.

Not a lady in Anne's position, anyway.

She twined her fingers tighter in the folds of her drooping shawl, drawing it back up over her shoulder. "I never asked you to remain constant to me. If . . . if that's what you're referring to."

Hartford took a decisive step toward her. Her full skirts bowed against his legs. "You did. You asked me to wait."

Her pulse surged into an unsteady gallop. He was so grave, so sincere, and so dangerously close she had to tip her head back to meet his gaze.

"I didn't," she said.

Not for six and a half years, at any rate.

At the time of Hartford's proposal, his grandfather had been set to leave on a yearlong expedition to the Himalayas.

One year.

It was the exact length of time a daughter was obliged to mourn a father.

After Papa's death, Anne had encouraged Hartford to accompany his grandfather. To travel with him to India and to leave her to her grief.

It had seemed the wisest course at the time.

There had been little point in Hartford's remaining to wait upon her in London, not when the whole of her attention was caught up in mourning her loss, and in looking after her soul-stricken mother.

He'd called on Anne in Grosvenor Square the day before he left, soberly attired and solemn with concern. He'd held out his hands to her as she'd entered the drawing room. Anne had taken them gratefully, clasping them tight.

"A year isn't so long, old thing," he'd said. "It may even be to our benefit. I'm told that absence makes the heart grow fonder."

"Some hearts might forget," she'd replied, already regretting her decision to let him go.

"Mine won't. Not ever. I'll wait for you," he'd promised. "And when I come back—"

"Yes," she'd agreed. "Yes."

Anne inwardly flinched to remember it.

Hartford *had* waited. But when he'd returned from the Himalayas, nearly thirteen months later owing to his ship having been delayed, she'd still been in her blacks. Life had changed for her. *Everything* had changed.

Hartford had changed, too.

He was no longer patient. No longer understanding. A few ill-thought words, and the old antagonism had blazed up between them, scorching everything in its path.

Looking at him now, standing over her in the moonlight, Anne imagined she could still see the scars she'd inflicted during that final argument.

They were scars that mirrored her own.

"Perhaps it was only me, then," he said gruffly. "Some gallant notion I had that we were meant for each other."

She shook her head. "Hartford—"

"Perhaps not even that." The shadow of a frown crossed his face. "The truth is . . . I tried to forget you. To move on with my life. But it was impossible."

Anne's heart quivered.

Skeptical she might be. Uncertain she was. But not immune. Not to him.

There would always be a part of her that craved his sweetness. It was a weakness in her. This unextinguishable desire to have him. To lean on him, as if he were a gentleman one could depend on to hold the course.

"It doesn't matter now," she said. "It was a long time ago. We needn't relitigate the past . . ." Her words faded to a whisper as he brushed his knuckles along the curve of her cheek.

"I told you in York," he said. "It isn't over."

Her eyes closed briefly against a swell of such raw yearning she didn't know whether to weep or to swoon.

He bent his head to hers. "It never has been. Not for me."

She felt his breath warm against her lips for a suspended moment before his mouth captured hers.

A muffled gasp. A flicker of doubt. And then . . .

Oh, and then.

Her lips softened, yielding beneath his as if they'd been waiting for him all this time.

A low growl of approval sounded in his throat. It reverberated within her, a thoroughly disconcerting sensation. She wanted—

But she didn't know what she wanted, only that she was in no hurry for this to end.

Hartford wasn't disposed to rush. His mouth angled across hers, kissing her slowly—achingly slowly—as if he were imprinting every second of the experience onto his memory.

Her legs threatened to sag beneath her. She reached up, circling his neck with her arms to steady herself.

In response, his arms curved around her waist, drawing her closer.

And she submitted to his embrace. To her own desires. Indeed, everything within her went warm and pliant.

Good Lord. Felix Hartford could kiss.

She had nothing much to compare it with, save his kiss under the mistletoe. But that had been the kiss of a younger man, as respectful as it was chaste.

This was another kind of kiss.

This was the kiss of a man approaching his thirtieth year. A man who had waited. Who had yearned as she had yearned.

Anne hadn't the experience to catalog the art of it, but every fiber of her being recognized it for what it was—slow, deep, knee-weakening perfection.

Or perhaps it was just that he was perfect for her.

An alarming thought.

She dragged her mouth away from his on an unsteady breath. "This is *not* a good idea."

"Isn't it?" He kissed her again. "It feels rather good to me."

She turned her head. "You're not thinking straight."

His lips found her cheek. "You may do the thinking. I'm going to continue kissing you."

In other circumstances, his words might have provoked a disgruntled laugh. But she couldn't succumb to his teasing. She wasn't an infatuated girl any longer.

Her arms slid from his neck, hands coming to rest on the front of his waistcoat. "It doesn't resolve anything between us," she said. "One can't simply kiss a problem away."

He drew back to look at her. His brows lowered. "Is that what we're doing?"

"I don't know *what* we're doing. One minute we're arguing, the next . . . this. It isn't at all reasonable. Just because there was something between us once—"

"*Was*," he repeated flatly.

"It doesn't give us an excuse to indulge our every inclination." She removed her hands from his chest. There was no way to disguise their trembling. "Though why we should still be having these inclinations, I don't know."

"I see." A hint of coolness infiltrated his voice. "Very well," he said. "Call it unfinished business."

Anne stiffened. She had the vague sense that he'd meant it as an insult. "What a coarse thing to say."

He released her waist, allowing her to back away from him. "You wanted reason. God forbid anything you do should fail to be sensible."

"And God forbid you should take anything seriously," she shot back. She gave her rumpled skirts a disgruntled shake. "I suppose we should all just forget our duties and obligations and give in to our whims all the day long?"

Anger flared in Hart's gaze. "As ever, you equate humor with lack of purpose."

"That isn't so," she said.

Was it?

Had she been unfair to him? Misjudged him?

Anne wasn't so unbending she couldn't admit that it might be the case. After what he'd confessed to her in York and, then again, this evening, she knew him to be taking one part of his life seriously.

"I realize you're more responsible than I thought you were," she said, marshaling her composure. "But how that applies to—"

"I blame your mother," he said.

Her head jerked back with a sharp inhalation of breath.

In his youth, Hartford had been known to escalate arguments with unsportsmanlike intensity, jumping from point A straight to zed without anything in between. It was a ruthless tactic. One that had the effect of thoroughly disarming his opponents.

Perhaps he hadn't changed so much after all.

"Don't you *dare* speak about my mother," she said.

"Someone must." The brief flare of anger in his eyes was replaced by an expression of grim certainty. "She's going to destroy your life."

"I'm warning you—"

"She's already bullied you into a shadow. And you've let her, as far as I can tell. Choosing this"—he cast a disgusted look at her black dress—"instead of joy. Even when it's right in front of your face, you're too bound up by your mother's rules to risk taking it."

It was no different from what everyone else in society believed. But to hear it from Hartford's lips—those same lips that had only a moment ago been kissing her so tenderly—was insupportable.

Anne's throat constricted with stifled emotion. "If that's what you think, may I say that you don't know me at all."

"I know what I've witnessed these past years. I've seen a girl who was once pure fire snuffed out as easily as a candle flame. *Willingly* snuffed out. You've put up no fight at all. And why? What is it you're afraid of, Anne?"

"I'm not afraid!" she burst out. "And I'm not bullied, either!"

He made a harsh sound of disbelief. "What would you call it, then?"

Turning her back on him, she strode further beneath the old oak's canopy of knotty branches, only stopping when she reached the trunk. Her hands were clenched tight in her shawl.

In the past weeks, her world had been battered by one wave after another. Evelyn gone. Julia gone. Joshua arriving to take Anne's home in Grosvenor Square just as he'd taken Cherry Hill.

And now Mama was faltering again.

Add to that the storm of Anne's renewed acquaintance with Hartford, and the dam could hold no longer. She found herself blurting out a secret she'd never shared with anyone.

"It's not about bullying," she said. "It's about control."

Fifteen

Hart stalked after her. He was in no frame of mind to interpret the subtle nuances of female language. After the kiss they'd shared, his brain had softened to the consistency of porridge. If it hadn't, he might have been capable of exercising a better restraint on his tongue. Instead, when she'd pulled away from him, he'd been provoked to incivility.

Worse than incivility.

But by God, how was a man meant to react in such circumstances? Just when he'd thought he was making progress with her. Just when she was, at last, back in his arms, her blasted mother had reached out through the darkness, exerting her power over Anne as effectively as a strong-handed groom gripping the halter of a spirited filly.

Power. Bullying. Control. Whatever Anne wanted to call it, the fact of the matter was, it was a damned nuisance.

"Is there a difference?" he asked, coming up behind her. "I can't see one from where I'm standing."

They were well beneath the canopy of the oak tree now. The branches filtered out the moon and the stars, leaving the pair of them in shadowed darkness.

She cast him a scornful glance over her shoulder. "Because you don't know anything about women."

"Undoubtedly. I still fail to comprehend—"

"I told you. It's about control. We ladies already have so little of it. What do you suppose one of us might feel if we lost it entirely?" She gave him another scathing look. "We would feel as if the world was in chaos, that's how. We would wish to take ruthless control of the only things we could—our households, our children, the very food we put into our mouths."

A glimmer of understanding brought Hart up short.

He moved to stand in front of her, forcing her to meet his eyes. "What control is your mother lacking in her life? She's one of the most formidable ladies I've ever known."

Anne folded her arms, drawing her shawl firmly about her. "My mother lost the love of her life. No matter how strong she was or how well she managed the situation, he slipped away from her. And she can never get him back. She's powerless. Can you imagine how that feels to a woman as strong as she is? To realize that, when it came to the point, she had no power at all?"

"That was almost seven years ago."

"What does time matter in relation to such a love?" she asked.

It was a question Hart had often posed to himself.

He was silent for a long moment. And then, "Was it dreadful after your father died?"

"It was." Anne's words were etched with remembered pain. "My mother's grief was overwhelming. There was no room for anything else. Not even my own grief. For a time, I was afraid I might lose her, too. I've never felt so entirely alone in my life."

There was a dull ache in Hart's chest. "You never said."

"How could I? After you left . . ." She gave a short, bitter laugh. "Half the time I didn't even know whether you cared anymore."

What in blazes?

He held her gaze. "I cared."

She looked steadily back at him, a hint of censure in her eyes. "You never wrote."

"For God's sake, Anne. How the devil could I have? I spent most of my time in the Himalayas camping up some mountain or other. Unless I drafted my correspondence with a burnt twig, and sent it to the nearest village on a yak cart, I don't see how—" Hart broke off. He fixed her with an accusatory glower. "You never wrote to me, either."

"You left no address. Where would I have sent my letters? To the same mountain? Via the same yak cart?"

"If you had, I might have known what you were going through. I might have—"

"What?" Her brows lifted. "Been a trifle more accommodating when you returned?"

A scowl threatened. "The point is, I had no way of knowing anything about your mother's condition. I couldn't very well discern it for myself. She's never once shown any sign of weakness."

"She never would. Not to you. But *I* have seen it. *I* have witnessed the full extent of her wounds. And knowing how she suffers—how she *still* suffers—I choose to be with her. To care for her. To give her what she lost when my father died, that sense of power and control."

Hart stared at her with building outrage. "It's *you* she controls."

"Rubbish," Anne said. "She does nothing I don't allow. Yes, it's tedious at times. But I wouldn't change anything. If you had been closer with your parents you would understand."

He straightened from the tree trunk. "You're right," he said, looming over her. "I don't understand. You've made yourself a martyr to a woman who, given enough incentive, might have recovered years ago."

"Recovered?" Anne scoffed. "Do you truly think anyone who has loved that deeply ever could?"

Hart privately conceded the point.

He hadn't recovered from losing her, had he?

But this was different. It wasn't a personal loss, causing pain only to oneself. It was a loss that was doing harm to someone else. Someone he cared about.

"There's more than one kind of love," he said. "There's the love a widow holds for her late husband. And there's the love she should have for her daughter."

"My mother does love me," Anne replied with unerring conviction.

He clenched his jaw. "If she loved you, she would *let you go*."

"She's not holding me! Everything I've done has been my choice alone."

"Some choice," he said. "You weren't meant to be anyone's shadow."

Anne drew herself up with all the mighty blue-blooded dignity of generations of Deveril women. Her face was set with a furious resolve. "I decide who and what I am, and no one else," she said. "You mistake me when you accuse me of being weak. A flame willingly snuffed out by another. As if my sacrifice had somehow diminished me. Quite the reverse. There's power in doing one's duty."

Hart was dazzled by her, smitten anew by her fierceness and her loyalty, even as he cursed her refusal to face the truth. "No one in society believes that you're being strong. From the outside, your situation appears exactly as I've described it. You're fooling yourself to think otherwise."

"This is what I give for society's opinion of me." She snapped her fingers in his face. "And this is what I give for yours." She snapped them again. "I care nothing about how I'm perceived. Only a weak person would do so. You would be advised to adjust your thinking in that regard."

"Anne—"

"Enough!" she cried. "Enough! We've spent years sniping back and forth, both of us bitter over what happened in the past. But it *is* the past. You said we must talk about it, and now we have. We can finally be quit of each other."

His heart lurched. By God, she was serious.

He took an abrupt step toward her. "Is that what you want?" he asked harshly.

She'd gone pale. It was the only sign of how upset she was. "Yes," she said.

He searched her face. "Even after that kiss?"

"*Yes*," she said again, with greater conviction. "Our unfinished business is finished at last. Let this be an end to it."

With that, she turned in a swish of skirts and strode back to the inn.

After their argument, and the knee-weakening kiss that had preceded it, Anne dreaded the return journey to London. She had no desire to be in Hartford's company, not even with her mother as chaperone. There was too much risk.

Another private parlor at a coaching inn. Another kiss or compassionate stroke of her cheek, and Anne's hard-won resolve might crumble. Mere proximity to him rendered her vulnerable. And she couldn't afford to be vulnerable, not now.

It would be different if he were reliable. If she could count on him to be a rock, a sure and steady presence in her time of trouble. But though Hartford was older and, admittedly, more responsible in terms of his family obligations, there was still a part of him that hadn't changed. Anne sensed it as surely as she sensed his attraction to her.

She couldn't trust him.

And when they were together, she couldn't trust herself.

Thank goodness for Julia.

When Anne arrived at Goldfinch Hall the next morning, her friend greeted her with news that was as startling as it was welcome. "When you return to London," Julia said, "I want to come with you."

Anne sat across from her on a blanket in the garden, holding the smallest kitten on her lap. The rest of the kittens gamboled between them under the watchful eye of their mother.

On the opposite side of the garden, Julia's three young stepchildren—the infamous illegitimate offspring of her new husband—played together as companionably as the kittens.

"To London?" Anne asked. "Whatever for? I thought you were happy here."

"I *am* happy," Julia said. "But I must sort some things out with my inheritance. *And* with my parents."

"Captain Blunt won't accompany you?"

"I must do it alone."

Anne regarded her friend with a dawning respect. This was a new Julia. No longer shy and anxious, she appeared bold, confident, and wholly determined. "How brave you've become."

Julia lifted one of the calico kittens to her face, pressing a kiss to its nose. "I suppose I have something to fight for."

"Your new husband?"

"Him, and the children. Our entire life here." Julia set down the kitten. "Will you let me come with you?"

"Of course," Anne said. The little black kitten on her lap hissed and spit at an encroaching sibling. Anne calmed her with a pat.

Julia smiled. "She likes you."

"The temperamental beasts of the world usually do."

"If you wish, I can send her to you when she's weaned. You could use a companion."

Anne's mouth curved with amusement. "A cat. Just what every spinster requires."

"You're *not* a spinster," Julia said. "You're practically the same age as I am. And I *will* send her to you. See if I don't."

"You may do as you please." Anne scratched beneath the kitten's chin with the tip of her finger. The idea of having a cat appealed to her more than she would have expected. "She matches my wardrobe, anyway."

The following day, when they departed for the railway station at Malton, Julia was with them. Mama made no complaint. Neither did Hartford. Except for a few dry remarks, he seemed resolved to keep his own counsel.

Anne was equally resolved to keep hers.

She focused all of her attentions on Julia. The two of them sat side by side, talking only to each other during most of the journey to York and then, after a change of trains and a night spent at a nearby inn, all the way back to London.

Hartford deposited the three of them in Grosvenor Square, along with their luggage and servants. He handed them down from the carriage himself, first Mama, then Julia, and, finally, Anne.

She reluctantly set her gloved hand in his, their eyes meeting briefly as she descended the steps. A flush of heat rose in her cheeks.

Drat that kiss!

It was impossible to look at him without thinking of it.

Hartford arched a brow at her, but for once, he said nothing.

It confirmed Anne's suspicions. She'd said she wanted to be quit of him. That she wanted that night in the moonlight to be the end of it. And he was respecting her wishes.

Perhaps he'd wanted it, too. So long as he felt some loyalty toward her, some remnant of unfinished business, as he'd called it, he could never move on with his life.

As for her own life . . .

Once inside the house, she passed Julia into the care of their capable housekeeper, Mrs. Griffiths. Then, after briefly conferring with Mama, Anne withdrew to her room, shutting the door behind her.

Alone for the first time in days, she sank down on the edge of her four-poster bed and promptly—and rather alarmingly—burst into tears.

Sixteen

"Is that the post?" the Earl of March inquired from the doorway.

Hart glanced up from riffling through his grandfather's morning correspondence. A footman had left it on the library desk not five minutes ago.

"It is." Hart held his driving gloves in one hand. He'd been on his way out when the post had arrived.

Grandfather entered the library, his hands still filthy from gardening. He wiped them, somewhat ineffectively, with a large handkerchief. "I'm expecting a letter from a man named Archer. A British perfumer operating out of Grasse. He's interested in my newest strain of tea roses. I don't suppose he's written?"

"He hasn't," Hart said.

Neither had Marcus, thank God.

Since Hart's return to London yesterday, he'd had no luck in tracking the boy down. Marcus appeared to have gone to ground. His mother and sisters claimed not to have heard from him in days, and there had been no sign of him at his favorite taverns or gaming establishments.

Hart hourly anticipated Marcus's appearance in Arlington Street. Either that or a letter sent to Hart's grandfather or uncle asking for money.

It was fear of the latter that had prompted him to look through his grandfather's post.

"Pity." Grandfather took a seat in the leather chair behind his desk. "You may put those letters down. I'll see to them later."

Hart obeyed him. "You have something more pressing to attend to?"

"Those Himalayan lilies are vexing me again."

Hart's attention was briefly diverted. He was no botanist himself, nor even a very passionate gardener, but he knew enough of plants to write his tongue-in-cheek column for *Glendale's Botanical Bi-Monthly.* Before leaving for Yorkshire, he'd examined the lilies and, on his recommendation, had helped his grandfather transplant them to better-draining soil.

"I thought the new watering regimen was a success," Hart said.

"There's been a minor improvement in the color of the leaves, but the dashed things still refuse to bloom. Lobb had a similar problem, as I recall. I'll send him a wire." Grandfather glanced up at Hart's driving coat and gloves as he withdrew a sheet of paper from the drawer of his desk. "You're off again?"

"I have an appointment."

"With Lady Anne, I presume."

Hart's smile wavered. He'd been trying not to think of her.

Trying and failing.

Her presence in his life had been so long-standing. So ubiquitous. Not as a sweetheart. Not even as a friend. But as a possibility. It was that to which Hart was accustomed. To the ever-present hope that, one day—given the right words, the right circumstances—she might return from her self-imposed exile, realizing that she still wanted him.

But she didn't want him.

She wanted an end to things.

Hart supposed he should want it, too. But he didn't, truth be told. Call it weakness. Call it sentimentality. Call it habit. Whatever it was, it had ensnared him in its web. He was having a devil of a time freeing himself.

"You presume incorrectly," he said. "I have no plans to call on Lady Anne."

"You needn't keep it from me if you have." Grandfather sharpened his quill with an ivory-handled penknife. "Brookdale may object to her, but I've always been rather fond of the girl."

"I wasn't aware you had any opinions on the subject."

"Why shouldn't I have? Arundell was a capital fellow. So is his widow, regardless of how she chooses to amuse herself." Dipping his quill pen in a pot of ink, Grandfather began to write out his message to Mr. Lobb. "As for the girl . . . she has spirit. An admirable quality. One she'd pass on to your children."

Hart smoothed his driving gloves in his hand. A frown notched his brows. He was plagued enough by thoughts of Anne. He didn't wish to be plagued by thoughts of their hypothetical children, too.

"If that's how you feel," he said, "I should tell you that I've invited her to Sutton Park for the holidays."

"Excellent," Grandfather muttered distractedly. "Will her mother be joining us?"

"I assume so," Hart said. *If* Anne was still willing to come. He was no longer certain she would.

After what had transpired between them in Yorkshire, he was tempted to release her from the obligation. It's what a gentleman would do.

But Hart was weary of playing the gentleman.

Bidding his grandfather good morning, he tugged on his gloves and departed the house. His curricle awaited him, Kestrel and Damselfly champing at their bits and shaking their heads in protest against the groom who had been walking them up and down the street in Hart's absence.

"They're in dangerous temper today, sir," the groom said.

"Nonsense." Hart gave each of his mares a conciliatory scratch on the nose as he crossed in front of them to mount his curricle. "They're full of fire, just how I like them." He gathered up the reins. "Stand away from their heads."

The groom backed out of the way in the nick of time.

Kestrel and Damselfly leapt forward in their traces into a brisk high-stepping trot. Hart expertly navigated them through the street. They wanted a good run, but he couldn't indulge them. Not today. He was destined for another, what was sure to be fruitless, visit to the Neales' house.

He drove in the direction of Chelsea, and from thence across the river to Battersea. It was an unobjectionable suburb, though far from a fashionable one. Approaching the turning for the Neales' modest neighborhood, he was obliged to slow his mares to make way for a passing dray. It was then he saw a familiar young lady standing at the omnibus stop. She was dressed in a plain gray gown, her pale face framed by a sturdy bonnet.

It was Ethel Neale.

Hart brought his curricle alongside her. "Ethel."

Her head jerked up. Her eyes went round as saucers. "Hartford! What are you doing here?"

"I could ask you the same question." His half sister was far from being a fashionable lady, but she was still a respectable one. And respectable females didn't loiter along busy roadways waiting for public transport. "Where are you bound for?"

"I'm . . . I'm going to visit a f-friend."

"That friend wouldn't be Marcus, would it?"

Ethel's gaze slipped guiltily from his.

Hart didn't wait for her to reply. The answer was evident in her face. Only loyalty to her older brother could prompt her to behave so recklessly.

"Climb in," he said abruptly. "Don't dawdle. We've made enough of a spectacle of ourselves."

Ethel hastily struggled up next to him. The moment she was settled,

Hart sprang his horses. She gripped hard to the seat. "Are you taking me home?"

"I am," he said. "Which gives you exactly five minutes to tell me where he is."

The sponging house was located in a narrow street off Chancery Lane. It was a tumbledown dwelling with bars both on the windows and arranged cage-like over the back garden. A sort of debtors' purgatory. Men of every class were detained within, where they were squeezed like the eponymous sponges until they yielded enough coin to pay their creditors.

Hart had some experience with such establishments. Not on his own account. He'd always been careful with his money. His university friends, however, had been markedly less so.

During the years he'd spent at Cambridge, Hart had known several gentlemen whose needless extravagances had landed them in sponging houses just like the one that now stood before him.

He paid a neighborhood lad to hold his horses and then, bounding up the steps, pounded twice on the splintered door.

It was opened by a greasy-haired fellow with gaps in his teeth. The bailiff, Hart presumed. Likely, this was the man's own house. Sponging houses were often private residences, modified to serve as places of temporary confinement.

"Marcus Neale, if you please," Hart said.

The bailiff gave an oily smile. "Right this way, milord."

Hart followed him up a flight of stairs and down a narrow hall. The sounds of men talking and laughing emanated from behind the closed doors that lined the way.

A sponging house wasn't as grim as a debtors' prison. Men were held here only temporarily, during which time they mingled together quite companionably. Those who managed to reach accommodation with their creditors were soon free again. The rest were destined for court and a longer period of incarceration in less hospitable surroundings.

The warden rapped on a door at the end of the hall before opening it. "Someone to see you, sir," he said with mocking deference. "Shall I send up some beer?"

Marcus's voice emerged from the depths of the darkened room in a furious growl. "No more beer, damn you."

"He's run up a bill, he has," the bailiff informed Hart. "A guinea a day for his lodgings, plus the charges for his breakfasts, dinners, beer, brandy, and tobacco—"

"Indeed," Hart said. "I shall summon you if I require a further accounting." Entering the room, he closed the door behind him.

It took a moment for his eyes to adjust to the dim light. When they did, he beheld a dingy little chamber, furnished with an old wooden table, a single chair, and a narrow bed.

Marcus Neale sat upon the edge of the sagging mattress, his elbows on his knees and his head in his hands. He was clad in a pair of breeches and a stained white shirt, absent his coat and neckcloth.

"I might have known it would come to this," Hart said.

Marcus slowly raised his head, his dark brown hair standing half on end. A look of disgust crossed his face. "And I might have known Ethel couldn't keep a secret."

"Ah yes. Your sister. I'm gratified you mentioned her." Hart lifted the wooden chair from the table and dropped it in front of Marcus with a thunderous clatter. "I found her standing on the side of the high street with most of the housekeeping money in her reticule, easy prey for any pickpocket, procurer, or roving lothario."

"The little fool," Marcus muttered. "I told my mother to send her in a cab."

Hart sat down in the chair to face his half brother. He might have been looking in a mirror for all that they resembled each other.

Everett Hartford had left his indelible stamp on both of his sons, passing on his great height, broad shoulders, and square jaw. The only difference between them was in age and expression.

"And what do you suppose would have happened had your sister arrived here to settle your tariff?" Hart asked. "How would your mother and sisters have managed 'til next quarter day with the housekeeping money gone?"

"You wouldn't let them starve."

"No. But it appears that you would." Anger lent a dangerous edge to Hart's words. "How much this time? It must be substantial to prompt you to wire me in Yorkshire."

Marcus's mouth curled in a sneer. "I'll wager that put the fear of God into you."

"You'd lose that wager. But you seem to have a talent for losing wagers, don't you? I ask again, *how much*?"

"Don't you want to know how I discovered where you were staying?"

Hart wanted very much to know, but he wouldn't give his half brother the satisfaction. He remained silent, still waiting for an answer.

Marcus expelled an angry gust of breath. "Five hundred pounds. There. Does that satisfy you?"

"Owed to whom?"

"My tailor and bootmaker. And . . . to Garrard's."

Hart raised his brows. Garrard's was a jeweler. An exceedingly expensive one. "What the devil were you buying at Garrard's?"

"A trifle," Marcus said. "What difference does it make?"

No difference at all, Hart supposed. The money was owed regardless of what had been bought with it. "Are those your only debts at present?" he inquired. "Or are there others I should be concerned with?"

"Tradesmen's debts? That's all of them."

"What about gaming debts? You've already been banned from

most of the respectable betting shops. I trust you haven't been venturing into any of the seedier establishments? You won't find them as obliging if you fail to settle your losses."

"But *you'll* settle them, won't you?" Marcus's sullen countenance contorted with resentment. "It's why you're here. You'd pay any sum to guarantee I keep my mouth shut."

Hart recalled Anne's warning about Marcus bankrupting him. At this rate, he might do so sooner rather than later. "Whatever I do, it won't be on account of your threats. In truth, boy, I've reached the limits of my patience with you."

"I'm not a boy," Marcus said wrathfully. "I'm nineteen."

"If you want to live to see twenty, you'll mind what I say." Hart brought his face level with his half brother's. "You may not like it—it may not be fair or just or reasonable—but you are *not* a gentleman of wealth or property. You're not the heir to an earldom or to anything that I'm aware. What you are—"

"I'm just as much a gentleman as you are."

"No," Hart said. "You're not. You might be eventually, but not at this rate. A gentleman doesn't permit his sister to make herself vulnerable on his behalf. He doesn't enrich himself at his mother and sisters' expense."

"If I had money of my own—"

"Might I suggest gainful employment? It does a great deal for a man's sense of self-worth."

Marcus looked at Hart as though he'd proposed that Marcus become an aeronaut. "You're telling me to get a *job*? Where? In some shop? My father would turn over in his grave!"

"I take leave to doubt it," Hart said with a humorless chuckle. "The more I know of our father's moral lapses, the less I believe anything could shock him."

"It's easy to laugh when you hold all the cards," Marcus replied through his teeth. "Well, mark this. I may not be legitimate, but my father *loved* me. He cared *nothing* for you."

Hart felt the truth of his half brother's words like a sharp knife twisting into his gut.

It was an indisputable fact. Hart's father hadn't cared for him. He hadn't cared for his mother, either. If he had, Marcus and his sisters wouldn't exist at all.

But here they were.

And here Hart was. The last thing he intended to do was reveal that Marcus had struck a nerve.

"I'm certain you're right," Hart said. And then he smiled. "Would that he'd cared enough for you to alter his will."

Marcus's eyes blazed. For a moment, it looked as though he might resort to violence.

Hart immediately regretted his words. He had no interest in this conversation devolving into fisticuffs. Never mind that the continuous jabs about their father's feelings—or *lack* of feelings—had begun to grate.

"Don't be an idiot," he said. "Do you think our father was wealthy? That he had some fortune put by from all his pamphlets and unsolicited editorials? He earned no money in his lifetime save the little he accumulated from the rents on his estate. It would scarcely keep you in cravat pins from Garrard's—or whatever it is you've been buying at the place."

"It wasn't a cravat pin," Marcus snarled. "It was a gift for a young lady."

"Is that what's been sinking you into debt? Presents you've bought for some highflyer? I knew you to be gullible, but I thought you smarter than that."

"She's not a—" Marcus broke off, hands clenching into fists. "Oh, to hell with your opinions! I don't give a damn for them. And I don't believe anything you say about my father's money."

"What you believe or disbelieve makes little difference to me." Hart stood. "Come. Get up and gather your things. I'll settle your affairs and return you to your family. We can discuss the rest of this sad business in more congenial surroundings."

Marcus didn't budge. He was still shaking with fury.

"*Now*," Hart commanded. "You've already wasted my morning. I'll not have you wasting the rest of my day as well."

At length, Marcus grudgingly got to his feet. He offered no words of thanks for Hart's generosity. Quite the opposite. "*One day*," he seethed as he collected his coat, "I'm going to remove that damned smirk from your face."

Hart's smile broadened. "You're welcome to try."

Seventeen

Anne brought Saffron down to a walk. His sides were heaving. Try as he might, the old stallion could no longer keep up with the likes of Stella's mare. Locket was too young and far too determined to win.

"You can't quit before the race has been run!" Stella called out, laughing as she circled back at a canter. She returned to Anne's side, the skirts of her stylish riding habit floating behind her.

Several of the other riders in the park shot disapproving glares her way. A lady shouldn't be galloping in Rotten Row during the fashionable hour. And she definitely shouldn't be laughing while doing it.

Anne leaned forward in her sidesaddle, the leather creaking as she stroked Saffron's damp golden neck. "His race was run years ago, I'm afraid," she said. "The old dear. He's quite ready to retire to the country."

Stella slowed Locket to a walk. Her cheeks were rosy behind the veil of her riding hat. "Meanwhile, Locket is still itching to take on all comers. Pity Julia couldn't join us."

"She'd have had to borrow a mount. She left Cossack behind in Yorkshire."

Stella shortened her reins, maintaining a close contact on Locket's mouth lest the mare leap forward again. "I still wish she might have come. I've seen so little of her these days."

The pair of them rode on, side by side through the throng, their grooms trailing dutifully behind them.

Unlike the mornings, when one had a semblance of privacy, the afternoon hours in Rotten Row were crowded with aristocratic ladies and gentlemen, young misses on the marriage mart, and overbearing sportsmen showing off their latest purchases from Tattersalls. Even the Pretty Horsebreakers were in attendance—famous courtesans known as much for their riding skills as for their other abundant charms.

Competence wasn't a prerequisite to taking part in the daily parade. Among the few accomplished equestrians were countless blunderers. Novice riders clung nervously to horses that spooked and shied at every breeze, and incompetent drivers mismanaged their teams, nearly colliding with one another as they passed.

It was no wonder galloping was frowned upon. Given the dubious skill of the various lords and ladies, most horses couldn't be trusted at any faster than a walk.

"Julia is very much about her own business these past days," Anne said. "Yesterday it was a visit to the solicitors, and today a visit to her parents' house. Who knows what tomorrow might bring?"

"She didn't wish you to go with her?" Stella asked.

"No, indeed. Julia is resolved to face her obstacles alone."

Anne was both proud of her friend's newfound independence and frustrated by it. She wanted to lend Julia her strength. To be there for her in the best way she knew how. But though Julia leaned on her to a degree, she would no longer permit Anne to fix her problems.

As if Anne could do so!

She wasn't even capable of managing her own problems at present. It was hubris to think she could manage those of her friends.

"Marriage has changed her," Stella observed when they'd ridden past most of the crowd and there was less danger of anyone eavesdropping.

"To be fair," Anne said, "I believe her marriage is less the cause of her change than the result of it."

"What do you mean?"

"Only that Julia has taken up the reins of her life. It's what prompted her to wed Captain Blunt in the first place. She's certainly happier for it."

"Perhaps we should follow her example," Stella said.

Anne flashed her friend a quizzical look. "Elope with a notorious ex–army captain?"

Stella affected to give the idea serious consideration. "If only we could be as confident of obtaining the same result. Just our luck, the villain we marry would end up being an actual villain and not a hero in disguise."

"It would be easier to tell the villains from the heroes if gentlemen didn't take such pains to hide their honest selves," Anne said. "Only think of how much time we waste in trying to ascertain who it is they really are."

"It isn't only gentlemen. My brother says every person has two faces—their true face and the one they choose to show to the world."

Anne instantly thought of Hartford and the face he'd chosen to wear. A roguishly smiling countenance that masked the depths beneath. After all these years, she'd barely scratched the surface of him. And now she never would.

She had seen to that in Yorkshire.

In the past two days, she'd resigned herself to the fact. What tears she'd shed had dried up as quickly as a summer storm. There was nothing left now but the same lingering bitterness that had plagued her since the infamous day she'd broken their engagement.

"Your brother says a great many things," Anne replied.

"He does," Stella agreed. "And he's lately found a companion to encourage his pontifications."

"Oh?" Anne gave her a curious glance.

"Miss Amanda Trent." Stella uttered the name as though it were a vile poison on her lips. Locket pranced beneath her, alert to her rider's slightest change in temper. "He met her at the ecumenical conference. She's expected in London for the holidays. My brother speaks of little else."

"You don't imagine he intends to—"

"I do," Stella said grimly. "I'm all but guaranteed to be their chaperone for a Christmas courtship. And when they marry, he'll have no more room in his household for his spinster sister any longer."

With a gentle press of her leg, Anne yielded Saffron closer to Locket. She sank her voice, anxious to offer her friend comfort. "I'm sure that's not true."

"It is." Stella's voice lowered to match Anne's. "He's already started mentioning the possibility of my marrying a widowed parishioner of ours in Derbyshire. The poor man is pushing sixty. 'He won't mind your gray hair,' my brother says. As if that were the only consideration!"

Anne hadn't known Stella's situation had become so dire. "What will you do?"

"What *can* I do? I haven't the luxury of taking the reins up as Julia has. I have no great fortune of my own, and there are no ex–army captains beating down my door. Had I any relations to turn to, I would leave London. Without me here to play chaperone, my brother's marriage plans might falter. But I have nowhere to go, regrettably."

"You can still leave London." So great was Anne's desire to solve her friend's problem, she didn't think of the consequences of her words. "I've been invited to a house party in Hampshire for the holidays. Perhaps you might accompany me?"

"Whose house party?" Stella asked.

Anne hesitated, belatedly realizing that she'd cracked open the door to a whole host of secrets. She slowly readjusted her reins, letting Saffron have his head. "The Earl of March's," she admitted.

As if on cue, a familiar curricle appeared in the distance, pulled by an equally familiar pair of matched chestnut mares. Hartford was driving them with his usual aplomb, his handsome face and tall, broad-shouldered frame immediately putting every other gentleman in the shade. With the sun glinting down on him and his horses gleaming like fire, he might have been the Greek god Apollo himself.

If, that is, Apollo had ever lowered himself to wearing bright plaid trousers and a garish wine-colored coat.

Ridiculous. Even Hartford's clothes were a lark.

How could Anne ever trust a man who turned everything into an object of fun?

But her heart didn't seem to care about his trustworthiness, or lack of it. On catching sight of him, it thumped so hard she wondered that Stella didn't hear it.

Hartford slowed as he approached. He was smiling. He was *always* smiling. But this time his smile didn't quite reach his eyes. "And then there were two," he said dryly.

"Hartford." Anne gave a stiff inclination of her head. "As usual, your powers of observation astound me."

"Your numbers are dwindling, my lady," he replied. "First Miss Maltravers vanished and now Mrs. Blunt? You're neither the Four Horsewomen, nor the three Furies any longer. What am I to call you instead?"

Anne urged Saffron forward. "Pardon us if we ride on while you exercise your feeble wit."

"I do enjoy a bit of exercise, ma'am," Hartford said as she passed. His voice dropped for her ears alone. "Long walks in the Yorkshire woods in particular."

"I would that you would walk straight into the sea," Anne snapped back at him before she could stop herself.

Hartford's smile transformed into a swift grin. This time it was genuine, reaching all the way to his eyes. "I am, as ever, eager to do your bidding." He touched the brim of his hat to her. "Good day, my lady. Miss Hobhouse."

Anne's stomach trembled as she rode away. She was grateful Saffron was no longer sensitive to her moods. Any other horse might have bolted to feel her so uncharacteristically out of sorts. But Saffron was old and dependable. He plodded steadily forward, too tired from his earlier gallop to do more than walk.

Hartford's curricle disappeared in the opposite direction, Kestrel and Damselfly springing into an exuberant trot.

Stella looked at Anne, brows elevating in question. "Will Mr. Hartford be in attendance at his grandfather's house party?"

Anne exhaled the breath she'd been holding. The urge to confide in her friend swelled within her. She could no longer restrain it. "He will. It was he who issued the invitation."

"And you accepted?" Stella was all amazement. "Do you like him after all, dearest?"

"I liked him once," Anne confessed. "But . . . all we do is quarrel. I fear we've quarreled so much we can neither of us forgive each other." There was a gnawing ache in her midsection. "Sometimes I think I hate him."

Stella smiled. "That's encouraging."

"How so? Hate is the very opposite of love."

"The opposite of love is indifference," Stella said. "If you can be riled by the fellow, it means you still care for him."

Anne was doubtful. "Is this more of your brother's dubious wisdom?"

"No," Stella said. "It's my own."

Eighteen

After leaving the park, Stella rode off toward St. George's Street with her groom, and Anne returned with hers to Grosvenor Square. Her mother was taking tea in the drawing room with some of her friends from the spiritualist society. Much to Anne's surprise, Evelyn Maltravers and her uncle, Mr. Fielding, were among them.

Evelyn rose, crossing the room to greet Anne. Her curvaceous beauty and dark auburn hair were enhanced by the exquisitely tailored afternoon dress she wore. It was a garment that could only have been made by Evelyn's beau, Mr. Malik.

Anne met her halfway. The two of them warmly clasped hands and kissed each other's cheeks.

"When did you return from Sussex?" Anne asked.

"Only this morning." Evelyn's soft hazel eyes twinkled from behind her silver-framed spectacles. "My aunt Nora sent me ahead so I might get a start on ordering my wedding clothes."

"Wedding clothes!" Anne gasped. After acknowledging the others in attendance, she drew her friend away to the relative privacy of a stuffed settee near the window.

They sat down beside each other, the skirts of Anne's black bombazine dress bunching against the swell of Evelyn's lustrous pearl-gray silk.

"I wanted to write you about Mr. Malik's proposal," Evelyn said. "But there's been no time. It was quicker to tell you in person."

"And you must," Anne said. "Though I warn you, you'll have to repeat it again for Stella and Julia's benefit."

"Is Stella back from Exeter already?"

"She is. I just parted from her in the Row. Julia's here as well. She's staying with us for a time."

"My uncle told me," Evelyn said. "I expected to see her when we arrived."

Across the room, Mr. Fielding gave a hoarse cough into his handkerchief. It seemed he was still recovering from his putrid throat. Mama was seated next to him on the green velvet sofa, her expression rapt as she joined him in conversation with her other guests, Lady Younger and Mrs. Blakely-Strange.

"Julia should be back from visiting her parents at any moment," Anne said. "She'll be delighted to see you—*and* to hear your good news. But first, my dear, you must tell me all."

Still holding Anne's hand, Evelyn glowingly related how Mr. Malik had traveled to Sussex to make her an offer of marriage. She didn't go into extraordinary detail, but one didn't have to be a clairvoyant to know that the manner of his proposal had been the stuff of dreams.

Anne smiled. "You're being admirably discreet."

"What more can I say?" Evelyn asked with a laugh. "It was excessively romantic. I suppose all proposals are."

"I expect yours was even more so," Anne said, "given the obstacles the two of you have had to overcome."

"I confess, they don't seem so daunting now I know we'll be facing them together." Evelyn beamed. "He's an excellent man, truly. We intend to take good care of each other."

"When will you marry?"

"In November."

"That soon! It doesn't give you much time to plan."

"We're less concerned with a grand wedding than we are with starting our lives together. It's that which is important to us, not the ceremony of the thing." Evelyn pressed Anne's hand. "Though I do hope, when I take my vows, my friends will be there to lend their support. It would mean so much to me."

"Of course we'll be there," Anne promised. "We wouldn't miss it for the world."

Evelyn went on to explain that her wedding was to be held at her uncle's town house in Russell Square, after which she and Mr. Malik would spend the night at Claridge's Hotel before leaving on a short honeymoon. "We can't stay away more than a few days," she said. "Mr. Malik has his dress commissions to think of."

"Where will you live?" Anne asked.

"We haven't decided yet. But we think somewhere near Hampstead Heath might suit, so long as we can find a house with enough room for Hephaestus."

Evelyn was devoted to her Andalusian stallion. He was a majestic beast, with a bright career ahead of him at stud.

"You're leaving him in Sussex until then?" Anne asked.

"He doesn't mind it," Evelyn said, blushing. "I've already taken ten more bookings for him."

An answering flush crept into Anne's cheeks.

She was still a little shocked by Evelyn's entrepreneurial spirit. Horse breeding wasn't an entirely respectable occupation for unmarried ladies. They weren't meant to know about the workings of such things. But Evelyn had been fiercely determined, doing whatever was necessary to secure her happily-ever-after.

She'd been the first of the Four Horsewomen to take up the reins of her life. Julia had swiftly followed her example. All that remained was for Anne and Stella to sort out happily-ever-afters of their own.

Anne was beginning to doubt whether she had the necessary courage.

Perhaps Hartford was right. Perhaps she *was* afraid.

She immediately dismissed the thought.

How could she countenance anything he said? He'd insulted her mother. He'd insulted *her*. And then today, he'd had the audacity to reference the kiss they'd shared when walking in the woods in Yorkshire.

The unscrupulous devil.

"I'm eager to hear the details of Julia's infamous elopement with Captain Blunt," Evelyn said.

"I'm certain she'll tell you when she returns," Anne replied. "Though don't expect anything more than a recitation of how deliriously happy they are in Yorkshire."

"*Is* she happy?" Evelyn asked.

Before Anne could answer, Horbury entered the drawing room. He cleared his throat.

Mama was pouring out the tea for her guests. "What is it, Horbury?"

"Captain Blunt to see Mrs. Blunt, my lady," Horbury said.

Anne's brows lifted. She and Evelyn exchanged a worried glance.

"Captain Blunt?" Mama flashed Anne a sharp look. "Has Julia summoned him?"

"I daresay she has." Anne had no inkling if it was true, but she'd rather not involve her mother in a potential scene. She stood, addressing the butler. "I shall receive him in the small parlor."

"Is something amiss?" Evelyn asked quietly as Anne moved to leave.

"I don't know," Anne admitted.

Making her way downstairs, she reminded herself that Julia hadn't departed Yorkshire in secret. On the contrary, Captain Blunt had been present to bid her farewell. His arrival in London after only two short days nevertheless signified a man who wasn't happy with his wife's absence.

Captain Blunt's disheveled appearance only confirmed Anne's suspicions.

He awaited her in the sunlit parlor, his suit rumpled, his jaw shadowed, and a battered Gladstone bag at his feet. "Lady Anne."

"Captain Blunt." She motioned for him to sit. "If you've come to see Julia—"

"I have." He remained standing.

"She isn't here at the moment. She's gone to call on her parents in Belgrave Square."

A scowl darkened his brow. "Alone?"

Anne sensed an accusation in the question. As if she'd somehow abandoned her friend in her time of need. "I like it no better than you do, sir," she said coolly. "But she insisted upon it. She's insisted on handling all of her affairs alone since she arrived in town."

"I'm obliged to you for the information." Picking up his bag, Captain Blunt turned to leave.

Anne stepped in front of him, temporarily blocking his way. She wouldn't permit him to go after Julia if he was in a temper. "You're not vexed with her, I trust?"

"I am, ma'am," he said. "Deeply vexed. I've lately discovered I can't live without her. If you will excuse me."

Anne moved aside, staring after him as he strode from the room. She'd rarely seen a gentleman so in danger of losing his composure.

None, that is, save Felix Hartford on the night he'd kissed her.

He'd been unshaven and disheveled, too.

"I want to be with you," he'd said gruffly.

The memory of it provoked another pang in her midsection. Dreadful things! Would they never stop plaguing her?

She returned to the drawing room. Evelyn had resumed her seat next to her uncle. Anne sat down in a nearby chair, offering a reassuring smile in answer to Evelyn's look of concern.

Mama broke off from speaking with Mrs. Blakely-Strange. "Well?" she demanded.

"It seems as though Julia will be leaving us," Anne said.

Mama nodded her approval. "Her husband means to take her home, does he? I can't say I'm surprised. Newlyweds shouldn't be parted in the early days of their marriage." She turned back to Mrs. Blakely-Strange, continuing their interrupted conversation. "You were saying something about the Egyptians?"

Mrs. Blakely-Strange sipped her tea, concealing a flinch at the lack of sugar. She was an older woman with a white streak in her dark hair and a propensity to adorn herself with a quantity of jet beads. "Yes, yes. The Egyptians. They're of great significance, of course. But we mustn't discount the Romans. I was discussing the subject only yesterday with Mrs. Frazil. She claims her sessions with the planchette are never so active as when she's near St. Paul's."

"St. Paul's?" Mama queried. "What does St. Paul's have to do with it?"

"Oh, but I thought you knew," Mrs. Blakely-Strange said. "Its location in Ludgate Hill was formerly the site of a Roman temple to the goddess Diana. Mrs. Frazil refers to it as a hill of power. She's conducted private readings for me at her lodgings there, and I must say I've noticed a difference."

Mama's eyes shone with interest. "Fascinating," she murmured. "To think. Right here in London."

Anne could see the wheels turning in her mother's mind. The idea of a "hill of power" had caught her imagination. Especially since it was located so very close to home.

Mama talked of little else during the dinner they shared with Mr. Fielding and Evelyn, and then again, the following morning after a beaming Julia—victorious in her efforts to obtain her inheritance—had departed for Yorkshire on the arm of a contented Captain Blunt.

"I'll have no long faces," Mama said after they had gone. "We've too much to occupy us today for you to be moping about after the loss of your friend."

Anne wasn't aware she'd been moping. She followed her mother back into the drawing room. "Do we have an engagement?"

"Mrs. Frazil has extended an open invitation to tea," Mama said. "We may as well go today as not." She rang the bell for Horbury. "It's past time you and I paid a visit to Ludgate Hill."

Ludgate Hill was only three and a half miles from Grosvenor Square, but it might have been one hundred given how long it took Anne and her mother to reach their destination. At midday, the congestion leading to St. Paul's Cathedral made the steep, narrow street all but impassable. It was clogged with a triple row of vehicles of every form, from the lowliest fruit cart to teetering wagons and overburdened omnibuses.

Amid the clouds of dust generated by the crush of conveyances, pedestrians attempted to cross the street, risking life and limb as they darted through traffic.

Peering out the window of their carriage as they ascended the hill, Anne observed a fellow nearly flattened by a careening hansom cab. "Goodness!" she exclaimed. "What extraordinary chaos!"

"The noise is deafening," Mama complained from the seat across from her. She was in an irritable mood owing to Mr. Fielding having declined her invitation to accompany them. Though he was much improved from the worst of his symptoms, he was still too ill at present to risk a long drive.

"It is, rather," Anne said. They'd been to Ludgate Hill in the past on occasion. It boasted the best warehouses. But they'd never visited at this time of day.

Shouts of cabdrivers and pedestrians filled the air, along with the clip-clop of hooves, the rattle of wheels, and the voices of countless people walking, shopping, and selling their wares.

The street was lined with all manner of shops—linen drapers, carpet sellers, tobacconists, and jewelers. It was also home to several rather depressed-looking houses. Sagging, ramshackle affairs, all jammed together, with little grace or dignity about them. It was in front of one of these that the Arundell carriage finally rolled to a halt.

Mrs. Frazil's house stood in the shadow of St. Paul's. Though somewhat dilapidated, its appearance was softened by the pale pink climbing roses that framed the doorway. The blooms emitted a sweet fragrance as Anne and her mother passed beneath them to enter the house.

A careworn housekeeper admitted them into the front parlor, where Mrs. Frazil was receiving. It was a colorful room, with no traces of black crepe in evidence, either in the decor or on Mrs. Frazil's person.

"Lady Arundell. Lady Anne." Mrs. Frazil rose from her tufted yellow chair near the window. She promptly dropped into a curtsy, the skirts of her lavender day dress pooling around her in a froth of pleats and ribbon bows. "It's a singular pleasure to welcome you to my humble abode."

There was an air of pantomime about the faded woman, as though she were a performer putting on a show for an audience. It was all of a piece with her powdered face, thinly plucked brows, and unnaturally red hair.

Anne suspected she'd taken to dyeing it.

"Please have a seat." Mrs. Frazil gestured to an overstuffed pink sofa across from her. "I'll order tea. My housekeeper has only this morning baked the most delightful little Turkish cakes."

"No cakes, thank you," Mama said as she and Anne sat down. "I don't hold with sweets."

Mrs. Frazil exchanged a few more words with her housekeeper before dismissing her. "Forgive my mistake," she said, returning to her seat. "I recollect that you don't approve of sugar."

"An unwise indulgence. As are so many things these days." Mama's gaze swept over the room with thinly veiled disapproval. "I must say, madam, your parlor is extraordinarily cheerful."

"It is, my lady," Mrs. Frazil said. "I find it restful to my spirits."

"Restful, you say?" Mama gave an elegant snort. "I'm astonished you can hear yourself think with all of the noise from the street."

"There is noise, to be sure," Mrs. Frazil acknowledged. "I often boast that the whole of the world passes by my door. Ladies and gentlemen from the best families, the tradesmen from whom I buy my linens, and the newspapermen who print my daily paper. There's wealth and want, crime and justice, and a greater array of people from distant lands than any you might encounter in Mayfair. I have no cause to seek them out. All I need do is look out my window."

Anne was accustomed to being silent during visits to various practitioners of spiritualism. She had little enough to contribute on the subject other than a healthy skepticism. As a consequence, she often drifted off in her head during her mother's conversations, thinking about letters she had to write or upcoming engagements she'd be attending.

Mrs. Frazil's words nevertheless caught Anne's attention.

It was true. Mayfair was not very diverse. Largely composed of the wealthy and titled, it functioned very much as an exclusive society. Anne had expressed her wish to remain there because it was familiar. Because she knew everyone and everyone knew her. And yet . . .

The same qualities that attracted her also provoked a certain discomfort.

Familiarity was all well and good, but not to the exclusion of everything—and everyone—else. There was a great wide world out there, full of all manner of people. Evelyn had embraced that world and found happiness as a result. Anne hoped she was no less open-minded than her friend.

"Do you have much congress with these people, ma'am?" she asked. "Or do you only observe them?"

Mrs. Frazil smiled benignly. "I speak with many who live in the

Hill in passing. But I confess, I prefer to view them from a distance. I require privacy to conduct my work with the spirit world."

"You don't find the noise distracting to your efforts?" Mama asked.

"Not at all," Mrs. Frazil said. "Ludgate Hill is life. Only listen to it, my lady. Tell me if the sound does not echo in your veins. Such potency can only be to the good."

Mama nodded slowly. "Mrs. Blakely-Strange informs me that it is a hill of immense power."

"It must be so," Mrs. Frazil said. "In Roman times, there was a temple here dedicated to Diana, goddess of the hunt. The vibrations . . ."

Anne's attention strayed as the conversation turned back to matters of spiritualism. She only resumed listening after the tea was served. As she finished drinking the bitter brew, she caught the tail end of something alarming her mother was saying to a very eager-eyed Mrs. Frazil.

". . . to view the house. It may transpire in the near future that it's desirable to be somewhere such as this, a place of life and potency, as you say, if only for a short time."

Anne's gaze jolted to her mother's face. "A house? What house?"

Mama gave her a look of reproof. "Have you not been attending? The house next door to this one is available to let. Mrs. Frazil is acting in the way of landlady." She returned her teacup to its saucer with a decided clink. "We'll have a look at the place after tea."

Anne's mouth opened only to close again. She couldn't interrogate her mother in front of a stranger. And even if she could, it would be unpardonably rude to disparage Miss Frazil's neighborhood to her face.

But honestly . . . Ludgate Hill?

It was too noisy. Too crowded. To dashed inconvenient.

If Cousin Joshua *did* evict them from Grosvenor Square next month and if Mama *did* let a house here, Anne would be entirely on her own. None of her friends would be able to visit her, not without great difficulty. There would be no more gallops in Rotten Row. No more strolls in Bond Street.

No more Hartford.

Outside of their journey to Yorkshire, Anne only ever encountered him in the park or at the various balls and society parties of Mayfair. It had been their sole contact since she'd broken her engagement with him so many years before. If she moved to Ludgate Hill, she'd effectively never see him again.

It was what she wanted, wasn't it? An end to things. And that's what this would be, and no mistake.

The prospect left Anne quite cold to the heart.

Nineteen

Lord and Lady Ramsey's ballroom was ablaze with candlelight. It reflected in the mirrored walls, glowed in the polished wood floor, and shimmered in the colorful silks of the ladies' skirts as their partners swirled them around the room to the strains of a lively polka.

As Hart entered, he counseled himself not to expect too much.

When he'd crossed paths with Anne in Hyde Park a week ago, she'd done nothing to encourage his interest. On the contrary, she'd been furiously uncivil, declaring her wish that he drown himself in the sea rather than continue to plague her.

It was hardly an expression of undying passion.

But it had been passionate nonetheless.

The sharp words had worked on Hart's low spirits as effectively as a tonic. They had taught him to hope again. And he'd lately discovered that a world without the hope of Anne was a very grim place indeed.

He searched the ballroom for her, his gaze drifting over the crush of ladies in jewel-hued gowns and gentlemen in stark black-and-white eveningwear. An orchestra was seated on a dais at the end of the room, energetic musicians playing at speed. Most of the guests were dancing.

Unsurprisingly, Anne wasn't one of them.

Hart strolled around the perimeter, intermittently pausing to exchange pleasantries with the dowagers, spinsters, and wallflowers who were seated at the edge of the ballroom. Anne could generally be found among them, sitting together with her mother or with her horse-loving friends.

But not tonight.

With a sinking feeling, he began to wonder whether she'd come at all.

"Mr. Hartford!" The elderly Dowager Lady Sawbridge beckoned to him with her fan. She was holding court from an armchair at the entrance to the cardroom, haranguing passing gentlemen into partnering one of her charges. "Why aren't you dancing? Are there not worthy enough young ladies among those you see before you?"

Hart gave her an apologetic smile. "Indeed, ma'am. I've been remiss."

"Then you must rectify your error. May I suggest Miss Thrapstone as a partner? She's been sitting these five dances and more."

Miss Thrapstone went scarlet with embarrassment. A spotty girl in her first season, she was perched on a chair beside the dowager, looking like she'd rather be anywhere else in the world but here.

"Miss Thrapstone." Hart bowed to her. "Perhaps you might grant me the country dance?"

Miss Thrapstone's eyes goggled. "B-but that's the supper dance."

"Then it will be my pleasure to take you into supper." Hart bowed to her again before walking on, silently cursing himself for not realizing.

He'd had some notion of asking Anne to dance the supper dance with him.

Not that Anne had ever accepted any of his invitations before.

He'd gone no more than a few steps when his cousin Mariah darted into his path.

"Hart!" The enormous skirts of her apple-green tarlatan gown swung around her in a whirlwind of flounces. "Have you seen my mother?"

"I have not." Hart cast a disapproving glance at the hideous brooch his cousin wore at her bosom. Made in the shape of a tropical flower with a gaudy ruby at its center, it complemented neither her gown nor the blooms in her coiffure. "Speaking of your mother," he said. "Her taste is impeccable. I can only assume this gawdy bauble was your own choice."

She covered the offending article with a protective hand. "Must you be hateful just now? I wanted to ask you a particular favor."

"I've already promised the supper dance. I can spare you a galop, but you might tip over from the weight of that monstrosity."

"I don't want to dance with you." Catching hold of his arm, she pulled him to a less crowded corner. Her voice dropped to a confidential whisper. "I want you to drive me to Richmond Park next Thursday. I've promised to meet a . . . a friend, and my mother has forbidden me the carriage."

Hart was immediately suspicious. His uncle had said Mariah was harboring feelings for a mysterious young man, and this request bore all the symptoms of an assignation. "A *gentleman* friend?"

Mariah didn't deny it. "You won't tell, will you?"

"Do I have the character of a talebearer?"

"No, but—"

"Why Richmond Park? Why not somewhere nearer home?"

"Will you drive me there, or won't you?" she demanded. "If not, I shall hire a cab or . . . or take an omnibus."

"Neither of which you've ever done before in your life," Hart pointed out.

"It's easy enough," she said. "I'm assured I won't have any difficulty."

"Assured by whom? Your gentleman friend?"

Her mouth clamped shut.

It was as good as an answer.

Hart made an effort at sternness. "You might ask yourself what sort of gentleman would encourage a young lady to risk her reputation in order to meet him. He can't think very much of you."

"You don't know him," Mariah said defensively. "And I'm not a young girl anymore. I'm a woman. If you understood—"

"What I understand about females could very possibly fit on the head of a pin. But I know the respect that's owed a young lady. If he cares for you, let him court you in a respectable fashion."

"He's going to. Indeed, he's promised that soon he'll approach my stepfather."

Hart was skeptical. His cousin was an heiress from a well-to-do family. A gentleman requesting to meet her in some remote corner of a park halfway across the city was likely no gentleman at all. "What is he waiting for?"

"He's had a bit of bad luck. He needs time to right his ship."

"A sailor, is he?"

"It's no laughing matter, Hart. If you could but comprehend what it's like to face adversity on the path to true love. Lord Byron wrote that—"

"Good God," Hart muttered. "Not Byron."

Mariah's face was stricken. "You have no finer feeling."

"I have plenty of feelings, fine and otherwise. But mawkishness is dangerous. It can lead one to make oneself ridiculous."

"I'm not making myself ridiculous," she replied. "I'm as capable of choosing my sweethearts as you are."

"My sweethearts don't ask that I put myself in danger on their behalf."

"No," she said with a rare flash of spirit. "They only make you accompany them on ill-advised rail journeys to obscure little villages in North Yorkshire."

Hart stilled. "And what, pray tell, does that mean?"

Mariah's courage failed her. "Nothing, nothing, I only want your help. I have no one else to—Oh!" Her eyes went wide. "There's Mama!

Don't tell her you've seen me." With that, she darted off, vanishing back into the crowd.

Aunt Esther appeared a split second later, looking coldly elegant in an unembellished silk gown. "Hartford," she said. "You haven't seen Mariah, have you? I've engaged her to dance the waltz with Lord Whatley and she's nowhere to be found."

Lord Whatley?

If that was the cause of Mariah's flight, Hart didn't blame her for absconding. The aged Lord Whatley might make a wise alliance in terms of politics, but he would make a poor husband for a featherheaded young girl.

"You might check the ladies' retiring room," Hart suggested.

"I shall." Aunt Esther hurried away.

Hart exhaled heavily. He had no wish to become entangled in Mariah's affairs this evening. His family had taken up enough of his time of late. There had been precious little left for himself.

What he wanted—what he *needed*—was to see Anne. It didn't matter that his cousin was probably right. That, in his pursuit of Anne, he'd likely made himself ridiculous.

More than likely, if he was being honest with himself.

He'd trailed after her for years, still wanting her. Still admiring her. Still measuring every other young lady against her and finding them wanting.

Perhaps it was wrong to hope. Perhaps he'd be wiser to do as she asked. To forget her. To finally let her go.

Increasingly discouraged, Hart abandoned the ballroom, making his way to the Ramseys' library. The evening stretched ahead of him in Anne's absence, a long expanse of emptiness until the supper dance.

He could do with a drink.

The tall paneled doors to the library stood closed. On opening them, he was at once assailed by a familiar lemon-tart voice. It drifted to his ears from a high-backed settee facing the fireplace.

"A temporary accommodation," Anne was saying. "Not a permanent one."

"But Ludgate Hill? Truly?" Miss Hobhouse's voice sounded from beside her in a soft murmur of sympathy. "You don't think she's serious about it?"

"It depends on what happens when he arrives," Anne said. "*If* he arrives."

Hart was tempted to eavesdrop, but he hadn't sunk that low.

Not yet, anyway.

He dramatically cleared his throat.

The two ladies were at once on their feet. Flames flickered from the silver candelabra that stood on the mantel behind them, illuminating them in a soft, candlelit glow.

Miss Hobhouse was garbed in a pale blue dress of some variety. Hart hardly noticed her. His attention was wholly and entirely riveted by Lady Anne.

She was wearing the same black watered silk ball gown she'd worn to a recent dance at Cremorne Gardens. A striking garment with a daringly low neckline, it exposed a lush expanse of her alabaster bosom and throat.

His mouth went dry.

"What do you mean by creeping up on a person?" Anne's sharp words were belied by the blush suffusing her face.

And Hart didn't think. He simply uttered the first thought in his head. The *only* thought in his head. "I mean to tell you," he said huskily, "that you are by far the most beautiful creature I have ever beheld."

Twenty

Anne's mouth fell open. "*What?*"

Beside her, Stella hastily collected her silk-fringed shawl and reticule. "Forgive me," she said, moving to leave. "I recall I've promised the next dance to . . . someone."

Anne hadn't the good sense to stop her friend from abandoning her. She was too busy staring at Hartford.

Her heart thumped hard as he advanced into the room.

He was never so dangerous as when he was in eveningwear. It was the only time his handsomeness was shown off to its full brilliancy, unmuted by garish patterns or colors. Anne didn't like to think she was influenced by such things, but . . .

Evidently, she was.

Behind him, Stella silently slipped out of the library. The door drifted shut after her with a click that Anne felt in her bones.

"Your friend has made a timely exit," Hartford observed. "Perhaps she knows something I don't?"

"A great many somethings, I shouldn't wonder," Anne replied. "Why on earth would you say such a thing in front of her?"

"You'd rather I said it privately?"

"Yes." She inwardly groaned. "I mean—no. Obviously."

A smile tugged at his mouth. "I'm usually not so indiscreet. But your dress . . . it's planted me a facer."

Anne felt a surge of self-consciousness. Not because she didn't look her best, but because she looked too well.

She'd worn black for so many years, she'd almost become used to invisibility. But her fashionable ball gown had taken the dourness of mourning and turned it into something seductive.

"This isn't the first time you've seen it," she said. "I wore it at Cremorne Gardens."

"Yes, I know. And I still haven't recovered."

Anne's pulse quickened as he came to a halt in front of her. "You can thank Mr. Malik. It's one of his designs. He's . . . he's Miss Maltravers's fiancé. They've recently become engaged."

"I know who he is," Hartford said gruffly.

"Well, then." Her chin lifted a notch.

"Well, then." He gazed down at her, an odd frown at the back of his eyes.

Anne had the impression that he was at a loss for words. A rare occurrence. "You haven't been drinking, I trust?"

"No. I don't drink overmuch."

"Yes. I'm sure you're sober as a judge."

"I wouldn't go that far," he said. "But I *am* sober minded. I don't overindulge. I don't amuse myself with music hall girls or—"

Anne took a reflexive step back. "Why are you telling me *that*?"

"Because," he said, closing the distance between them, "despite everything, you seem to be operating under the illusion that you can't trust me."

She huffed. "I wonder what would have given me that impression?"

The frown in his gaze became more pronounced.

Or perhaps it was only a trick of the candlelight.

Lord and Lady Ramsey disapproved of gaslight. Instead, they illuminated their Cavendish Square mansion in old-fashioned style with beeswax candles dripping from chandeliers, wall sconces, and a great many strategically placed candelabras.

The library danced with candle flame, resulting in seductively shadowed corners, darkened alcoves, and an atmosphere that was decidedly—and rather uncomfortably—romantic.

Anne took another step back. There was a window seat nearby. It faced the door, making it seem somehow safer than the secluded settee where she and Stella had been huddled together talking. As she inched toward it, Anne was conscious of Hartford matching her step for step, like some great gorgeous beast stalking his prey.

"I'll have you know," he said, "that I've recently solved all manner of family problems. I've paid to have new drains completed on my estate. I've bailed my half brother out of gaol. And I've—"

"Your half brother was in gaol?" Anne latched on to the opportunity to change the subject with a desperate grip.

Hart stifled a grimace. "Not gaol exactly. It was a sponging house in Chancery Lane."

"Good Lord." Anne sat down in the window seat. It was swathed by heavy velvet draperies, drawn back to reveal a view of the Ramseys' torchlit rose garden. She felt a decided coolness seeping through the glass. It raised gooseflesh on her bare arms and shoulders. "How did that come about?"

Hartford sank down beside her, making no attempt to preserve a respectable distance between them. A fold of Anne's full skirts caught under his muscular thigh, trapping her next to him as surely as a butterfly in a net.

"He has expensive taste," he said. "And an expensive sweetheart, apparently. The money he doesn't lose betting on the horses, he spends at various shops. I've had a stern talk with him and the rest of his family. We discussed his finding employment. Or rather, *I* discussed his finding employment. In any case, they know where I stand."

Anne tugged her skirt free of his leg. "I hope they took you seriously."

"There's no reason they shouldn't."

She gave him a speaking look.

"I'm not always jesting, you know," he said.

"It seems that you are."

"Why? Because I laugh too much?"

"Because you engage in one foolish enterprise after the other," she said. "Shall I enumerate them?" Plenty of incidents came to mind. "In April, you practically killed yourself in a curricle race with Lord Rushton."

"The stories about that race have been vastly overstated," he said dismissively. "Rushton only lost a wheel."

Anne continued, undeterred. "Then there was the catastrophe at Vauxhall, when you volunteered yourself as a passenger on one of the balloon ascents, only to have it crash down in the middle of Hertfordshire. For a full day, no one knew whether you were alive or dead."

He gave her a look that was hard to read. "That was nearly four years ago."

To Anne, it might have been four days. She could still recall the helpless despair she'd felt during the twenty-four hours Hartford had been missing. And she could well remember what she'd felt when he'd been found. She'd wanted to strangle him with her bare hands for putting her through such distress.

But she hadn't been able to do anything.

She'd had no right, either to scold him or to throw her arms around him in relief. The next time she'd seen him, it had been in Hyde Park. He'd teased her just as he always did, and she'd snapped back at him in return. There had been a deep cut over his left eye. The sight of it had provoked a queer hollowness in her chest.

"Very well," she said, nettled. "What about all the absurdities you spout in your columns? 'No good has yet been derived from ignoring our mutual history.' What nonsense."

"I was talking about the Roundheads and Cavaliers," he said. And then, with a flash of a roguish grin, "Anyway, I wrote that for *your* benefit."

"What about your other columns? All those sarcastically florid phrases and sardonic observations? Talking about the 'glorious benefits of prolonged abstention on the masculine constitution,' for heaven's sake. As if you're privy to some private joke at the rest of the world's expense."

Hartford's gaze intensified. "You've been reading them."

Anne didn't like the way he was looking at her, as if he'd discovered something important that he hadn't known before. "You know I have. It's how I discovered who you were." She warmed under the weight of his regard. "You use *vouchsafe* too much, by the way. Along with your pseudonyms, anyone might recognize you."

"No one else has," he said. "And that bit about masculine abstention was only printed this morning."

Anne flushed. "Your point?"

"My point is, that despite your disapproval, and despite the fact you've already made use of them *and* me, you're still reading my columns."

"One can scarcely avoid them."

"In a temperance magazine?" A smug smile edged his mouth. It was almost as provoking as his mocking words.

"It's good you can be so pleased with yourself," she said. "It saves me any guilt I might have had in feeling the opposite."

"You don't approve of my amusements."

"I don't. They show a profound lack of seriousness, both in yourself and in reference to the feelings of other people."

"It's harmless fun," he said. "Even the most well-functioning machine requires a mechanism for letting off steam."

"It's hardly harmless. Some of the reviews you write in the *Weekly Heliosphere* are downright cruel. The authors of those novels are real people. You could be ruining them with your flippant words, without any more thought given to the exercise than you give to any other of your larks."

Hartford's smile slowly faded. "I'm sorry for it," he said. "Or rather, I'm *not* sorry. It isn't a sin to find amusement in life. Not everyone can be as humorless as your father was."

Anne blinked. His words seemed to come out of nowhere, taking her completely off her guard. "What gives you the right—" Her tongue tripped over itself in swift-rising outrage. "First you insult my mother, and now you insult my father—"

"It's not an insult. Your father was—"

"Steady. Reliable. Someone who always did what he said he would and who always, always kept his promises."

"Yes, I know. A saint."

"Not a saint," Anne retorted. "A man whom we could depend on."

Hartford's expression turned thoughtful. "And you can't depend on me," he said. "That's the crux of it."

"No, I can't. And no amount of compliments or . . . or *kisses* will make me do so."

A lick of heat flared in his blue eyes. "Perhaps I haven't complimented you enough." He bent his head toward hers. "Or kissed you enough."

Anne immediately set a hand on his chest to hold him back. His heart thumped rapidly beneath her palm. A disconcerting sensation. It was entirely at odds with his self-assured demeanor. "Don't," she said, a breathless note coming into her voice. "I can't think straight when you kiss me."

His nose brushed hers. "Thinking is overrated."

She curled her fingers in the creamy silk of his waistcoat. "You *would* say that."

A laugh rumbled in his chest like a lion's purr, but he didn't press his advantage. He remained where he was, unmoving, yet still close enough to take her mouth with the slightest effort. He smelled of expensive shaving soap. Of mint and leather and memory.

And Anne wanted to kiss him. She wanted it quite badly. The aching desire was warm and fizzing in her veins, drawing her closer to him with every beat of her heart, making the temptation almost unbearable.

But she couldn't do it. It wasn't safe.

He wasn't safe.

She rested her forehead against his, a soft breath trembling out of her.

Hartford's large hand slowly covered hers on his chest. He flattened her palm against his heart. "Do you feel that?"

She managed a slight nod, her own heart thumping as heavily as his.

"I'm extraordinarily healthy, Anne," he said. "I'm not going to die in a curricle race or a balloon crash. I'm not going to die full stop."

She jerked back sharply to meet his eyes. "*Everybody* dies."

"Eventually, yes. But I expect I'm going to be around for a very long while. I promise you that."

"You can't promise it. No one can."

"*I* can." His strong fingers curved around hers. "You can depend on me."

Anne's defenses began to weaken.

She shored them up again with recollections of the past. Of how he'd hurt her when she was at her most vulnerable. Of how he'd let her down. It wasn't difficult. The pain he'd inflicted was ever near the surface.

Depend on him? He was the last person on earth she could depend on!

He must have felt the change in her. A frown notched his brows. "I'm not so different from the man who proposed to you all those years ago."

No, she wanted to answer. *And that's the problem.*

"We're both different." Her hand fell from his chest, sliding free of his grasp. "Utterly and inexorably changed. All of this"—she gestured to the negligible space between them, a space that was even now pulsing with attraction—"is just a remnant of what we once were to each other."

Hartford's handsome features etched with frustration. "This remnant, as you call it, is very close to driving me insane."

She stood abruptly. "That's *your* problem."

"Yes," he said, surging to his feet. "Because you're not affected by any of this *at all*."

Anne let out a bitter laugh. "Of course I'm affected. I'm not made of stone. But I shall overcome it. Just see if I don't."

Twenty-One

It was exactly one week before the first column appeared. Anne discovered it at breakfast in the newly delivered issue of *Glendale's Botanical Bi-Monthly* that Horbury had set beside her plate with the rest of her morning post.

After Hartford's words to her at the Ramseys' ball, Anne was quite tempted to dispose of the magazine altogether. She'd parted from him in high dudgeon, returning to the ballroom (after a brief stop in the ladies' retiring room) only to find him there smiling, socializing, and roguishly devil-may-care, as though he hadn't just confessed that his unresolved feelings for her were driving him mad.

The dratted scoundrel.

He'd even danced the supper dance with a young debutante—a spotty, awkward young lady in her first season. He'd been obliged to dine with her, too, something he'd done with extraordinary good humor, gracing the stammering girl with the full force of his charming attention all through their meal in the supper room.

As Anne had watched him with her, a peculiar warmth had settled in her breast.

Hartford might not be as serious or sober minded as he claimed. He might not be wholly trustworthy. But he was kind. And kindness counted for a great deal in this world.

Perhaps it was that which had made Anne begin to soften toward him. Even so . . .

She wasn't some fawning nitwit to be reading a gardening journal just because it contained a paragraph of drivel he'd penned for his own amusement.

But Anne didn't dispose of the magazine.

Despite her misgivings, she turned to Hartford's column. To her consternation, it contained none of the sarcastic flourishes and sly insults that usually characterized his writing. Indeed, it seemed as though this particular gardening article had been written about her.

FROM THE GARDEN OF MR. H. TIDEWATER

Cardiocrinum giganteum, *or the giant Himalayan lily, is a difficult specimen. She requires inordinate patience on the part of the gentleman gardener who would seek to cultivate her. From seeds, the lily may take as many as six and a half years to reach maturity. A slow process. During this protracted wait, lesser men will be tempted to give up and turn their attention to showier, more easily won blooms. But take heart: those who persevere in their devotion to this rare and formidable plant will eventually be rewarded with the showiest of flowers, unmatched in their splendor. Tend her well. Prune her heart-shaped leaves, keep her soil damp, and do not crowd her too closely in the garden. Be patient, be diligent, but above all, my good sirs, be not discouraged.*

Anne chewed her lip, biting back a reluctant smile as she lowered the magazine to the table. She supposed *she* was the Himalayan lily and *he* was the gardener. Foolish man. Either way, his message was clear.

He wasn't giving up on her.

Hart regarded William Webb from across the small table in the dining room of the railway hotel near Euston station. He was a man of middle years, with tightly curling black hair framing a broad face darkened to deep umber by the sun. Fresh off the train from Borrowdale, he was still in his traveling clothes—a loose brown coat and plain wool trousers.

Webb had the management of the Parfit Plumbago Crucible Company's mines in Cumberland. He'd come to London to meet with Hart and the other shareholders. It was a meeting that was slated to take place in the morning.

"I appreciate your talking to me first," Hart said.

The low murmur of conversation swirled around them, punctuated by the clink of glasses and cutlery.

"Happy to, sir." Webb's words were edged in a thick Cumbrian burr. "It's nothing I wouldn't say to the others."

As always, Hart appreciated the man's brutal honesty. It's why he'd hired him five years ago. That, and because of his unique intelligence.

Webb had been born and bred in Cumberland. The son of a black washerwoman and an illiterate Whitehaven sailor, he'd labored in the pits as a boy, learning the business of mining firsthand.

It was from Webb that Hart had learned the worst of what children experienced in the mines. Boys as young as ten were lowered down, sometimes hundreds of feet into the pits, via precarious baskets and ladders. Once inside, they were stuck underground for half the day in poorly ventilated darkness, consigned to crawling through narrow tunnels on their hands and knees and pulling heavy loads behind them.

The dangers were considerable.

Children were often injured. Some even died as a result of falling down open shafts, being caught in collapses, or drowning in flooded pits.

Hart wasn't interested in having anyone's death on his conscience, least of all a child's. He'd long insisted that the company limit the use of children underground. It hadn't been a popular stance with his partners, but Hart had doggedly adhered to it.

Webb agreed with Hart, both in theory and practice. He was a man who shared Hart's vision for a fairer, more compassionate relationship between the plumbago company and the mining community.

"It's like I said," Webb told him. "They'd gladly break their backs for you. There's that much goodwill among the miners."

If there was, it was owing to Webb's influence. He had an innate gift for inspiring loyalty among the workers, whether it be the rawest lad or the most cantankerous and intractable of the old-timers. The men respected Webb's steadiness and skill. They knew he'd never steer them wrong.

"But it isn't a question of hard work," Webb went on. "The mines are in good fettle, but they can't produce what they don't have."

Hart nodded. He more than comprehended the issue.

His partners in the crucible company had been pressing for expansion in Cumberland. They were convinced that it was Hart's limitations on the hours miners could work, and his restrictions on the use of children in the pits, that were hindering production. But it wasn't that at all. The fact was, there simply wasn't enough plumbago to be had anymore. Not enough to keep up with demand.

"My partners will want to see for themselves," Hart said.

"They're welcome to return with me to Borrowdale," Webb replied. "Talk with the miners and the other men. I'll take them down to the pits myself."

Hart couldn't envision his aged partners going anywhere near the pits, let alone descending down into them.

But someone would have to.

Unlike Hart, the others wouldn't be as willing to take the word of an uneducated workingman like William Webb. Not if Webb's opinions went against their interests.

Which left only one solution.

Hart didn't much care for it. He hadn't planned on leaving London in the near future. He was in the middle of a campaign for Anne's heart. A written campaign this time, but a campaign nonetheless. It involved his remaining in town. To win her, he had to see her. He had to make her see *him*.

A few pointedly written articles in the various journals he contributed to, and he was confident she would be provoked into a response. And even if she wasn't, it would keep him in her thoughts—a constant, irritating reminder, like a pebble lodged in her slipper—making it all the more difficult for her to overcome her feelings for him.

Perhaps it was a juvenile tactic. Or possibly an unwise one. But Hart was running out of options where Anne was concerned.

He couldn't forget her. And he refused to let the hope of her go. Whether she was willing to admit it or not, she wanted him just as much as he wanted her.

He'd realized something at the Ramseys' ball. Something he probably should have recognized from the start. He felt a fool for not having seen it before.

Anne was terrified of losing the people she cared about.

It was why she scorned his recklessness. It was why she'd remained at home.

Her father's death had shaken her badly. Worse than she'd likely ever admit.

Hart had attempted to reassure her. He'd promised her he wasn't going to die. And he'd meant it. It had been ages since he'd engaged in anything riskier than a curricle race.

Until now.

A trip down into the pits was far from safe. Quite the opposite.

But there was nothing for it.

Hart made up his mind. "I doubt my partners will take you up on that offer," he said. "But I will. When you return to Borrowdale in the morning, I'll go back with you myself."

The next column appeared exactly one week after the lily column, and the next one a week after that. Each of them was worded in a similar fashion. Whether Hartford was writing about gardening, the temperance movement, or literature, he seemed to be subtly addressing his precarious relationship with Anne.

She read his latest offering in the morning room, seated alone by the window, while her mother and Mrs. Griffiths went over the menus for the week, just as they did every Sunday. It was a review of a new collection of poetry in the *Weekly Heliosphere*, written under yet another of Hartford's ridiculous water pseudonyms.

THE LITERARY TRAVELS OF MR. BILGEWATER

> *On this month's stop on our reading journey, your humble guide must warn you against stepping over the treacherous cliffs of oversimplification. Case in point: the painful poetic scribblings of Mr. E. Arbuthnot. In his latest collection of verse, Arbuthnot writes of love as though it were as airy and insubstantial as spun sugar, the sort of juvenile fancy that dissolves at the first quarrel. In doing so, he fails to convey the earthy complexity of adult emotion, the very realness that stands the test of time, serving to vouchsafe a visceral response in the reader. Maturity lends substance to feeling. I recommend the author do a little maturing before he gifts us with his next volume of treacle.*

A frown crept into Anne's face.

Hartford's words vexed her more than they comforted her. It was reassuring to know she was still in his thoughts, but . . . was this how he categorized their broken engagement? As some childish quarrel that paled in comparison to the physical attraction they still felt for each other? Something she was, in her feminine naivete, oversimplifying to the detriment of them both?

If that were the case, he didn't understand their past at all.

Anne would have liked to tell him so, but the prospect seemed unlikely. She hadn't seen Hartford in weeks. He'd been strangely absent from the park, and he'd made no appearance at any of the various society engagements she was obliged to attend with her mother.

Presumably, he had business out of London. Something to do with his investments, perhaps. Or some difficulty he was sorting out with his father's illegitimate offspring. It was none of Anne's business, she knew. Still . . .

She couldn't stop herself from wondering.

"Anne," her mother called to her from across the room. She was seated behind her dainty papier-mâché writing desk, marking the sample menus Mrs. Griffiths had given her. "Shall we order chicken or beef for tomorrow's dinner? I seem to recall that he prefers the latter."

Anne didn't need to ask to whom she was referring.

In the past weeks, Mama had been fretting over Joshua's visit with increasing intensity. According to the letter he'd written in June, he was meant to be here tomorrow, but he'd sent no further word. No additional letters had arrived. Not even a telegram from Cherry Hill informing them of his departure.

It was yet another sign that he considered the Grosvenor Square house quite his own. He wasn't a guest arriving to stay, he was the Earl of Arundell finally coming home.

Anne felt vaguely ill to think about it.

But being heartsick about the future didn't stop it from coming. Better to face it with a stiff upper lip than to cringe from it like a coward.

Besides, Joshua may be the new Earl of Arundell, but Anne was still the old earl's daughter. She had no intention of putting Papa's memory to shame.

"Beef," she said. "And lots of it. Cousin Joshua has a healthy appetite."

"Beef, then." Mama marked one more change to the menus with her quill pen before handing them back to Mrs. Griffiths.

The housekeeper departed the morning room with a curtsy.

Mama set down her pen, leaning back in her black-lacquered chair with a sigh. "I've a headache coming on," she muttered to herself.

Anne rose and went to her. She examined her mother's face with concern. "Would you like one of your headache powders?"

"That won't be necessary. They give little enough benefit these days." Mama massaged her temple with her fingers. "I suppose he *is* coming."

Anne felt the sudden sting of tears at the backs of her eyes. "Yes," she said. "I believe he is."

"I don't know why he would wish to. The season is over. Everyone is leaving for their country estates to begin the shooting. He might have stayed at Cherry Hill. The grouse were always plentiful this time of year. Your father and I were never so happy as when—" Mama stopped. Her voice fractured with inexplicable sorrow. "It's all slipping away."

"No," Anne objected softly.

"I can see it quite clearly," Mama said. "First Cherry Hill and now Grosvenor Square. He's taken every refuge. Every memory."

Reaching across the desk, Anne clasped hold of her mother's hand. She grasped it tightly. "Papa isn't this house, no more than he was Cherry Hill. He isn't any one place. He's part of us. He'll stay with us wherever we go."

"A pretty thought."

"It's the truth," Anne said. "Joshua may come tomorrow, but he can't take anything from us. Not anything that matters. We'll still have our memories—*and* each other."

Mama pressed her hand. There was an odd catch in her voice. An emotion she rarely gave voice to. "I don't know what I'd do without you, my girl," she said. "If anything were to happen to you—"

"You needn't worry on my account, Mama," Anne said. "I'm strong enough to bear whatever comes. As strong as you and Papa."

"Indeed," her mother said. "You've inherited the best of us." She squeezed Anne's hand once more before releasing it. "Perhaps I might use a headache powder after all. Pray go and tell Mrs. Griffiths to make one up for me."

"Of course." Anne straightened. She had no doubt but that she'd just been summarily dismissed.

Her mother didn't want reasonable arguments. She didn't even seem to want reassurance. Anne wasn't certain what else to offer her except diversion. Another visit to Ludgate Hill? Another séance or session with the planchette?

As ever, Anne was quite willing to do whatever it took.

It was enough for now that her mother had acknowledged the value of Anne's presence. That she'd recognized Anne was here for her, an ally in the fight to come. They may only be women in a world governed by men, but there were two of them. And when women banded together, they could make empires tremble.

Anne reminded herself of that fact as she descended the stairs to the ground floor. She crossed the entry hall toward the door that led down to the kitchens. Before she could reach it, the door opened and Horbury emerged. He looked unusually out of sorts.

"My lady? A package has arrived for you."

Anne cast a glance around the hall. The table that usually held such deliveries was empty. "Where is it?"

"I've taken the liberty of placing it in the pantry," he said. "You might better view the creature there."

Creature?

Anne's mood perked as she followed Horbury down the servants' stairs to the house's expansive kitchens. The door to the butler's pantry was closed. An insistent mewling seeped out through the cracks at the hinges.

Her face spread into a smile. Good heavens! Julia had actually done it. She'd sent Anne a kitten!

Horbury opened the door to the pantry. Inside, a screened wooden traveling box sat atop a small table. A fluffy black kitten peered out from within, its eyes the color of molten gold.

"A footman escorted her here all the way from Yorkshire." Horbury handed Anne a note. "He brought this along with her."

Anne cracked open the red wax seal, swiftly reading the enclosed lines.

My dearest Anne,

This is Alice (what the children and I have been calling her). She's the smallest of the litter and also the boldest. She enjoys milk, cream, and chopped beef, which my husband says you must procure from the butcher and <u>not</u> from the cat's meat man (who lamentably uses horse meat). For her private relief, I recommend a discreet tray of sand in your dressing room.

Your devoted friend,
Julia

"The poor lad," Horbury went on as Anne read. "His hands and face were scratched bloody. I fear he tried to comfort the vicious little she-devil."

Anne folded the note and tucked it into the pocket of her black crepe skirt. "She's not vicious. She's frightened." Unlatching the door to the box, Anne reached in and gently extracted its hissing and spitting occupant. "Shh," she murmured as the kitten clawed its way up her bodice to perch on her shoulder. "Easy, little friend. You're home now."

Horbury's usually impassive face betrayed a trace of alarm. "Are you keeping her, my lady?"

"Of course I am," Anne said. "We she-devils of the world must stick together, you know."

Twenty-Two

Hart sat across the long oak table from Mr. Parfit, Mr. Goodbody, and Mr. Acker in the Battersea manufactory's small conference room. Together, they made up the four largest shareholders of the Parfit Plumbago Crucible Company. They weren't friends by any means, but thus far they'd managed to get along pleasantly enough together.

Until today.

From the moment Hart had arrived at the riverside gates of the factory, civility had been at a premium. It was his own fault. Not for the first time, he refused to fall in with the majority view.

He'd spent most of the past weeks in Cumberland, visiting the company's plumbago mines with William Webb. When not at the pits, Hart had been in the company's offices in Borrowdale. There, he'd hammered out production figures with a series of bleak men who'd imparted even bleaker information.

Hart had expected his partners to meet the news with anger and disappointment. They had been set on an expansion in Cumberland and would now be forced to alter their plans. What Hart hadn't expected was that, in his absence, they'd have formulated another plan entirely.

"The solution is clear," Parfit said impatiently. An imposing older man with a full set of graying side-whiskers, he was the public face of the company. It was a fact that often had him acting as though he were truly in charge. "If the company is to survive, it requires international expansion."

Goodbody and Acker grunted their wholehearted agreement. The former was a gouty, balding man of sixty and the latter a plump, white-haired fellow with a walrus mustache. They were businessmen, born and bred, who—like Hart—had invested in the crucible company in its earliest days.

"The site in Ceylon is ideal for what we require," Goodbody repeated for what must have been the tenth time. "The site's manager has assured me of it."

"He's already completed most of the blasting and tunneling," Parfit said. "Initial estimates project the mine will yield as much as eight hundred tons per annum, with an estimated annual profit of two thousand pounds."

"If we start there," Goodbody added, "we'll be well placed to expand even further."

Acker eagerly bobbed his head. "First Ceylon, and then—"

"And then, nothing," Hart said. "Not so long as certain standards aren't met."

Goodbody blustered. "But we have no other alternative. You've said yourself that the Cumberland mines won't meet projected demand."

"The mines in Ceylon promise to produce treble the amount of plumbago," Acker said. "Not to mention the savings to us in employing local workers—"

"By which you mean women and children," Hart said.

Parfit gave a dismissive snort. "They're glad for the opportunity to earn a wage."

"Quite right," Acker agreed. "They line up for the chance to work in the mines, right along with the native men."

"And in exchange you propose we reward them with backbreaking labor and unsafe conditions?" Hart shook his head, refusing to countenance the idea. "Sinking shafts and digging tunnels must be done with precision. Safety measures must be taken. Particularly if we're going to allow women and children into the mines. I won't have their lives on my conscience."

"Damn your conscience, man!" Parfit barked. "This is industry, not Sunday school!"

"Why must it be a matter of conscience?" Goodbody attempted a conciliatory tone. "We'd be breaking no laws. Everything would be perfectly in order."

It was true enough. Slavery had been outlawed in Ceylon in 1844. What workers they employed there would be paid for their labor. But it wouldn't be enough. That was the entire point of it. Skirting standards, exploiting the miners, and giving absolute discretion to tyrannical loadmasters was all part of the business plan. None of it was, strictly speaking, against the law.

But just because something was legal didn't make it right.

"No," Hart said. "I won't agree to it. There are better options here at home."

"Where you've already affected our profits," Parfit said. "We're so hemmed in by your compassion in the pits, we can make no headway. And now you would prohibit our international expansion?"

Hart fixed the man with a glacial stare. "Limiting the hours a day a British child toils in a plumbago mine has hardly ruined our business. As far as I can tell, the only result of it has been to burnish our reputation in the mining communities. The people know we're fair. They know our workers aren't disposable commodities to us."

"Yes, yes, that's all very laudable," Parfit said scornfully. "I conceded to it, didn't I? But we're talking about Ceylon, not Cumberland. I'll not have us expending a fortune in sending engineers to sink mines and milk-veined nursemaids to oversee them. Our entire purpose is to make money, not to lose it."

"They'll be grateful for the work there," Acker added. "And think how much more we could earn in profits!"

"*More?*" Hart repeated. "Who among us needs more? Certainly not I. Not if it means compounding the suffering of the most vulnerable among us. We none of us require it. Business is flourishing. That's the very issue, isn't it? Business is so grand we must discover new sources of plumbago? Very well. Let us do so here at home."

"By God, sir," Parfit said through his teeth. "I'll not be moralized at by a boy fresh out of the schoolroom."

Hart was surprised into a short laugh. "Not that fresh, sir. As for moralizing—" He shrugged. "I own fifty-one percent of the company."

Parfit's face turned the color of a ripe tomato.

Goodbody hastened to smooth things over. "Surely, we can negotiate. If we can all agree—"

"There's no room for negotiation," Hart informed him. "The three of you have known my position from the start."

"A lofty position," Acker remarked. "Is it one you take in your other investments? Do you refuse sugar in your tea? Do you confine yourself to homegrown wool and cotton? Or is thwarting our company the sole expression of your morality?"

"I do the best I'm able under the circumstances," Hart replied, undeterred. "And when given a choice in the matter—when given power over the lives of others—I choose to err on the side of basic humanity."

"Go yourself, then," Parfit said.

The room went silent.

"If you won't be satisfied that the business is up to your standards," Parfit continued, "then take management of the operation in person. Run it there as you see fit. Only get it up and running."

Hart was briefly taken aback. "You're suggesting I move to Ceylon?"

"Why not?" Acker said, quickly warming to the idea. "Why shouldn't you be the one to go? You have no wife. No children. Of all of us, you're the one best equipped to remove to a foreign clime."

"Will you consider it?" Goodbody asked. "It would be an acceptable compromise."

Hart immediately thought of Anne. "I'm unable to leave England at present."

Parfit leaned across the table. "Unable or unwilling?"

"Both," Hart admitted.

His three partners all exploded at once, their voices raised in various expressions of frustration and outrage.

"Your fastidiousness will rob us of thousands of pounds in income," Parfit said.

"It will send us straight to the poorhouse!" Acker declared.

"I doubt that," Hart said. "Parfit has a new town house in Brook Street. Goodbody just finished refurbishing his Dorset estate, and you, Acker, are as well-fed and prosperous as a Russian princeling. Don't tell me any of you will feel the pinch from staying out of Ceylon."

Acker blustered. "We may not feel it in the short term, but—"

"Those workers would," Hart said. "It would make their lives a misery. If that's how the three of you wish to do business—"

"*Business!*" Parfit erupted, slamming his fist down on the table. "That's what this is! The sooner you understand that and stop acting the gentleman—"

"But I *am* a gentleman," Hart said. Rising from the table, he collected his hat. "The sooner you understand *that*, the better off this company will be."

"And that's to be the end of it, is it?" Parfit asked furiously.

"I'll explore other options." Hart opened the door to leave. "I advise you to do the same."

He exited the manufactory through the riverside gate, emerging out onto the road that ran alongside the south bank of the Thames. It was empty at present, save for a few children playing down by the water.

Hart walked until his temper cooled.

He hadn't brought his curricle today. Kestrel was favoring her right front. Hart suspected she had a bruised hoof pad, possibly from a stone she'd picked up. The groom who had been tending the two horses in Hart's absence hadn't been as fastidious at checking their hooves as Hart was himself.

After arriving back in London yesterday evening, he'd immediately repaired to the stables. There, he'd stayed up late into the night, soaking Kestrel's hoof and treating her sore leg with liniment. Bishop had made a pallet for him. It's where Hart had slept, only rising at dawn to wash and change in preparation for his meeting with the other shareholders.

Drat them all and their antiquated views.

Money was all well and good, but a man had to sleep at night.

Pity there were no possibilities here at home. Remaining in England was quite the best solution to the dilemma. Unless . . .

Perhaps the others might agree to explore mining opportunities further north? There had long been rumors of plumbago deposits in the Scottish Highlands. Granted, it would mean starting entirely from scratch—not only finding a promising vein, but expending the necessary capital to buy the rights to it, and sink a shaft. It was an expense the partners would doubtless expect Hart to subsidize as part of a potential compromise. One he'd be more than willing to pay, provided he could find a company representative game enough to lead the expedition. A man who could be trusted to uphold the company's standards. *Hart's* standards.

William Webb instantly came to mind.

Webb was a hard worker, both diligent and compassionate. And like Hart, Webb was unmarried and had no children. He had nothing to tie him to Cumberland, save his position in the company's mining operation.

Hart scanned the road for a hansom cab. He needed to get back to Mayfair. He would write to Webb without delay. Or, better yet, send the man a wire.

But it wasn't only mining business that made Hart impatient to return home.

He had an overpowering desire to see Anne.

It had been three weeks since they had last crossed paths. Three weeks since he'd begun his campaign for her through his columns.

Had he remained in London, he might have seen her response to his efforts firsthand. Instead, he'd spent the past weeks wondering, with a burgeoning sense of apprehension, whether Anne was intrigued by his columns or whether she'd taken them as further proof of his lack of seriousness.

It was that which he was thinking of when he registered the sound of footsteps swiftly approaching behind him.

"Marcus Neale?" a thick male voice queried.

Hart stopped and turned.

By then, it was already too late.

The first blow hit him out of nowhere, a thundering crack across the side of his head. Stars burst in front of his eyes. He staggered back, blinking to clear his vision.

There were three men altogether. Big ugly bruisers, differing only slightly in size. They swiftly moved to surround him. One of the men—the smallest of the bunch—held a cudgel in his hand. The leather-wrapped club was stained with Hart's blood.

"It's him all right," the biggest one said.

The second largest one grinned. "Afternoon, guv," he said. "Mr. Royce sends his compliments."

Hart spat blood. His head was ringing. "I'm not entirely sure who Mr. Royce is," he said cordially. "But I'm happy to return his consideration." And drawing back his fist, he delivered a staggering right cross to the fellow's jaw.

A sickening crunch rent the air. It was followed by a high-pitched shriek.

"He broke my teeth!" the villain bellowed.

"You were supposed to stun him," his compatriot replied.

"It's going to take more than that," Hart said, casting a fleeting glance at the cudgel. "I've been told I have an exceedingly thick skull."

The second and third man came for him at once.

Hart fought them with a strength and athleticism honed from years of boxing and fencing. He was agile for a man of his height. It was both a blessing and a curse. Had he succumbed earlier, the beating he took may have been less brutal.

As it was, he gave as good as he got, leaving all three of his opponents battered and bloodied by the end of it. He might even have prevailed if he hadn't lost track of the smallest man.

While Hart was cracking the largest brute's nose with his forehead and jamming his elbow into the second fellow's ribs, the third villain managed to slip behind him with the cudgel.

The resulting blow brought Hart to his knees. Another blow followed and then another.

"Get him into the carriage," a voice commanded.

And then there was only darkness.

Anne brought Saffron to a halt as she entered the darkened stables behind the Deveril house in Grosvenor Square. Swinging her leg over the pommel, she dismounted without assistance, her booted feet landing softly on the straw-covered floor. Her groom came forward to take Saffron's reins.

"Give him a rubdown, would you?" Anne said, stroking Saffron's neck. "And an extra portion of oats. He's earned them today."

"Yes, my lady." The groom led Saffron away to untack him.

Anne removed her rumpled hat and filthy gloves as she slowly followed them. A midmorning gallop had lifted her mood. It had also left her covered in gray horsehair, smudged with dirt, and damp with perspiration beneath her habit.

It served her right for agreeing to trade horses with Stella.

Riding Locket had been no easy feat. The mare was as fast as quicksilver, and equally as difficult to control. After ten minutes in the saddle, Anne had begun to doubt her capabilities as a horsewoman.

It had been small comfort that Evelyn was facing a similar struggle with her own borrowed mount—a rawboned bay from her uncle's stable.

"My father used to say that, for every horse, there is but one rider," Evelyn had said, laughing as the big gelding hopped and bucked. "And I am *not* this horse's rider."

"At least he's moving," Stella had replied from her place atop a dozing Saffron. "Your stallion won't budge, Anne!"

"He requires strong encouragement," Anne had said. "Whereas *your* horse—"

"Locket objects to strength," Stella had told her. "She needs a featherlight touch."

"Any lighter and she'll bolt all the way to Bridgehampton," Anne had replied.

The three of them had laughed and rode and enjoyed one another's company. There had been no talk of gentlemen. Nothing of Hartford, or Mr. Malik, or of Stella's overbearing brother. A reprieve, truly, though a trifle bittersweet for the absence of Julia.

Anne had needed it desperately.

Cousin Joshua was supposed to be coming today. He and his mother's train should reach London in the early afternoon, if the railway schedule Anne had consulted was to be relied upon.

Though what would happen when they arrived at Grosvenor Square was anyone's guess.

The best Anne could do was prepare herself. She needed a bath and a change of clothes. Her chemise and riding stays were sticking to her skin, and she very much feared that she smelled—and not in a pleasant way.

"Lady Anne?" a masculine voice inquired.

Anne stopped where she stood, pulse leaping as a tall, broad-shouldered figure detached from the shadows and moved to block her path.

It was a young gentleman. A stranger. And yet . . .

There was something about him that struck her as oddly familiar.

Sinister as his sudden appearance was, he was well-dressed and well-favored, with dark brown hair and a face marked by a square jaw and penetrating blue-gray eyes.

"You *are* Lady Anne?"

"I am." She masked her brief moment of fear with a tone of indignation. "And who are *you*, sir? And what do you mean by accosting me in this manner?"

Removing his hat, he took another step toward her only to come to an uncertain halt. His double-breasted waistcoat had a large dark mark stretching across the lapel. Anne realized, much to her alarm, that it was a smear of dried blood.

She took a step backward. A cry for help hovered on her lips. Her groom was a mere few feet away. He could reach her in a moment if need be.

"*Wait.*" The man moved closer. "Don't scream. Please. I'm . . . I'm Marcus Neale."

Anne's eyes widened. Marcus Neale? *Good Lord.* No wonder he looked so familiar. It was Hartford's spendthrift half brother!

"I suppose you've heard of me," he said.

By some miracle, Anne managed to keep her countenance. "Whether I have or haven't, it gives you no right to spring up on me out of nowhere. You might have applied at the front door."

"Hartford wouldn't have liked that. He doesn't want anyone of your sort to know of my existence. I gather you're the only one who does." Mr. Neale's fingers moved restlessly on the brim of his hat. "He asked me to give you a message."

A frown notched her brows. "I don't understand. What message? And why on earth would he send *you* of all people?"

"Because he's been hurt. Grievously hurt."

The stain on Mr. Neale's waistcoat took on new meaning. *Terrible* meaning. Good gracious. It must be Hartford's blood!

Images of a gruesome curricle accident materialized in Anne's mind.

Her mouth went dry. "Hartford is hurt? But how—"

"Some villains accosted him on the road. I found him by the Thames but half an hour ago. He won't permit me to fetch his grandfather—*my* grandfather. And he won't allow me to summon a physician. He wants only you. He asks you to . . ."

Her stomach clenched with apprehension. "What?"

Mr. Neale squared his shoulders as if bracing himself to deliver a piece of extraordinarily bad news. "He asks you to send him a clergyman."

The blood drained from Anne's face. For a moment she feared she might be sick.

She didn't succumb to the impulse. She'd never before lost her nerve in a crisis, and she wasn't about to start now.

"Where is he?" she asked.

"I've taken him to a tavern at the Battersea Wharf. If you could send the clergyman there, I daresay it would give him comfort in his final moments."

Final moments?

Anne shook her head. "No."

Hartford wasn't devout. Not that she was aware. And she refused to believe he'd found religion on his deathbed.

Besides, he couldn't die. He'd promised her.

Sweeping the skirts of her black riding habit over her arm, she turned toward the street, all thoughts of Cousin Joshua's impending arrival forgotten.

"Never mind the clergyman," she said, striding to the door. "I'll go myself."

Twenty-Three

Hart squinted up at the unfamiliar wood-beamed ceiling. His head was throbbing, and the sickening iron-tinged aroma of blood hung heavy in the air.

He had no idea where he was or how he'd come to be here. All he knew was that he was lying flat on his back atop what must surely be the most uncomfortable mattress in five counties. It didn't help that his ribs were aching, one of his eyes was half-swollen shut, and his nose was likely broken, making it difficult to breathe.

Somewhere outside his field of vision, a person moved quietly about the room. Hart couldn't for the life of him imagine who it was.

In truth, he couldn't remember much of anything after he'd blacked out.

There had been a carriage. A closed four-wheeler, inside of which he'd been pummeled rather severely. At some point, he'd regained consciousness just long enough to register the door of that carriage opening and the wind whipping his face as he'd been unceremoniously pitched out onto the road at speed. After that . . .

Only darkness.

"Lie still," a lady's voice commanded.

A tremor of soul-quaking recognition went through him.

"*Anne?*" The name emerged in a hoarse croak.

The lady it belonged to appeared over him a moment later.

Her golden hair was falling from its pins, and her gown—*a riding habit?*—was stained and rumpled. She looked as though she'd galloped here at breakneck speed, forgetting her hat and her gloves.

Forgetting her common sense.

He struggled to rise. "What the devil—"

Her hand came to rest on his shoulder. His *bare* shoulder. Hart felt her soft touch like a lightning strike through his vitals.

Good God. Where in blazes was his shirt?

"I told you not to move," she said, gently restraining him. "Didn't you hear me?"

He sank back on the pillow in grudging defeat. Anne's touch was soft enough, but there was no mistaking the strength in it. He'd seen her hold back a stallion with no more than a crook of her fingers on the reins. Curbing the addled impulses of a wounded, half-naked man was surely child's play to her.

It made it no easier to accept his circumstances.

"My shirt," he rasped.

"Hush." The mattress dipped as she sat down beside him on the edge of the bed. She brought a wet cloth to his face, dabbing at the dried blood on his temple. "I had to cut it off. It was the only way I could ascertain the damage. I feared you'd broken your ribs—or worse."

Hart's gaze was riveted to her face as she tended him.

Her expression might almost have been businesslike but for the redness rimming her eyes.

Good Lord. She'd been weeping. And recently, too, by the look of it.

Weeping over *him*.

The realization brought a lump to Hart's throat.

"You do realize you're the most infuriatingly unreliable man in all of creation?" she asked in a conversational tone. "Only a few short weeks ago you promised me you wouldn't die and yet . . . here we are."

He caught her hand, stilling it on his face. His own hand was battered, knuckles raw and bloody. "Where?"

"A room above a tavern somewhere in Battersea. The Eagle? The Bull?" Her shoulder lifted in a delicate shrug. "I haven't the foggiest. Your brother brought me here. I didn't stop to read the sign."

"My brother?"

"Mr. Neale. I've sent him to fetch some supplies from the chemist's shop. Pray he doesn't make a thorough hash of it. He's a strapping boy, but I doubt his fortitude. He couldn't look at you without turning green."

Marcus.

Hart's hand fell from Anne's. Disjointed scraps of memory returned. Images of Marcus appearing on the bank of the Thames, his face bleach white as he'd stood over Hart.

"It's this head wound of yours," she said. "My father always told me they bleed like the dickens. It's quite frightening to see."

Hart flinched as the wet cloth met the cut on his temple. He vaguely recalled one of the villains hitting him there with a leather-covered cudgel. "Did you—"

"Bring a clergyman?" She frowned down at him severely. "I most certainly did not."

He gave her a muddled look. He seemed to have lost the thread of the conversation. "Why would you?"

"Because you asked me to. That's what your brother said, anyway. According to him, you wished me to summon a vicar to ease your passing or some such nonsense. He claims you were quite insistent upon it."

Hart stifled a low groan as Anne blotted the blood from his head wound. "Not a clergyman," he managed to say. "*Bishop.* You were supposed to send Bishop."

"Your valet?" Anne's frown transformed into a fleeting smile of relief. She rose from the bed. "Well, I must say that makes a good deal more sense."

Hart followed her with his gaze as she crossed the small inn room to the washstand. "Bishop knows how to patch me up," he said. "But . . . I couldn't have Marcus going to Arlington Street to . . . to fetch him. I needed you to do it. Otherwise—"

"Yes, I see." She dropped the bloody cloth into the chipped porcelain basin. "You were being practical."

It had been more than practicality. Hart wasn't too proud to acknowledge the fact to himself, even if he couldn't yet admit it to her.

"I didn't mean for you to come," he said. "I wouldn't have expected you to—"

"Naturally I came."

"But . . . why?"

Her back was to him as she rung out the cloth. "Why do you think?"

His heart gave a hopeful thump. "But your reputation—" He broke off, his mouth gone dry. "If anyone knew you were here—"

"No one knows save your brother." Anne returned to the bed, sinking down beside him once more. She brought the wet cloth to the dried blood on his cheek. "And if you believe for a moment that my reputation matters one whit when measured against my devotion to a friend, you haven't been paying attention."

A friend.

That's what he was to her. Not her sweetheart. Not her beloved. Just a friend. It wasn't nothing, but . . .

It wasn't enough.

"This could ruin you," he said.

She stroked the cloth along the curve of his brow. "I could ruin myself dancing the waltz three times with the same gentleman or visiting the theater unchaperoned. At least this is something useful."

"Anne . . . if anyone finds out—"

"They won't." She stretched across him to bathe the blood from his hair. The voluptuous swell of her bosom, bound tight in the black cloth bodice of her habit, brushed lightly over his naked chest.

Hart briefly closed his eyes against the sensation. Bloody hell. Pain was one thing, but this . . . this was torture. "*Anne*."

"Why in heaven were you attacked?" she asked, oblivious to his distress. Her fingers ran through his blood-clotted locks—the most delicious feeling. "It can't have been a robbery. You still had your signet ring and your purse."

Hart marshaled his throbbing senses. "It wasn't a robbery. It was a band of thugs sent to rough up Marcus."

She drew back. "This is your *brother's* fault?"

Hart had no illusions on that score. "The men who accosted me called out his name. They had the look of half-witted ruffians sent from an underground gaming house."

"My goodness," she said, lowering the cloth. "I suppose he owes them money?"

"Undoubtedly. It was my misfortune to meet them first. They mistook me for Marcus and proceeded accordingly."

"You don't look *that* much like your brother."

"No, indeed," he said. "I'm much more handsome."

Anne gave him a look of reproof. "Not anymore you aren't," she replied frankly. "Those half-witted ruffians, as you call them, have made mincemeat out of you."

Hart suppressed a grimace. All things considered, he'd rather Anne not have seen him in this pitiful condition. But there was no use in repining. "There were three of them," he informed her. "And I did fight back, you know."

"I realize." She picked up one of his hands, cradling it so tenderly it made his chest tighten on a spasm of pleasure that was almost pain. "Your knuckles are completely raw." She dabbed at them ineffectively with the cloth. "You'll have to soak them."

"Bishop will sort me out." Hart's fingers curled gently around hers. "I'll be fit as a flea in no time."

Anne stared down at his ravaged hand for a long moment. "I'd no notion your brother's vices could be a danger to anything more than your pocketbook."

"Nor did I," Hart admitted. "Not that it would have altered my responsibility for him."

"Is that the cause of all this? Your desire to be more responsible?"

"I'd like to blame it on that," he said. "To tell you that responsibility was going to be the death of me. The truth is . . . after everything that's passed . . . I suppose I've begun to care for the lad." It was a surprising admission, even to himself.

"Your feelings aren't reciprocated as far as I can tell."

"It makes no matter." He gave her a slight smile. "It's long been my misfortune to care for people who don't care for me in return."

Anne's sherry-brown gaze jerked sharply to his. "You don't include me on that list?"

He huffed a humorless laugh. "Yours is the first name on it, old thing."

"Idiot." Her eyes glittered with unfathomable emotion. "I care for you. I've *always* cared. A fair bit more than you care for me, I'd wager."

Impossible, Hart wanted to say.

But he couldn't say a word. He could only look at her, his aching heart beating like a smith's hammer.

She continued in a fierce undertone, her words edged with the rough scrape of tightly leashed emotion. "If I hadn't cared, you couldn't have hurt me as you did when you returned from India. That day at Grosvenor Square . . ." Her brows knit into a troubled line. "The things you said—the way you *looked* at me. I was already brittle as glass, but you—you broke my heart into a million pieces."

Anguish twisted in Hart's gut, making his voice a hoarse rasp. "Anne . . ." His hand tightened reflexively on hers. "I never meant—"

"But you *did*," she said. "I was all alone. My father was gone. My mother was falling apart. I had every burden in the world on my shoulders and no earthly idea how to manage them. I didn't need your dratted ultimatum. All I wanted was for you to walk through that door and take me in your arms. To tell me I could lean on you awhile. That I didn't have to bear it on my own." She slipped her hand free of his, rising from the bed in an agitated rustle of skirts. "Don't tell me I didn't care. No man on earth has ever been loved the way I loved you, Felix Hartford."

Hart's throat worked on a convulsive swallow. Her impetuous words, uttered in obvious irritation, ran through his heart and mind in a continuous, life-altering refrain.

No man on earth has ever been loved the way I loved you, Felix Hartford.

For the first time in his nearly thirty years, Hart was at a loss. There was too much pain between them. Too much regret. He despaired of saying the wrong thing. "What do you wish me to—"

"Nothing." She returned to the washstand, resting her hands on the wooden surface for several seconds as she composed herself. "Absolutely nothing."

He stared after her in muted torment.

No man on earth has ever been loved the way I loved you, Felix Hartford.

If his head weren't ringing and he weren't suffering the aftereffects of blood loss, he might have been able to come up with a clever reply. A witty gibe or a teasing remark. But that's not what she wanted, was it? She wanted—*needed*—something else.

At the moment, he was ill-equipped to give it to her.

"Oh, where is Mr. Neale with those bandages?" she muttered, throwing the bloody cloth back into the basin with a splash. "If he doesn't show his face in the next ten minutes, I shall be compelled to wrap your wounds with strips of your shirt."

"Bishop will tend to me," Hart said. "You're not obliged to play nursemaid."

She flashed him a narrow glance over her shoulder. "Someone had to look after you. I believe your nose is broken."

A prickle of heat rose up Hart's neck. Damn his vanity! "I believe you're right," he replied tightly. "Bishop will set it."

"I shall summon him when I return to Grosvenor Square," she said. "As soon as your brother gets back, I'll have him hail me a hackney cab."

Hart's gaze swept over her habit. The fashionable black riding costume hugged her every curve as seductively as the embrace of a lover. "I thought you rode here?"

"Hardly." She returned to the bed. This time, she didn't sit. She merely stood there, too far away for him to reach her. "I'd just returned from the Row when Marcus appeared in the mews to tell me that you'd been hurt. I didn't think to change. No doubt I should have done."

"Those are white hairs, not gold," he observed. "You weren't on Saffron?"

It was a trivial conversation, given the magnitude of what she'd just confessed to him. Good Lord. Not five minutes ago, she'd spoken of love! And now they were speaking of Bishop, and Marcus, and . . . horsehair?

"No," she said, smoothing her skirts. "I traded him for a gallop on Miss Hobhouse's gray mare. Saffron is getting too old for such sport. He's nearly eighteen."

"You shall have to retire him and find another mount."

"On no account. I shan't ever replace him, no matter how old he gets." Her expression turned wry. "It's one of my failings, I daresay. Once I choose a partner, I stick with him until the bitter end."

Anne felt the warmth of Hartford's gaze all the way to her toes. It took a staggering effort to keep her countenance.

She didn't know how she managed it.

Her reserves were all but empty. She'd been on the edge of panic since Mr. Neale had come to fetch her, so caught up in keeping control of her emotions she'd scarcely uttered more than three words altogether during their entire journey from Mayfair. And when she'd entered the tawdry room above the tavern, when she'd clapped eyes on Hartford, a wave of such despair had washed over her, Anne had very nearly buckled beneath it.

Even now, blessedly conscious and cleansed of most of the dried blood that had marred his handsome face, Hartford's appearance still made her go weak at the knees. And it wasn't only because he was so terribly hurt. It was because he was *vulnerable.*

He looked like a great wounded tiger lying atop the narrow bed. Battered, bloody, and shirtless. Temporarily at her mercy.

Anne would have liked to enjoy her power over him, however brief. Instead, the minute Mr. Neale had left them alone, she'd found herself battling an onslaught of tears.

Ridiculous.

It helped immensely to know that Hartford hadn't wanted her. That her name had only sprung to his lips by necessity. The only reason he'd mentioned her at all was that he'd wanted her to fetch his dratted valet, Bishop.

But of course he had.

That hadn't stopped Anne from blurting out one inanity after the other since he'd regained consciousness, rendering herself as vulnerable as he was.

She felt an absolute fool.

"It *is* a failing," Hartford agreed solemnly. "But you're not alone in it."

She arched a brow. "Is that a fact?"

"Indeed. It rather reminds me of a column I'm writing for the *Zoological Annual*, about a black swan who lived at Empress Josephine's Château de Malmaison in the early part of the century. A widower swan. After his mate died, he refused every effort at pairing him with another. And there were plenty of others. The keeper introduced an endless succession of beautiful white swans into the canal where the black swan lived. The black swan chased them all away. He could find none to compare with his black-feathered love."

Anne's cheeks burned. She had the suspicion he was laughing at her again. "You and your columns," she said crossly. "What do you mean by writing such things? Am I supposed to be flattered?"

His mouth quirked faintly. "Amused, at the very least."

A brisk rap at the door prevented Anne's reply. She went to open it, admitting Mr. Neale into the room. He had a harried look about him. "You took your time," she remarked, shutting the door after him.

"The shopkeeper was an interfering old busybody." Mr. Neale thrust an overflowing bag of supplies into her arms. "Practically accused me of being involved in a duel gone wrong or something equally nefarious. I had to buy half his stock to shut him up."

"Perhaps he recognized a villain when he saw one," Anne said as she set the items down on a small wooden table. "I understand this is all your fault."

"*My* fault!" Mr. Neale removed his hat. "If Hartford would have minded his own business for a change—"

"Hartford *was* minding his own business," Hartford said from his bed. "And he's conscious now, so you may address your impertinence to him, if you please."

Mr. Neale strode hastily to his brother's bedside. "You're awake! And . . . you're without your shirt. How did—"

"Never mind my shirt," Hartford said. "I only require my valet. Lady Anne will fetch him for me. You may see her safely into a cab."

Anne turned to face him from across the room. An objection hovered on the tip of her tongue. She wanted to remain to bandage his wounds herself. To assure herself that he was truly going to be well.

But Hartford was right. She'd already lingered too long.

In the chaos of the last two hours, she'd set aside any concerns about herself, or what it would do to her reputation if she were discovered alone in a room above a tavern with not one but two unmarried gentlemen. She'd spared no thought for the men in the taproom below, any one of whom might be a servant or someone otherwise employed in proximity to people of fashion. They'd all seen her as she'd passed through their midst on her way to the stairs that led up to Hart's room.

Anne was readily identifiable. The barest description would be enough to start the gossip spreading. It was a prospect she hadn't considered at all in the moment.

Her reputation wasn't the only thing she'd disregarded.

She'd completely overlooked her obligations to her family. Cousin Joshua's visit had paled in comparison to the urgency of Hartford's condition. And as for Mama . . .

Anne had all but abandoned her.

The possible repercussions of her behavior were only now beginning to sink in.

"You're right," she said. "I must return home at once."

Hartford held her gaze with uncommon solemnity. "I shall call on you in Grosvenor Square within the week."

Anne's stomach tensed. "I don't know why you should."

It was a lie, and they both knew it. She saw as much in his eyes.

There was every reason he should call on her. And it wasn't because she'd confessed that she'd been in love with him, or because she'd told him that he'd broken her heart into smithereens.

No.

It was because he believed she'd compromised herself in coming here.

He may be a rogue and a rascal, but Felix Hartford was a gentleman to his marrow. There could only be one purpose in his threatened visit to Grosvenor Square.

Unless Anne was very much mistaken, he was going to propose marriage to her.

Again.

Twenty-Four

Any hope Anne had cherished of returning home before her cousin's arrival was obliterated the moment the hansom cab rolled into Grosvenor Square. Two carriages were stopped in front of the house, the second one brimming with luggage. Footmen in Arundell livery were dutifully unloading it, carrying leather trunks and monogrammed cases up the steps into the hall.

Her stomach sank.

She was already egregiously late. Her tardiness had only been exacerbated by the return traffic across the river, and by the stop she'd been obliged to make in Arlington Street. Luckily, Bishop had been at his leisure. He'd at once comprehended the urgency of the situation, promising her he would fly to his employer without delay.

That was Hartford taken care of. As for Anne . . .

Her battle was yet to come.

"You may stop here," she instructed the driver.

He pulled up beside the black iron fence that masked the servants' entrance. Disembarking from the hansom, Anne discreetly slipped down the stairs to tap softly at the kitchen door. It was opened by a young scullery maid.

"Milady!" She bobbed a curtsy as she stepped back to allow Anne entry. "The whole house has been looking for you."

"I expect they have." Anne ducked inside. "Where is my mother?"

Horbury emerged from the butler's pantry to answer her. "Her ladyship is in the drawing room, my lady, with the earl and Mrs. Deveril. Shall I tell her you've returned?"

"No, indeed." Anne hurried past him. "I'll tell her myself once I've changed."

Using the servants' stairs, she made her way up to her bedchamber. Jeanette was inside, seated by the window, one eye on her sewing and the other on Anne's new kitten. The diminutive feline was perched in the window, her fluffy black tail flicking lazily as she dozed.

"My lady!" Setting aside the petticoat she was mending, Jeanette stood. "Your mother has been asking for you."

"Yes, I know." Anne crossed the room to give the sleeping kitten a soft scratch under the chin with the tip of her finger. A tiny rumbling purr emerged in response.

Anne's anxious heart warmed at the sound of it.

In the days following her new pet's arrival in Grosvenor Square, Anne had been prompted to change the kitten's name from Alice to Eris. Much like the eponymous Greek goddess of chaos, the tiny creature had the unfortunate habit of wreaking havoc wherever she set her paws. None of the upholstery had been safe from her. She'd even taken to climbing the silk-covered walls. Anne's mother hadn't been best pleased.

"Shall I fetch your black bombazine?" Jeanette asked.

Anne unfastened the bodice of her habit. "Yes, and be quick about it."

Fifteen minutes later, freshly washed and changed, Anne descended the stairs to the drawing rom. A lady's voice drifted out into the hall amid the clink of porcelain. Not her mother's voice, but that of another woman, speaking with all the imagined authority of her position.

"I've told Arundell time and again that he must assert himself," the lady said. "But my son has a tender heart. 'Tis his only weakness."

"Now, now, Mother," a gentleman replied with indulgence. "You will make me out to be a man who is ignorant of his rights, and you know nothing could be further from the truth."

Entering the room, Anne found Mrs. Deveril seated on the green velvet sofa beside her son.

Cousin Joshua glanced up as Anne came to join them. "My dear cousin. At last." Setting aside his teacup, he rose and sketched her a bow. "Time has altered you so I wouldn't have known you."

Anne inclined her head to him. "Whereas *I* would recognize you anywhere."

The new Earl of Arundell looked exactly the same as he had at Papa's funeral: pale, thin, and positively brimming with poorly concealed avarice.

It was no secret that he and his mother had eagerly anticipated the death of Anne's father. They had no great fortune of their own. No wealth or property to speak of. Their entire future had hinged on Joshua's ascension to the title.

"Anne," Mrs. Deveril sniffed, making no move to rise. She was a slender reed of a woman, with a narrow face and tightly pinched mouth. "Still in black, I see, just like your mother."

Anne acknowledged the odious woman with a rigid dip of her chin before moving to join her mother. "My father is greatly missed, ma'am."

"Oh, I don't doubt it," Mrs. Deveril said with a titter. "His death has left the two of you with no gentleman to manage things. I do pity you."

Mama's face was an emotionless mask as Anne sat beside her. She didn't appear upset or even angry. Indeed, her expression might have been chiseled from stone.

Belated guilt settled over Anne like an iron-lined cloak. In her haste to rush to Hartford's aid, she'd thoroughly abdicated her responsibilities to her mother. As a result, Mama had been left to face her worst fears alone. It was unpardonable.

"I apologize for my tardiness," Anne murmured to her.

"We shall address it later," Mama replied. Her eyes were hard as flint. Whatever had transpired in Anne's absence, it plainly hadn't been of a pleasant nature.

"Happily, my son is here now." Mrs. Deveril cast a glowing look of adoration at her pallid progeny. "As the head of the family, he will gladly assume management of your affairs."

"Indeed, my lady." Joshua's gaze fell briefly to Anne's bosom as he resumed his seat. "It will be my pleasure to take them in hand."

Anne locked eyes with him, unflinching, until he looked away.

The odious little toad. He wasn't fit to shine her father's boots.

"A generous offer," Mama said curtly. "But an unnecessary one. My man of affairs has matters under control."

"My son will meet with him, of course," Mrs. Deveril said.

"Of course," Mama replied.

Joshua addressed Anne. "Your mother informs me you were out riding."

"I was." Anne offered no further elaboration. This wasn't a social call. This was a blatant seizure of power.

Never mind that it wasn't illegal. That Joshua had every right to assume control of Grosvenor Square, Cherry Hill, and every other square inch of property owned by the earldom. For all the disrespect inherent in his and his mother's manner, it may as well have been a coup d'état.

"You must be parched," Mrs. Deveril remarked, reaching for the silver teapot. "Allow me to pour you out a cup of tea."

Anne's lips compressed. It was Mama who should be doing the pouring. As the Dowager Countess of Arundell, she was the most senior lady present. But Mama uttered not a word of censure. It would have been ill-bred to speak out under the circumstances.

"I spend most of my time at Cherry Hill in the saddle," Joshua said as his mother poured. "The late earl kept a fine stable."

"It was his greatest joy," Mama said.

"Oh yes. That's apparent," Joshua replied. "Though mere joy in a thing is no guarantee of that thing's success. One must be ruthless as well."

Mama's eyes narrowed. "In what way ruthless?"

Joshua gave a dismissive wave of his hand. "I've had to sell off some of the older horses this year. No point in keeping mounts who can't handle the fences, isn't that right, Mother?"

"You know best, my dear." Mrs. Deveril passed a teacup to Anne.

Anne accepted it, but she didn't drink. Her teeth were clenched too tightly to accommodate the passage of a single drop.

Her cousin had been selling off the old horses? Horses Papa had bought? Ones that Anne had likely ridden in her youth?

Everything within her coiled with murderous outrage.

Oh, if she were a man—!

But she wasn't. She was only a woman. A lowly unmarried daughter of an earl at the mercy of the laws of primogeniture. She felt the unfairness of it to her core.

"I look forward to making a similar inventory of the horses you've elected to keep in town," Joshua continued, ignoring the lethal glimmer in Anne's eyes. "You've a great golden stallion, I understand? A warmblood?"

Anne's hand tightened on the handle of her teacup with such reflexive force she wouldn't have been surprised if the porcelain shattered beneath her fingers. "Saffron doesn't belong to the earldom. He belongs to me."

"I will examine his papers, naturally," Joshua said. "In the meanwhile, I'm sure you won't object to me taking him through his paces."

Anne opened her mouth to do just that, but was forestalled by her mother.

"You may examine the papers of all our bloodstock, along with the account books and household ledgers, at your leisure. Everything is in readiness for you, as are your rooms." Mama stood abruptly in an imperious sweep of black crepe. "Mrs. Griffiths will take you to them."

The housekeeper appeared at the door to the drawing room as if by magic.

Mrs. Deveril set down her teacup with a look of irritation. "How commanding you are, Rosamund," she said. "You forget your place."

"On the contrary, madam," Mama said. "I'm fully aware of the position I hold in this household, *and* in society. Mrs. Griffiths? Please show his lordship and Mrs. Deveril to their rooms."

Cousin Joshua rose along with his mother. "I feared we would have a battle on our hands in relation to my rights," he said in mournful tones. "I'm grieved to think it might be the case."

"We are all grieved, sir," Mama retorted icily. "Deeply grieved. Mrs. Griffiths?"

"This way, my lord." The housekeeper ushered the new earl and his mother from the room.

Anne watched them go. The moment they disappeared from view, she set down her teacup and faced her mother. "Mama—"

"No excuses." Mama sank down beside her. "And no more apologies. It can't be undone."

"But I *am* sorry." Anne spoke the words with all sincerity. "I should have been here sooner to lend my support."

Her mother's face remained unreadable. "Do you realize where Mrs. Griffiths is taking that boy?" She didn't wait for an answer. "She's taking him to your father's room."

Anne sucked in a breath. "Surely not!"

"Oh, yes. His wretched mother had the temerity to ask for it explicitly. She claims your cousin would have done so himself were he not so tenderhearted. As for allowing it—" Mama gave a short, brittle laugh. "They need no permission from me. Your cousin could cast us into the street this very moment if the impulse took him. And be sure he will, my girl, within a fortnight, unless I'm much mistaken."

Anne shook her head numbly. She could believe anything of her cousin, but not this. Not so soon. She wasn't prepared.

They weren't prepared.

They hadn't leased another house in a fashionable street in Mayfair. They'd made no arrangements with their servants or their stablemen. They hadn't packed a single bag.

"The only question before us," Mama continued, "is whether we allow ourselves to be driven from our home in disgrace or leave this place with our dignity intact." Her face was set with an implacable resolve. "I know which I shall choose."

"Where will we go?" Anne asked.

But she already knew the answer. She'd known it ever since their visit up the hill to St. Paul's so many weeks ago.

"Where *can* we go on such short notice?" Mama asked. "It must be to Ludgate Hill."

Hart sprawled in a chair in the small room above the tavern, stifling a grimace of pain as Bishop finished tying off the bandage he'd wrapped snugly around Hart's ribs.

"Is that all you have to say for yourself?" Hart asked his half brother.

Marcus sat on the edge of the bed in the same surly posture he'd adopted at the sponging house. The only difference was in the paleness of his face—the same white-about-the-mouth look he'd borne ever since discovering Hart unconscious alongside the Thames.

It was the one saving grace of this debacle. Perhaps, at last, Marcus had been shocked into altering his behavior.

Though one wouldn't know it by his tone.

"What else?" he replied petulantly. "I've already told you I owe them money."

"Fifteen hundred pounds," Hart said.

A weary sort of rage washed over him.

While his business partners in the crucible factory were earning money hand over fist, Hart was losing it at an equally rapid rate. And it was all owing to Marcus.

Was his bastard half brother trying to ruin him? To render him bankrupt—or worse?

Hart ran a hand over the side of his face. Bishop had managed to stitch up Hart's head wound, plaster his cuts, reset his nose, and bind up all the rest of his injuries, but Hart was still aching in every limb.

The worst pain, by far, was in his pocketbook.

"Eight thousand if you count the sixty-five hundred pounds I've already paid out on your behalf." Hart winced as Bishop assisted him into a clean shirt. "Are you even capable of comprehending the value of such a sum?"

"What's done is done," Marcus said with a sullen shrug.

Bishop gave an almost inaudible sniff of disapproval.

Hart couldn't blame his valet for taking offense. Bishop earned thirty pounds per annum. A generous wage, but one that was nothing in comparison to Marcus's debts.

"It's more than a workingman could earn in several lifetimes," Hart said. "And you've squandered it at the tables."

Marcus flushed. "Not at the tables. It was at the races. I was assured the horses I chose would win. They were prime goers who—"

"And you were persuaded they were unbeatable? Based on what? Your copious knowledge of horseflesh?" Hart could have shaken his half brother senseless. "By heaven," he said, "I should let those villains have you and be done with it."

"I'd have gladly taken a beating from them," Marcus retorted sourly, "if it would have saved me one of your tedious sermons."

Hart felt the unholy urge to laugh. It was either that or break something, and his fists were too battered at present to support the latter activity.

Bloody hell. This is what Marcus had reduced him to. To sermonizing. One couldn't help but appreciate the irony.

Hart slowly stood so he could tuck his shirt into his trousers.

Thank God Bishop had brought him a change of clothes. It was going to be difficult enough explaining his appearance to his grandfather without arriving back in Arlington Street in a blood-spattered suit.

"Mr. Royce?" Hart said. "Is that his name? I seem to recall the three ruffians referencing the fellow before they fell on me like a pack of jackals."

"Gabriel Royce," Marcus said. "He has a betting shop in St. Giles."

"*St. Giles?* Good God, man."

It was one of the worst slums in London. Dangerous, too. Most respectable people wouldn't risk setting foot in the place.

"You told me to stay away from the clubs," Marcus shot back defensively. "Where else was I to turn?"

"You might have tried abstaining," Hart suggested. "It's generally the best course when one has no money left to wager."

Marcus glowered. "You left me no choice," he said. "How else am I to earn my fortune? And don't say that I should find a job. Not when I've heard tale of gamesters winning an estate on the turn of a card, or of financing one through strategic picks at the track. I'm as capable of doing so as the next man."

Hart muttered an oath. "Is that what you think you're doing? Gambling for a chance to make yourself a wealthy squire? Have you no brains in your head, lad? I sometimes wonder what the point was in sending you to school."

"Why did you? If you didn't want me to be anything. If you didn't want me to aspire to more."

"I wanted to set you on the right path in life," Hart said. "To secure a future for you, regardless of the legitimacy of your birth."

"By sending me to a boarding school in Plymouth? A school filled with other men's bastards?" Marcus's face mottled with muted hurt and anger. "If all I was fit for was the shop, you should have left me in my mother's care."

"It's your mother who's filled your head with these tomfool ideas in the first place," Hart said. "There's nothing wrong with the shop. And there's more to a man than the origins of his birth. I've seen lesser men rise above their parentage to make something of themselves. You could, too, if you'd only rid yourself of this notion that I, or anyone else in the world, owe you a damn thing."

Marcus surged to his feet. "I don't know why I'm listening to you—*or* why I'm still here. You have everything you require. Your valet. Your brandy. Your blasted sticking plasters. And I already brought you your lady. You've no need of me."

Hart's mood sobered at the mention of Anne. "Yes, you did bring my lady here," he said. "To a gentleman's room in a wharf-side tavern."

Bishop avoided Hart's gaze as he helped him into a fresh waistcoat. The valet was well acquainted with Hart's interest in Lady Anne Deveril. A good servant knew things before his master knew them himself.

"Are you implying I offended her sensibilities?" Marcus snorted. "That termagant? She'll survive."

"Be careful how you speak of her," Hart advised softly. "I've a little fight left in me yet."

Marcus's smirk vanished at the unambiguous note of warning in Hart's voice. "I meant no insult," he grumbled. "But you're mistaken if you think her shocked by the experience. When we left here, she read me a lecture the entire way down the stairs to the street. She may be a beauty, but I wouldn't wish her on my worst enemy." A flicker of renewed malice curled his lip. "Now I think of it, she's perfect for you."

"That may be the first sense you've spoken all day," Hart said as he collected his coat.

There was a battle ahead on every front. He didn't relish the challenge. But he had no intention of shrinking from it, either. First, he'd deal with Marcus. Then the shareholders at the Parfit Plumbago Crucible Company. And then . . .

Then he would deal with Lady Anne.

"Bishop?" he said. "Settle my tab with the barman and procure me a cab back to Mayfair. After that, I need you to go to the telegraph office. I've an urgent wire to send to Borrowdale. You can take the message down before you leave."

"Yes, sir," Bishop replied. He went to find a pencil and paper.

"What about me?" Marcus asked. "Where am I to go?"

"Go home," Hart commanded. "Dine with your mother and sisters. Enjoy their company while you can."

Marcus's face darkened with suspicion. "What's that supposed to mean?"

"It means," Hart said, "that tomorrow, we're paying a visit to St. Giles."

Twenty-Five

The west end London slum of St. Giles was objectionable for many reasons, not least of which was the stench. Open drains and teeming refuse conspired to make the air all but unbreathable. If that weren't enough to deter a respectable person from paying a visit to the squalid maze of narrow, intersecting alleyways that made up the rookery, then its inhabitants surely were.

Amid the dissipated men, gin-soaked women, crying infants, and broken-down ex-soldiers who populated the crooked streets, there was danger lurking in every shadow.

And there were plenty of shadows here, even at midday.

Hart was alert to every one of them. "How did you find this place?" he asked Marcus as they turned down yet another fetid alleyway.

"A fellow recommended it to me when I was in my cups," Marcus said. He darted another guilty glance at Hart.

Hart didn't have to ask what had prompted his brother's uncharacteristic expression of remorse. The answer had been evident in Hart's shaving mirror this morning. His face, which yesterday had been marred by only cuts and scrapes, was now a mass of unsightly bruises.

The worst of it was that both of his eyes had been blacked, an unfortunate result of having his nose broken. It was really quite shocking to see, even from Hart's jaded perspective. He couldn't imagine what his half brother must be thinking of it.

Or what his grandfather was going to think.

Fortunately, Grandfather had been out last evening attending a dinner with his horticulturalist friends. Hart had narrowly avoided meeting him on his return, and then again this morning by the simple expedience of departing the house two hours before breakfast. But there would be no avoiding him forever. And no avoiding Uncle Brookdale, either.

Not to mention Anne.

Hart's mouth flattened into a frown at the thought of seeing her again. He'd promised to call on her within the week. A call he'd now have to make looking like he'd just gone ten rounds with a prizefighter.

"Are you certain you're well enough for this?" Marcus asked for the third time.

Hart sidestepped a puddle of unidentifiable effluvia.

He *wasn't* well. His ribs ached, his head was throbbing, and his right arm was inexplicably swollen at the shoulder. In truth, he wasn't fit for much of anything.

Not that he had a choice.

"You'd rather we wait until Royce's henchmen give you a set of bruises to match mine?" Hart asked.

"No, but—"

"Excellent," Hart said tightly. "I'd as soon get this over with."

Marcus didn't speak again until they reached their destination. "It's just there," he said, indicating a narrow building crammed between what looked to be a gin shop and a brothel.

A hulking gorilla of a man stood guard at the door. He drew himself up at their approach.

"What d'you want?" he asked.

"Your employer." Reaching around the fellow, Hart rapped twice on the closed door with his walking stick.

The guard didn't budge. "Is Mr. Royce expecting you?"

"He should be," Hart said.

He knew enough of the criminal element of society to understand that their leaders kept themselves remarkably well-informed. If Royce was anything other than a bumbling fool, he'd have learned of his henchmen's error not long after Hart had been left alongside the river. Royce would doubtless comprehend that there were repercussions for such a mistake.

Hart was counting on the fact.

Within seconds, the door behind the guard opened and a scrawny, oily-haired youth poked his head out. His gaze flicked to Marcus with a glimmer of recognition. "It's all right, Tim. I know this bloke." He grinned at Hart. "And I heard about this one."

The guard grudgingly stepped aside, permitting Hart and Marcus to pass.

"Mr. Royce said as how you might be coming by." The youth led them through the door. "You're the sporting gent what broke Walsh's jaw and sent Murphy to hospital."

Hart followed him inside. "If Walsh and Murphy are who I think they are, then they had it coming."

Marcus stayed close as they made their way through the smoke-filled interior of the shop. It was crowded with rough-looking men of various shapes and sizes. Many of them were lingering outside of a closed door at the back as though waiting their turn to meet with the person inside.

The loquacious youth cut through the throng to knock at the door. "Mr. Royce, sir? It's that toff from Battersea come to see you."

A guttural voice answered, "Let him in."

"After you, guv," the youth said, opening the door.

Hart entered along with Marcus.

Inside, a man in his shirtsleeves sat behind an enormous carved oak desk. His hair was black as coal, his swarthy face cloaked in the shadows cast from a high window. He smiled, revealing a flash of strong white teeth. "Felix Hartford. I told the lads you'd be stopping in."

"I'm gratified you recognize me," Hart said. "A pity your men didn't."

"They're paying the price for it, ain't they?" Mr. Royce gestured to the wooden chairs in front of his desk. "Sit. Unless you're here to go another round?"

"With you?" Hart availed himself of a seat. "That can't be very efficient business."

"It's been known to happen," Royce said. "And I flatter myself that it's very efficient, if you take my meaning."

Marcus sat down nervously beside Hart.

"Dispatching one or both of us isn't going to result in Mr. Neale's debt being paid," Hart said. "That is, if you were successful at the task." He paused. "How are your three henchmen, by the way?"

Mr. Royce gave a sudden laugh. "Poorly," he said. "Damned poorly. But you already know that." He sat back in his chair. "I suppose you're here to settle up?"

"That depends on what you call settling up," Hart replied. "Mr. Neale may have owed you fifteen hundred pounds yesterday morning, but as far as I'm concerned, that debt has since been offset by a great inconvenience to myself."

Marcus looked horrified. "*Hartford*—"

"How much reduction in the principle can I expect for my condition?" Hart asked, ignoring his half brother. "I shall provide an inventory of every bruise if need be."

Royce chuckled. "I've been looking into you, Hartford. Grandson of the Earl of March. Man about town. You used to enjoy a wager now and then, but not at the tables, I hear."

Hart didn't deny it.

"One of my contacts tells me you once bet on a balloon coming down within fifty miles of Hemel Hempstead. Then, you leapt into the basket yourself to see the bet was won. Something of a risk-taker, ain't you?"

"Your point?" Hart asked.

"I'll give you a reduction in what's owing," Royce said. "We can wager for it."

"I'm obliged to you for the offer," Hart replied, "but I'm not interested in balloons anymore."

"And you won't place the sum on another go at the races?"

"On a horse that I don't know? Ridden by a rider I've never met?" Hart's mouth curved in a dry smile. "Clearly you haven't learned as much about me as you think you have."

"You're something of a horseman," Royce said.

"I rarely ride."

"But you drive. That's what I heard. Got yourself a sweet little curricle and a matched pair of prime fillies." An unholy glimmer sparkled in Royce's black eyes. "Tell you what I'll do. I'll wager you the fifteen hundred pounds owing plus an additional five hundred on a curricle race between your fine horses and my own nags."

That got Hart's attention. "You'd wipe out the debt if I won?"

"Plus another five hundred pounds for your troubles," Royce said. "What do you say?"

Hart's eyes narrowed. He was beginning to comprehend how Marcus had been roped in to his ill-advised bet at the track. "I say that a successful gambler would only bet such a sum on a surety," he answered. "You must be confident your team can win."

"And you're not confident in yours?" Royce shrugged. "Suit yourself, milord. You can always hand over the full fifteen hundred now."

Hart would have been inhuman if he weren't tempted. But that's how wagers were won—by tempting unwitting fools into the treacherous waters of deep play. Once, he might have allowed himself to wade in for the pure sport of it. But he wasn't a reckless young man any longer.

He couldn't afford to be.

And not only because of the money, but because of Anne.

He'd promised her he wouldn't come to any harm. It was a promise she'd reminded him of only yesterday, her face taut and her eyes red-rimmed from tears as she'd bathed the blood from his cheek.

Hart's chest tightened to recall it. He'd understood then what he'd only begun to comprehend at the Ramseys' ball. Lady Anne Deveril, who had for so long seemed to him to be strength personified, desperately needed someone to be strong for *her*.

It was that for which she couldn't forgive him. Not the cruelty of his words all those years ago, but the absence of his action. In the moment when her strength had failed her, when she was at her weakest and most vulnerable, he had been too consumed by his own hurt and disappointment to rise to the occasion.

He'd let her down, abandoning her during the greatest crisis of her life. In the intervening years he'd consoled himself with the fact that Anne was strong enough to bear anything. She didn't need him. She didn't need anyone.

But it wasn't true at all.

She needed the best version of himself he could muster. He may be nearly seven years too late, but Hart was determined to give it to her.

"Not the full fifteen hundred," he said. "We'll settle it at a thousand, along with a promise that Mr. Neale will never set foot in St. Giles again."

Marcus hung his head in shame.

"You speak for him, do you?" Royce looked between the two of them. "What is he to you, Hartford? A poor relation? A family bastard?"

The latter provoked Marcus to flinch.

Royce's face lit with calculation. "I might have guessed," he said. "There's resemblance enough for it."

Hart kept his countenance. He'd been fully aware of the danger in accompanying Marcus here today. It threatened to lay bare their connection to each other, exposing it to a villain who might very well exploit the knowledge for financial gain.

But there had been little alternative. Not when Marcus couldn't be trusted to satisfy the debt on his own.

Hart could only hope that the risk would be worth the reward. "Does it matter?" he asked.

"It might do," Royce said. "If the information's valuable."

Marcus opened his mouth to reply.

Hart silenced his half brother with a look before answering Royce himself. "If it were, do you imagine for a moment that I'd have accompanied the lad here myself?"

Royce considered the question. "Don't expect you would," he said at length. "Unless you're a fool." He folded his hands on his desk. "Very well. A thousand pounds it is. You don't have it with you, I presume?"

"I'll get you a bank draft," Hart said, rising from his chair.

Royce's smile returned. "By tomorrow noon," he said. "As for him"—he jerked his head at Marcus—"if he so much as attempts another wager in any of my shops, I won't be answerable for his life."

A quarter of an hour later, back in a hansom cab trotting swiftly away from the rookery, Marcus sat back in his seat with an exhalation of naked relief.

"Thank you," he said. "I never meant—"

"I'm sure you didn't," Hart replied. "But in these circumstances, I'm afraid an apology isn't quite good enough."

"What else can I offer?"

Hart leveled a flinty stare at his brother in the shadowed interior of the cab. "You can repay me the money I've expended on your behalf the same way you'd have been obliged to repay Royce. With your life."

Twenty-Six

Anne withdrew another heavy, leather-bound tome from the shelf of her father's library. She wasn't allowed to take any of them with her. Not a single blessed one. It didn't prevent her from opening the weighty book and bringing the seam of the pages to her nose.

She inhaled deeply, filling her lungs with the final remnants of her father's scent—old ink, fading paper, and the lingering odor of expensive pipe tobacco. It was all that was left of him in the room, the memory-provoking fragrance that clung within the pages of his treasured books. Joshua's presence had eradicated all the rest of it.

In a week's time, he'd made Papa's library his own, settling in with his mother to review the accounts during the day and then returning in the evening to drink and to smoke for hours on end. Once a shrine to Papa's memory, the library now reeked of Joshua's foul cigars.

It broke Anne's heart.

What was left of her heart, anyway.

It had been breaking by degrees with every passing day.

She'd told her mother that Papa's memory couldn't be taken from them, but that's what it felt like. Soon it would be gone. And then what would they have left?

Closing the book, she slid it back onto the shelf.

Seeming to sense Anne's melancholy mood, Eris jumped down from the chair where she'd been dozing and came to rub along her mistress's skirts with a delicate mew.

Anne bent to pick her up. Eris met her halfway, anchoring herself with her tiny claws to climb up Anne's skirts.

Eris loved to perch on Anne's shoulder—a height the kitten could only reach by scaling the fabric of Anne's clothing. It was an unfortunate habit, but one Anne hadn't discouraged.

Gently dislodging the little creature's claws, Anne lifted the kitten to cradle in her arms. She rubbed her cheek against the soft fur of Eris's head. An outsized purr emerged in response.

The library door opened. "Anne?" Mama said. "What are you doing hiding in here?"

Anne turned. "I'm not hiding. I'm saying goodbye to Papa's books."

Mama entered the room, the skirts of her black crepe day dress rustling behind her. During the course of the past several days, she hadn't once dropped the air of dignified imperiousness with which she addressed Joshua and his mother. Nevertheless . . .

The cracks were beginning to show.

Mama's eyes were shadowed, and there was a decided tension about her tightly pressed mouth. "I haven't the luxury for such sentimentality," she said. "I've too many obligations pressing down on me."

Anne's fingers idly stroked Eris's small back. "I thought we had everything in hand?"

"There's always more to attend to," Mama said. "I have packing to finish with Hortense, a meeting with my man of affairs, and then a luncheon in Russell Square with Fielding and Mrs. Blakely-Strange." She crossed the room to the library window. "I trust you're at leisure to receive morning callers?"

Morning calls were typically received between the hours of one and three in the afternoon. It was a tedious business unless one was anticipating friends—which Anne wasn't.

"Are we expecting anyone in particular?" she asked.

Mama drew back the curtain, peering outside with a distracted frown. "The usual fawning sycophants. That wretched boy and his mother have been paying visits all over town. Return calls should be forthcoming."

"Of course," Anne said. "I shall deal with them."

Since the new earl had made it known he was settling in town permanently, it seemed that everyone in Mayfair was eager to curry favor with him. It didn't matter that Joshua was a man of little grace and even less maturity. His title was enough to gain most people's good opinion.

Mama let the curtain fall closed again. "Excellent," she said. "I'd as soon be well out of it today."

"Are you feeling unwell?" Anne asked.

"How else to feel? They've taken your father's room, his library, his seat at the table. And yesterday, that boy had the temerity to send his lawyers to ask after the legal validity of my jointure."

Anne inhaled a sharp breath. "Great God. Whatever for?"

Mama's countenance was rigid. "To see that I'm not taking a penny more from the estate than what I'm entitled to."

Anne was rendered speechless by the insult. Her mother's jointure was their sole means of support. It was how they maintained their stable. How they paid their servants and settled their tradesmen's bills.

Mama returned to the door. "Never mind it. We shall be gone soon enough." Her gaze dropped to Eris, seeming to register the kitten's presence for the first time. "Why is that kitten still here? You promised me you would make arrangements."

Anne's arms tightened protectively around Eris. "Yes. I know I did."

Cats were expressly forbidden in the house they'd leased in Ludgate Hill. Something about fear of the carpets being soiled or some such nonsense. As if Anne and her mother weren't intending to replace the entirety of the furnishings! But Mrs. Frazil would not be swayed.

Poor Eris would have to go back to Julia. Either that or to Stella or Evelyn. Anne hadn't yet broached the subject with any of them. She'd been loath to face the necessity of it.

In only a short while, Eris had managed to claw her way, hissing and spitting, into Anne's affections. The thought of losing her . . .

"It must be done, Anne," Mama said before departing the library. "It *all* must be done."

A few moments later, after depositing Eris safely in her bedchamber, Anne glumly made her way to the drawing room. Mrs. Deveril was already there, presiding over the tea tray.

"Well," she said as Anne came into the room, "I'm pleased to see you haven't entirely abdicated your duties. Unlike your mother. She's been absent every morning this week."

"My mother has many engagements." Anne took a seat. "Her social calendar is full through the next three months."

Mrs. Deveril sniffed. "I would venture to say that, for the ladies in our family, duty must come before frivolity. And if that frivolity is of a dubious sort—crystal balls and whatnot—we would be wise to—"

"*I* would venture to say, ma'am, that such sentiments are best left unsaid," Anne replied. "Unless you wish to repeat them in my mother's hearing?"

Mrs. Deveril pursed her lips. "I wouldn't dream of causing offense."

Anne was gratified to see that, despite her mother's depressed spirits, Mama still had the power to intimidate the likes of Mrs. Deveril.

Would that it were enough to carry the day.

But a lady's firm disposition and adamantine strength of will mattered little when weighed against hundreds of years of British inheritance law.

The house belonged to Joshua and his mother now. Anne and her mother had been relegated to the role of unwelcome guests.

"Is my cousin not joining us today?" Anne asked.

"Arundell has taken one of the horses out," Mrs. Deveril said.

"Has he?" Anne's shoulders tensed. She'd expressly forbidden her cousin from riding Saffron, but that hadn't stopped him from making use of the other horses in their stable. "He might have told me."

"He has no reason to do so," Mrs. Deveril said. "It's *his* stable now. You and your mother would do well to remember it."

"We could hardly forget," Anne said. "He still might have mentioned it as a courtesy."

"Surely you don't begrudge him a little morning air to clear his head? He needed it after everything he's been through with your mother since we arrived. She challenges him at every turn." Mrs. Deveril poured Anne a cup of tea, warming to the subject. "I don't desire a confrontation, but he's right to be concerned for her state of mind—*and* for yours. All of this black and this troubling obsession with the dead. It threatens to create a scandal for my son. We would both feel easier if Lady Arundell would retire to the dower house. It's the appropriate thing to do, don't you agree?"

Anne most emphatically did *not* agree.

The dower house at Cherry Hill consisted of a small lodge at the furthermost edge of the property. In years past, it had been occupied by one of the retired family servants—an aged housekeeper from Anne's childhood. The very thought that Mama would be happy in such a remote country dwelling, no better than some old retainer sent out to pasture, beggared belief.

"My mother will never leave London," Anne said. "She has an active life here. The country would be a misery to her."

"Will she be any more content outside of Mayfair? Will you?" Mrs. Deveril proffered the teacup to Anne. "You're still handsome, my dear. Arundell was telling me so only this morning. You might yet make a match if you would only sweeten your temper."

"No thank you," Anne said, declining the tea. "On both counts."

Horbury entered the drawing room with a delicate cough. "Mr. Hartford to see Lady Anne, ma'am. I've taken the liberty of putting him in the small parlor."

Anne's pulse jumped. In all her distress over her situation at home, she'd forgotten Hartford's threat to call on her.

Good Lord above. He must be here to propose!

It was entirely unnecessary—and so she would tell him. There had been no hint of scandal arising from her visit to Battersea. No malicious whispers or threats of exposure from any of the men who had been drinking in the taproom. Indeed, given her reckless behavior (and barring the usual rumors about her eccentricity), Anne's reputation remained in surprisingly good order.

"The small parlor?" Mrs. Deveril echoed peevishly. "What have you done that for? I've provided ample instruction on how I'll receive my visitors. Show Mr. Hartford up at once."

Anne stood. "But Mr. Hartford is *my* visitor, ma'am. I shall receive him in the small parlor." She crossed to the door. "Thank you, Horbury."

Horbury bowed. He accompanied her from the room and down the stairs. "I must warn you, my lady. The gentleman's appearance is . . . most alarming."

Anne's brows lifted. "Do you mean that he's black and blue all over? I'm not likely to be shocked by that."

But when Anne entered the sun-filtered parlor, with its plump velvet chairs and elegant little tables of inlaid satinwood, she was confronted by a sight that stopped her cold.

Hartford stood by the window, garbed in an uncharacteristically sober suit. The sunlight illuminated his face. He wasn't only bruised, he was sporting a pair of black eyes, a swollen, disjointed nose, and a gash at his temple sewn up rather gruesomely with a row of white silk thread sutures.

She froze on the threshold. Her throat tightened painfully. "Good heavens."

Hartford's blue eyes held a glimmer of humor. "It's not as bad as it looks."

"It could hardly be worse," Anne remarked. She addressed the butler: "Thank you, Horbury. That will be all."

Horbury bowed before withdrawing, leaving Anne alone with Hartford.

She bit her lip as she looked at him, her body going hot and cold by turns.

This wasn't the Hartford she knew, the dashing, outrageously handsome gentleman who clothed himself in plaid trousers and garish mulberry coats. This was the same wounded tiger she'd encountered in the cramped inn room above the tavern in Battersea. A man who was more of a threat to her injured than he'd ever been to her at full strength.

She ventured a step toward him. "Did Bishop—"

"He reset my nose and sutured my wounds," Hartford said. "With luck, in a month's time, I'll be myself again."

"What did your grandfather have to say?"

"I told him it was a carriage accident." Hartford gave an eloquent grimace. "Not entirely a lie, now I think of it. Those villains did throw me out of a carriage, I seem to recall."

Anne's countenance crumpled. Emotion, too long suppressed, crashed over her in an unforgiving wave. It wasn't just Hartford's appearance. It was everything—her mother, Joshua, Mrs. Deveril, Eris, and Ludgate Hill.

Bringing her hands to her face, she choked back a sudden sob.

Hartford reached her in three strides.

And then she was in his arms.

He gathered her close, enveloping her in the unyielding strength of his embrace.

She was too overcome to resist him. Nor why should she wish to? He was warm and strong and safe. And she needed him desperately.

Her shoulders sagged, her body melting into the shelter of his arms.

"Poor old thing," he murmured against her hair. "It's not my face, is it."

It wasn't a question. She answered it nonetheless, giving a mute shake of her head, lest her voice betray her tears.

"It's all right, sweetheart. You don't have to say anything." His large hand moved over the curve of her spine in a soothing caress.

Her eyes squeezed shut. She pressed her cheek to the lapel of his black cloth waistcoat. He smelled of horses, harness oil, and new leather. Reassuring fragrances. They reminded her of all she loved best in life. All that was still good and happy in this world. And he was somehow all mixed up in it.

Felix meant happiness, that's what he'd told her. He'd been only partially in jest.

"So, your cousin has arrived at last," he said. "And brought his mother with him, I hear."

She responded with a muffled choke of acknowledgment. Moisture stung at her lashes. She was reluctant to stir from his arms.

"Have things been dreadful?" he asked. "But they must be so, else you wouldn't be turning to me." He brushed his lips over her temple, his voice a low-pitched murmur. "Damn the lot of them. They're not worth a single one of your tears."

"I'm not crying," she sniffled.

"Of course not. Furies don't cry. They rage." Bringing a finger under her chin, he gently tipped her face to his. "Why don't you rage at me awhile? I can withstand it."

She bleakly met his eyes. "I'm too dispirited to rage at anyone."

He frowned. "You begin to concern me."

"I concern myself," she admitted.

His eyes searched hers. His expression set with a sudden resolve. "Very well, then," he said, releasing her. "Fetch your hat and gloves. I'm taking you for a drive."

Hart cast another worried look at Anne as he turned his team into the park. He hadn't had the privilege of driving her in a very long while. Since their broken engagement, she'd have rather drunk poison than climb up beside him in his curricle. But today she'd uttered no objection. She'd permitted him to hand her up into the seat just as though it were the veriest commonplace.

For him, it was anything but.

He was acutely conscious of her body beside him, the swell of her skirts crowding his legs and the intimate brush of her arm against his. She was still and quiet, gazing out at the passing trees and the curving waters of the Serpentine with an expression of preoccupation.

Kestrel and Damselfly were joyfully energetic—fairly champing at their bits after a few days of enforced rest. Hart's swollen shoulder ached as he handled the reins. It was still paining him whenever he exerted himself.

And he'd been exerting himself to no end this past week. When he wasn't writing letters to Cumberland or to the crucible company's contacts in Inverness, Hart had been in company with the Neale family, attempting to sort out their futures.

Or rather, Marcus's future.

At present, Marcus was convinced that Hart was going to press him into the army. Hart hadn't disabused him of the notion. The fact was, Hart didn't know yet *what* he was going to do with the lad. He had an idea or two up his sleeve, but it all depended on what happened with William Webb.

Webb was definitely interested in Hart's proposition to lead the company's possible expansion into Scotland. He'd wired back almost immediately in response to the telegraph Hart had sent on the day he'd been attacked in Battersea. But a wire was a poor means of conveying the particulars of a proposal. For that, Hart had relied on a lengthy letter.

He was awaiting Webb's reply. Until he received it, Hart was at a standstill. So was the Parfit Plumbago Crucible Company.

So was Marcus.

It wasn't entirely a bad thing to let the lad stew for a while. With luck, the fear of being forced into the army would temporarily curb his behavior. As for the crucible company, Hart was confident they would accept his Scotland proposal, providing certain criteria were met.

The whole of it had been occupying the entirety of Hart's energies for days.

But not today. Not now he was with Anne. Now, all of his attention was focused on her.

"I've been treating Kestrel's right front," he said by way of conversation. "She was off recently. But she's better now, as you see."

"They've matured handsomely," Anne said. "I knew they would."

"You knew better than I. Back at Sutton Park, all I saw were a pair of scraggly, mischievous fillies."

"You want a bit of mischief in a horse. It gives them a sparkle."

"I do like a female with sparkle," Hart said.

Anne didn't seem to register his teasing. She resumed staring out at the lake, her black-gloved hands folded tight in her lap. "Joshua is selling the elderly horses at Cherry Hill," she said abruptly.

"He what?" Hart gave her a sharp glance. "When did this happen?"

"It's *been* happening. And I can do nothing about it. I can do nothing about anything."

"I'm sure that isn't true."

Anne didn't reply. She again lapsed into silence, lost in her own thoughts.

"Do you know," he said, "I believe I'm beginning to understand the trouble."

"With the horses?"

"With you."

She gave him a weary look. "I'm in no mood to argue."

"It's not an argument. It's a fact. You've lost control of your situation—your cousin, your home, your mother."

Her face hardened to marble just as it always did whenever he dared mention her mother.

"There's only one thing to do in such a case," he said.

"And what's that, pray?"

"You told me the answer yourself in Hardholme. You said that when a lady loses control of the essentials of her life, she must compensate by taking ruthless control of the only things she can." He drew Kestrel and Damselfly to a halt. "Come," he said. "It's past time you took hold of the reins."

Anne's brows flew up. "You're not suggesting I drive your curricle?"

"It's not a suggestion," Hart said as Kestrel and Damselfly danced impatiently in their traces. "Shall we switch seats? I always find it easier to drive from this side."

She didn't budge. She was too busy staring at him as though he'd lost his mind. "But . . . you don't let anyone drive your team. Not ever. It's a point of pride with you."

His mouth tipped in a lopsided smile. "You're not just anyone."

Twenty-Seven

Anne would be lying if she said she wasn't tempted. She'd long admired Hartford's mares, and she fancied herself an excellent driver. She nevertheless demurred. "I couldn't. What if—"

"What if, what if," he repeated dismissively. "Since when did you flinch from anything?"

She gnawed her lip. She may have been brave in the past, but she didn't feel so bold today. Not with Mama to worry about, and Eris, and the impending move to Ludgate Hill.

"Besides," he said, "you'd be doing me a service. My shoulder is aching like the devil. I doubt I can continue driving us without aggravating it further."

"What's wrong with your shoulder?" she asked.

"Didn't I mention it? My grandfather insisted his physician examine me. The fellow says I must have dislocated my shoulder at some stage and then popped it back in again when I fell onto the road. A dashed nuisance."

She eyed his shoulder with prompt concern. Despite their bitter history, it still caused her pain to think of how he'd been beaten and thrown from a carriage. She hated the very idea of his being hurt.

"I'd no idea," she said.

"How could you?" He offered her the ribbons. "Are you going to take them or not?"

Anne swiftly made up her mind. "Very well." She stood, bracing her hand on the back of the seat. "Move over."

With a great deal of fumbling and a brief tangle of her skirts around his legs, she and Hartford switched places. She sank down in his seat and took up the reins. The two mares were prancing nervously, so full of restless energy that it vibrated up the ribbons, communicating everything they felt straight into Anne's hands.

A thrill went through her.

"Not too heavy," Hartford said. "They like a gentle touch, with a bit of power at the back of it."

Anne adjusted the reins. "They're quite powerful themselves."

He stretched his arm out behind her along the back of the seat. "They're testing you," he said. "Show them what you're made of."

A reluctant smile tugged at Anne's mouth. "Walk on," she said, giving a cluck of encouragement. The mares leapt forward, springing into an animated trot. Anne caught her breath. "Goodness!"

"That's it," Hartford said encouragingly. "You know what you're doing."

Her confidence swelled as she guided Kestrel and Damselfly back onto the avenue. The mares moved with lofty energy, fairly floating along the path. They were as sensitive to Anne's fingers as the strings of a finely tuned harp. "Oh, they're heaven!"

"As close to it as one can find on four legs," he agreed.

A gentleman mounted on a large hunter stopped to goggle at them. Indeed, they seemed to be drawing the eye of everyone in the park. It wasn't yet the fashionable hour, but the weather was fine and it was late enough in the day that many were out walking, riding, and driving.

Anne felt the scandalized stares of a quartet of aristocratic matrons in a barouche, a stylish lady mincing along with her groom, and two young lordlings out for a canter.

"By Jove," one of the young men remarked loudly as Anne drove past, "is that a lady driving Hartford's curricle?"

"It can't be," his companion replied. "He'd never allow it."

Hartford couldn't have failed to hear them, but he evinced no reaction. His attention was on Anne and his horses. "Take them to the right," he said. "There's a secluded stretch over the rise where you can give them their heads."

Anne obeyed him, driving the mares further away from the fashionable traffic. She didn't notice how far they'd gone until the noise of the growing crowd faded and there was nothing but the brisk clip-clop of the mares' hooves and the chirp of birdsong to break the silence.

"Now," Hartford said.

With another cluck and a soft tap of the whip, Anne sprang the team into a canter. When they offered a gallop, she didn't restrain them. She let them fly.

And that's exactly what it felt like: flying.

Wind whipped at the black gossamer netting of her oval-crowned hat, stinging her face as the curricle soared behind the mares. Had flames appeared beneath the vehicle's wheels, she wouldn't have been at all surprised.

No wonder Hartford was mad for his team. Driving them was thrilling. Powerful. And so wildly exhilarating that it burned away all traces of sadness, doubt, and misery. One felt rather like Helios must have felt, driving his chariot of the sun across the sky.

"Draw them back a little," Hartford said. "Ease them into the turning."

She tightened her fingers on the reins. The mares mightily resisted. Anne was briefly jolted forward.

Hartford's arm dropped to her waist, holding her steady in the seat. "Ask them again," he said. "I won't let them pitch you out."

Her heartbeat quickened at his touch. She again tightened the reins. This time, anchored by Hartford's strength, Anne succeeded in slowing the mares into the turn. They tossed their heads against her grip as they fell back into a trot. "Easy," Anne said. "Easy."

"That's it," Hartford said. "They're listening now."

Her stomach trembled with the threat of butterflies. She wished he would remove his arm from her waist. At the same time . . .

It was rather nice.

More than nice. It was actually quite wonderful.

Hartford wasn't interfering with her influence over the horses. He wasn't commanding her or attempting to seize control. He was just there—big, strong, and solid—lending her the full power of his support. The result was that she felt braver. Stronger. As though she were capable of anything.

"Shall I bring them back to a walk?" she asked.

"No. They can trot awhile yet." A note of solemnity crept into his voice. "It will give me a chance to talk to you."

She cast him a fleeting glance. "I can't talk while I'm driving. Not sufficient for conversation."

"I'll do the talking," he said gravely. "All you need do is listen."

Hart hadn't intended to speak to Anne out of doors, and definitely not while she was handling the reins of his curricle. He'd imagined they'd talk in the small parlor. That he'd tell her everything he'd planned to say within the privacy of those four walls.

But when he'd seen her so sad and dispirited, when she'd let him hold her and comfort her, sagging against his chest in her weariness, he'd known that the Arundell town house wouldn't do. He needed to get Anne away from that old mausoleum.

And perhaps this was best after all, here under the vaulted sky, amid the trees and the warmth of the summer sunshine. This way, at least, she couldn't argue with him or attempt to keep him from saying what he must. She was too preoccupied with handling the horses.

Hart slid his arm from her waist, moving away from her on the seat. She was staring straight ahead, focused on navigating the mares. His gaze settled on her profile; the long frill of her dark lashes, the elegant slope of her cheek, and the voluptuous curve of her pink meadowsweet mouth.

A spasm of affection clenched his heart, making it ache as keenly as his injured shoulder.

Hart had been thinking about her ever since they'd parted. About the fact that, despite all the years of arguments and acrimony, she'd flown to his side the moment she believed him hurt. He'd been thinking about what she'd said to him as he'd lain, shirtless and senseless, on that narrow inn bed.

No man on earth has ever been loved the way I loved you, Felix Hartford.

He'd spent the past week feeling like the biggest fool on the planet.

"When I saw you in Battersea," he began, "I told you that you could expect me to call on you within a week."

"I remember," she said. "But if you think you're obliged to propose to me merely because I compromised myself in coming to your aid, you may think again. There's been no gossip on that score. And if it should ever arise, I won't require a gentleman to redeem my honor. I'm entirely capable of—"

"I'm not going to propose," he said. "I'm going to apologize."

She flashed him a sharp look. "I *beg* your pardon?"

"Yes, I know. I'm quite amazed myself." The humor in his tone vanished as quickly as it had appeared. It was replaced by a solemn resolve. "Or rather, I'm not amazed. I've wanted to tell you . . . that is, I've known for some time how much I was in the wrong."

"On what occasion?"

"I'm serious, Anne."

"I wish you wouldn't be." She checked the mares as they offered another canter. "You unnerve me when you're serious."

"I'm sorry for it," he replied. "And I'm sorry—*deeply* sorry—for how I behaved when I returned from India."

The mares broke stride again.

Anne muttered an unladylike oath under her breath as she struggled to regain control.

Hart covered her hand with his on the reins, helping her to slow them. "Perhaps we should stop after all?"

Her lips compressed. "I suppose we must if you're going to keep talking nonsense."

With his assistance, she brought the team to a halt alongside a stand of trees.

They were far from the other riders and drivers now; alone, deep within the wooded recesses of the park. It was as close to privacy as they were likely to get anywhere.

He set the brake.

"Is this truly necessary?" she asked.

"I'm afraid it is," he said.

She turned to face him on the seat. "Well, then?" Her impatient tone was belied by the subtle flush of color rising up her throat.

Hart regarded her steadily. "I've thought a lot about that day. As have you, it seems. During our journey to Yorkshire, you recalled my unfortunate words with startling clarity."

"I could hardly forget," she said.

"I've not forgotten, either. That childish ultimatum I gave you and the things I said afterward . . . Anne, you must know I didn't mean any of it."

Hurt glimmered at the back of her eyes, a faint but visible remnant of the pain he'd caused her. "Then why did you say it?"

"For the same reason you said what you did, I suspect." He gave her a brief, rueful smile. "We were too young."

Emotion welled within Anne's breast. Her gaze fell from Hartford's in confusion. How could she look at him when he was saying such things to her?

He was right, of course. They *had* been too young. Still . . .

"It's no excuse," she said.

"No, it isn't. But it helps to explain it. You were grieving your father, and I was still grappling with the revelations about mine. We weren't best equipped to handle ourselves."

"It was you who—"

"Yes," he said. "I must shoulder the lion's share of the blame. I was older. I should have exercised more care with you." His voice lowered with tender intensity. "My only defense is that I wanted you too much to see reason."

Anne's throat closed so she couldn't speak.

"That day at Grosvenor Square, I was in a dreadful mood," he said. "I'd been feeling for a long while as though I was alone in the world, absent any family of my own. I suppose you could say I felt abandoned. Ridiculous, I know. I wasn't a child. But having you had come to mean everything to me."

She shook her head, at last finding her voice. "Hartford—"

"It was what brought me back to England. The one hope that sustained me in my darkest moments. And when I finally returned to you . . . I couldn't bear to wait any longer."

"You didn't seem to want me at all," she said.

"I was angry because *you* didn't seem to want *me*. Not enough to forgo any other concern. I felt as though you were doing the same thing my father had done. You were forsaking me in favor of someone else. Someone better. Worthier. Someone who had the whole of your heart."

"But it was my *mother*."

"It didn't matter who it was. Not at the time. I was already nursing my wounds. When you said you had to remain at home, I lashed out—stupidly, cruelly." His words were gruff with genuine regret. "I had a great deal of growing up to do. I'm sorry it was at your expense."

She swallowed hard. If he could admit his fault, then so could she. "I wasn't blameless on that occasion. As you well know."

His gaze drifted over her face, sending a quivery sensation through her stomach. She wished he wouldn't look at her like that. It made it difficult to formulate a single coherent thought.

"What did you say to me that was untrue?" he asked.

"I won't repeat it."

"You don't need to. The words you uttered on that occasion are burned into my soul. I've been endeavoring ever since to prove every one of them wrong."

She must have betrayed a flicker of doubt. His columns had come to mind.

A smile edged his mouth. "I won't claim to have altered my character entirely. That would be impossible. But I've changed in every way that matters. I'd hate to think I must give up every source of amusement in order to prove myself responsible. But if I must—"

"I never objected to your good humor," Anne said. "I only wished I could depend on you. I needed you when you returned to London. My life was—" She stopped herself. There was no sense in relitigating the past. "It doesn't matter. It was a long time ago. We were young, just as you said. Young and naive. We didn't . . ." Her words trailed off as Hartford's large hand came to cup her face.

His eyes held hers with aching tenderness. "You told me that you loved me," he said. "In Battersea. You said that you'd loved me then as no man has ever been loved before."

Anne gazed back at him. She'd never felt so vulnerable in her life. "I did love you."

"Then give me another chance," he begged her. "Let me show you that I've changed. That you can rely on me now as you couldn't then."

"I already know you've changed," she said. "Your relations with your half brother and his family are evidence enough of that. Though why my good opinion should count for anything—"

"Your good opinion is the only one that matters to me," he said. "I still care for you, Anne. I still want you in my life."

"I *am* in your life."

"Not like this. I want to be your friend again. Your true intimate friend." The pad of his thumb moved gently over the curve of her cheek. "I know I've hurt you. I know you don't trust me anymore. But please, let me try to make it up to you. Let me call on you in Grosvenor Square."

Anne trembled beneath his touch. "You can't."

"Why not?" A spasm of anguish crossed his face. "Is it because you can't forgive me?"

"It's because . . . it's too late." Tears burned in her eyes. She refused to let them fall. "We're leaving Mayfair. I thought you'd have heard the news by now."

Hartford's hand slowly slid from her cheek, leaving her cold. "I haven't heard a thing. I've been closeted with my business associates all week—and with the blasted Neales, attempting to sort out Marcus's affairs. I haven't so much as picked up a newspaper."

"I doubt it's made the papers yet, but it's true enough. My cousin and his mother want us to retire to the dower house at Cherry Hill."

His brows snapped together in an immediate scowl. "The devil you will."

"Of course we won't. But we *are* leaving Mayfair. My mother has taken a house in Ludgate Hill."

"*Ludgate Hill?*" He was incredulous. "Are you joking?"

"I wish I were. Mama is convinced it's a hill of power. Something about a Roman temple that once existed on the site of St. Paul's. She's already let a house there from one of her spiritualist acquaintances."

"My God," Hartford muttered.

"We're almost finished packing. All that remains is to sort out our stable and to make arrangements for Eris—"

"Who in blazes is Eris?"

"My kitten. Mrs. Blunt sent her to me as a gift from Goldfinch Hall." Anne's voice cracked. "The worst part is, I've become so terribly fond of her. And now I must find another home for her in town, else she'll have to be sent back to Yorkshire." She bit her lip. "I don't suppose you would consider . . . ?"

"Giving a home to your cat?" Hart's mouth tipped up at one corner in an ironic smile. "I gather she's named after the goddess of chaos?"

"She is," Anne admitted.

He gave a short laugh. "Well, why not? I suppose it's a start."

If Anne hadn't been holding the ribbons, she'd have flung her arms around his neck in gratitude. "Thank you," she said. "You don't know what it means to me, Hart."

"Hart, am I? My self-interested act of kindness is already paying dividends."

"Don't tease."

"I'm not." His smile dimmed, his eyes once again growing serious. "I'd do anything for you, my dear. Don't you know that by now?"

Her heart turned over. "I didn't know it."

"Then let me show you," he said. "May I call on you in Ludgate Hill?"

Anne felt a resurgence of familiar reluctance. It was a hesitation born of an old hurt. A pain she'd nursed for years into a steadfast strain of bitterness. She wasn't entirely confident she could overcome it.

But he'd said *call* on her, not *court* her. Whatever his feelings might be, he wasn't offering anything more than a resumption of their friendship—for now.

"Very well," she said at last. "But it won't be very convenient for you. The road up the hill is terribly congested at the best of times. You'd be stuck between omnibuses and fruit carts for ages."

His blue eyes shone with single-minded determination. "I've waited nearly seven years for you. Do you really believe for a moment that a little traffic is going to keep me away?"

Twenty-Eight

Hart finished reading the letter he'd received from William Webb with a feeling of intense satisfaction. Webb wasn't only willing to go to Scotland, he was eager to do so. If the expedition was successful, it would be an advancement for him. A chance at a new life in a position of even greater authority. All that remained was for Hart to confirm the decision with his partners at the crucible company.

Somehow managing to find a pen and paper amid the tremendous clutter of his grandfather's desk, Hart dashed off letters to Parfit, Goodbody, and Acker, calling for a meeting for tomorrow. After signing and sealing them, Hart summoned a footman to see that they were delivered.

The servant appeared in record time. "Lord March is asking for you, sir," he said as he collected Hart's letters. "He's in the garden."

"Of course he is." Hart exited the library to find him.

At this hour, Grandfather was usually in his greenhouse. The vast glass structure was situated at the edge of his gardens. Most of the flowers that surrounded it were fading as cooler weather set in, but the interior of the greenhouse was alive with color.

Grandfather was just emerging from behind it, his face lit with excitement. "It's happened at last!" he said. "Come and see!"

Hart followed his grandfather behind the greenhouse to the patch of partially shaded earth where the two of them had transplanted the Himalayan lilies earlier in the summer.

The three large plants were arrayed in a line, spaced yards apart. They were massive by any measure, as formidable as they were rare. Adorned with glossy, dark green leaves, the sturdy spikes rose up several feet from the ground, nearly reaching Hart's shoulders.

"Here." Grandfather led Hart around the back of the nearest lily. "What do you think of that?"

A single trumpet-shaped flower came into view. The creamy white bloom was exotically beautiful, with petals furling back to reveal a vibrant, reddish-purple heart.

"You were right to recommend a change of soil," Grandfather said. "That's all it took, you see. It didn't want perfection or refinement. It wanted good wholesome earth, with no alterations to it. We've been coddling it, that was the problem. But now it's finally come into its own, I'm confident more blooms will follow."

Hart bent to smell the lily. He was met by the heady fragrance of rich vanilla. It reminded him of something.

Of someone.

"Nearly seven years we've had to wait," Grandfather went on proudly. "But we've done it. We've seen it bloom at last." He looked at Hart in glowing expectation. "Well? Have you nothing to say, lad?"

"Only this." A smile spread over Hart's face. "It's about damned time."

Later that afternoon, Hart stopped in at Grosvenor Square to collect Anne's kitten. The Arundell house was a flurry of activity, with maids rushing about, footmen hauling trunks down the stairs, and bags stacked haphazardly in the hall.

Lady Arundell was absent, and Anne was rushed off her feet.

She joined him in the morning room within minutes of his arrival, her eyes shadowed and her hair fraying loose from her coil of golden plaits. She held a screened wooden box in her arms. Inside of it, a small black kitten crouched on what looked to be one of her mistress's black-dyed cashmere shawls.

"She's frightened," Anne said as she presented the box to him. "You must be patient with her. And you mustn't let her out of the house until she knows the lay of the place. She'll get lost in the city otherwise."

Hart listened intently as Anne exhorted him on all of the kitten's various likes and dislikes. She was attached to the little creature. That much was plain. There were no tears and no protracted farewells, but he knew enough of Anne to recognize the tension in her countenance.

"You can trust me with her," he assured her as he took charge of the box.

You can trust me full stop, he wanted to say.

But promises were just words. The only way to prove to Anne that he was trustworthy was by being trustworthy.

"We leave tomorrow," she said. "I haven't a moment to spare. There's still much to be done."

"I won't keep you," he said.

She offered him a faint smile before taking her leave.

Hart carried the box out to his waiting curricle. He set it up on the seat and then, after a word to the groom who had been holding the horses, vaulted up beside it. He was just taking up the reins when a sharp movement caught the corner of his eye.

He jerked his head to investigate. Since his encounter in Battersea, he'd become sensitive to the slightest threat. But looking across the square, he found no band of villains sent to pummel him. It was only a boy.

A *familiar* boy.

He stood, fidgeting, against a lamppost, his cap pulled down over his brow and his scrawny frame half-hidden by a neighboring tree. It was the loquacious youth from Gabriel Royce's betting shop.

No sooner had Hart spotted him than the lad darted away across the green, quickly disappearing from view.

Hart felt a creeping sense of apprehension.

Either the boy was here purely by coincidence or Royce had sent him to follow Hart with a purpose. If the latter was the case, there could be only one explanation.

Hart recalled how Royce's eyes had glittered with calculation on learning that Marcus might be a bastard relation of the Earl of March's. No doubt Royce was interested in expanding his knowledge on the subject. Once he learned the truth, he could use it as he saw fit, to blackmail Hart—*or* a member of his family.

Brookdale at once came to mind.

A man in Royce's position stood to benefit from having a member of Parliament beholden to him.

"Hartford?" A slender, fair-haired gentleman approached on a large bay gelding, arresting Hart's attention. "I thought that was you."

"Arundell," Hart said.

He'd met the new earl for the first time only recently. The two of them were members of the same club in St. James's Street. One of Hart's friends had introduced them in passing. Hart had been leaving at the time, and had exchanged no more than three words with the man. It had been enough for Hart to get the measure of him.

"That's a fine pair of fillies you have there." Arundell brought his horse to a clumsy halt alongside the curricle. He eyed Kestrel and Damselfly with rank admiration. "Did you find them at the sales? I haven't seen anything as prime during my visits, more's the pity."

Hart immediately thought of Anne and what she'd confided to him during their drive in Hyde Park. "I understand you've been to the sales a great deal recently."

"Had to," Arundell said. "Been listing some horses from my estate. Not that anyone's biting. Might have done better to sell them straight to the knackers."

Hart's jaw tightened imperceptibly. "I might be interested."

Arundell let out a loud guffaw. "In those old nags? You can't possibly want one of them."

"No, indeed," Hart replied. "I want them all."

"I won't have any tearful goodbyes," Anne said as she walked Evelyn and Stella out of the marble-tiled hall of the house in Grosvenor Square for the very last time.

Mr. Fielding's carriage awaited Anne's two friends in front of the house. The gentleman himself was still inside with Anne's mother. Anne had thought it prudent to leave Mama alone with him. It seemed only fair that she should have the same privacy to say her goodbyes that Anne had been afforded.

It was only on account of Joshua and Mrs. Deveril's absence from Grosvenor Square that they had any privacy at all. The new earl and his mother had gone to Bond Street to procure themselves new wardrobes. They weren't expected back until later in the afternoon. By then, Anne and her mother would be gone.

Anne supposed she should be grateful Joshua hadn't remained to make sure she and her mother weren't absconding with the family silver. A small mercy. It was difficult enough saying goodbye without doing it in the presence of a warden.

"This isn't goodbye." Evelyn hugged her tightly on the stone front steps. The skirts of her white foulard dress bunched against Anne's severe black silk.

"No, indeed." Stella embraced Anne in her turn, pressing a kiss to her cheek. "We're going to see you again quite soon."

"Yes, we are," Evelyn said. "My uncle has threatened to call on you both in Ludgate Hill as early as Thursday."

"We'll barely be settled," Anne said. "Though my mother won't mind it. She's happy to receive your uncle at any time."

Stella tugged on her dyed kid gloves. They were an exact match for her plain, dark blue gown, with its modest collar of starched cambric. "They're devoted to each other," she observed. "One wonders—"

"One does," Anne said. "But I can't imagine the thought has ever crossed Mama's mind."

Evelyn smiled. "You don't give her credit for finer feeling?"

A carriage rolled by in the street, the clatter of the horse's hooves ringing out amid the other sounds in the square—the shouts of a servant calling a greeting to another, and the merry shrieks of two small children out walking on the green in company with their nurse. The sky was overcast, the weather markedly cooler, but it wasn't yet intemperate enough to keep people confined indoors.

"Naturally I do," Anne said, sinking her voice. "But not in *that* direction. She's still in love with my father."

"A lady can have multiple great loves in her life," Evelyn replied.

Stella pulled a face. "I shall count myself lucky if I have just *one*."

Laughing, the three of them descended the steps to the street. Evelyn and Stella climbed into the carriage with the help of Mr. Fielding's footman.

Anne stood at the open door. "It isn't as though I'm moving to Newcastle," she said. "We shall find ways to meet, I promise."

Behind her, Mama and Mr. Fielding emerged from the hall, mid-conversation.

". . . for you, as well," Mama was saying as they descended the steps to the street.

"You are too good," Mr. Fielding replied.

"Nonsense," Mama said. "You will always be welcome in my home wherever I might go. And if the spirits are as well-disposed in that area as Mrs. Frazil and Mrs. Blakely-Strange assert, who knows but that Ludgate Hill might not be a benefit to us both?"

He bowed over her hand. "I bid you a safe journey, my lady."

Mama remained at Anne's side as Mr. Fielding departed in his carriage with Anne and Stella. "Poor man. He's distraught at the thought of my leaving Mayfair. One would think I was relocating to the moon."

"It rather feels as though we are," Anne said. "Ludgate Hill seems an entirely different world."

"I pray it will be," Mama replied, "for I have grown weary of this one." The moment the carriage disappeared from the square, she moved to go back inside. "Don't dally, Anne. There's still much to be done before we leave."

"Yes, Mama." Despite her mother's directive, Anne remained behind, lingering on the bottommost step.

She was loath to return to the house.

In the past week, it had taken on the air of an inhospitable hotel where she and her mother were staying without benefit of having paid their bill. A sorry state of affairs, to be sure.

Anne felt it keenly.

Since returning from her drive with Hartford last week, a constant dull pain had taken up residence in her chest. She seemed to be as tormented by the thought of remaining in Grosvenor Square as she was at the prospect of leaving it. The result was a sort of emotional purgatory.

It hadn't helped that Joshua's mother had hired a fleet of new servants, making the once-comfortable household feel even more unfamiliar.

Horbury, Mrs. Griffiths, and Hortense had resigned in order to remain with Anne's mother. So, too, had Anne's lady's maid, her personal groom, and several of the maids and footmen. They'd all gone ahead to Ludgate Hill to ready the house and to set up the small stable, which consisted of Saffron, a team of coach horses, and an aged saddle horse that Joshua might otherwise have disposed of.

Perhaps by the time Anne and her mother arrived this afternoon, the strange little house would feel like a home? Anne prayed it would.

With a sigh, she turned to ascend the steps.

"Lady Anne?" a sugary-sweet voice inquired. "Upon my word, how changed you are from when I last saw you in the park."

Anne stifled an inward groan. *Good Lord*. It needed only this.

Steeling herself, she turned on the steps to face Lady Heatherton.

The viscountess was dressed in a fashionable violet silk afternoon gown. A near neighbor of theirs in the square, she lived but four houses down from the Arundell mansion. It made it impossible to avoid her.

And avoiding Lady Heatherton was what Anne had thus far advised her friends to do. Not because Anne was intimidated by the woman, but because she and her friends had their reputations to consider. There had seemed no point in provoking Lady Heatherton into a senseless attack.

But Anne didn't care much for her reputation at the moment.

She'd put up with Viscountess Heatherton all these years because she'd had to. Because Lady Heatherton was a woman of rank and fortune. But she was a vile snake for all that. A spiteful woman who frequently amused herself by sinking her fangs into Anne and her friends.

Once it had seemed to be only petty cruelty, but after Lady Heatherton's behavior toward Evelyn and Mr. Malik at Cremorne Gardens, and then toward Stella in the park, Anne was disposed to think it something worse.

"Have you been ill?" Lady Heatherton asked in the same syrupy tone of faux concern. "You look so pale and sickly."

"I'm quite sure I don't," Anne replied.

"My eyes don't deceive me," Lady Heatherton said. "You're sadly altered, poor creature."

The viscountess's pinch-faced lady's maid hovered behind her, displaying an avid interest in her employer's conversation. Anne had no doubt but that the exchange would be faithfully reported in the servants' hall this evening. By tomorrow, it would likely be running through all of Mayfair.

Anne didn't intend to come out the loser in the tale.

"You might consider a visit to an oculist," she suggested. "I'm told that age inevitably affects one's vision."

Lady Heatherton's smirk faltered. "There's nothing wrong with my eyesight. Anyone can see that you're leaving Grosvenor Square. Leaving Mayfair, I'm told."

"We are."

"And never to return?" A glitter of spite brightened the viscountess's face. "Such a pity. And you an unmarried girl of advancing years. How will you continue to move about in society from such a great distance away? It won't be convenient, will it, to travel all the way here from . . . where did my maid tell me? Ludgate Hill? Among the drapers and silk mercers?" She burst into laughter.

"I'm gratified that you'll miss us," Anne said dryly.

"Oh, I won't. Not in the slightest." Lady Heatherton's laughter trailed away. "You and your mother have lorded your positions over the rest of us too long for my comfort. The only thing that could bring me more pleasure than seeing the back of you would be if you'd take your abhorrent little bluestocking friends along with you."

"I wonder that anything can give you pleasure," Anne remarked.

Lady Heatherton's smile vanished. "*What* did you say?"

Anne lifted one shoulder in a careless shrug. "Only that you're an unhappy woman. And there's nothing so tedious as an unhappy person who takes out their unhappiness on everyone around them. You've become a bore, frankly. I advise adopting a hobby."

"Why you self-righteous little—" Lady Heatherton took a furious step toward her.

Anne stood her ground. "Sheathe your claws, madam," she said, "lest I be tempted to unsheathe mine."

Lady Heatherton's face flushed red. "Are you—Is that a threat?" She advanced another step. "You have no position any longer. No place in society whatsoever. Your situation has changed forever. And you have the audacity to—" She sputtered with outrage. "Just who do you think you are?"

Anne drew herself up, her spine as rigid as an iron bar. "*I* am Lady Anne Deveril, daughter of the Earl and Countess of Arundell. And no matter where I live, *that* is something that will *never* change."

With that, she turned her back on the woman and, head held high, returned to the house.

Mama was in the hall ordering one of the maids where to put a stack of bandboxes. "Who was that outside?" she asked as Anne entered.

"Lady Heatherton." Anne gave her skirts a shake. "I'm afraid we had words."

"Did you?" Mama was temporarily diverted. "I trust you weren't too brutal."

"Not at all," Anne said airily, mounting the stairs to her bedroom. "I hardly touched her."

Twenty-Nine

A muffled yelp emerged from Hart's dressing room. A moment later, Eris stalked out on stiff legs. Her black fur was fluffed up so she looked twice her tiny size. Bishop came after her, nursing a bloody scratch on his hand.

Hart paused in the act of knotting his neckcloth. "I thought I told you not to pick her up?"

"She was sharpening her claws on your new driving jacket, sir," Bishop said, aggrieved. "I sought only to remove her."

"She doesn't care to be removed against her will," Hart said. "You can't touch her unless she permits it."

Bishop glared after the kitten as she wound herself around Hart's legs. "How am I to know when she permits it?"

Hart tapped his chest with his finger. In response, Eris leapt onto his trouser leg. With the athleticism of a miniature panther, she clawed her way up his clothes to perch on his shoulder. She butted her head against his cheek.

"You'll know," Hart said.

He prided himself on the progress he'd made with the temperamental kitten. All it had taken was a few dishes of warm milk, some soft words, and the invitation of a hot water bottle placed under a quilt.

Nearly a week later, Eris was sleeping in Hart's bed each night, greeting him with a raspy little purr each morning, and regularly making herself at home on his shoulder.

Hart was convinced the kitten was half parrot.

"Will Lady Anne be retrieving her soon?" Bishop asked hopefully.

Removing Eris from his shoulder, Hart dropped her gently onto the bed. She promptly curled up in Anne's black cashmere shawl, a garment that occupied a permanent space beside Hart's pillow. "I shouldn't think so." He picked up his coat. "But don't despair. She'll come round to you eventually."

Bishop flashed him a doubtful look. "If you say so, sir."

Shrugging on his coat, Hart exited his chamber. He made his way to the drawing room, where his family had gathered for preprandial drinks.

Aunt Esther sat in an upholstered chair beside Grandfather, sipping a glass of sherry. Mariah was seated a distance away, her arms folded and her face contorted in a childish pout.

Brookdale stood in front of the ornate marble mantel. He was discussing politics, as usual. Something to do with the upstart Liberal opponent he'd defeated in his recent borough election in Hampshire.

He stopped midsentence as Hart entered, brows beetling in swift disapproval. "Felix," he said. "Those bruises are disgraceful."

"Really?" Hart bent to kiss his aunt's cheek in greeting. "I thought they lent me a certain charm."

"Don't heed him," Aunt Esther said. "We all know your injuries are mending as quickly as they can. But . . . if you could manage for the bruises to fade a little faster—"

"My constitution is doing its utmost, ma'am," Hart said.

"Sit down, my boy," Grandfather said. "See if you can cheer up your cousin." He motioned to the sofa before resuming his conversation with Brookdale. "Cobb is no gentleman, that's plain."

"If he were, he'd have taken his loss with good grace," Brookdale said. "Instead, he's hunting for the slightest hint of anything untoward in my past. He thinks to discredit my moral authority in some way."

Grandfather gave a dismissive chuckle. "He'll be disappointed. Our family tree may display occasional sprouts of eccentricity, but I'm happy to say that immorality has never taken root among the Hartford line."

"Indeed." Brookdale took a drink of his sherry. "I've told him to do his worst. My conduct in both my public and private life is beyond reproach. There's nothing he can dig up that could possibly do me harm."

Hart did his best to ignore the conversation.

He didn't like to think of his uncle's political career. Not when there was a looming threat to it on the horizon.

That youth of Royce's had appeared again recently. He'd been lurking in Rotten Row two days ago when Hart was out driving his mares. Hart could no longer dismiss it as coincidence. It couldn't be. Not twice in as many weeks.

Royce must have sent the lad.

But until the man made his next move, Hart could do nothing but watch, wait, and try to keep his wits about him.

It was easier said than done. He was already extending himself to the utmost balancing the needs of the earldom, his business, and his heart. Add Brookdale's political career and the uncertain future of the Neale family, and it was altogether too many balls to keep in the air.

No man could keep juggling indefinitely. Not even Hart.

He took a seat next to his cousin.

"Did you really have a carriage accident?" she asked him with evident suspicion.

"You sound as though you don't believe it."

"I don't," she said. "You would never crash your curricle."

"I appreciate your faith in my driving. But it wasn't my curricle. It was a dilapidated coach I had the misfortune of riding in during a brief journey across the river."

"You look like someone pummeled you."

Hart grinned. "Do I? What an exciting life you must think I lead."

"Any life is more exciting than mine," she said petulantly. "I'm being kept prisoner in Mount Street."

"On what charge?"

"You wouldn't understand," she said. "And I wouldn't tell you anyway. Not after how you behaved to me at the Ramseys' ball."

"Because I wouldn't drive you to Richmond Park?" He gave her an assessing look. "Don't say you attempted to go on your own?"

"How could I? My maid refused to accompany me, and the omnibus was so crowded and filthy—"

"You actually boarded an omnibus?" Hart was surprised. He hadn't credited her with the necessary courage.

"I didn't board it exactly."

"Ah."

"But I waited for it and saw the state of it when it arrived. What else could I do but go straight back to Mount Street? It was dreadful. I was obliged to walk the entire way. And in my new green Morocco boots, too! I scuffed the leather. *And* I tore the hem of my new petticoat."

Hart was unmoved by his cousin's sartorial suffering. "Consider it a just punishment for your poor judgment," he said. He hated to think what other harebrained schemes she might be concocting in her impressionable young brain. "I trust your seafaring admirer has since given up on you?"

Mariah flushed. "I told you, he's *not* a sailor. And I won't say another word about him if you insist on making him a figure of fun."

"Has he asked you to meet him somewhere else?"

"Has Lady Anne asked *you* to meet *her*?" Mariah retorted with a flicker of spirit.

Hart's gaze narrowed. "We'll leave Lady Anne well out of this."

"What's that about Lady Anne?" Brookdale asked.

"Lady Anne?" Grandfather echoed. "Is this about her joining us in Hampshire for the holidays?"

Brookdale was aghast. "You've invited her to Sutton Park?"

"Lady Grantley tells me that Lady Anne was seen driving your curricle in the park last week," Aunt Esther volunteered. "I told her it couldn't be so. That my nephew doesn't even allow his groom to drive his horses. But Lady Grantley insisted it was true."

"It *is* true," Mariah said. "Miss Dodson told me the same. She said Lady Anne was driving at breakneck speed and that Hart had his arm around her."

Brookdale's expression turned thunderous. "He *what*?"

Hart stifled a sigh of resignation. Why was it that every family gathering seemed to turn into a referendum on his personal life?

Rising from the sofa, he went to the drinks table and poured himself a large glass of sherry. "I wouldn't believe every piece of tittle-tattle you hear from the society gossips," he said.

"Is there any shred of truth in it?" Grandfather asked.

"Some," Hart acknowledged. "I did let Lady Anne drive my mares."

The room fell quiet. When Hart finally turned around, drink in hand, he was met by the stunned faces of his family.

It was Aunt Esther who finally broke the silence. "Lady Arundell and her daughter have left Grosvenor Square. There was no sign of them at all when I called on the earl and his mother yesterday. He was excessively attentive to Mariah, wasn't he, dear?"

"Yes, Mama," Mariah said. "He said how sorry he was to have missed my debut. But he's promised to host a ball next season and says that I shall choose the day."

Aunt Esther beamed. "Wasn't that civil of him?"

"Vastly civil," Brookdale said. "But what about this business with Felix and that black-clad Deveril woman?"

Grandfather regarded Hart with a thoughtful expression. "What does it all mean, my boy?"

"Only that we've resumed our friendship," Hart said. A foolish smile edged his mouth. He still couldn't quite believe it himself. "I'll be calling on her tomorrow in Ludgate Hill."

And if she wanted to take the reins again, Hart would bloody well let her do it.

Thirty

If you're that worried about his welfare," Mama said, glancing up from the letter she was writing, "you might think of sending him home to Cherry Hill."

Anne stood at the door to the cramped parlor, her hair and gown rumpled. She'd just returned from the small stable behind the house, where she'd spent the past hour in a futile effort to get Saffron settled.

Despite Joshua's desire to keep him, Anne had easily shown that the great golden stallion belonged to her alone. Thanks to her father, she had the papers to prove it. He'd been adamant that Saffron be registered in her name. The bond between horse and rider was sacrosanct, he'd said. Wherever Anne went in life, Saffron must go with her.

Though Papa could never have envisioned that she and Saffron would one day find themselves living in Ludgate Hill.

The stallion had been uncharacteristically ill-tempered since they'd arrived, no doubt owing to the diminished size of his loose box and the constant clamor from the street.

He was unhappy here.

So was Anne at the moment.

"Cherry Hill isn't our home anymore," she reminded her mother.

Mama resumed writing. "No. You're right, of course." Her quill scratched busily over the paper.

"Mama?" Anne prompted in rising irritation.

Her mother looked up again distractedly. "What is it, my girl? Not more complaints about that stallion of yours? I've told you, if you wish to keep him, he'll have to make the best of things here. As will we all."

"For how long?" It was the same question Anne had asked her mother yesterday and the day before.

The house in Ludgate Hill was a fraction of the size of their house in Grosvenor Square. And it wasn't only the lack of space that required acclimating to, it was the drafty fireplaces, the dreary position of the rooms, and the excruciatingly narrow staircases that wound up, up, up to the teetering floors above.

The former tenant had been a merchant. A man possessed of vulgar taste, if the garish fixtures and ill-chosen paper hangings were anything by which to judge.

Mama set down her pen. "Really, Anne," she said in exasperation. "Have you nothing else to do but plague me? My head is starting to ache."

Anne didn't wonder. The past three nights, her mother had resorted to laudanum to ease her into sleep. Anne knew because she'd been the one to administer it. It was either that or leave the bottle in the custody of her mother's maid.

But laudanum was too dangerous for that.

Her mother had never taken an overdose of the stuff, not even at her lowest ebb. But Anne had always feared she might, if only accidentally.

The fear had never entirely left her.

It was why she insisted on managing her mother's medicine herself. Better that than risk losing her mother altogether.

"It isn't me causing your megrim," Anne said. "It's all this din. The noise from the street is unceasing."

"The noise doesn't trouble me."

"That's not what you said when we first called on Mrs. Frazil. You said there was so much activity in Ludgate Hill that a person couldn't hear herself think."

"There are times," Mama declared, "when that's a blessing."

Anne advanced into the room. She hated to add to her mother's worries. But it wasn't only her mother who was affected by coming here. Anne must advocate for her horse, for the servants, *and* for herself.

"Mrs. Griffiths tells me she heard of a house to let in Green Street," Anne said. "Perhaps after we've stayed here a short time, we might remove there?"

"Back to Mayfair? With our tails between our legs? I think not. We neither of us would be happy residing in the shadow of our old life. Not now your cousin has taken charge of it." Mama massaged her temple. "No, no. My decision has been made and I stand by it. I've taken a six-month lease. We'll remain that long to start. It will be good for us. You'll see that once you and your horse have settled in."

Anne couldn't entirely dispute the logic of her mother's decision. It was true, if they'd remained in Mayfair, they would have been marked for their fair share of humiliation. Driven from their home, forced to witness Joshua's ascension to societal power while she and Mama were reduced to living on the fringes. It wouldn't have been comfortable. Indeed, it would have been downright demeaning.

Still, Anne couldn't accept that they must make such a drastic alteration in residence. They might have gone to Bloomsbury, for goodness' sake. Or to Hans Town. Either would have been less jarring than a move to Ludgate Hill.

"And after six months?" she asked.

"I'm contemplating a visit to Greece or Italy," her mother said. "Fielding might be persuaded to accompany us as our escort."

Anne's shoulders drooped. She'd hoped for a different answer. "Mr. Fielding is very obliging."

"He's a good friend to me." Mama picked up her quill. "If that's all?"

It wasn't all, but Anne saw no point in pressing her mother further. Not at this particular moment. "I might take a walk down the hill," she said.

"Go, by all means, but take Jeanette with you." Mama returned to writing her letter. "I won't have you wandering about unescorted."

"Yes, Mama." Departing from the parlor, Anne went upstairs to her bedroom to retrieve her hat and her gloves. "I'm going for a walk," she informed her maid.

Jeanette scurried to retrieve her bonnet. Tugging it on her head, she followed Anne down the stairs, face set in the same mournful lines as when they'd departed Grosvenor Square.

Horbury opened the front door for them, letting in a great rush of noise from the busy road.

As Anne stepped outside, it enveloped her in a mighty embrace. But it wasn't the noise that surrounded her. Indeed, noise was only a by-product of it.

It was energy. A contagious sort of vigor that caught one's spirits up like a tidal wave and buoyed them along on its swell.

Anne had felt it before. It was the very heartbeat of London. A rhythm she'd experienced on previous shopping excursions to the Hill, or when she'd called at the busy offices of the *London Courant* in Fleet Street. It was the energy of any large city, teeming with business and industry. But this time, Anne wasn't merely a visitor passing through on a short errand. This time, she was a part of it.

"It's not safe to walk in this place," Jeanette complained as they ventured along the edge of the road. "You'll get flattened by a carriage."

"On the paving stones? I think not."

Ludgate Hill might be outrageously busy, but it wasn't uncivilized. Indeed, once one grew accustomed to the crowds of pedestrians and the traffic in the street, the arrangement of the shops was really quite convenient.

Anne walked past a clockmaker's, a jeweler, and the painted windows of a tobacconist. It was another overcast day as August came to a close, the sky darkening above with the threat of rain.

The weather had no effect on the activity of the street.

Ladies and gentleman of every description bustled past her. Men of business in three-piece suits, ladies in fashionable dresses, and women and children in humbly woven rags. Fruit sellers bellowed from the sides of their fruit carts, and cabdrivers shouted at vehicles blocking their way.

There was a pastry cook and confectioner's shop situated on the next corner. A sign in the window proclaimed the proprietor as "a purveyor of cakes to Her Majesty." Anne should have walked on, but the smell of baked goods lured her like a siren's song.

Surely a brief look around would do no harm.

She entered the front of the shop. It opened to additional rooms at the back—a soup room and a busy tearoom where several people were seated enjoying refreshment.

An attendant hastened to assist Anne. He directed her to a polished wooden counter that held a selection of tiny cakes, artfully shaped marzipan, and a colorful array of French macarons.

Anne purchased a pink macaron for herself. She all but inhaled it before departing the shop. The sugar sank into her tongue, along with the delicate taste of almonds and rose water. If she hadn't been on a public street, she might have swooned at the unadulterated pleasure of it.

A stationer's shop was next. Filled with paper, leather-bound ledgers, and beautifully tinted note cards, it smelled almost as divine as the pastry shop had. A glass case at the front held quill pens, engraved penknives, and silver seals.

After perusing the wares, Anne selected a packet of wafers, a bottle of blue India ink, and a new silver nib for her pen. The shop's proprietor, a small man with a heavily waxed mustache, boxed and wrapped her purchases for her as carefully as any shopkeeper in Bond Street.

She next passed a straw-hat shop with a smart little hat in the window. It was trimmed with narrow bands of cherry-red silk, and accented by a cluster of red velvet flowers.

Anne had a sudden vision of herself wearing it with a colorful new habit.

Red, Hartford had said. That was the shade he wanted her in.

Anne wasn't yet ready to go as far as a red habit. But the red trimmings on the hat were bright enough in comparison to the unrelieved black of her dress. It seemed a sin to even consider trying it on.

Anne immediately resolved to do just that.

Entering the premises, she was greeted by a young shop assistant with gleaming black hair bound up beneath a ruffled cap. Her accent was edged with a cockney lilt.

"Can I help you, ma'am?"

"That hat in the window," Anne said. "I'd like to try it on."

The shopgirl at once obliged her. Retrieving the hat, she escorted Anne to a low padded stool in front of a small gauze-draped table at the back of the shop. A gilded looking glass stood atop it.

Sitting down, Anne removed her dull black hat. The shopgirl settled the new one in its place, tilting it back in the current style. She artfully arranged the wide cherry-red ribbons in an extravagant bow beneath Anne's chin.

Anne scarcely recognized her reflection. She'd worn black so long, she'd forgotten what it looked like to see herself in color. The red brightened the whole of her countenance, lending a brilliancy to her complexion and a beguiling shine to her eyes. She looked radiant.

"Do you like it, ma'am?"

"Very much so," Anne said. "Is it of your design?"

The shopgirl's golden complexion suffused with a blush. "Oh no," she replied. "This isn't my shop. I'm Mrs. Crackenthorpe's assistant. She's teaching me the trade."

"What do you think, Jeanette?" Anne asked her maid.

"It's very becoming, my lady," Jeanette replied.

The shopgirl's eyes widened at Anne's honorific.

"I shall take it," Anne said.

The shopgirl offered a flustered curtsy. "Yes, my lady."

With the boxed-up hat added to their growing pile of purchases, Anne left the shop to continue down the hill. The city stretched beneath her in all its chaotic splendor, and the dome of St. Paul's rose majestically behind.

A strange kind of elation took over her heart. It was only a hat, but coupled with the effects of the sugar and the energy of the street, the purchase of it felt like an act of pure rebellion.

Good Lord, but she was tired of being confined! She wanted life—*real* life—in all its vividness and clamor. Even if it was unfamiliar at first. Even if it made her feel ignorant and untutored about the greater world around her.

Despite all its sadness and uncertainty, life at the moment seemed very much worth living.

"Lady Anne," a familiar deep voice hailed her from the street.

Anne came to a surprised halt. Her already-quaking heart performed a disconcerting somersault as Hartford pulled his curricle up alongside her. He was dressed in plaid trousers and a dark wool driving coat, his tall beaver hat sitting at a rakish angle.

"What are you doing here?" she asked.

"I'm on my way to call on you," he said. "Or have you already forgotten our conversation in Hyde Park?"

Her cheeks heated. She was conscious of Jeanette's keen attention. "I haven't forgotten."

Behind him, the driver of a wagon shouted for Hartford to stop blocking the road.

Hartford ignored the man. His attention was entirely fixed on Anne. "Would you like to come up?"

Anne didn't hesitate. "Yes, I would, actually."

He offered her his gloved hand and she took it.

Jeanette gaped at the pair of them. "My lady?"

"You may take my purchases back to the house," Anne said as she climbed into the curricle. "Tell my mother I've gone for a drive with Mr. Hartford. I'll return soon."

"Yes, my lady."

Hartford's eyes briefly met Anne's as he started his mares. "I take it you'd rather I not call at the house?"

"Not today." Anne settled herself on the seat beside him. "I'm not ready to go home just yet."

Hart steered his team back into traffic. He'd planned to commence his campaign for Anne's heart with as much respect and formality as he could muster. A call at her house to start, complete with compliments delivered to her mother.

But Anne, it seemed, had other ideas.

Hart didn't mind it. Indeed, all things considered, he preferred being alone with her. And here, at least, in a busy street, far from his regular stomping ground, there was less chance of being hounded by that boy of Royce's who had been plaguing Hart's every footstep.

"Where would you like to go?" he asked.

"Anywhere," she said. "You decide."

"Will Lady Arundell not mind it? Your being out this way unchaperoned?"

For the first time in Hart's memory, Anne didn't bristle at the mention of her mother. Her demeanor was unusually bright—and uncharacteristically unconcerned.

"It's an open carriage," she replied. "My reputation is safe with you."

I'm *safe with you*, she might have said.

Hart's chest expanded on a ridiculous surge of pleasure. "Very well," he said.

With a cluck of encouragement and a tap of the reins, he urged his mares up the hill. Kestrel and Damselfly sprang into a trot, tossing their heads at a cart horse that ventured too close and flattening their ears at an impertinent gelding pulling a hansom. The same qualities that made them fast also made them sensitive to the slightest incursion on their presumed territory.

Above them, the dark clouds in the sky loomed ever closer. The air was thick with the scent of impending rain.

Hart prayed the weather would hold.

"How are you finding life in Ludgate Hill?" he asked as he guided the mares around a slow-moving dray.

"It's certainly different," Anne said.

"Is that bad?"

"Not all of it," she said. "In fact, I'm beginning to see the benefits of living in such a place. But . . ."

"But?"

"The house *is* very cramped. The servants are complaining. Saffron won't settle. And . . ." She hesitated before admitting, "I don't know that the location has been as beneficial to my mother's state of mind as she'd hoped it would be."

"I'm sorry to hear it," he said. "Has she been . . . ?"

Ill? Grieving? Melancholy?

Hart didn't know how to categorize what ailed Anne's mother. In truth, the idea that Lady Arundell wasn't invulnerable was still taking some getting used to.

"She can't sleep," Anne said. "And her familiar spirit has left her."

He failed to contain a chuckle. "As bad as that?"

"It's no laughing matter. Dmitri was a great comfort to her."

He gave her a doubtful glance. "You believe he existed?"

"Of course not," she said. "But the thought of him has got my mother through many a difficult period. He was a kind of confidant. Someone to whom she could unburden herself."

"Has she considered keeping a journal?"

"I don't know. I've never asked her. I daresay I should have done." Anne shook her head as if ridding herself of unwanted thoughts. "I didn't want to talk about any of this. I don't know why I brought it up!"

"Force of habit," he said.

It must be a difficult one for her to break. Since the death of her father, Anne had been consumed by her mother's needs.

Hart wasn't unsympathetic. Not anymore. Not after the way Anne had fallen tearfully into his arms when he'd called on her that day in Grosvenor Square.

They continued up the hill, his mares making slow but steady progress. Hart was conscious of Anne's skirts pooling against his leg, and of her silk-encased arm brushing his as he handled the reins. She didn't flinch from the contact. Quite the reverse. She appeared perfectly at ease beside him.

"How is Eris?" she asked. "Is she acclimating well?"

"She's made herself at home," Hart said. "Both in the house and out of doors." He deftly avoided a pedestrian crossing the busy road. "When she's not shredding my coats or terrorizing my valet, she's taken to visiting my grandfather's garden. The greenhouse holds particular appeal."

"Oh no." Anne gave a rueful laugh. "Lord March must be furious."

Hart smiled, recalling his grandfather's horror at finding the kitten using his flower beds as a privy. "Not to worry. I'm confident Eris will redeem herself. She has a sweetness to her beneath all that bluster."

"She does," Anne agreed. "She vastly improves on acquaintance. If you persevere with her, you'll see I'm right."

"I know you're right," he said. "It's the same thing I told my grandfather. The difficult females are always the ones most worth winning."

Anne gave him an arch look. "And you have a vast experience with difficult females, I suppose?"

"Some," he acknowledged humbly.

"Do they all sweeten to you in the end?"

His mouth hitched. "Ask me again after our drive."

Thirty-One

They'd gone no more than a short distance when the clouds burst and their drive was interrupted by a sudden downpour of rain.

Hart was obliged to improvise.

He took her to St. Paul's. There, he entrusted his horses to a nearby livery stable while he and Anne entered the vast cold interior of the church.

Not the most romantic spot to commence a courtship, but Anne didn't seem to mind it.

Trailing a distance behind a long-winded clergyman who appeared to be leading a tour of his parishioners, she stopped at her leisure to examine the various statues and monuments that lined the church's dignified walls. With her black silk gown and lusterless black hat, she might easily have been mistaken for some poor chap's beautiful young widow.

"I've only been here once before," she confided in a hushed voice. "And not since I was a girl."

"No?" Hart followed her, his hands in his pockets.

Admission to St. Paul's was free, excepting the library, the crypt, and the whispering gallery. As a consequence, between daily services, the church was full of visitors from near and far, admiring the paintings, statuary, and the serene beauty of the dome.

It wasn't privacy exactly, but it was a variety of it. The sort one could find only in a crowded room of tourists, each of whom was engaged in exploring some architectural wonder or other. They scarcely noticed Hart's and Anne's existence.

She glanced back at him. "Does that surprise you?"

"After the length of your residence in London? Yes, it does," he said. "You always seemed to be striding about from one place to the other. Every time I encountered you, you looked as though you were in command of the whole world."

"A tiny world," she said. "It stretched only to the boundaries of Mayfair."

"You ventured further in London on occasion."

"Yes. Visits to my mother's charity school in Wimbledon. Picnics in Richmond Park. Sketching trips to some Roman ruin or other. All of it well chaperoned and surrounded by other fashionable people." She stopped in front of a statue of Sir Joshua Reynolds. "Nothing very daring, was it?"

Hart couldn't account for her strange mood. "Ladies of your position aren't meant to be daring."

"I suppose that's reserved for poor women and ladies who aren't sporting honorifics."

"They have less to lose, certainly."

"They have *everything* to lose. Whereas I—" She paused. "I seem to have taken no risks. Not like Miss Maltravers. Not like Mrs. Blunt."

"Ah," Hart said, coming closer to her. "You're speaking of romantic risks."

"Any risks. Of all my friends, I'm in the best position to make changes to my life. To alter the world around me. And I've done nothing at all. I've been stuck here." A frown etched her brow. "I might as well have been buried alongside my father."

Hart snorted. "What rot."

"Is it? You accused me of much the same on the road to Yorkshire."

"I was talking rubbish," he said. "Trying to get a rise out of you."

It was partially true. His words to her then had been fueled by bitterness as much as by honesty. He'd wanted to wake her up to her situation. To remind her of all that she'd relinquished in order to remain with her mother in a perpetual state of self-imposed mourning.

"It wasn't completely rubbish," she said, walking on.

He followed. "What about doing your duty?"

"I still believe in doing my duty. I always will. But there are times when . . ."

"What?" he prompted softly.

Her bosom swelled on a deep breath. "Sometimes I find myself railing against the lack of power I have in my present situation. I'd like to occasionally make decisions for myself. To choose how and where I stable my horse. To decide where I'll live and how I'll order my day. I want—"

"You want control," he said.

"Yes, I suppose I do." She looked up at him bleakly. "When I learned Joshua was selling off the old horses at Cherry Hill, I offered to buy them. But, as he so kindly pointed out, I have no place to put them. My mother and I haven't room in our own stable, and the expense of stabling them somewhere else in London would be unthinkable at present." She sighed. "In any event, it doesn't matter. I was too late to save the horses. He's already sold them all. Every last one."

"I know he has," Hart said. "I'm the one who bought them."

Anne's eyes flew to his. "*You?*" She came to an abrupt halt. "But . . . why?"

Hart stopped. "Why do you think?"

A flush of color swept up her throat. It was the only sign that his words had flustered her. After a few taut seconds, she resumed walking. Hart kept pace at her side.

"Where are they now?" she asked.

"I've had them sent to Sutton Park," he said. "There's plenty of pasture for retired horses on the estate. And I know how well you trust the wisdom of my grandfather's head groom."

"I don't know what to say."

"Don't say anything," he answered. "I didn't do it to earn your gratitude or to put you under some sort of obligation to me. I did it because . . ."

"What?"

He shrugged. "I wanted to make you happy."

An unreadable emotion passed over her face. "Thank you, Hart. Thank you. I—"

"No need to thank me. I'm sure you'd have done it yourself if it was within your power."

"I wish I could have done," she said. "I wish I had an estate where I could have sent them to live out the rest of their lives in peace. Some property wholly under my command."

"You require a household of your own."

"I do."

"You can easily obtain one," he said. "You need only marry."

She fell silent for a moment. "But that wouldn't be my household, would it? It would be my husband's house. He would have final say in all of my decisions. I would be forced to defer to him."

"Which is why, when you're inclined to take a husband, you should choose a man who won't attempt to dim your light. A man who isn't intimidated by you. One who will let you burn as brightly as you wish."

"Does such a gentleman exist, I wonder?"

"I believe there might be one such man in the world," Hart said gravely. "But only one, I'm afraid."

She gave him a speaking glance. "How convenient."

He smiled at her. "It is, rather."

Anne didn't respond to his flirtation. Instead, warmed by his words as much as she was by his reassuring presence, she walked on through the cathedral.

This was how Hart had won her the last time. Not through flowery compliments or grand romantic gestures, but by talking with her and listening to her. She and Hart had always had an ease about them. An effortless, intimate banter that never failed to make her smile. One minute he was teasing her, and the next he was stealing her heart away as skillfully as a sneak thief.

But no.

He hadn't stolen anything. Her heart was already his. It had been for years. There had never been another.

She came to a halt when she reached the memorial to Admiral Nelson. The marble statue stood on a round pedestal, adorned with reliefs of sea gods and flanked by a large lion.

The sea gods were partially unclothed. Anne's eyes lingered on the carved planes and grooves of the centermost figure's bare chest.

An image of Hartford's chest materialized unbidden in her mind. The way he'd looked, shirtless, on the bed above the tavern in Battersea.

Heat crept into her cheeks at the memory of it.

It had been the first time she'd seen a man's naked chest outside of a museum or the pages of a history book. She'd thought, as she'd cut away his bloody shirt, that nothing could surprise her. But Hartford's chest had put all those Grecians and Romans to shame. It had been lean, muscular, and as well chiseled as any ancient sea god.

"Admiral Nelson's body is down in the crypt," he said, walking up on her left side. "We could view it if you like. It's only sixpence."

Anne willed away her blushes. "It's dark down there. We'd be obliged to take a lantern—*and* a guide."

"You're right," he replied. "Not very conducive to conversation."

"Precisely," Anne said.

It was more agreeable aboveground, even if they had to keep their voices low. Despite the crowds, the shadows of the great church were still vastly more private than it would be if they'd returned to the house to take tea in her mother's small parlor.

Anne realized all at once how much she wanted privacy with him.

Their time together on the road to Yorkshire had spoiled her.

She gazed up at the marble face of Nelson's statue. "Did Mrs. Neale really compare herself to his widow?"

Hart's leg brushed against the swell of her skirts as he came to stand beside her. "She enjoys the melodramatic. Though I suspect there were some aspects of her affair with my father that might contain similarities. He did seem to care for her and their children more than he did for my mother and me. Marcus claims he loved them."

"Do you think it's true?"

"Probably." He considered the subject with a troubled frown. "My father was constrained to marry my mother. She was well-bred, from an excellent family, with the right sort of aristocratic pedigree. It was a match that had been planned from their nurseries. But Mrs. Neale was his own choice. A selfish one, but his all the same. The children he had with her merited his affections."

"He still failed to provide for them in his will."

"I doubt he expected to die. It's one of those things a man's always putting off, isn't it? Amending his will? My father never altered his from the time he married my mother. It's how I inherited Barton Court."

Anne smiled faintly at the mention of Hart's tumbledown ancestral estate in Somersetshire. It was a small property and quite remote. His father had let it fall into neglect during his lifetime. Hart had used to speak of the place with contempt.

"You always said you'd sell it the moment it became yours," Anne reminded him. "I was surprised when you didn't."

"You shouldn't have been. It was meant to be ours."

Her brows lifted. She hadn't known that. Indeed, she'd never even thought of it. Barton Court was leagues away from her mother. Leagues away from anyone they knew. "You were intending to whisk me off to Somersetshire? To keep me all to yourself?"

"That was my nefarious plan, yes. Do you disapprove?"

She didn't answer. Not directly. "You'd have hated living in the country."

"I could have stomached anything if you were with me," he said. "And it wouldn't have been all the year round. We could have come to London during the season or visited Bath. Anywhere you pleased."

"I notice you don't remain there now, not for any amount of time."

"I've no reason to. Not alone." Hart's face was uncharacteristically solemn. "When you broke our engagement, I wanted to sell it. I went there a month later with that very purpose in mind."

"But you didn't."

"I couldn't abandon the place," he said. "Not entirely."

"No more than you could abandon Mrs. Neale and her children," Anne remarked.

Hart wasn't only responsible, it seemed. He was deeply, intrinsically decent. One would never guess it. His roguish manner was as much a mask as his perpetual good humor.

She wondered how deeply his father had hurt him.

How deeply *she* had hurt him.

"Unfortunately not," he said. "It seemed a better plan to repair the place in hopes that eventually the estate would be self-sustaining. As for the Neales . . ." Hart regarded the statue of Admiral Nelson, a pensive look in his eyes. "Someone had to do something for them. It may as well be me."

"What will you do with your brother?"

"Send him away," he said bluntly.

"To Barton Court?"

"Lord no. Marcus is too green to be trusted in England. My grandfather would liken him to one of those plants that take years to mature. One that would do better in a different soil."

"You're not in any danger in the meanwhile, are you?" she asked. "Those villains who accosted you won't be coming back?"

Hartford went quiet. "I don't expect so," he said at length. "They only wanted money. That's all anyone ever seems to want from me these days."

She gave him another weighted glance. "Not everyone, surely."

He smiled at her.

Such a smile!

"Tell me, old thing," he said as they walked on, "is this fulfilling your hopes for a pleasant outing? A stroll among all these cold monuments to moldering saints and dead heroes?"

Anne took his arm. She could have responded with sarcasm or evasion. She could even have remained silent. Instead, she gathered her courage and confessed the simple truth. "I enjoy being with you, Hart."

His expression softened with solemn tenderness. "And I with you. Wherever we are." He covered her hand with his. "But when next I call on you—"

"You intend to call again?"

"That's the idea," he said. And then: "I mean to court you, Anne."

A quiver of feminine alarm went through her. She'd anticipated his aims, but to hear them spoken aloud was quite another matter.

Good gracious.

She'd scarcely acclimated to the idea of resuming their friendship. Of talking with him instead of arguing. Of *flirting* with him.

But courtship wasn't mere flirtation—teasing words or stolen kisses beneath the mistletoe or on moonlit country walks. Courtship was a stepping stone toward marriage. A formal, public declaration of a gentleman's intent.

"You can't be serious," she said.

"I've never been more serious." Hart stared down at her. "Let me court you properly. Let me make my intentions plain. Unless . . ." A glimmer of doubt crossed his face. "Do you object to anything more than a renewal of our friendship?"

Anne's heart thumped hard. She felt rather like a rider on a horse she couldn't control—half-exhilarated and half-terrified to her soul.

But there was no thrill in life without the risk of a little danger.

She'd be a coward to choose safety now. Not if it meant denying herself the one thing she wanted most.

And she'd already denied herself too long.

She was tired of living without him.

"No," she said at last. "I don't object."

Thirty-Two

"I'm sorry Evelyn couldn't come," Stella said, linking her arm through Anne's.

The pair of them strolled at a leisurely pace through the Egyptian Room of the British Museum, the heavy wool skirts of their gray and black day dresses brushing against each other as they walked. Gone were the light cottons, muslins, and summer-weight silks of August. The autumn cold had necessitated a stark change in wardrobe.

Anne's lady's maid, Jeanette, trailed after them, a handkerchief pressed to her nose as if she might catch something from the antiquities.

Up ahead, Anne's mother stood in front of one of the glass-enclosed exhibits, deep in conversation with Mr. Fielding and Mrs. Blakely-Strange.

"Evelyn will join us for luncheon at Mr. Fielding's residence when we return," Anne said. "I'm sure she'll have much to tell us about the progress on her wedding clothes."

"Do you suppose it's unlucky for Mr. Malik to make her bridal gown?" Stella asked.

"Evelyn makes her own luck," Anne said. "So should we all."

Stella smiled. "Is that what you're doing with Mr. Hartford?"

Anne blushed at the very mention of her erstwhile foe.

Over a month had passed since Hartford had taken her to St. Paul's. Since then, he'd been calling on her regularly in Ludgate Hill. Courting her, if it could be called that, though they'd had scarcely any privacy owing to the weather.

Instead, Hartford had taken tea with Anne and her mother on multiple occasions. He'd lent his services in escorting her mother to a spiritualist gathering in Kensington and a dreary lecture on ancient Roman history in Albemarle Street.

And he'd sent flowers.

Bouquets of the most beautiful blooms. Not only roses, but chrysanthemums, out-of-season bluebells and daffodils, and once, even a spray of enormous lilies. Himalayan lilies, he'd told her. The very ones he'd written about in his column.

Mama had taken it all as a courtesy from a family friend. She was that absorbed in the activities of her own life. For as much as Hartford had come calling, so, too, had Evelyn's uncle. Indeed, Mr. Fielding's visits had been more frequent and of far longer duration.

"That's not luck," Anne said. "That's . . . I don't know what to call it. Dogged perseverance, I suppose."

She wished it might be more.

Stella nudged her. "What has he sent you today?"

"A bouquet of violets," Anne said.

"That symbolizes faithfulness."

"Does it?"

"That's what it says in the *Language of Flowers*." Stella had lately been reading the popular publication. It ascribed meaning to every variety of bloom. Gentlemen sometimes used it to send secret messages to the young ladies they favored. "And it's all of a piece with the other bouquets. White roses for hope, bluebells for constancy, and daffodils for unrequited love."

"What does a lily mean?" Anne asked.

"Purity or benevolence, I think." Stella scrunched her nose. "Or perhaps that's the potato?"

Anne huffed a short laugh. "Who on earth would send a lady a potato?"

"Not everyone has a grandfather with a hothouse full of out-of-season flowers," Stella pointed out. She hesitated before asking, "Have you told your mother yet?"

"I'm not hiding anything."

"Yes, but . . . have you talked to her?"

Anne cast a glance back at her mother. "No," she confessed. "Not yet."

She was reluctant to disrupt the fragile equilibrium of their new life. Mama had ceased relying on laudanum to sleep. She was focused again now. Busy and purposeful. It didn't hurt that Mrs. Frazil had been giving Mama positive messages through the planchette.

As for Anne, the energy of life on Ludgate Hill had proven addictive. She'd taken to riding Saffron through the busy streets, or to venturing out on long walks to explore the sights and the shops. Unlike Mrs. Frazil, who preferred to view the masses from a distance, Anne found it thrilling to be a part of the vast throng. It made her problems seem smaller somehow, reminding her that she was but a tiny part of a much wider world.

"What about you?" she asked. "How are matters coming at home?"

"My own luck has been against me," Stella replied morosely. "It's why I've so rarely come to call. My brother is never willing to lend the carriage, and you know how poorly Locket behaves on busy streets. I've been stuck in the house for ages."

"The weather has us all stuck inside," Anne said.

Autumn had set in with a frightening bluster—wind, rain, and darkened skies. It was enough to make anyone miserable, especially if that person preferred the freedom of being out of doors on their horse.

"At least you have the excitement of living in Ludgate Hill," Stella said. "In George's Street, there's nothing happening at all, except for my brother sniping at me from morning 'til night. He's been in high dudgeon ever since he agreed to allow me to come to Lord March's house party."

"Ah yes. The house party." Anne's expression sobered. "I'd almost forgotten."

So had Hartford, she feared. He hadn't mentioned it in ages. Perhaps the bargain they'd made that day in Arlington Street had slipped his mind?

"You *are* still going?" Stella asked.

"Are you?" Anne asked. "Your brother won't change his mind?"

"I fear he might," Stella said. "He only permitted me to join you today because he believes our outing to be of educational value. Sometimes I think he wants to see me unhappy."

"His desires have nothing to do with your happiness." Anne tucked her hand more firmly in Stella's arm as they passed a display of animal mummies. "You're the mistress of your fate."

"I'd like to be," Stella said. And then she shivered.

"Poor dear." Anne squeezed her arm. "Is it that bad?"

"It isn't my brother's foul mood that makes me tremble. It's these gruesome creatures. I know I shall have nightmares for a week." Stella gave an eloquent shudder at one of the cat mummies that stared sightlessly at them from behind the glass. "Would your mother object if we removed ourselves to one of the other exhibits? Something less frightening?"

"I'm sure she'll understand. So long as we take Jeanette with us." Quickly procuring her mother's permission, Anne steered Stella toward the exit. "Shall we have a look at the Grecian sculptures?"

"The drawings," Stella said decisively. Next to riding, sketching was her favorite pastime.

Anne smiled. "As you wish."

The two of them made their way to the King's Gallery, Jeanette trudging sullenly behind. There, they passed a contented half hour admiring the prints and drawings in the museum's latest exhibition. One drawing in particular caught their eye. It was a study of trees by the Flemish painter Van Dyck, made in brown ink softly tinted with watercolor.

Stella stopped to look at the understated piece. "What are your views on this one, Anne?"

Anne came to a halt beside her. "It's rather pretty."

Stella's brow furrowed as she examined it. "It is," she acknowledged. "At the same time, it's rather—"

"It's dull." A gentleman's voice sounded at their backs.

Anne and Stella turned sharply to face the voice's owner standing behind them.

But he wasn't standing.

The dark-haired young man was sitting, and not on one of the benches in the gallery, but in some manner of wheeled chair. He held a sketchbook on his lap.

Stella cheeks flushed pink as she looked at him. "You find Van Dyck's work to be dull?"

"This drawing is," the gentleman answered. There was a wry humor in his face not too dissimilar from that in Hartford's countenance on occasion. A threat of razor sharpness that could cut just as easily as it could amuse.

Anne tugged gently at Stella's arm. It wasn't the thing to converse with a strange man, even about art. Especially if that stranger was clever and handsome. "Come," she said. "Let us away."

Stella held fast, her attention momentarily riveted by the man. "I can think of few artists superior to Van Dyck."

The gentleman seemed equally fascinated by Stella. He stared at her, a hint of color visible high on his cheekbones. Clad in a plain suit and carelessly knotted cravat, he appeared little older than they were themselves, though he carried himself with the confidence of a much older man.

"Turner is superior," he answered without hesitation.

"You can't compare the two," Stella said. "They're nothing alike."

The gentleman gave a short laugh. "Thank God for that."

Stella's blush darkened. She despised being made a figure of fun. "You're young," she said, goaded to a rare display of incivility. "I daresay you haven't yet learned to appreciate the works of the Flemish masters."

"*You're* young," the gentleman replied, seemingly without malice. "And yet your hair is gray."

Stella's jaw dropped. "I *beg* your pardon?"

"That's quite enough," Anne said at the same time. She stepped in front of Stella, her spine stiff and her tones as frosty as any she'd ever employed with a stranger. "Really, sir. Do you suppose a discussion about art is an invitation to make personal remarks?"

"I meant no offense," he said. "I approve of contrasts. Shades of gray in particular." He addressed Stella: "You should see Whistler's new piece at the Berners Street Gallery."

"We shall do nothing of the sort," Anne informed him. She again tugged at Stella's arm.

This time Stella complied. "Oh, how could he?" she whispered as they hurried away. "To mention my hair! It was too cruel."

"Ignore him," Anne said. "A stranger's sentiments are of no consequence to us."

"He seemed to know a great deal."

"Because he volunteered his opinions about art? Men are always opining on subjects they know nothing about. It doesn't make them experts."

"But he was an artist himself," Stella said.

"A very brazen one." Anne steered her friend back toward the Egyptian Room. "I'm amazed you indulged his impudence as long as you did."

"So am I," Stella said. "But he looked at me so strangely. I suppose I was intrigued." Her face turned thoughtful. "What kind of painting do you imagine we'd find at that gallery he mentioned?"

Anne huffed. "One by Mr. Whistler, apparently. Whoever *that* is."

The French walnut mantel clock in the small parlor of the house on Ludgate Hill struck three o'clock. It was the signal that Hart must go. A formal call didn't last above twenty minutes.

And his calls on Anne were nothing if not formal.

Outside, the weather had worsened. Rain streamed down the damask-draped windows in an endless drizzle, the clap of distant thunder shaking the glass.

Hart returned his empty teacup to the inlaid wooden tray. In the past month, he'd drunk enough black tea to float a British warship. Such was the price of courting Anne in this tediously respectable manner.

It was his own fault.

He was the one who had resolved on conducting himself as formally as possible.

He'd decided from the beginning that there would be no more blurring the lines between friendship and courtship. No more doubt about what he wanted from Anne or what he was offering her in return. He'd resolved that, this time, he was going to do things right.

His visits had been so regular—so steady and dependable—that even his St. Giles's shadow had caught on. Hart had spotted the scrawny lad several times, lurking in the Hill, during his calls on Anne. It had done nothing to improve Hart's mood.

"Shall I freshen your cup?" Lady Arundell briefly paused her monologue on the history of Roman temples in England to reach for the silver teapot. She was seated across from him on the velvet sofa, her wide black skirts spilling around her in a relentless sea of black crepe. "You'll want to hear about the London temple to Diana before you go."

"Mama," Anne said from her place beside her mother. "Would you mind very much if I took Hartford out to the stable?"

Hart was instantly alert. Anne hadn't said above ten words since he'd arrived. Her mother had dominated the entire conversation, just as she did during all of his visits.

"In all this damp?" Lady Arundell asked. "Whatever for?"

"I want him to have a look at Saffron's foreleg." Anne stood abruptly, meeting his eyes. "I'd value your opinion."

"Of course." Hart rose to follow her from the room, only pausing once to bow to Lady Arundell.

Anne kept a brisk pace, not even stopping to collect a bonnet or shawl before ducking out the back of the house. She crossed the muddy patch of garden to the gate that led to the house's small stable.

Hart strode to keep pace with her through the driving storm. By the time they reached the dry interior of the stables, he was wet with rain.

So was Anne.

Raindrops clung to her face and hair and dampened the fabric of her plain black dress.

She gave a breathless laugh as she came to a halt in front of Saffron's loose box. "I was afraid she'd stop us."

"No chance of that." Hart shrugged off his wool coat. "Here." He draped it across her shoulders, drawing it snugly over her chest. His fingers lingered there. "You'll catch your death."

Her cheeks went pink, whether from exertion or from blushes, he couldn't tell.

"Thank you," she said.

He gazed down at her for a long moment, his fingers still curled in the lapels of his coat.

There was no one else about. No sign of any grooms, stable lads, or the coachman. There was only the two of them.

So Hart did what he'd been wanting to do ever since the last time he'd done it so many months ago in Yorkshire. He brought his head down to hers and kissed her.

Thirty-Three

Hart felt Anne's breath catch in her throat. But she didn't recoil from him. She leaned into his touch, her lips yielding to his with infinite sweetness.

She tasted of rain and strong English tea. Of everything he wanted in life and could never get enough of.

His fingers tightened, holding her captive in the folds of his coat. But Anne was no one's prisoner. She kissed him back in equal measure, stretching up to meet the searching heat of his mouth with warm, half-parted lips.

Hart's blood caught fire. His voice was a husky rasp. "Anne. Sweetheart, I—"

Saffron chose that moment to swing his large golden head over the door of the loose box. He bumped Anne's cheek with his bristly nose, giving her a soft snuffle of welcome.

Hart dropped his hands from his coat, freeing Anne so she could turn to greet her horse. "A timely interruption by your chaperone," he said.

Anne laughed as she reached up to stroke the stallion's forelock. Her face was awash with color.

Hart desperately wanted to kiss her again.

Who was he fooling? He wanted to lock himself in a room with her for a month.

His mouth curved in a reluctant half smile. "Is something really wrong with his foreleg?"

Anne patted the stallion's golden neck. "No, indeed." She flashed Hart a rueful look. "Do you think me a dreadful liar?"

"What I think," he said, coming closer, "is that if I had to listen to one more word about the dubious merits of ancient Roman temples in London, I'd have been forced to do something drastic."

"Such as?"

He stroked Saffron's shoulder. "I might have been provoked into reminding your mother that I'm courting her daughter, not sitting for a lecture on spiritualism."

Anne's gaze slipped from his, but not before Hart detected a glimmer of guilt in her eyes.

It confirmed something that he'd only suspected up to now. "You haven't told her, have you?"

"That you're courting me?" Anne was suddenly very focused on untangling a knot in Saffron's flaxen mane. "It's obvious, surely."

"Do you know," he said, "I'm not so certain it is. Not to your mother."

From his first visit, Hart had marked Lady Arundell's strange lack of interest in his intentions toward her daughter. She'd voiced no thoughts at all on the subject. Instead, she'd talked of spiritualism, history, and the latest articles published in her favorite journals.

There had been no time to discuss anything else. Not during visits of such short duration.

In the beginning, Hart hadn't pressed the matter. His truce with Anne had still been too fresh. Too fragile. But a month had passed. More than a month if he counted their trip to St. Paul's. Had Anne told no one at all?

It wasn't a necessity, no more than it was that he should ask her mother's permission. A suitor didn't typically approach a young lady's parents until he was prepared to make her an offer of marriage. Nevertheless . . .

Hart felt a distinct flicker of uneasiness.

Was Anne still in doubt of him?

"Would you like me to speak with her?" he asked.

Her eyes met his with swift alarm. "Heavens, no. It must come from me."

Hart chose his next words with extraordinary care. He had no desire to provoke a quarrel. "Anne—"

"I can see what you're thinking," she said before he could begin. "You're thinking I've kept it from her for some ominous reason."

"Have you?"

"No. It's plain to anyone what you're about in calling here so often."

"But not to her, apparently."

"I suppose she doesn't want to see it. And . . ." Anne's brows notched in a frown. "The truth is, I've been reluctant to make her. Things have been going so well lately. She's more herself again."

"Have you told anyone?" he asked.

"I've mentioned it to Miss Hobhouse. And I do mean to tell my other friends eventually. As for the rest of society . . ." She gave him a wry look. "Pity the season is over. One or two waltzes at a ball and a few outings in the park and all of Mayfair would know you had designs on me."

He smiled. "All of Mayfair already knows. They knew it the moment I let you drive my curricle."

Anne smiled at him in return. And then she laughed. "Goodness. I daresay you're right."

Hart stared at her, transfixed. She was so bright and beautiful. So rain-rumpled and completely at her ease. If she hadn't already captured his heart forever, he'd have lost it then as surely as he was breathing.

He touched her cheek. "I don't care about them. I care about *us.* I don't want us to make the same mistakes we did before."

Then, they'd kept their feelings a secret, except from each other. They had waited to tell their friends and their families. It had made it all the easier to break their engagement.

"Do you think we would have reconciled?" she asked. "If our attachment had been made public, I mean?"

"We might have felt duty bound to try," he said. "Though I doubt I could have persuaded you to forgive me at the time. I was so grievously in the wrong."

"We both were. But we're older now, and wiser, I hope. We won't be so silly this time." She curled her fingers around his, holding his hand softly against the curve of her cheek. "I'll talk to my mother."

Anne remained with Hartford in the stable only a few minutes longer before he insisted on escorting her back to the house.

He was determined to play the gentleman.

Anne allowed it, just as she had for the past month, though it meant he'd been as formal as a stranger to her.

But there had been nothing formal about that kiss.

His mouth had captured hers with the same searing intensity of the kiss they had shared in Yorkshire. But this time . . .

This time, Anne had been an active participant. She'd kissed *him* as eagerly as he'd kissed *her*. It was an extraordinarily powerful thing to kiss a gentleman. To feel his breath catch and his large frame quake with longing.

She'd realized in that moment that kisses were more than pleasurable. They were revealing. No one looking at Hartford would know how much he wanted her, but a few moments of their lips clinging together, of their breath mingling and their pulses pounding in delirious harmony, and Anne was in no doubt.

Her blood was still fizzing merrily on account of it as she walked him to the door. He was still in his shirtsleeves, his coat draped possessively around her shoulders.

Mama was in the vestibule when they entered, preparing to leave for a visit with Mrs. Frazil. Her mouth flattened into a disapproving line at the sight of them.

Anne hastily slipped out of Hartford's coat and handed it back to him. "I'm obliged to you for the protection against the rain."

"Not at all." He shrugged his coat on with seeming unconcern. "I shouldn't like you to catch a chill."

"You're very considerate, sir," Mama said. "I trust you'll come again when the weather improves?"

"You may depend on it." Hartford bowed to her. "Good day, ma'am." And then, taking Anne's hand in his, he pressed a kiss to it. "Good day, Lady Anne."

Heat crept into Anne's face. No one kissed hands any longer. It was an exceedingly old-fashioned gesture. One to which Hartford lent unmistakable meaning.

Mama stared after him in amazement as he took his leave. When Horbury closed the door, she turned on Anne. "I thought you couldn't stand the man's company?"

"I couldn't," Anne said.

"Yet you were eager enough to whisk him away to the stables. And to wear his coat, apparently. Hadn't you a shawl at hand? Or a proper bonnet? To allow such liberties with a gentleman you profess to dislike—"

"I don't dislike him."

"That's not the impression you gave during our journey north."

"I suppose I've changed my mind," Anne said. "A woman can."

"*Anne*." Mama's voice contained an unmistakable reprimand. "What in heaven is going on between the pair of you?"

"Nothing. He's my friend, that's all."

"The way he looked at you . . ." Mama's brow creased. "I never noticed it before, but—"

"Mama, really," Anne said. "Must we discuss this in the hall where any of the servants might hear?"

Her mother was belatedly recalled to a sense of propriety. "No, indeed. We shall discuss it this evening."

It was as good as a threat.

In all the chaos of the afternoon, Anne hoped her mother might forget. Mama had her visit with Mrs. Frazil, and later, a small dinner party with Mr. Fielding, Mrs. Blakely-Strange, and some other of her friends from the spiritualist society.

But that night, when she and Anne were once more on their own together, alone in the parlor after their dinner guests had gone home, Mama again broached the subject.

"Has Hartford made overtures to you?" she asked the minute the servants had withdrawn.

Anne nearly dropped her teacup. "Overtures? Of a romantic nature, do you mean?"

"What other kind are there?" Mama finished pouring out her own cup of tea. "I daresay it's my fault for accepting his escort to Yorkshire, and for encouraging you to dine with him at that wretched inn."

"That hadn't anything to do with it."

"Then what, pray? He came to the house in Grosvenor Square twice in as many days before we left. I did wonder at his motivation. It's been a long while since our families were on terms of intimacy. And all of his visits this autumn—equally obliging, but I've never known him to be so attentive to an old friend of his mother's."

Anne saw no point in dissembling. "He's been coming to see me, Mama," she said. "He cares for me."

"*Hartford?* The same boy who used to pull your plaits?"

"He isn't a boy anymore. He's a grown man."

"I can see *that.*" Mama sounded vaguely put out by the fact. "I suppose he's considered handsome. A Corinthian of a sort. Sporting-like and all of that. Is that why you fancy him? Because he can drive a gig with a bit of flair?"

"It doesn't hurt," Anne said frankly.

Mama sat back in her chair. "How long has it been going on? This . . . this flirtation?"

"It's not a flirtation. It's not anything yet. But . . ." Anne set down her cup, afraid she might inadvertently spill her tea. "There *was* something between us once. The two of us were very fond of each other before Papa died. Had things been different, I . . . I might have married him."

Mama inhaled a deep breath. "Upon my word. I never dreamt—"

"No one did. We only admitted our feelings to each other in the days before Papa passed away. And then, after he was gone, everything was turned on its head. Hartford went away with his grandfather and I stayed in London with you to mourn."

"And when he returned?"

Anne had no intention of going into any detail. Some hurts were too private to share. "We had a terrible falling-out. It's taken a long while to repair the breach."

"But you have, it seems."

"We're making an effort," Anne said. "He's invited us to Sutton Park for Lord March's house party in December."

"A house party at Sutton Park?"

"I'd like us to go, Mama. And I'd like to bring Miss Hobhouse along with me for company. I trust you won't object?"

"How can I do so, if he's courting you? That *is* what he has in mind, I assume." Mama rubbed a hand over her brow as though staving off another headache. "This is my fault. I threw the two of you together. I forced you into his company over and over again. I thought he was as a brother to you."

"Do you disapprove of him greatly?" Anne asked.

"I don't know what I think of him." Mama paused, seeming to recall something. "Your father did say once that he thought Hartford's quizzing was good for you. You had a tendency to be too serious as a girl. Arundell often remarked on it. I suppose he knew even then. He had a way of knowing these things."

A pang of acute loss constricted Anne's chest. "Papa was very perceptive."

Her mother's eyes glistened. "I wish I might consult with him on this matter. Or Dmitri, if he would ever deign to return. I don't know why he's abandoned me now when I need him most."

"Maybe you *don't* need him anymore," Anne suggested. "Maybe that's why he's gone."

"Nonsense. You've seen for yourself. I've been at my wit's end ever since that odious cousin of yours first threatened to come to London."

"You haven't," Anne said. "You rallied marvelously. You found another house for us. You removed us from Grosvenor Square with remarkable efficiency. And you never once permitted Joshua or his mother to put you out of countenance. Not publicly, anyway. You've been terribly strong."

Mama's bosom heaved on a sigh. "A woman grows tired of being strong. Sometimes she requires a man to lean on." She moved to rise. "I believe I'll retire early this evening. The day has left me unusually fatigued."

Anne stood. "Shall I come up to assist you?"

"No, no, my dear," Mama said. "I won't be requiring my laudanum tonight. I must have a clear head. I need to think."

Thirty-Four

"What do you mean Webb won't suit?" Hart's voice rose with increasing anger. "He's the best man we have in England!"

Hart sat, along with Parfit, Acker, and Goodbody, at a table in the back room of the Bull and Gate, an unassuming tavern in the center of town. They'd had a meeting scheduled at the crucible factory this morning, but none of them had been inclined to cross the river during the storm. The tavern had been a compromise. It was, in a manner of speaking, neutral ground.

It was also the establishment where William Webb was lodging after having arrived in London yesterday evening. He awaited them in the taproom, eager to formalize plans for his departure to Inverness next month.

Hart had no intention of disappointing the man's expectations.

"We already decided he was the right man for the job," Hart said. "He's traveled here on the strength of our promise to him. If we go back on our word—"

"We're not going back on our word." Parfit sat across the table, bundled up in a heavy overcoat and muffler. He balanced an ebonized cane in one gloved hand. "All we've said is that we won't have him as the first point of contact in Scotland."

Acker nodded his agreement. Like Parfit, he was girded against the storm in several layers of thick wool. "Only consider," he said. "Is he really the face we want on our new mining operation?"

Hart stared at Acker in disbelief. "You object to his face?"

"No, no," Goodbody interjected quickly. "Though you must agree that sending him on his own to haggle with Highlanders might reflect poorly on us."

"Because of his parentage," Hartford said. It wasn't a question.

Goodbody went ruddy with embarrassment. He'd been late to their meeting. His bald head was still gleaming with droplets of rain. "We all like Mr. Webb. He's an invaluable asset. But he's no businessman."

"He has no education," Acker said.

"What has that to do with competence?" Hart asked. "Webb may not have been formally educated, but he's more than made up for it with intellect and determination. If our Cumberland mines have prospered at all, it's owing to him."

"He must go, naturally," Parfit said. "Once he's settled, we have confidence he'll be fit to manage the business. But it's unthinkable for him to go alone at the start. Who would take him seriously?"

"We've discussed it among ourselves," Acker said, "and we've all agreed that you must accompany him."

"*I?*" Hart was tempted to laugh. "We're back to that again? I've already told you, I've no intention of leaving England."

"You won't have to remain in Scotland," Goodbody clarified. "We only ask that you stay long enough to see Webb established, and to secure any mining rights."

"A reasonable compromise, you must agree," Acker said. "Your presence will lend weight to Mr. Webb's position."

"You needn't stay above a month," Goodbody added.

Hart slowly shook his head, even as he privately acknowledged that they had backed him into a corner. He was now in the unenviable position of having to choose between his own selfish comfort and the future of both William Webb and the crucible company.

A compromise, indeed.

It was nothing of the sort.

"You'd be back by Christmas," Acker said.

Parfit smiled complacently. "And after all of the restrictions you've placed on the company's expansion, it really is the least you can do to accommodate our interests."

A quarter of an hour later, Hart related the bleak news to William Webb over a pint of ale at a small table in the corner of the smoke-filled taproom.

Webb didn't appear surprised. "I did wonder, sir. Me going up there alone. The locals won't know me from Adam. It'd be easier to throw my weight around with one of you behind me."

Hart frowned. "Then you're in favor of the idea?"

"If it wouldn't put you out too grievously, sir. It would be a good start for me. A stamp of approval, like."

Hart couldn't conceal his disappointment. Removing to Scotland for a month meant leaving Anne in the middle of their courtship. Abandoning her when she needed him most.

An unsettling proposition.

It was eerily similar to what had happened nearly seven years ago. Then, he'd left England for India, certain that he held Anne's heart. On returning, nothing had been the same.

"I'd rather hoped you'd be too offended to accept," Hart said.

Webb's mouth tilted in a prosaic smile. "If I took offense at every slight thrown my way, I'd not last long in this business. Best not to take these things to heart, I've found. It's the work that's important. Do well enough, and you earn men's respect in time."

"You're confident you can so far from home?"

"Oh, aye," Webb said. "Got a knack for it, if you don't mind me saying so."

"Why not? It's the truth." Hart took a long drink of his ale. When he'd finished, he set down his mug. "Once you're settled in Scotland, perhaps you might consider taking on an apprentice."

"I might. Do you have someone in mind, sir?"

"As a matter of fact," Hart said, "I do."

Grandfather issued a brief introduction as Hart entered the library. "Hartford, this is Mr. Archer of Hayes's Perfumes. Archer, my grandson."

Mr. Archer stood. A strapping gentleman with dark hair, clothed in a gray sack coat and trousers, he looked more like a sportsman than a perfumer. "Mr. Hartford. A pleasure."

Hart crossed the room, Eris trotting at his heels as faithfully as a spaniel. The temperamental black kitten was larger now than when she'd arrived, but not by much.

"Mr. Archer." Hart shook his hand, smiling. "Have we you to thank for Hayes's Lavender Water?" The popular eau de toilette had once been in all the shops.

"That was my wife's family," Mr. Archer said. "The business has expanded since then, I'm pleased to say. We're no longer confined to lavender products."

"It's why Mr. Archer has returned to England. He's interested in my new tea roses. The ones that received such acclaim last season." Grandfather motioned to a chair. "Sit down, my boy. Join us."

Hart hadn't a great deal of time. He'd only just returned from his meeting at the public house. He still had to wash and change before driving to Ludgate Hill to call on Anne.

He didn't know how he was going to break the news to her.

Good Lord, he hadn't even told her yet how he made his money.

As far as Anne was aware, Hart supported himself on the remnants of his inheritance, the profits from his small estate, and through whatever he made on the patents he'd invested in.

He'd never mentioned anything to her about being in trade. As confessions went, it was on par with being a criminal. At least, as far as most people in fashionable society were concerned.

Hart felt a leaden weight in his stomach at the prospect of admitting it to her. Not because he was ashamed of his work, but because he'd grown accustomed to keeping it separate. Just as he kept the Neale family separate. Just as he kept his duty to the earldom. It was how he maintained control of it all.

But there was no more holding the disparate parts of his life at arm's length. In the past months, they'd been intermingling with alarming regularity. The crucible company, Marcus, Anne, Brookdale, Mrs. Neale, and Grandfather. Not to mention Hart's St. Giles's shadow. The boy hadn't been appearing with frequency of late, no doubt owing to the weather, but Hart had still seen him skulking about on occasion, eager for a glimpse of something he could report to Gabriel Royce.

That the whole of it hadn't yet blown up in Hart's face was a minor miracle.

"Mr. Archer will be joining us at Sutton Park in December, along with his wife and brother-in-law," Grandfather said as Hart sat down. "The three of them have come to town early."

Archer resumed his seat. "We have friends in Half Moon Street," he explained. "We're staying with them until it's time to depart for Hampshire."

Eris sidled around the legs of the chairs, first rubbing on Hart's trouser leg and then on Archer's.

"Forgive my cat," Hart said. "She's a creature of many moods."

"Not at all." Archer reached to briefly scratch Eris's head.

Hart opened his mouth to warn him, but there was no need. Eris permitted Archer's touch, appearing to give the gentleman her tacit stamp of approval.

Archer smiled. "My family keeps a cat. I find them to be discerning characters."

"That they are," Hart said. "You spend most of the year in Grasse, I understand."

"We do," Archer replied. "Though my brother-in-law has lately expressed a desire to return to England. He's something of an artist."

"Oh?" Hart feigned interest as the discussion shifted from the London art world back to roses. He listened for the next quarter of an hour as his grandfather and Mr. Archer discussed the suitability of Grandfather's new tea rose for rose water and perfume.

Hart was just preparing to make his excuses when his grandfather's butler appeared at the door of the library.

"I beg your pardon, Mr. Hartford. There's a lady to see you."

Anne.

Hart was at once on his feet.

"I've put her in the blue salon," the butler said.

"Forgive me." Hart inclined his head to his grandfather and Mr. Archer before exiting the room, Eris fast at his heels.

He strode down the hall to the blue salon, thus named for its blue-silk-papered walls and blue-damask-upholstered furnishings. But when he entered, it wasn't Anne who was awaiting him.

It was her mother.

Hart stopped short. "Lady Arundell." He bowed. "This is unexpected."

Lady Arundell stood in front of the settee, as grand as Queen Victoria and equally as humorless. She wore her usual uniform of black crepe. Her silver lorgnette was clutched in one hand.

"I should think it the very opposite," she said frostily.

"Ma'am?"

Raising her lorgnette to her eyes, she perused the length of his person through the glass. Whatever she saw seemed to disappoint her. When she lowered the lorgnette, her lips were compressed in a frown.

"You're a deeper one than I gave you credit for, Hartford."

Eris chose that moment to leap from the floor directly onto Hart's shoulder. It was a trick she'd mastered during the past months and one she now offered without express invitation. Hart automatically removed her, conscious all the while of Lady Arundell's appalled stare.

"Not excessively deep, I assure you," he said, depositing Eris in a chair.

"So you claim," she replied. "A convenient facade, this devil-may-care, merry-hearted man-about-town. But you've been playing the long game, it seems." Her eyes bored into his in unmistakable challenge. "Are you or are you not courting my daughter?"

Hart suppressed the sudden urge to grin.

Good Lord. Anne had actually told her!

"Well?" Lady Arundell demanded.

"I am, my lady," he said.

She glared at him for a long moment. "I must tell you, sir, that I find this an extraordinary impertinence. That you should be paying your addresses to my daughter without so much as a word to me on the subject. Did it never occur to you to ask my permission?"

"It did occur to me," he said. "But I saw no reason to speak to you explicitly when my intentions were so abundantly plain."

Her ladyship was having none of it. "And is it true that you courted her in a similarly secret fashion before my husband died?"

Anne *had* been talking, it seemed.

Hart was glad of it. More than glad. It meant she was serious about him. Serious enough to risk discomposing her mother.

"It wasn't a secret," he said. "I intended to ask Lord Arundell's permission before he died. Regrettably, his death prevented—"

"You might have asked *mine*," Lady Arundell said. "The very fact that you didn't speaks volumes about your character."

"That was years ago, ma'am."

"A long game, as I said."

His jaw hardened at the blatant accusation in her tone. As though he'd been messing about with her daughter's affections. As though his heart hadn't been breaking for Anne every day since they'd parted all those years ago in Grosvenor Square.

"It's not a game to me," he said stiffly.

"I trust it isn't, sir. I'll not see my daughter trifled with." Lady Arundell stepped closer, standing tall, as formidable as any outraged father. "Know this. My husband may be gone, but my daughter is still under *my* protection. You'll not find me inadequate to the task."

"My intentions are honorable, my lady. They've never been anything less where your daughter is concerned. And may I tell you—" He stopped himself before he said too much.

"What do you wish to say?" Lady Arundell asked. "Some accusation about my conduct as a parent, I don't doubt. You would accuse me of being overprotective. Of guarding my daughter too closely, perhaps, and thereby preventing your aims."

Hart had resolved not to address Anne's mother in anger, no matter the provocation. But he could hold his tongue no longer. "You haven't protected her *or* guarded her. Not as well as she deserved. You've been too absorbed in your own concerns. Anne has suffered as a result."

Lady Arundell paled. "How dare you?"

"I dare because I care for her. I've seen her diminished by her devotion to you. A devotion that appears to me to run in only one direction."

"You know nothing of my devotion to my daughter."

Hart made an effort to rein in his temper. "No," he said. "Forgive me. You're right, of course. All I know is that I wish to make her happy again. I should like to have your permission to try."

"Happy *again*?" she repeated. "You imply she isn't happy now?"

Hart didn't answer.

Lady Arundell's countenance was taut with offended dignity. "Very well. You may court her if she's amenable. I'll not stand in your way. I'll even permit her to attend this house party at Sutton Park in December, with my chaperonage. But make no mistake, sir, the man who wins my daughter's hand will be something more than a handsome whip."

A handsome whip?

Hart had been called worse.

It was no less insulting.

"I'm confident I have more to recommend me than my ability to drive a curricle, madam," he said. "*Or* my handsomeness, such that it is."

She snorted. "Oh? And what have you done to show yourself serious? What plans have you made? What diversions have you sacrificed? You have a modest estate in Somersetshire, but you keep no house in town. You live with Lord March in the same careless manner as when your parents died, God rest their souls. They raised you to know your duty, but since the loss of them, you've existed only for your own pleasure."

Hart had heard such charges before, from his uncle Brookdale primarily, and even from Anne herself. But to hear them from Lady Arundell—the very person Hart blamed for separating him from the woman he loved—struck a very different chord.

"With respect," he said, "you don't know anything about my responsibilities."

"No more than you know of my parenting," she retorted. "But we will say no more on the subject at present." She tucked her lorgnette into her sleeve. "I've no intention of falling out with you, Hartford."

He stood, his spine rigid, as she moved to leave. "Nor I with you, my lady."

"Then we are agreed. I shall permit your attentions to my daughter, and you . . ." Lady Arundell fixed him with a haughty stare. "You shall endeavor to deserve her."

Thirty-Five

"You've resigned your column in the *Weekly Heliosphere*!" Anne said the instant Hartford gave his mares the office to start.

The sun was peeping out from behind the clouds, and the relentless October rain had ceased, if only for an hour or two. It was enough time for a short drive up the hill.

Hartford had collected her at half past one. Anne had no sooner climbed into his curricle than she taxed him with what she'd discovered on opening her copy of the *Weekly Heliosphere* at breakfast that morning.

Mr. Bilgewater's column had contained no literary review this week, only a mocking farewell.

> *To my esteemed readers: I bid you adieu and good fortune on your literary travels. Alas, I can no longer vouchsafe my services as your guide. The siren song of connubial bliss compels me to give up my weekly column and turn my attention to pursuits matrimonial. As Goethe once wrote in* The Sorrows of Young Werther*: the heart alone makes our happiness. It is to matters of the heart which I now turn my attention.*

"I've given up all of my columns," Hartford said, looking straight ahead as he drove.

"*All?*" Anne's brows lifted in astonishment. "But why?"

He cast her a significant glance. "I'd have thought that was obvious."

It wasn't. Not to her. His mocking words about "pursuits matrimonial" and "matters of the heart" had been so much ridiculous fluff. He was nowhere near ready to propose to her.

And she was nowhere near ready to accept him.

"I'm sure it amused you to no end to write what you did," she said. "That doesn't mean I believe it. There must be some better reason for giving them up."

"Better than you?"

"No." She shook her head. "I won't take responsibility for this. I never asked you to sacrifice your pleasure on my account."

"It was no great pleasure," he said. "It was humorous, that's all. But I haven't the time for it any longer, no more than I do for curricle racing or placing ill-conceived wagers on balloon ascents. The truth is, except for as a means of courting you, writing those columns has long ceased to be anything other than a nuisance to me."

Anne went quiet.

Hartford had been behaving strangely ever since her mother had called on him in Arlington Street. Anne had only learned of the visit after the fact. She'd elected to remain at home when Mama had left to meet Mr. Fielding for a spiritualist lecture at Lady Younger's house in Mayfair. While in the vicinity, Mama had taken the liberty of dropping in on Hartford. She'd made no secret of the visit. Indeed, she'd confessed it to Anne the moment she'd returned to Ludgate Hill.

In the aftermath, both Mama and Hartford had been behaving with excruciating formality, not only to each other but to Anne as well.

Anne didn't care for it one bit.

"Is it something my mother said when she called on you last week?" she asked. "I know she must have been stern with you."

"How is your mother?" Hartford inquired with exacting civility.

"Improved. Ludgate Hill seems to suit her after all." Anne refused to be diverted. "I hope you know that I would never expect you to give up—"

"What *do* you expect from me, Anne?" he asked abruptly.

She blinked. "What do you mean?"

"It seems you require nothing very much. No proofs that I've changed. No assurances of my affections. You've asked all of two things of me since you crossed the threshold of my grandfather's house this summer." He enumerated them as he navigated his team up the hill. "You asked me to write something about Blunt's estate in Yorkshire in my column in the *Spiritualist Herald*, and you asked me to take charge of your kitten."

"I needed nothing else."

"Do you need me? I wonder. Do I have anything at all to offer you?"

"What an odd thing to say." She regarded him with a frown from beneath the wide brim of her black-ribboned hat. "Are you trying to provoke a quarrel?"

"I'm trying to determine where I stand with you."

"You're courting me, aren't you?"

"Yes," he said. "But what about the future?"

A hackney cab cut in front of them, causing Hartford to bring his horses up short. It was another busy day on the hill. The triple row of vehicles climbing toward St. Paul's was packed with donkey carts, advertising vans, and every imaginable specimen of hired vehicle and private carriage.

"If you're at all serious about the future," Anne said dryly, "you might have tried quoting from another of Goethe's novels. One that isn't about the miseries of unrequited love."

"Perhaps I can relate to that misery."

"You do realize that Werther dies in the end?" she said. "Anyway, you never claimed to love me."

"*You* never claimed to love *me*," he retorted. "Not until the day I was lying half-dead in Battersea. And only then, after the fact."

"You expected me to tell you at the time? I was sixteen. By the time I knew my own heart, you were halfway up a mountain, cataloging lilies in the Himalayas. And when you returned—" She stared at him in sudden realization. "Good heavens, you *do* want to provoke a quarrel!"

His large hands tightened reflexively on the reins. Kestrel and Damselfly shook their heads at the unwelcome restraint. Hartford immediately loosened his grip.

"What I want," he said, "is to know that if I go away for a time, the same thing won't happen to us that happened before." A muscle clenched in his cheek. "I can't lose you again."

Anne's expression softened. She understood all at once what the source of the problem must be. Her mother's visit had made him uncertain of himself—*and* of Anne's feelings. This vexing formality was his effort at proving himself worthy of her. Of showing both her and her mother that he was a sober and serious-minded individual.

He was in desperate need of reassurance.

"Don't be an idiot," she said.

"I mean it," he replied. "I've waited for you for too long. If I lost you now, I'd—"

"You're not going to lose me," she said. "Not unless you do something unforgivably stupid." She turned her face back to the busy road. "As for the future . . . if you wish to know what it holds, you must consult Mrs. Frazil or Mrs. Blakely-Strange. For myself, I can make no promises."

"Of course you can't," he replied unhappily.

"No more than you can," she retorted.

Hartford flashed her a solemn look. "I would promise you the world if I could."

Anne's pulse fluttered. She could deal with a teasing Hartford. A serious Hartford was more difficult to handle, especially when he was plying her with heart-quaking compliments.

She wanted him too much, that was the problem. She wanted his sweet words, his heated glances, his kisses. And it wasn't only when she was in his company. She found herself longing for him when they were apart, as well. It made every moment they were together fraught with an underlying tension, as potent as gunpowder, easy prey to any fallen spark.

Had they been alone, Anne might have been daring enough to do something about it. But there was no privacy to be had on the busiest street in London, in the middle row of afternoon traffic.

"I don't want the world," she informed him. "Your friendship will suffice." She paused. "And your kisses, too, if you're so inclined."

He flashed her a scorching glance. "I'm always inclined where you're concerned."

Anne was very much in danger of blushing. But she couldn't regret her bold words. Not when they seemed to have boosted Hartford's mood.

His mouth lifted up at one corner as he guided his mares past an omnibus.

"A smile at last," she said in mock amazement. "I feared my mother had permanently put you out of countenance."

"If she had, I'd have only myself to blame. I'm the one who asked you to talk with her."

"Are you sorry I did?"

"No," he said. "I want you to know I'm taking this seriously."

"I already know that. You needn't give up your columns to prove it to me. Indeed, I'm rather vexed you have. I was beginning to enjoy your attempts at flirtation."

He gave her an arrested look. "Were you?"

"Yes, I was," she admitted. "Despite better judgment, there's a part of me that's always been attracted to your penchant for foolishness. So long as it isn't mean-spirited. And so long as it doesn't involve you risking your neck."

"Huh," he mused. "I had no idea you found my antics anything but irritating."

"Well, now you do." Anne wanted him to be happy. To be himself. That was the man she'd lost her heart to, not some sober-minded individual with no sense of fun about him. "Don't give up all of your columns for my sake," she entreated. "If you're trying to prove yourself to me—"

"Not just to you," he said. "To your family. To your friends."

"Speaking of my friends . . ." Anne hesitated.

Julia, Stella, and Evelyn all knew that Hartford was courting her, but Anne had yet to make any sort of grand confession about what she felt for him. Only Stella seemed to suspect how thoroughly Anne had lost her heart.

"What about them?" Hartford asked.

"Miss Maltravers's wedding to Mr. Malik is next Monday," Anne said. "Perhaps you might escort me to it?"

Hart's smile broadened. It wasn't a betrothal announcement in the papers, but as public declarations went, it was a hell of a start.

"It would be my honor," he said.

"Excellent." Anne folded her hands in her lap as they continued up the hill, turning her face to the sky. Sunlight glistened in the strands of golden hair that peeped from beneath her severe black hat.

Hart's spirits lifted as he looked at her.

He'd been in a foul mood since learning he'd have to travel to Inverness in a fortnight. A mood that had only been worsened by the exchange he'd had with Lady Arundell.

Since her visit, Hart had felt every ounce of his own unworthiness. It was an all-too-familiar feeling. Growing up, he'd been forever in his parents' black books, marked down in their minds as a boy who lacked the qualities they valued most. He had never been serious enough or intelligent enough. Not when measured by their high standards.

It had taken years for him to appreciate his own value. But after

Lady Arundell's words, he'd doubted himself once again. With that doubt had come a consuming fear of losing Anne.

He wanted to be worthy of her.

It's why he'd resigned from his columns. Why he'd been trying to conduct himself with sober, dignified decorum during the last week of his courtship.

Anne hadn't seemed to appreciate his efforts. Rather the reverse.

Hart liked her all the more for it.

Perhaps he wouldn't give up his columns after all. Not altogether.

"We proceed apace," he said, only partially in jest. "I've commenced courting you. I've been dressed down by your mother. And now I'll be escorting you to an event with your friends."

"Next, we must attend one of *your* family functions," Anne said. "I have a feeling you've been as guilty of handling your relations with kid gloves as I have been with mine."

Guiltier, Hart nearly replied, for he still hadn't told his family about Mrs. Neale and her children. He still hadn't told them about his crucible business. He was reluctant to do so, despite Marcus's threats and the looming menace of Gabriel Royce. The consequences to his family would be too great.

The consequences to himself were equally grave.

Sometimes it seemed there was no one on earth who knew him for who he really was. No one except Anne. And even she didn't know the whole of it.

Hart had been meaning to tell her. He *had* to tell her. He couldn't leave for Scotland without her knowing the truth.

He brought his mares to a walk behind a slow-moving cart. "I'd like to show you something," he said. "Would you be at liberty to take a long drive with me? Later next week, perhaps, if the weather clears?"

"I don't see why not."

"Your mother may not approve."

"She isn't likely to object now you're courting me. Not so long as our outing is in an open carriage." Anne smoothed her gloves. "Do you have somewhere in mind?"

"I do," he said resolutely. "There's something I wish to show you in Battersea."

She gave him a look of surprise. "You wish to introduce me to the Neales?"

Hart stiffened. Introducing Anne to Mrs. Neale was the last thing he'd been thinking of. "God no," he said.

Gentlemen's mistresses and their baseborn children didn't mix with polite society. Their very existence—though it might be privately acknowledged—was a public affront. No delicate-minded lady would dare expose herself to it, and only a villain would ask her to. It would be an unpardonable insult.

But Anne wasn't any ordinary lady.

"I'd be happy to meet your sisters," she said. "And to renew my acquaintance with your brother. We didn't meet under the most auspicious circumstances."

Didn't Hart know it. Marcus still referenced the lecture he'd received from Anne that day at the tavern. A termagant, he'd called her. He wasn't half-wrong. But this time . . .

This time Anne's fury had been engaged in Hart's defense.

She cared for him. She'd *always* cared for him.

He wanted no more secrets between them.

"Very well," he said. "If it's truly what you wish, we'll stop in on the Neales first."

Evelyn's wedding to Mr. Malik took place on a rainy Monday morning at her uncle's town house in Russell Square. Mr. Fielding's drawing room had been decorated for the occasion, with orange blossoms framing the doorways and adorning the front of the room where a young, bespectacled clergyman was poised to read the wedding service from the *Book of Common Prayer.*

Mr. Malik stood beside him, awaiting his bride. A tall, well-made gentleman, with black hair and rich copper-colored skin, he was dressed in an immaculately cut black suit.

Anne would have expected nothing less from the gifted tailor and dressmaker.

She sat in the third row of seats, in company with Stella and Julia. The three of them were bookended by Hartford and Captain Blunt.

Several chairs and padded benches had been brought in to accommodate the wedding guests. They were all of them full. The small ceremony had drawn friends and family from all across England—and from every stratum of society.

Julia had traveled down from Yorkshire with Captain Blunt. Evelyn's aunt Nora had journeyed up from Sussex, along with Evelyn's younger sisters, Augusta, Caroline, Elizabeth, and Isobel. Mr. Malik's cousin, Mira, was present with her fiancé, Mr. Jones. The famous solicitor Mr. Finchley and his wife, Jenny, were in attendance. So was a hard-faced young seamstress named Miss Rawlins, and several other young ladies who looked to be of the same working-class stock.

Anne's gaze drifted over the diverse array of guests as she awaited Evelyn's appearance. Say what one would about marrying outside one's class, the newly minted Mr. and Mrs. Malik would have the full support of their close friends and family.

"I'm so nervous," Stella said in a low voice.

"So am I," Julia whispered back. "I feel as though it's *me* who's getting married."

"You're already married," Anne reminded her.

"Oh, I know *that*." Julia flashed a blushing look at her stern, battle-scarred husband. She'd been holding his hand since the moment of her arrival, their fingers threaded in an intimate clasp. The two of them were so obviously in love with each other.

Meanwhile, Anne had released Hartford's arm the instant she'd sat down.

She'd never been as romantical as Julia. Not publicly, anyway.

It was enough that Stella and Julia had witnessed Hartford escorting Anne here today. There was only one thing to be gleaned from such an action. Anne's friends had been quick to discern it.

"It's said that one wedding brings another," Stella remarked to Julia as the ceremony began. "First yours, then Evie's."

Julia smiled impishly at Anne. "Who will be next, I wonder?"

Anne merely lifted her brows.

A brief moment later, Evelyn entered on her uncle's arm. Stella stifled a gasp, and Julia whispered, "Oh, how beautiful she is!"

Evelyn wore a gown of Mr. Malik's design. It was a creamy white glacé silk, with a plain bodice, dainty pearl buttons, and undersleeves of delicate white tulle. A gleaming white satin ribbon sash was tied in a bow at her waist, and a wreath of orange blossoms was pinned in her hair.

Surely there was never a lovelier bride.

As Evelyn joined Mr. Malik at the front of the room, Anne's mouth curved in a trembling smile.

No, she wasn't as romantical as her friends. It didn't mean her heart was any less full. Indeed, she'd been brimming with private emotion ever since Hartford had collected her this morning in Ludgate Hill.

He sat beside her now, garbed in a relatively subdued pair of pinstriped trousers and a matching striped coat. His bruises were gone, a slightly crooked nose the only remnant of that bleak day in Battersea. It made him even more handsome, if that was possible. Dearer to her than he'd ever been before.

As the ceremony commenced, she reached for his hand. Hartford's fingers promptly engulfed hers.

"Dearly beloved," the clergyman began. "We are gathered together here in the sight of God, and in the face of this congregation, to join together this man and this woman in holy matrimony . . ."

Thirty-Six

"We're not accustomed to entertaining, my lady," Mrs. Neale said from her wing chair near the fireplace. "Indeed, no one of your rank has yet stepped foot into my parlor."

"I'm pleased to do so, ma'am," Anne said. "I've been eager to make the acquaintance of Mr. Hartford's sisters."

Hartford sat, stone-faced, beside Anne on the chintz sofa in the Neales' modest parlor.

As promised, he'd arrived in Ludgate Hill on the first clear November day after Evelyn's wedding to drive Anne to Battersea. He'd been in one of his serious moods again. Anne couldn't think why. She already knew the worst of his father's sins.

And it wasn't that bad, really.

The Neales' house in Battersea was small but neat, and Hartford's sisters, though lacking in fashionable conversation, were quite prettily behaved. The eldest, Ethel, was a demure, raven-haired beauty, and the youngest, Ermintrude, a plump-cheeked fifteen-year-old in a printed floral frock. They had greeted Anne with matching curtsies and no little curiosity.

Even Marcus was on his best behavior. He'd bowed to Anne and inquired, a bit awkwardly, after her health.

Indeed, since her arrival, they'd all treated her with uncommon civility.

All except for Mrs. Neale.

The mistress of the late Everett Hartford was a faded Venus, with a chip on her shoulder so large Anne was amazed the woman didn't fall out of her chair from the weight of it.

"I'm sure there are many who would like to make our acquaintance," Mrs. Neale said acidly. "But Mr. Hartford has forbidden my children mingling with society. It makes no difference to him that his father doted on my children. My son was Everett's particular favorite."

Marcus had no visible response to his mother's assertion. Seated with his sisters on the matching chintz sofa across from them, he was more focused on his older half brother. He'd been shooting narrow looks at Hartford ever since they'd arrived.

The two girls were another matter. They were both of them fixated on Anne. She felt the weight of their fascinated gazes moving over every inch of her, from the top of her rolled coiffure to the unflounced hem of her black crepe gown.

"Have you known Hartford long?" Ethel asked.

"Most of my life," Anne said. "Our mothers were childhood friends."

Mrs. Neale flushed red at the mention of Hart's mother.

"Are you in mourning?" Ermintrude blurted out.

"*Trudy*," Ethel said under her breath.

"It's all right," Anne said. "I *am* in mourning, after a fashion. My father passed away. And, of course, we must all be grieving the loss of Prince Albert."

Ethel's eyes went round. "Did you know him, my lady?"

"I did not," Anne said. "But I held him in the highest esteem. We have him to thank for the Great Exhibition, and for so many other wonderful things. He was a visionary, you must agree."

Mrs. Neale was stiff as a ramrod in her seat. "I wouldn't dare venture an opinion about such an illustrious figure." She looked at Hartford. "I have learned my place, haven't I, sir? You have spent nine years in reminding me of it."

Hartford responded to Mrs. Neale with implacable calm. "Lady Anne is not here to be made victim to your grievances, madam."

"You wouldn't like that, would you?" Mrs. Neale snapped back at him. "Me telling the truth for once."

"Mother, please," Ethel said.

Marcus stood abruptly. "Can I speak with you?" he asked Hartford. "Privately?"

Hartford's brows lowered. He looked as though he was going to refuse.

Anne forestalled him. "Please do," she said. "I'll be perfectly well on my own."

"Are you certain?" he asked.

Anne smiled, first at him, and then at Ethel and Ermintrude. "Quite certain."

Hart stepped out into the Neales' small garden with Marcus. The moment the door closed behind them, Marcus turned on him.

"How much longer?" he demanded. "I've already spent months dangling at your pleasure. I can bear it no more."

Hart leaned against the back wall of the house. He folded his arms. "I believe you can," he said. "Consider it an enforced period of rustication. It happens to the best of us."

Marcus paced the muddy patch of garden in a small circle, visibly working himself up into a state. "It's not rustication. It's imprisonment."

If it was, it was one of Marcus's own making. Only his guilt over what had happened to Hart that day by the river had kept Marcus from getting himself into more trouble.

"There are no bars on the windows, that I can see," Hart said. "You're free to leave whenever you wish."

"To do what? I have no income. You've cut off my last penny."

"Your needs are well provided for."

"Oh yes, very well," Marcus said bitterly. "I haven't the money to buy so much as a bouquet of flowers for my young lady. What am I expected to offer her now? I can't even tell her what's to become of me because you haven't deigned to tell me yourself."

Hart had no pity for the lad. "If your young lady only cares about what you can buy her, then you're well shot of the girl."

"If you would increase my funds—"

"You've had money enough of mine for a lifetime. You're presently in debt to me for over seven thousand pounds."

Marcus glowered. "Which I'm to repay with my life, you said."

"I meant it. Every word."

Marcus lost a bit of his color. "So, what are you waiting for? Send me to sea already! Or to Russia or India, or wherever it is they ship soldiers to die."

"You're no use to me dead."

"Then what?" Marcus asked. "It's torture what you're doing."

Hart supposed it might be. A variety of it, anyway. It was difficult to lose control of one's future. But left to his own devices, Marcus would have had no future at all.

"Very well," Hart said. "I have an idea of sending you to Scotland."

Marcus stopped pacing to stare at him. "*Scotland?*"

"I know an excellent Englishman who'll be taking up a position there. He requires an apprentice. It would be hard work, but you'd learn the business from the ground up."

Marcus looked horrified by the prospect. "Why should I wish to?"

Hart straightened from the wall. He strode forward. "Because," he said, looming over him, "I want you to make something of yourself. I want you to learn a skill—to have work you can take pride in. There's no satisfaction to be had in the way you've been living, only ruin and disgrace."

"You don't know anything about my life," Marcus shot back. "How can you? You've led a life of plenty. First Eton, then Cambridge. The favored son. The wealthy heir. Laughing at my misfortunes from your great height as though I were nothing but dirt under your boots."

"Is that what you believe?" Hart hesitated all of a second before enlightening him. "You've often said that our father loved you best. That he cared nothing for me. And you're right. He didn't care about me. I was a disgrace. The family joke, good for nothing but driving a curricle with a modicum of skill."

Marcus snorted.

"It's the truth," Hart said. "He left me only a few thousand pounds and a crumbling estate in Somersetshire that demanded more money than it earned. The only recourse for me was to find employment. Which I did."

"You would never—"

"Oh yes," Hart said. "I *work*. I've had to. It's how I pay for this house. How I keep your mother and sisters in some degree of comfort. It's how I've been paying all of your blasted debts."

Marcus's throat bobbed on a swallow.

Hart continued relentlessly. "There was no way to follow in our father's footsteps. I was never that man. I had to go another way, and so must you. You can't spend what's left of your life struggling to be something you're not. Find something else to do. Something that will make you happy."

"Why the hell do you care about my happiness?"

"Because, you utter pain in the arse," Hart said, "you're my brother."

Marcus's face crumpled. He looked away. When next he spoke, his voice was hoarse with suppressed feeling. He sounded very young. "What kind of business is it in Scotland?"

"The kind with a future." Hart set his hand on his brother's shoulder with a reassuring grip. "Tell me," he said, "what do you know about plumbago mining?"

Anne held tight to Hartford's hand as he assisted her up into the curricle. They had been no more than twenty minutes at the Neales' house. A respectable afternoon call, though admittedly a little uncomfortable. But Anne didn't regret the experience. Indeed, it had been rather illuminating.

This is what Hartford had been doing since he'd discovered the truth of his father's betrayal. He'd been holding this little family together—without thanks or acknowledgment. He'd been keeping them safe and preserving their dignity.

Every word Mrs. Neale had uttered during Anne's brief visit had convinced her of the truth of it. Hartford cared for all of them, and he'd received nothing for his trouble but accusations, abuse, and requests for more money.

Still, he'd kept on, adhering to his responsibilities no matter the insult. Hartford was that good at his core. That unwaveringly steadfast.

Anne was both impressed and unsettled by the revelation.

Is this how it had been with the two of them?

Anne had asked nothing from him since she'd broken their engagement—not until the day she'd visited Arlington Street—but she'd offered him plenty of insults. She'd refused to dance with him. To talk with him. To give him her smiles or her understanding.

Yet, he'd persevered, despite it all. Always there for her. Always waiting.

"He never misses an opportunity to do you a service," Julia had said.

Anne's heart was heavy in her breast—weighted down with guilt and regret.

"How were they?" Hartford asked the neighborhood boy he'd enlisted to hold his mares. He seemed to be acquainted with the young lad.

"Right as rain, guv," the boy said.

Hartford tossed the lad a silver thruppence. "Until next time."

The boy caught it with a grin.

Hartford crossed to the other side of the curricle. "Do you know," he said as he climbed up beside Anne, "that's the first time I've left that house of my own volition. On every other visit, Mrs. Neale has thrown me out after the first quarter of an hour."

Anne arranged her voluminous black skirts. "She's embarrassed."

"Mrs. Neale?" Taking up the reins, Hartford guided his team into the street. "She's a venomous harridan with delusions of nobility."

"She is," Anne said, "but only because she's so deeply ashamed."

He shot her a sidelong glance. "You're not going to tell me you feel sorry for her?"

"Anyone must do so. She has three children by a man who never married her. And now she's left to depend on that man's son—a gentleman of wealth and breeding."

"Not much wealth any longer," he said with a wry smile.

"More than they have," Anne replied. "You hold the whole of their future in your hands. And it's clear you dislike the woman."

"Of course I dislike her. She abuses me every time I call."

"You wouldn't feel any animosity toward her otherwise?"

"I feel . . ." A frown crossed his brow. "I don't know. I suppose I'm angry with them all—my father, my mother, Mrs. Neale. They none of them behaved well. The rest of us have had to suffer as a result of it."

"You and your brother and sisters?"

"And everyone else."

"Your sisters are lovely, by the way," Anne said. "Shy, but very sweet. They'd benefit from going out into society."

"What society? They're illegitimate."

"There must be some events they can attend in Battersea. Local assemblies or—"

"It would never work. Middle-class morality is worse than

anything in the more fashionable districts of the city. The moment some enterprising busybody works out the reason the illusive Mr. Neale has never made an appearance, I and my sisters stand to be publicly humiliated."

"Why did you not insist they move somewhere further away?" Anne asked. "Somewhere they could better pretend to respectability?"

"That was my first inclination," Hartford said. "But Mrs. Neale refused to quit London. I had a devil of a time getting her to leave the little house in Chelsea my father had leased for her. If she could have afforded to stay there, she would have done. Battersea was a compromise."

Hart trotted his mares onto Church Road. The residential district, with its modest houses and shops, slowly gave way to the busy industrial area located along the river.

"Would your grandfather be very offended to know of their existence?" Anne asked.

"That's one way of describing it." He paused. "I fear it would kill him."

"He idolized your father that much?"

"If he didn't while he was alive, he certainly does now." Hartford's mouth twisted with bitter humor. "The snow-white reputation of the esteemed moralist Everett Hartford has only grown after his death. He was, apparently, a man too good for this world."

"No human being is *that* good," Anne said.

"Some are."

"Nonsense. If we didn't make any mistakes, we'd have no need to be forgiven." She looked out with a frown at the passing scenery. There were no more houses, only market gardens, distilleries, and manufactories. "Where are we going?"

Hartford was focused on the road, his face set with grim determination. "I told you. There's something I want to show you."

"By the river? But it's only tradespeople hereabouts."

A small factory loomed ahead on the waterfront. It was situated in a riverside yard, a large placard at the front proclaiming its name: *The Parfit Plumbago Crucible Company.*

Hartford slowed his horses, bringing them to a halt outside the gates. "I know," he said. "I'm one of them."

Thirty-Seven

Anne stared at him. Her lips parted as though she wished to say something, but no words came out. Hart feared he'd rendered her speechless.

But it was too late to turn back now.

He forged ahead, regardless of the consequences. "This is why I wanted you to come with me to Battersea. Not because of the Neales or because of anything to do with my father's sordid legacy, but because of me. I wanted you to see what I've been doing with myself since you broke our engagement."

She turned from him to look out at the factory. "You don't mean to say that this is *yours*?"

"As a matter of fact, it is. Fifty-one percent of it, anyway. Mr. Parfit is one of my partners, along with two other gentlemen, Mr. Goodbody and Mr. Acker. We formed the company in '57, a few months after I returned from the Himalayas. It all started with something I saw at the Great Exhibition. I had the notion of investing in it, but my life was set on another path. I didn't—" Hart broke off. He was rambling now and he knew it. "Have I shocked you?"

"No," she said. "That is, you have a little. But not because you're in trade. I already assumed—"

He started. "Did you?"

"Well, yes. You said in York that you had other sources of income. Common, you called them. What else could you have been referring to?" Her brows knit. "What I don't understand is what all this has to do with our broken engagement?"

Before Hart could answer, a workman emerged from inside the gates.

"Mr. Hartford!" He came forward, removing his cap. "Ma'am." He bobbed his head to both of them. "Are you stopping in on us today, sir?"

"I might be, Sam." Hart looked at Anne in barely concealed anticipation.

It was foolish, he knew. Possibly even self-defeating. But he wanted Anne to know he'd done well for himself. That he wasn't the useless, empty-headed nothing of a gentleman she'd accused him of being all those years ago.

"Would you like to see it?" he asked.

Her lush mouth curved in a slow smile. "It seems you'd like to show it to me."

"I would," he said. "Very much so."

"Very well," she said.

Sam took hold of the horses' heads as Hart jumped down from the curricle. Hart walked around to Anne's side. Rather than taking her hand, he caught her by the waist and lifted her easily to the ground.

Her breath trembled out of her at his touch. He trembled a little, too, knowing he was poised on the precipice of baring his soul. Of revealing all that he was and all that he still felt for her.

"Shall I walk them?" Sam asked.

Hart reluctantly released Anne's waist. "If you please," he said. "We won't be long."

Anne slipped her arm through his as they passed through the gates into the factory yard.

The sprawling buildings of the plumbago factory rose up around them: chimney shafts, storehouses, the potters' room, and rooms for grinding, mixing, and drying the clay used to make the company's crucibles.

Hart escorted Anne across the yard. The ground became blacker as they approached the sorting and mixing rooms, an unfortunate result of the plumbago used in their products.

It was the same black that covered the clothes of the factory workers who passed them, hurrying about their business. They were humble but diligent men, unaccustomed to the sight of a lady on the premises. Some of them gawped at Anne's golden beauty. Others doffed their hats at Hart in recognition.

Hart nodded to them, but he didn't stop. "It all started at the Great Exhibition," he said. "There was a gentleman there from America exhibiting a new kind of crucible. He claimed it would revolutionize the industrial world. I thought it an exaggeration, naturally, but the man's enthusiasm was contagious. I didn't forget him."

"The Great Exhibition was over eleven years ago," Anne said.

"I know." Hart could easily recall the sense of wonder he'd felt as he had examined the various inventions on display at the Crystal Palace. "I was all of nineteen. My father and mother were still alive. They'd laid out my future to a certainty. After university, I was to marry and set up house in the country, somewhere far away from London, where my reckless habits would do no more harm to my father's excellent reputation."

"The hypocrite," Anne muttered. She was immediately contrite. "I'm sorry to say so, but he was. They both were."

"As I soon discovered," Hart replied grimly. "Within two years, they were gone, and I'd learned the truth of my father's character."

"You must have been so . . ." Again, she couldn't seem to find the words.

"I was disillusioned," he said. "I won't claim I wasn't. But I wasn't inclined to deviate from their plans for my future. I had you to aspire to. And I had inherited Barton Court. I was poised to end my days a country squire."

She gave him a wry look. "A country squire, indeed."

He covered her hand with his. "It mattered little in the end. When you broke our engagement, the life I'd envisioned for myself was gone in a puff of smoke. I was shattered. I didn't care anymore about my future or about my reputation. I didn't care about Barton Court."

"Surely you cared a little," she said. "You didn't sell it when you had the chance. You told me as much that day at St. Paul's."

"No, I didn't sell it," he said. "But I mortgaged it to the hilt."

Anne stopped. "You *what*?"

Hart urged her forward. She reluctantly complied, still gaping at him as they continued on.

"I borrowed against it for everything it was worth," he said. "And then I gambled that money—along with what was left of my inheritance—on this."

He looked out at the warehouses and chimneys in front of them, still vaguely amazed at the audacity of the risk he'd taken, not only with his own future but with that of his tenants and his family.

"I contacted the American I'd met at the Great Exhibition," he said. "I paid him a substantial sum to obtain the sole rights to manufacture his crucible in England. And then, with the rest of my money, I opened this factory."

"You spent everything you had?" She was aghast.

"It still wasn't enough," he said. "I had to partner with three older businessmen. Parfit was a banker. Acker was newly retired from a soap manufactory. And Goodbody had owned a string of chemist shops. The three of them had knowledge I didn't. But I was keen to learn."

"My Lord, Hart." Anne dropped her voice as they passed two plumbago-blackened workmen. "You could have bankrupted yourself. You could have lost Barton Court."

"I know," he said. "But I didn't." He guided her to one of the outbuildings. "Come and see the storeroom."

Still holding his arm, Anne walked with him into the cool interior of the warehouse. It was filled with row after row of shelves that held various sizes of cylindrical, metallic-gray vessels. Crucibles, she assumed.

Two workmen were busy stacking them onto one of the shelves against the wall. At the sight of Hartford, they stopped to remove their caps and bob their heads in greeting. They seemed to recognize him as someone in authority.

"Can you give us a minute, lads?" Hartford asked.

"Yes, sir," the older man said. Setting aside their work, the two men hurried from the warehouse, leaving Anne alone with Hartford.

"When we started," he said, "we had only a brick kiln, a millhouse, and a single horse to grind the clay. Five years later, we've improved the outbuildings, expanded the property, built a new wharf wall, and replaced our horse with a thirty-five-horsepower steam engine."

Anne inhaled a deep breath as she gazed at the countless rows of crucibles. Hartford gazed right along with her.

He was proud of this place, she could see. It was evident in the way he carried himself, and in the way he looked about him, like a prevailing hero surveying his kingdom. There was satisfaction in that look, edged with the inevitable sadness of loss. Of the memory of whatever he'd sacrificed to attain his ends.

Good heavens.

He'd mortgaged his estate for this. He'd risked gambling away his very birthright as surely as if he'd placed a wager at the gaming tables.

That was the Hartford she'd known in her youth. A man willing to dare anything to achieve his aims, however dubious. But this was a completely different scale of daring. Hartford hadn't just risked his birthright, he'd risked everything: his wealth, his property, his position in society, and his place in his family.

To be in trade was to, effectively, be dead to one's relations. Indeed, for a young lady who stooped to marrying a tradesman, it *was* a manner of death. She was nevermore received by her parents or siblings. She was never acknowledged at all.

Anne was as aware of this as Hartford must be.

"I had no idea you were doing any of these things," she said.

"No one did. I've had to keep all of it a secret—both the risk and the success of it."

"You must have longed to share it."

"Sometimes." He gave her a faint smile. "I often wished I could tell you."

There was so much poignancy in his words. So much regret.

Anne felt the familiar ache of yearning. The same feeling she'd had for him all these years.

Her arm slipped from his as he walked to one of the shelves and extracted a medium-sized vessel.

He cradled it in his hand. "Do you know what a crucible does?"

She slowly came to join him, her full skirts sweeping over the storehouse floor. "It melts things, doesn't it?"

"It doesn't only melt them. It purifies them. Whatever is put in this container is distilled down to its essentials. All that's useless and meaningless is burned away in the heat." He passed the crucible to her so she could examine it. "A crucible made with a mixture of clay and plumbago burns it away twice as fast. That's a savings of both time and money for steelmakers, shipbuilders, and the gentlemen of the railway. It's an industry-changing invention."

Anne held the crucible carefully. It was solid and heavy in her hands. "You're the only one manufacturing them?"

"In England, yes. The fact is, we can't keep up with demand. Our mines aren't producing quickly enough. We're obliged to expand."

She gave the crucible back to him. "I didn't realize they could be so valuable."

"Infinitely valuable. Crucibles burn away the dross." He returned the vessel to the shelf, his fingers lingering for a moment. "Sometimes, I fancy that's what has happened to me."

She studied his face. "How do you mean?"

His hand fell back to his side. "All of this—everything that's occurred since the moment my mother called me into her bedchamber and told me about my father's betrayal. I lost faith. I lost heart." His eyes met hers with rueful humor. "I lost you."

Anne stilled. Her breath caught in her throat as he reached to brush a stray curl of hair from her temple. He tucked it back into the confines of her black bonnet.

"I suppose that sometimes you have to be put into the fire to realize what's truly important to you," he said. "It burns everything else away. Melts you down to your finest parts. In the end, all that was left of me were my responsibilities—and my love for you."

Her mouth trembled. "Hart—"

"Don't say anything." His fingers traced the curve of her cheek. "Not yet."

"You can't expect me to—"

He silenced her with a kiss.

Anne gave a muffled protest as his lips met hers. It quickly transformed into a murmur of pleasure. She brought her hands to his chest.

They had no guarantee of privacy here. Anyone might walk in on them.

But Hartford didn't seem to care. His mouth captured her every breath, her every sigh, shaping to her lips with a tenderness that sent a wild rush of heat through her veins.

If this is what kissing him was like, she trembled to think how all the rest of it would be.

Perilous thought!

Fortunately, he didn't prolong the encounter. If he had, she might have succumbed, regardless of the consequences.

His brow came to rest gently against hers. "If I don't tell you now, I might never say it."

"You've already told me—"

"Not *that.*" His voice deepened. "Good God, Anne. You must know how I feel about you. That's never been the difficult part. Not for me."

She slid her hands up the front of his wool waistcoat. "What, then?"

"Leaving you," he said. "I have to go away next week. I have company business in the north of Scotland. There's no way to avoid it."

She drew back to search his eyes. "How long will you be gone?"

"Possibly a month."

"*A month!*" Anne's heart plummeted like a stone.

No wonder he didn't wish her to make any promises or declarations of her own. He'd known what was coming. And he'd known exactly what it meant.

This was how it had ended the last time. At the very moment they'd been poised to achieve their happily-ever-after, he had gone. Their feelings for each other hadn't been strong enough to withstand the separation.

"Most of it will be spent exploring mining opportunities in the Highlands," he said. "I'll be on the move, with no fixed address once I depart from my hotel in Inverness. It will be difficult for me to receive letters, but I intend to write to you every day."

"You don't have to—"

"*Every day,*" he repeated, making the words a vow. "I'll be home in time for my grandfather's house party. I shall go straight to Hampshire from the station. If you return my feelings, meet me at Sutton Park. Don't come otherwise."

Her mouth went dry. "But we had an agreement—"

"I don't care about that anymore," he said. "I should never have demanded something in exchange for helping you. I didn't require it. I'd do anything you asked of me, Anne. Anything at all." His gaze held hers. "I've loved you without fail the entire time we've been apart. Even when I was infuriated with you, I loved you. If you come to Sutton Park, let it be because you feel the same and for no other reason. And for God's sake—" He cradled her face in his hand. "Wear whatever you wish. Black, red, any color on earth. I require no more concessions. All I want—all I've *ever* wanted—is you."

Anne swallowed hard. She didn't wish to wait. She wanted to talk to him now. To resolve things if they could.

But he was right.

This was neither the time nor the place. And even if it were, she doubted she'd be capable of summoning the words. Her thoughts were scattered in every direction.

"It isn't a terribly long time," he said. "And I—"

She gripped the fabric of his waistcoat in warning. "If you tell me that absence makes the heart grow fonder, Felix Hartford, I shall *not* be responsible for my actions."

He smiled. "I won't tell you, then." He pressed another kiss to her lips before stepping back from her. "Come," he said brusquely, offering his arm. "Let me show you the rest of the factory."

Thirty-Eight

Anne settled herself across from Stella inside the carriage as it rolled away from Mr. Fielding's house in Russell Square.

Mama was still inside with Mr. Fielding, closeted in his study just as she'd been from the moment she and Anne had arrived. He required Mama's assistance in reviewing some obscure Latin text. Something to do with the Romans or the ancient Egyptians.

Anne had been left on her own for much of the visit, languishing in the drawing room over a pot of plain black tea as the rain streamed down the windows.

Evelyn was no longer in residence. After their brief honeymoon, she and Mr. Malik had moved to a small farmhouse in Hampstead. Evelyn's aunt and sisters had gone as well, returning to Sussex not long after the wedding.

Anne had no one to keep her company.

Luckily, she'd drunk no more than one cup of bitter tea before it had occurred to her to summon Stella.

Stella had been an infrequent caller at the house in Ludgate Hill. The journey was too much of an ordeal for her without benefit of a carriage. But George's Street was an easy distance from Bloomsbury. In no time at all, Stella had arrived, damp, rosy-cheeked, and smiling.

Anne had promptly obtained her mother's permission to use the carriage so she and her friend could do some shopping.

"Shall we stop at Hatchards?" Stella asked. "Or would you rather visit Bloxham's Books in Charing Cross? Julia prefers it."

"Neither," Anne said. "We're going to Mr. Malik's dress shop in Conduit Street."

Stella smiled. "Do you need a new gown?"

"I need a new everything," Anne said bluntly.

Stella's expression turned quizzical. "Whatever for?" she wondered. "The London season is over."

"It isn't for the season. It's for Lord March's house party."

"You *are* still going, then?"

"Of course I am." Anne didn't know how anyone could be in doubt of it.

But Hartford had been.

He seemed to be operating under the delusion that there was a chance she'd refuse him.

Anne couldn't entirely blame him. She'd disappointed him in the past, just as he'd disappointed her. What happened next would be a matter of trust.

They were each of them making themselves vulnerable. He had done it first, confessing his feelings for her without hope of having them returned. And now she must do it, too. She must leave no doubt in his mind that she cared for him as he cared for her.

There had been little opportunity for it in the letters she'd sent to him these past two weeks. Though she'd written with affection, she hadn't dared bare her soul, not when she was uncertain of her words reaching him. He'd stopped in Inverness for only a short while. The rest of his time had been spent traveling deep in the Highlands—unable to reliably receive the post.

It hadn't prevented *him* from communicating with *her*. True to his word, he'd written to her daily, reporting on the weather, the people he'd met, and the humorous encounters he'd had with the locals.

They weren't love letters by any means. Hartford wasn't one for syrupy sentiment. But his feelings for her lingered between every line.

Anne could see it. She could feel it. He missed her dreadfully.

Just as she missed him.

"The weather in Hampshire will be miserable," she said. "But I daresay Sutton Park will be done up festively enough. I'll not cast a funereal shadow over the holiday with all my black crepe and bombazine."

Stella leaned forward eagerly in her seat. "You intend to buy something in another color?"

"I was thinking of red," Anne said.

"Red!" Stella's eyes went wide. "You jump in with both feet, don't you?"

"Should I wade in more slowly? First with pale pink and then with rose? I'd never be so fainthearted." Anne surveyed her friend. "Will you order a new gown as well?"

"I think I might," Stella said. "I've been saving my pocket money. And I do mean to make a good impression for once. No one will know me at Sutton Park. No one except you and Mr. Hartford." A frown puckered her brow. "Will he think I'm ridiculous?"

"Hartford is too busy being ridiculous himself to notice it in anyone else," Anne said, smiling. "Why? What do you plan to wear?"

"It's not my clothes. It's something else." A flush suffused Stella's face. "I ordered a bottle of hair dye through the post."

"Good gracious," Anne said. "You can't be thinking of using it?"

No lady of quality would ever resort to using dye. Like powder and rouge, it was something reserved for the lower orders—actresses, prostitutes, and women of dubious character.

"I'm tired of having gray hair," Stella said.

"But it's you," Anne said. "You're *you*. Anything else would be nothing but make-believe."

"What's wrong with a little make-believe?" Stella asked.

"Nothing, except that the people you meet won't be seeing you for who you really are."

"That's the problem," Stella said. "They don't see *me* at all. One look at my gray hair and they dismiss me out of hand. No one notices my face or my figure or whether I'm clever, or amusing, or a good horsewoman. I'd like a chance to shine without my hair getting in the way of it."

"*I* see you," Anne said. "Anyone who can't doesn't deserve you."

"*You* are a dear," Stella replied. "Pity you can't marry me."

"Is that what this is about? You want to find a husband?"

Stella sat back in her seat. "I don't want a husband. I want my freedom. And marriage is, ironically, the only way to get it. If this dye can help me, I'll happily try it."

Outside, the clattering of wheels and steel-shod hooves rose to a crescendo as their carriage joined the fashionable traffic of Bond Street. The rain hadn't stopped anyone from visiting their favorite shops. Horses whinnied and coachmen shouted out to one another amid the sounds of splashing puddles.

"What color did you purchase?" Anne asked.

"Circassian gold," Stella said. "It's supposed to turn my hair a radiant shade of auburn."

Anne couldn't conceal a wince. She instantly thought of Mrs. Frazil and her garishly dyed locks. "Oh, Stella—"

"Don't," Stella said. "This may be my only chance to make an impression."

"It may not be the impression you're aiming for."

"It would be something. And so long as no one knows me there, I can't see what it would hurt."

"I suppose not," Anne said. "But why auburn, for heaven's sake?"

Stella took a deep breath. "I went to the Berners Street Gallery."

"The *what*?"

"The gallery that that impertinent man at the British Museum mentioned to us."

Anne gasped. "You didn't!"

Stella was shamefaced. "I did."

"And?" Anne prompted, curious in spite of herself.

"I saw Mr. Whistler's painting," Stella said. "It was of a woman—a pale lady in a white dress standing against a white background. There was no color about her at all, except in the shade of her hair."

"Let me guess," Anne said. "Auburn?"

Stella nodded bleakly. "There was nothing to her otherwise. She was pale and empty. A wraith staring out at nothing."

"Not a pretty picture, then?"

"An unsettling one." Stella sighed. "Oh, Anne. I should never have gone to see it. I might have known he meant the comparison as an insult."

Recalling the handsome young man in the wheeled chair, Anne wasn't so certain. "He *was* impertinent," she acknowledged, "but I don't think he intended any offense."

"How else to take it?"

"He looked as though he was thunderstruck by you," Anne said.

Stella stared at her in disbelief. "He did not."

"That's what I thought, anyway," Anne told her. "Whatever that painting looked like, I daresay he meant it as a compliment. Artistic gentlemen must suppose a lady wants to be compared to obscure, unsettling works of art."

Stella fell quiet for a moment. "*Was* he a gentleman?"

"He appeared so. He was dressed respectably enough. And he was well spoken. But who can say, really? I've never encountered him before." Anne smiled. "You won't really dye your hair, will you, dearest?"

Stella's shoulders set with resolve. "I fully intend to."

"What about your brother?" Anne asked. "Won't he object?"

"He needn't know about it," Stella said. "The pamphlet promises the dye will wash out within a week. I'll apply it the night before we leave for Hampshire. I can hide it with the aid of a woven net and a hat. My brother will never be the wiser." She made a face. "I doubt he'd notice in any case. He doesn't see me, either, except as a manner of secretary. And even *that* doesn't merit his regard."

"Sisters are expected to be of use," Anne said. "So are daughters." She glanced out the carriage window as they approached Conduit Street, thinking about her mother's insistence on having a gentleman to lean on.

"Is your mother being very demanding of you?" Stella asked with concern.

"No more than usual," Anne said. "But she's a traditionalist for all her eccentricity. To her, a husband or a son would be of infinite value. Whereas a daughter—" She hesitated, reluctant to confess the truth of it. "Daughters are meant to sacrifice themselves. We give up our own dreams for our families. We stay at home when we're needed. We marry where we're told. And we're supposed to do it all without complaint, and without benefit of acknowledgment. Whereas a man—"

"When a man gives up the smallest thing for his family, he's hailed as a hero," Stella said. "It's unfair. A woman's life is no less meaningful. And our sacrifices are no less valuable."

"No, indeed," Anne said. "They're more valuable, for we have more to lose."

The carriage came to a halt in front of Mr. Malik's shop. Anne and Stella disembarked with the aid of the footman. Jeanette had traveled on the outside seat alongside him. She scrambled down to follow them into the gaslit shop.

The modest showroom was furnished with a pair of leather chairs, a trifold mirror, and a tall counter of polished mahogany. A curtained door behind it led to the workrooms at the back of the shop.

It was a small business as yet, but one that was growing rapidly in popularity. According to Evelyn, her new husband had lately taken orders for mourning gowns from several of the Queen's ladies in waiting.

Anne wasn't surprised. Mr. Malik had a talent for elegant simplicity.

He was also quite adept at choosing the most flattering fabrics and colors. She was eager for the benefit of his advice.

But a short moment later, it wasn't Mr. Malik who emerged from behind the curtain. It was his cousin, Mira. She was a pretty young woman, with black hair and olive-green eyes, wearing a beautifully tailored dark wool dress.

"My lady." Miss Malik inclined her head. "Miss Hobhouse. How may I help you?"

"Miss Malik," Anne said. "Is Mr. Malik not available? I have a large order to place, and I'm anxious to consult with him."

"I'm sorry, but he isn't here at the moment," Miss Malik said. "He's at the palace."

"Oh, heavens," Stella breathed. "How terribly exciting!"

A proud smile touched Miss Malik's mouth. "He has another commission."

"Will he be back this afternoon?" Anne asked.

"I can't promise it, my lady," Miss Malik said. "Can I be of assistance?"

Anne didn't wish to offend her. Miss Malik was a gifted seamstress in her own right. Indeed, it was she who was responsible for much of the intricate embroidery and delicate trimming on Evelyn's eveningwear.

"I require two ball gowns," Anne said. "As well as several day dresses, and a carriage gown for a long rail journey next month."

"Yes, my lady. We have a selection of new weaves in black crepes, poplins, and watered silks."

"Not black." Anne set her gloved hands on the edge of the wooden counter. "I prefer red."

Miss Malik's brows swept upward, but she made no comment on the drastic change in color. "Do you have a particular shade in mind?"

"I was hoping your cousin could tell me." Anne paused. "Or you, if you're able."

Miss Malik regarded Anne with a thoughtful frown. "Not scarlet, I think. And claret would drain the life from your face. It must be crimson, or a darker shade of orange red." She went to one of the shelves. "We have a new crimson velvet that would be suitable for a ball."

Anne exchanged a glance with Stella. Crimson velvet wasn't just bright, it was lush and tactile. Sensuous, even. To wear it, Anne would be making a statement indeed.

"Crimson velvet, then," Anne said.

Miss Malik pulled out several darker rolls of fabric, eventually revealing a gleaming bolt of rich crimson red. She withdrew it from the shelf. As she did so, a roll of eye-catching silk fabric tipped forward from behind.

The second fabric wasn't red. But it was glorious.

Anne's pulse quickened at the sight of it. "And that one."

Miss Malik picked up the colorfully patterned fabric with a doubtful look. "For a ball gown, my lady?"

"No," Anne said with unassailable certainty. "We must use that to make my carriage gown."

Later that afternoon, back in their house in Ludgate Hill, Anne stood in front of the small dressing table in her bedroom as her maid assisted her out of her damp clothes. Open boxes were heaped upon the bed behind her, spilling over with red stockings, gloves, hats, fans, and several petticoats—the spoils of Anne's shopping trip with Stella.

It was this her mother saw upon entering Anne's room unannounced.

Mama came to an immediate halt. "Anne?" She looked at the open boxes. "What is the meaning of all this?"

Anne waved Jeanette away. The maid hastily exited the room, leaving Anne half-undressed and alone with her mother.

"I don't object to your shopping," Mama said. "But to purchase underthings in such a color—"

"Not just underthings." Anne crossed the room, wearing only her corset, corset cover, and mud-stained black skirts. "I've bought other items as well."

Mama picked up one of the hats—a red velvet chapeau trimmed with red berries and shimmering red crystal beads. She stared at it in slow-dawning understanding. "Don't tell me you've ordered gowns in the same shade?"

Anne's stomach tightened on a rush of anxiety. She'd been dreading this conversation.

But there was no use in drawing things out. She'd already made up her mind.

"Several," she said. "They should be ready in time for our departure for Hampshire."

Mama's face was stunned. "You mean to give up your blacks."

It wasn't a question.

Anne answered anyway. "Yes. I do."

"And in such a dramatic fashion?" Mama shook her head. "What about your father?"

"It's been seven years, Mama," Anne said.

"I *know* how long it's been." Mama tossed the hat back onto the bed with uncommon force. "Is this Hartford's doing?"

"It's my own decision."

"Don't insult my intelligence, my girl. The brazenness of the color alone announces his influence. He's never taken anything seriously in his life, least of all the obligations one owes to one's family."

Anne took a swift step forward, instantly rising to his defense. "Indeed, you're mistaken. He's more responsible than anyone gives him credit for. And he has a great respect for his family."

Her mother scoffed.

"It's true," Anne insisted. "Believe me when I tell you, Mama, that he takes on a great deal."

"What has he ever taken on save another dare or a wager? Even his decision to accompany us to Yorkshire was impulsive at best. He has no fixed principles. Nothing to recommend him except a pleasing aspect and a certain skill with the ribbons." Mama's expression darkened. "I should never have sanctioned this courtship. I might have known it would lead to disaster. To be sure, I *did* know it and willfully blinded myself to the consequences."

"Nonsense," Anne said.

Mama looked at her sharply. "I *beg* your pardon?"

"Nonsense, I said. Hartford has principles. If he appears to be reckless and cavalier, it's only a facade he wears to mask the truth."

"What truth might that be, pray?"

Anne hesitated.

She couldn't tell her mother about Mrs. Neale and her children. Anne would never break Hartford's confidence on that subject. But the crucible factory was another matter.

"He's a businessman, Mama," she said. "A successful one. He's part owner of a crucible company in Battersea."

Mama's mouth dropped. "He *what*?"

Anne soldiered on. She wasn't ashamed of Hartford's occupation. Rather the reverse. She proudly described his factory, with its vast warehouses and mechanisms for grinding, mixing, and baking the clay. She told her mother about the unique role of plumbago in the process, how valuable the crucibles were to shipbuilders and the railway, and how the business would soon be expanding mining operations to Scotland.

"He's been working at it for five years in secret," Anne went on. "And he's unable to share what he's achieved with his family or other people of fashion. It's unjust, is what it is. To have to refrain from owning one's success, simply because the first rank of society looks down on any man who works for a living."

Mama appeared both impressed and appalled. "Do you mean to say that, all this time . . . the boy has been in *trade*?"

"I suspect many gentlemen will be in trade before the end of the decade," Anne said. "They'd be foolish not to invest in factories or the railway. The world is changing, Mama. A man can't insulate himself against progress, no more than a lady can. Surely you must agree. It's why you brought us to Ludgate Hill, isn't it? To live among the common people? To appreciate the value of their energy and industry?"

Mama's brow creased. "Yes, but . . . a factory in Battersea?"

"He's done well for himself, Mama. I wish you could see that. I wish everyone could see it."

"What of Barton Court?" her mother asked. "Does he mean to give it up?"

"Not at all. He's made numerous repairs to it. I understand him to be a good and conscientious landlord." Anne paused, adding, "Though anything would be an improvement after how badly his father left the place. The fact is, Hartford has had countless messes to clean up on his father's account."

"I can well believe it," Mama murmured. "Everett Hartford was more interested in moral matters than with earthier concerns."

Anne didn't know about *that*. As far as she was aware, Hartford's father spent a great deal too much of his time on earthy matters, as evidenced by his three illegitimate children.

"The point is," she said, "regardless of his father's errors, Hartford has never shirked his duty."

"Will he remove to Barton Court once he's wed?" Mama asked. The idea seemed to give her a ray of comfort. "You did love the country so. How you wept when we were obliged to quit Cherry Hill!"

"I do love the countryside. I always have."

"And you would be content to marry a tradesman?"

Anne's cheeks heated. "He hasn't proposed to me yet," she said. "But if he did . . ."

If.

After all, Hartford may well come back from Scotland in a different frame of mind than when he'd left, just as he had when he'd returned from the Himalayas. He might, after a period of thought, unhindered by the proximity of their attraction, decide that his feelings had changed.

But Anne's feelings hadn't. Not in almost seven years. She was no longer afraid to admit it.

"I care for him, Mama," she said. "I care for him just as you cared for Papa."

Her mother sank down on the edge of the bed. Tears sprang to her eyes. "Oh, but I miss him dreadfully."

Anne hurried to her mother's side. She sat down beside her. "So do I," she said, slipping her arm around her. "Every day I miss him."

"I loved him so."

"And he loved us," Anne said. "He wouldn't wish us to be unhappy. Not even for a moment. He wouldn't want us mourning him forever."

"I don't want to mourn him. I want him to come back to me."

"Oh, Mama."

"It's a foolish desire, I know." Mama brought her arm around Anne's shoulders, drawing her close. "The dead are always with us. Everywhere we look and everywhere we go. But they linger just out of reach. 'Tis the most maddening fact. To feel their presence, but never to touch them. Never to have the blessed safety of their arms. The door, once shut, doesn't open again, I fear. Not until we join them in the grave."

Anne's throat tightened with emotion. "You're not eager to do so, I trust."

"No, indeed." A rare note of regret penetrated Mama's voice. "I'm sorry if I've caused you alarm on that score, my dear."

"You have," Anne said. "I sometimes feared—"

"You needn't have. I've not yet been reduced to such misery." Mama brushed a tear from her cheek. "But I've made you miserable, haven't I?"

"No," Anne objected softly.

"I've held you close for fear of losing you, just as I lost him."

"You'll never lose me," Anne promised. "I'll always be here for you, Mama. I would never abandon you in your time of need."

"My need has been very great, indeed."

"Your love was equally great. It's right you should mourn it."

"Me, perhaps, but not you, my girl. You're young yet. You can't be forever looking backward." Mama's face became thoughtful. "Perhaps it *is* time you shed your blacks. You have your future to contemplate. As for myself . . . I trust you won't be offended if I keep to mine."

"I won't be offended," Anne said. "I only want you to be happy."

"Foolish child." Her mother hugged her close, pressing a kiss to Anne's hair. "How could I be otherwise with you as my daughter?"

Thirty-Nine

Hart stood in the receiving line, next to his grandfather and uncle, in the entry hall of Sutton Park.

The grand gothic-style house, with its carved stone arches and vaulted ceilings, had been lavishly decorated for the holidays. Pine boughs and artfully arranged garlands of holly and ivy, their leaves tipped in artificial crystals to mimic the coming frost, draped every window, doorway, and mantel. The greenery glittered with red and gold ribbons, gilded acorns, and gold-foiled fruit.

If that wasn't enough to inspire the Christmas spirit, the merriment of the guests and the fragrance of new pine and freshly baked gingerbread cake drifting through the corridors would surely do so.

Hart had arrived last night uncertain of his reception. He'd been gone a little over a month, leaving Marcus on his own in Battersea, with only his mother and sisters to guard him from his worst instincts. It was enough time for all manner of crises to have erupted—revelations about the Neale family, the crucible factory, or a blackmail threat from Gabriel Royce. Hart half expected to be met by a passel of angry relations demanding his blood.

Instead, he'd encountered a household in relatively jolly spirits.

Brookdale was already in residence, along with his wife, stepdaughter, and his three young sons, who were presently consigned to the upstairs nursery. The rest of the guests were arriving today. They'd been turning up with frequency for the last hour.

There were titled relations, country squires and their wives, gently bred ladies and gentlemen farmers, bookish botanists, and a scattering of tradesmen.

Mr. Archer had come with his wife, Laura, and her brother, Edward Hayes. Mr. Hayes used a wheeled chair. He'd been accompanied by a manservant who assisted him with maneuvering the stairs.

One by one the guests had been welcomed, and one by one the servants had seen them up the sweeping oak staircase to their rooms. They would all meet again at this evening's ball. It was to be the formal opening of the house party, with a twenty-piece orchestra and a lavish champagne supper.

Grandfather no longer entertained with frequency, but when he did so, he spared no expense.

Hart smiled and bowed to another young lady and her parents. Aunt Esther had made good on her threat to invite a selection of eligible young misses. Never mind that Hart was already courting Lady Anne.

"May I remind you," Aunt Esther said as the young lady and her parents moved down the receiving line, "Lady Anne is not here."

Hart needed no reminding. Every time the doors had opened, the rain blowing in another group of guests, he'd look for Anne, and every time he'd been disappointed.

His long absence from England may yet prove to be the death of his hopes, just as it had been the last time.

For the Parfit Plumbago Crucible Company, however, it had been worth it. After nearly a week of exploration, an old map had led them to a remote Highland glen near Loch Ness. There, an exploratory dig had revealed a deep vein of plumbago. The discovery had been promising enough to set things in motion. More promising still, the no-nonsense owner of the land had seemed as impressed with William Webb as Hart had always been. It augured well for their new venture.

But nothing could rid Hart of this damnable feeling of apprehension over all the rest of it.

His personal life might not equate to much on a balance sheet, but it was of infinitely more value to him. Without Anne, the rest of it didn't mean a thing.

He'd nearly given up on her coming, when the doors opened once again and Lady Arundell entered in all her majesty. Anne and Miss Hobhouse followed her. The three of them were swathed in heavy cloaks and bonnets against the rain.

Hart's chest tightened on a spasm of relief. But it wasn't only relief he felt as he looked at her. It was profound, heart-clenching happiness.

This was her answer to what he'd told her at the crucible factory.

She loved him, too.

She may not have said it in words, but she was saying it with her actions. She'd come here because she wanted him, not just for a moment, but forever.

Hart couldn't imagine a greater feeling of joy.

And then, Anne removed her cloak.

Anne heard several gasps as the maidservant assisted her out of her wet outer garments. It was difficult to tell whether one of those gasps had been Hartford's. Anne rather feared it might have been.

To be sure, she'd been rather shocked herself when she'd first tried it on.

The blue-and-red-silk-plaid carriage gown was flawlessly cut. Made with a formfitting bodice, it embraced Anne's figure as sweetly as a love letter, sweeping down over her hips in an artfully draped spill of voluminous skirts. The pattern was bold, and perhaps out of character, but it flattered her hair and her complexion, and when combined with the elegance of Mr. Malik's tailoring, produced a dress that was assured to catch the eye of everyone who saw it.

But Anne was concerned with only one set of eyes.

After straightening her skirts and smoothing her hair, she took a steadying breath and turned to face him.

Hartford had stepped out of the receiving line. He bore the look of a man transfixed.

Anne offered him a tentative smile.

His mouth curved into a swift grin. The expression lit his face, making his blue eyes glow as they never had before. He strode across the hall to greet her. "Anne. You look—"

"Yes, I know." She took his outstretched hands. "Like an absolute peacock."

"Beautiful, I was going to say." He held her hands tightly in his. "My God, but I've missed you."

She smiled up at him, her heart full of emotion. "I've missed you, too."

"Hartford," Lady Arundell said. "Pray stop monopolizing my daughter. We've had a long journey and are eager for our rooms."

"Forgive me," Hartford said.

Anne didn't let him release her just yet. She prompted him to her with a tug on his hands. He immediately bent his head. "Please don't remark on Miss Hobhouse's hair," she whispered.

Hart's brows lifted, but he didn't question her. "Of course not."

Anne gave him a decisive nod before letting him go. Behind her, Stella had removed her bonnet, revealing thick tresses, the color of warm apricot, bound up in a heavily woven net.

It wasn't exactly garish. Indeed, if one didn't know Stella, they might think the shade rather suited her.

But Anne didn't think so.

Stella wasn't at all herself. She seemed an absolute stranger. Some romantical creature in a painting, not the strong, silver-haired Fury that Anne knew and loved.

During their journey, Anne's mother had scolded Stella severely for dyeing her hair. But if Hartford was surprised, he didn't show it.

He seemed to be wholly and completely focused on Anne. Remaining close to her side, he escorted them to greet his relations.

"You've discarded your mourning blacks, I see," Lady Brookdale said. "I must say, I approve."

"You look charmingly, my dear." Lord March clasped one of Anne's hands in both of his. "Plaid is such a cheerful pattern. I often remark on it to my grandson."

"Miss Hobhouse," Mariah said. "You seem different."

"Miss Spriggs." Stella curtsied. "Do I? I daresay it's this foul weather."

"Oh, it's beastly!" Mariah exclaimed. "Has it affected the roads, do you think? Will people coming from London be very much delayed?"

"All of our guests have arrived," Lady Brookdale said. "Lady Arundell's party is the last of them."

Lord Brookdale bowed to Anne's mother. "Your ladyship."

"Brookdale," Mama said, looking down her nose at the man. "Still amusing yourself in Westminster, are you?"

"We must all have our little diversions, madam," Brookdale said coolly.

"Some more interesting than others," Mama replied. She moved down the line to speak with Lord March. The earl dropped Anne's hand to address her mother.

"But *do* you think the roads will become impassable?" Mariah inquired, this time posing the question to Anne.

"What's all this about the roads?" Hartford asked. "You haven't invited your mysterious suitor to the party, have you?"

Mariah blushed to the roots of her hair. "Oh, why must you be so horrible!"

"Ignore him," Anne said. "You'll only encourage him otherwise."

Hartford traced a finger down the back of Anne's plaid-silk-encased arm. "Speaking of encouragement . . ."

Heat pooled in Anne's belly. She could scarcely keep her countenance. "The roads are in a poor state," she said, "but far from impassable. And there's nothing wrong with the trains. Ours was running exactly on time."

Mariah's shoulders sagged with relief.

"Mariah?" Lady Brookdale beckoned to her daughter. "Come here. Your grandfather was saying . . ."

The conversation drifted away as Anne turned back to Hartford. "You're very wicked," she said.

"I am," he agreed. "Will you dance the opening dance with me at the ball tonight? It's a waltz."

Her heartbeat quickened. She hadn't waltzed with him since she was sixteen. Indeed, she hadn't danced with him at all. On every occasion he'd asked her, she'd refused him.

But not this time.

"I will." She smiled. "With pleasure."

Forty

Anne's room on the third floor of Sutton Park was surely one of the prettiest in the house. Papered in China blue silk, it was furnished with rich Aubusson carpeting, a dainty walnut secretary stocked with all manner of writing implements, and a four-poster bed draped in a luxurious blue-and-gold-damask canopy. Best of all, the windows looked out over the stables. Before the sun had set, she'd caught a glimpse of some of the retired horses from Cherry Hill gamboling in the pasture.

If Anne hadn't already recognized her feelings for Hartford, she would have recognized them then without a shadow of ambiguity. She wasn't only *in* love with him. She *loved* him.

How could she not?

She suspected he'd chosen this room specially for her. He was always thinking of her. He always had been.

"You don't like it," Stella said morosely. She stood in front of the full-length pier glass, examining her reflection. Candlelight shimmered in the mirror, illuminating her new ball gown and the equally new color of her hair.

Anne came up beside her. She set a hand on her friend's bare arm. "It isn't that. It's just that I'm not used to it."

"But I don't look too foolish, do I?" Stella wore a ball gown of white crepe over delicately embroidered white silk. It was another of Mr. Malik's peerless creations. To complement it, Jeanette had arranged Stella's hair in an elaborate roll at her nape, accented with pearl beads and an aigrette of spun glass.

"No more than I do, I hope," Anne said. Her own gown was as bright as Stella's was pale. Made of rich crimson silk velvet, it was cut low off her shoulders, with short sleeves, a dainty gold-clasped velvet belt, and double skirts festooned with black floral embroidery and red velvet roses. "We both of us are out of character this evening."

"Not you," Stella said. "You're radiant. I'm . . ."

"Ethereal," Anne said. "Luminous. As pretty as a painting."

"The Mr. Whistler painting, perhaps." Stella turned to pull on her elbow-length gloves. "Perhaps someone will actually ask me to dance for once?"

"I'm confident they will." Anne fetched her own gloves. "Hartford certainly will. And he's an excellent dancer. When Evie waltzed with him during the season, I couldn't help being jealous."

"Of Evie?"

"Of the pleasure of dancing with him."

"He's asked you to dance often enough," Stella reminded her.

"I know," Anne said. "But tonight will mark the first time I've accepted him in seven years."

"It's all very romantic," Stella said.

"I hope it will be." Anne fluffed her skirts. "Shall we?"

The two of them left Anne's room and made their way down the oak staircase. Christmas music floated up from the ballroom—violins, oboes, and horns. The orchestra was warming up their instruments with a rendition of "Here We Come A-wassailing."

Hartford awaited them at the bottom of the stairs. He was heart-stoppingly handsome in his black-and-white eveningwear. When he saw Anne, he grinned as broadly as he had when he'd first beheld her in plaid.

"Ladies." He bowed to them. "May I say that you both look splendid."

"Thank you," Stella said, blushing.

Anne only smiled.

Hartford's gaze lingered on her face. "I little imagined how well red would suit you, my lady."

"Nor did I," Anne said. She looked behind him. "Have you seen my mother?"

"Lady Arundell is already inside the ballroom with my grandfather." Hartford offered them each an arm. "If you'll permit me to escort you in?"

Stella gratefully set her hand on his sleeve. Anne did the same with his opposite arm, allowing him to guide them down the hall and through the wide-open carved wooden doors that led into Sutton Park's gothic ballroom.

It was as grand as Anne remembered, with its ornate plasterwork ceiling and intersecting plasterwork vaults. Italian white marble fireplaces flanked the room, mirrors fixed above them to reflect the three magnificent crystal chandeliers that hung overhead.

Like the rest of the house, the ballroom was decorated for Christmas. There were greenery and ribbons everywhere. At the opposite end of the ballroom, the musicians sat on a dais.

"If you'd care to dance the opening waltz, Miss Hobhouse," Hartford said, "I have a gentleman whom I'd be pleased to introduce you to. He's a near neighbor of my grandfather."

"Oh yes," Stella said eagerly. "I do so want to dance."

"He's just there." Hartford turned his head in the direction of the chairs and benches that surrounded the polished wood dance floor.

The seats were already occupied by several elderly ladies and gentlemen, along with the requisite clusters of wallflowers, aged bachelors, and spinster companions. Among them, not far from the doors to the terrace, a handsome, dark-haired gentleman sat in a wheeled chair.

Anne recognized him in the same instant that Stella did.

Stella stifled a gasp.

"Not to worry," Hartford said. "He must have stepped into the cardroom. Shall I go and fetch him? We have a few minutes before the opening dance."

"Please do," Anne said, releasing his arm. The second Hartford was gone, she hurried to Stella's side.

Stella turned her back on the room, her face flaming. "What is *he* doing here?"

"I don't know," Anne said. "Except for that day at the museum, I've never seen him before in my life."

"I'm mortified!"

"You have no reason to be. You look beautiful and—"

"My hair and gown are almost identical to that painting he recommended to us," Stella said in a trembling under-voice. "He'll take one look at me and burst out laughing."

Anne took Stella's hand. "He wouldn't dare."

"I must away." Stella pulled free of Anne's gentle restraint. "I need a moment to compose myself."

"Stella, wait!" Anne called.

But it was too late. In a flurry of white silk skirts, Stella fled the ballroom.

Hartford reappeared a moment later. "Where is Miss Hobhouse?"

"She needed some air," Anne said. "Where is your grandfather's neighbor?"

"I can't find him, the blackguard. He's probably slipped out to have a smoke." Hartford regarded her with concern. "Is something the matter?"

Anne looked across the ballroom. "Who is that gentleman by the terrace doors?"

He followed Anne's gaze. "Mr. Edward Hayes. Teddy, I believe he's called. He's the brother-in-law of a perfumer my grandfather has invited. Something of an artist, I understand. Why do you ask?"

"Miss Hobhouse and I crossed paths with him at the British Museum one afternoon. He put her quite out of countenance."

"Oh? I wouldn't have thought him the type." Hartford frowned. "Shall I speak to him?"

Anne was touched by the gesture.

Hartford wasn't only protective of her, he was protective of her friends as well. He'd looked after Julia in Anne's absence and was prepared to champion Stella, too.

But there was no need this time.

"It wasn't like that," Anne said. "He only flustered her. She'll be back any minute, I'm certain. Miss Hobhouse is made of stern stuff."

"I don't doubt it."

The Christmas music ceased, and the orchestra commenced the beginning notes of the first waltz.

Anne's heart swelled. It was Strauss.

Hartford extended his hand. "Would you do me the honor?"

In answer, she settled her hand in his.

He slid his arm around her waist, drawing her close—dangerously close. "I've wanted to do this every time I saw you, at every ball for the past six and a half years."

"Seven now." She caught her breath as he swept her into the first turn. Her skirts swirled around her in a graceful arc of crimson velvet.

"I'm not counting anything after the day you appeared in Arlington Street," he said. "When I found you there, standing in my grandfather's library, I thought I was dreaming."

"Not for long, I presume," she said. "I scolded you enough to wake you up."

"You were magnificent."

Anne nearly lost track of the steps. It had been so long! She'd danced with other gentlemen, of course, but nothing could compare with being back in Hartford's arm. He was firm and steady and smooth, blessed with an innate gracefulness that made every dip and turn akin to floating on air.

The waltz had formerly been considered scandalous. An antiquated view, or so Anne had always believed. But she now understood why it had once shocked the fashionable world. It was an embrace of sorts, made all the more thrilling by the throb of her pulse and the blood-stirring swell of the music.

Her fingers tightened on Hartford's shoulder as they whirled across the polished wood floor.

"Look up at me, love," he said gently. His large hand was strong at her back, a warm imprint on her skin through the bodice of her ball gown. "Trust me. I won't steer you wrong."

"It isn't you. It's me." Her eyes met his. "It's against my nature to let someone else take charge."

"You can lead if you wish."

She stifled a laugh. "No, thank you. At least," she added, "not when we're dancing."

It was his turn to smile. "I'd follow you anywhere, sweetheart."

Anne relaxed into the strength of his hold. Trust wasn't natural to her where Hartford was considered. It wasn't easy. But she gave hers to him now absolutely. With it came a lightness she'd never felt before.

She wasn't leaning on him. She wasn't depending on him to guide her or look after her.

No. That wasn't it at all.

They were equals. Partners. Each of them a perfectly matched complement to the other. It made dancing a pleasure. It made *everything* a pleasure.

They no longer spoke, only looked into each other's eyes. A smile played at Hartford's lips, but his gaze was warm enough. She felt the heat of it thrumming in her veins.

As the strains of the waltz began to soften and the first dance came to a close, he bent his head to her ear. "Will you join me in the library?" he asked. "There's something very particular I'd like to ask you this evening."

Her heart beat hard.

"*May* I ask it?"

"Yes," she said. "You may."

When the music stopped, he retained her hand, holding it warmly in his. The two of them made their way toward the doors that led out into the hall.

They'd gone no more than a few steps when Hartford came to an abrupt halt. The color drained from his face as though he'd seen a ghost.

Anne followed his gaze. What she saw made her stomach sink. "Oh no," she said under her breath. "What is *he* doing here?"

It was Marcus Neale. He stood just outside the doors, clothed in black-and-white eveningwear. And he wasn't alone.

He was with Mariah.

Forty-One

The whole of it was, all at once, crystal clear. Hart wondered how he could have been so blind as to fail to recognize it before.

Marcus was Mariah's secret beau, of course.

It was he who had bought her the garish brooch she'd worn at the Ramseys' ball. He who had exhorted her to meet him in Richmond Park. He was the mysterious gentleman struggling to "right his ship."

This was how Marcus had learned where to telegraph Hart in Yorkshire. Mariah must have told him. She was Marcus's sweetheart. His unwitting dupe, very likely.

Hart didn't want to believe it. He and Marcus had left things on good terms. They'd seemed to better understand each other. And now this?

"You didn't invite him?" Anne asked.

"I did not," Hart said, still holding her hand. "I'll see if I can minimize the damage."

But it was too late.

Brookdale joined Mariah and Marcus at the door, Aunt Esther close behind him. Their faces were taut with barely controlled anger.

Hart's blood went cold.

The repercussions of this meeting were more far-reaching than

Marcus could possibly comprehend. Hart wasn't ready to confront them yet. But after nine long years of secrets, it seemed he no longer had a choice in the matter.

"I fear we're past the minimizing stage," Anne said.

"I fear you're right," he answered gruffly. "I have to face things."

She pressed his hand with a reassuring grip. "We'll face them together."

Hart nodded once, his throat too constricted to speak. This was meant to be the night he proposed to her. Instead—once again—family had gotten in the way of things. Last time it had been hers. This time it seemed it would be his.

They wove their way through the crush of guests assembling for the next dance. By the time they reached the door, Marcus, Mariah, Uncle Brookdale, and Aunt Esther had already gone. They were headed for the library.

Hart and Anne followed. Grandfather and Lady Arundell emerged from the crowd of guests to join them in their pursuit.

"What's all this commotion?" Lady Arundell asked, clutching the skirts of her black crepe ball gown. "Has something happened?"

"It's that mysterious young man of my granddaughter's," Grandfather said. "Did you get a look at him, my boy?"

Hart didn't respond.

He and Anne crossed the threshold into the library, Grandfather and Lady Arundell a mere footstep behind them.

The Sutton Park library was a vast cathedral-like space, with a ceiling that rose two stories high. Leather-bound books lined the walls, and groupings of comfortable chairs were arranged in various nooks, both on the richly carpeted lower level and high above it in the iron-railed gallery that ringed the library's second floor.

Uncle Brookdale stood with his wife in front of the cavernous hearth, facing down Marcus and Mariah. "This is not how it's done, sir," he boomed. "To conduct an affair by stealth, meeting my daughter in secret. Corresponding with her! You, a man whom we have never met, and who has never extended the courtesy of paying his addresses in a respectable manner."

"Who are your people, sir?" Lady Brookdale demanded. "Who are your mother and your father?"

Hart went to join them, Anne at his side. Lady Arundell and Hart's grandfather followed in their wake.

"Did you come here intending to disrupt this house party, young man?" Grandfather asked. "This is my home, sir. Guests come by my invitation or not at all."

"*I* invited Mr. Neale," Mariah said. "If you'll let me explain—"

"Neale, is it?" Grandfather looked to Lady Arundell. "One of the Surrey Neales?"

"The Surrey Neales only have daughters, as I recall," Lady Arundell replied. "And this young man bears no resemblance to them. Though he *does* appear familiar . . ."

"Not to me, he doesn't," Aunt Esther retorted.

"My intentions are honorable," Marcus said. He drew himself up with all of the sober dignity of a prospective suitor calling on a young lady's parents. "I'm in love with your daughter. I hope, one day, to be in a position to make her an offer."

"You are a stranger, sir," Brookdale said. "And yet you have the temerity to speak of loving my stepdaughter? Of hoping to make her an offer? As though we would ever countenance such a match! We've never been introduced to you or seen you about in society. We have no knowledge of your name, your birth, or your character."

"Nor do we require it," Aunt Esther added hotly. "Your conduct alone proclaims you a villain."

Hart came forward. "I can't speak to his conduct," he said, locking eyes with his half brother. "But I can apprise you of his parentage."

Uncle Brookdale turned on Hart in a towering fury. "You're acquainted with this blackguard?" His face went scarlet. "I might have known! Was it you who arranged this scandalous affair? Was it another of your despicable amusements? I suppose you thought it comical to pair up my stepdaughter with a—"

"Hartford had nothing to do with this!" Marcus said, raising his voice. "Miss Spriggs and I met by chance. We didn't even know each other's names in the beginning."

"It's true," Mariah said. "I was walking in Hyde Park with my maid when I tripped and dropped my novel into the Serpentine. Mr. Neale leapt in to retrieve it for me. He was excessively gallant."

Marcus's face betrayed a flicker of remorse. "I wasn't long returned from Plymouth," he said to Hart. "I didn't realize who she was until later. By then, my feelings were such that I couldn't sever the connection."

Hart believed him. And it wasn't only because of Marcus's penitent expression. It was because his confession explained so much. Since returning from school, Marcus had been desperate to make himself into a gentleman. All of those ill-advised wagers and clothing and gifts bought on credit. He must have done it, however foolishly, with Mariah in mind.

"We've been meeting when we can," she said, clinging to Marcus's arm. "But nothing untoward has happened, I promise. We only sit and talk with each other or go walking alone in the park."

Aunt Esther threw up her hands. "How can a daughter of mine be so senseless? To have risked your reputation in such a hoydenish fashion. Have you no care for Brookdale's career?"

Brookdale remained focused on Hart. "Well? Do you have nothing to say for yourself?"

"Only this," Hart answered. "Marcus Neale is not unknown to me. He's the son of Mrs. Neale of Battersea, a former lady's maid to my mother, and of—"

"A servant's child?" Lady Brookdale staggered backward as if from a blow.

"Pray, let him speak, ma'am," Anne said sharply. "Nothing can be gained by these constant interruptions."

"What right have you to even be in this room?" Aunt Esther flung back at her. "This is a family matter!"

"Too right, madam." Lady Arundell swept to Anne's side, as formidable as ever. "And as my daughter is contemplating a connection to this family, she has as much right to be here as anyone."

Anne gave Hart a bracing look. "My dear boy, what are you waiting for?"

The tightness in Hart's chest eased. With Anne beside him, he felt stronger. As though he could take on the world.

Straightening to his full height, he faced down his aunt and uncle. "Marcus Neale is the son of Mrs. Neale, and of my late father, Everett Hartford."

"Ah," Lady Arundell murmured. "That explains the resemblance."

Once mentioned, the likeness was impossible not to see. The assemblage looked between Marcus and Hart and back again, seeming to come to the realization at the exact same time.

What happened next was pure pandemonium.

Uncle Brookdale bellowed in outrage, Aunt Esther fainted into a heap on the hearthrug, and Grandfather turned the shade of bleached linen. For a moment it appeared as though he, too, would fall into a swoon.

Hart was immediately at his side. Taking his grandfather's arm, Hart assisted him to a chair. "I'm sorry," he said. "I didn't want you to find out this way."

Uncle Brookdale hoisted Aunt Esther from the floor. With Lady Arundell's help, he managed to lift her up onto the library sofa.

Mariah dropped into a chair, her countenance a little green. "Mr. Neale . . ." she whispered. "Do you mean to say that . . . you're my *cousin*?"

"Cousins!" Aunt Esther, who had temporarily revived from her swoon, promptly slumped into another faint.

Marcus crouched down beside Mariah. "We're not cousins. Not by blood. We're only related by marriage. There's nothing to prevent us being together." He took her hand. "Forgive me. I would have confessed to the connection the day we met, but I didn't dare risk revealing the circumstances of my birth."

Anne glanced at Hart as she loosened his grandfather's cravat. "Fetch him a stiff drink, would you?"

Hart went to the drinks tray and swiftly poured out a large measure of brandy. He brought it back to his grandfather, holding the glass as he took a sip.

"This young man is *not* my brother's son," Brookdale said. He wafted a handkerchief over his prone wife. "Everett would never—"

"Nonsense," Lady Arundell said. "Only look at him. Anyone can see Everett's stamp on the boy."

Grandfather stared at Marcus. The truth slowly registered in his eyes. "Everett had another child."

"Three children, my lord," Marcus said. "I have two younger sisters."

"Don't listen, Father," Brookdale cut in. "It's rubbish, all of it. Everett was a moral man. He honored his marriage vows."

Hart couldn't suppress a laugh.

Brookdale's brows snapped together. "By God, if you make a mockery of this—"

"It was my father who made a mockery of us," Hart said. "He *wasn't* a moral man. I'm sorry for it, but there it is. He kept a mistress for over a decade during his lifetime. He sired three children on her, all of whom were left without a penny after his death."

"He loved us," Marcus said. "Whatever his failings, I know it to be true."

Grandfather took another drink of his brandy. His eyes found Hart's over the rim of the glass. "How long have you known of this?"

Hart's jaw tightened. He'd rather anything than have this conversation. But Anne had been right. The secret wasn't the Hydra. It was the Augean stables.

It was time to wash the place clean.

"For nine years," he said. "My mother confessed it to me in the days before she died. She'd known for some time, apparently. It was a source of great bitterness to her."

Grandfather blinked. "Why didn't you tell me?"

"Because you're so blasted proud of him," Hart said. "You were always talking about how much comfort his morality gave you. And because of Uncle Brookie's career. I knew the damage it could do to him politically. In my own way, I was trying to protect the family."

Brookdale stared at him. "*You* were protecting *us*?"

"Not only that," Hart admitted. "I was ashamed of the truth. It didn't speak well of my mother and me, did it? We must have been a grievous disappointment to him."

Anne set her hand on his shoulder. "You're far from a disappointment."

"She's right." Grandfather leaned back in his chair with a weary sigh. "There were signs of Everett's proclivities long before you were born."

"Father," Brookdale protested. "There's no call to sully my brother's name."

"He had a roving eye in his younger days," Grandfather said. "You know it as well as I do, Brookie. I had to bail him out countless times when he was at Oxford. I thought he'd mended his ways. It was *that* which made me proud, the change he'd wrought in his life. He'd embraced his new philosophy with such fervor. Such uncommon zeal."

"Many do who actively engage in hypocrisy," Lady Arundell remarked. "The more fervently the righteous oppose something, the more you can be certain they're engaging in the behavior in private."

"Mama," Anne said quietly. "Your observations are hardly helpful at present."

"No, no." Grandfather patted Anne's hand. "She's right, my dear. I've seen it time and again. I might have recognized it in my own son had I taken the trouble to look. I was blinded by my love for him."

Brookdale sank down on the sofa beside his prone wife. "A mistress and three children," he muttered. "Cobb will waste no time in making this the news of the day."

"No one else knows of it, sir," Marcus reassured him. "Except for my mother and sisters. And possibly Mr. Royce. I've seen one of his men following me about."

Hart gave Marcus an alert look. "You, too?"

"Royce?" Lady Arundell echoed. "Who's Royce?"

"He has a betting shop in St. Giles," Hart explained. "Marcus owed some money to the man, and I went to pay it. It's how Royce learned of our connection."

"*Gabriel* Royce? The notorious London criminal?" Brookdale lost what was left of his color. "I'm ruined."

"Come here, lad," Grandfather said to Marcus. "Let me have a look at you."

Marcus reluctantly left Mariah's side to come and stand in front of his grandfather. His hands were shaking. "Sir."

Grandfather's eyes glimmered. "You have the look of him," he said. "And your sisters? Do they resemble you?"

"To an alarming degree," Hart informed him. "I shall take you to meet them if you like."

"No, you will *not*," Aunt Esther said, regaining her senses. She struggled to a sitting position on the sofa. "Have none of you comprehended how sordid this all is? How very crass and vulgar? There can be no connection between our families. And as for a union between my daughter and this . . . this presumptuous, penniless, bast—"

"He won't be penniless for long," Hart interjected before his aunt could give voice to the word. "He's embarking on a new business venture, aren't you, Marcus? With hard work and dedication, I expect that, in a few years, he'll have made his fortune."

"That's why I came here," Marcus said. "I'm sorry, Hartford, but I had to see Mariah before I go. We've been unable to meet in London for nearly a month. This was my last chance to speak with her. I had to explain. I thought no one would notice me in the crowd."

"Where are you going?" Mariah asked.

"To the Scottish Highlands," Marcus replied. "Hartford has arranged a position for me there."

Brookdale's eyes narrowed at Hart with suspicion. "Who the devil do you know in the Highlands?"

"What sort of position?" Grandfather asked at the same time.

Hart exchanged a brief glance with Anne. She gave him a slight nod. He took a deep breath. "I have the honor of being a majority partner in the Parfit Plumbago Crucible Company," he said. "We're in the process of expanding our mining operations to Scotland."

Anne's face shone with pride. "He has a wonderful factory in Battersea, my lord," she said to his grandfather. "The crucibles it produces are of great value to British industry."

"Good God, man," Brookdale uttered. "You're in trade!"

Aunt Esther moaned. "Take me to my room, Brookdale. I require my maid and my sal volatile."

"Trade?" Grandfather examined Hart's face, searching for any sign that he was jesting. "Can it be true?"

"You've ruined us all," Brookdale said. "My political career, our family's reputation, and my—"

"Didn't you hear my daughter?" Lady Arundell interrupted. "Hartford is a success! He's finally stuck to something of worth—for the first time, I might add—and is on the brink of wealth and status. He's a gentleman of the new age. I should think you, of all people, would appreciate his achievement."

"I? Appreciate a tradesman in the family?" Brookdale's lips compressed. "I assure you—"

"You're a politician," Lady Arundell said. "Where does the future power of England lie but within the mechanisms of industry and invention? Prince Albert would have embraced such innovation. Unless you're setting yourself up in moral superiority to the late Prince Consort—"

"Indeed, I am not, madam," Brookdale said tightly. "But the realities of our position—"

"If you're quite finished," Aunt Esther said. "I've already told you that I require assistance to my room. Will no one take pity on my poor nerves?"

"I must return to the ball," Grandfather said. "My guests will be wondering where I've got to. We daren't risk any more gossip."

"I'll accompany you," Lady Arundell said stoutly. Taking his arm, she helped him from the chair. "All will be well, March. We've weathered worse storms than a trifling litter of by-blows and a tradesman or two. Only think of your grandson and my daughter—our two great families joined together at last!"

Grandfather's face softened. "It is cause for celebration, ma'am, I agree."

Brookdale struggled to assist his wife up from the sofa. He couldn't manage to lift her on his own. The two of them were too similar in size.

"Permit me," Marcus said.

"Oh no." Aunt Esther shrank back against the sofa cushions.

"Pray let him, Mama," Mariah said. "He's ever so chivalrous."

Marcus scooped Aunt Esther up easily in his arms. "It's no trouble, ma'am," he said gallantly. "You're lighter than a feather."

"I'll go with you," Mariah said. She trotted along at Marcus's side as he carried her mother from the room.

Brookdale trailed after them, looking back only once. "A tradesman!" he exclaimed. "Heaven forfend!"

And then they were all gone, the library door swinging shut behind them.

Hart was left alone with Anne. He looked down at her, a trifle dazed. "The Augean stables," he said.

And then he laughed.

This time there was no bitterness in it. There was only imminent relief. He felt like a cart horse who had, at long last, been relieved of a burdensome load.

Anne didn't join him in laughing. She reached up to frame his face, her small hands gentle but possessed of infinite strength. *She* wasn't a burden. She was an ally. A friend. The companion of his heart.

"What were you going to ask me?" she inquired.

Just like that, all of the cares of the world melted away. Even the book-lined walls of the library faded into the background. There were only the two of them, in front of the fire, bathed in the soft glow of flickering candlelight while the tempest raged outside.

But the timing was no longer right for a romantic proposal. Not with his family up in arms. Not with Marcus to deal with, and his uncle and grandfather to placate.

It struck Hart then that the timing would never be right. Not for either of them. But that was the precise beauty of their partnership. Nothing else need be perfect in their lives because they were perfect for each other. Together they could face any obstacles, weather any storm.

"I wondered, old thing," he said softly, "if you might consider marrying me?"

"I *have* considered it."

"And?"

"Yes," she said. "I will marry you, Hart."

Hart exhaled an unsteady breath. His voice, when he spoke, was thick with emotion. "You will? Truly, Anne?"

"Yes." She tugged him down to her and kissed him. "Yes, yes, yes."

His arms came around her in a fierce embrace. He kissed her back, deeply, passionately, murmuring love words and promises against her lips. "My darling. I swear I'll make you happy."

He felt her smile. "You already have," she said.

There were no more words then. Only Anne in his arms, her lips pressed to his, the two of them together at last with no obstacles or barriers between them.

"Your mother was wrong, you know," he said a long while later.

Anne's lashes lifted. She looked up at him dreamily. "Was she?"

"The crucible company isn't the first time I've stuck to something of worth," he informed her. "I stuck with you, didn't I?"

"Yes, I suppose you did."

"I never gave up the hope of you. Not once in all these years." His voice deepened with emotion. "I love you to the ends of the earth, sweetheart. To the heavens and beyond. All I require is but a fraction of that devotion returned, and I shall die a happy man."

"Foolish." She cradled his face. Her sherry-brown eyes had a peculiar shimmer in them. "Don't you know that you're the love of my life?"

Hart's chest tightened. His mouth found hers once more, and he kissed her again, with all the love in his heart.

The sound of the orchestra seeped through the doors, playing first a lively country dance and then a vigorous polka. How much time passed, Hart didn't know, but it was long enough for their absence to be remarked upon.

"We shall have to rejoin the ball soon," he said, nuzzling her cheek. "Regrettably."

Her fingers threaded in the hair at his nape. "When we're married, our kisses will never have to end."

"When we're married, I'm never going to let you out of my sight." He drew back to look at her, his words a solemn vow. "I intend to spend every hour of every day with you."

"Every hour of every day?" She gave a soft laugh. "We shall argue. We shall drive each other mad."

Gazing down at his beautiful, golden-haired Fury, Hart was unable to suppress a grin. "My dearest love," he said, "I'm heartily looking forward to it."

Epilogue

Somersetshire, England
Summer 1863

Anne held tight to the reins of Damselfly's bridle as the temperamental mare once again reared up on her hind legs. "This is *your* fault," she said to her husband. "Had you backed her as a three-year-old—"

Hart took charge of Damselfly's reins. "She *was* backed as a three-year-old. She's merely out of practice."

Absent his hat and coat, he stood beside Anne in the secluded arena behind Barton Court's ancient stone stable block. The sleeves of his white linen shirt were rolled to his elbows, revealing the sinewy muscles of his forearms. Before coming outside, he'd been at his desk in the library, occupied in writing one of his anonymous columns. They were still published occasionally—all of them for Anne—each line layered with flirtatious double meaning.

"There's no shame in begging off," he said.

She cast him a speaking glance as she moved to Damselfly's left side. "Nonsense. I'm more than capable of riding her. You said yourself that she was perfect for me."

Having calmed Damselfly, Hart assisted Anne into the sidesaddle, tossing her up into the seat with the same effortless strength as he held his mare. "I was trying to console you after you retired Saffron. I'd no intention of you risking your neck."

Anne hooked her right leg over the pommel. The skirts of her garnet habit fell over her limbs in a graceful sweep of jewel-bright wool. "My neck is perfectly fine," she said. "So long as you hold her steady."

She sounded braver than she felt.

Saffron had been unsaddled for the last time only a fortnight ago. It had been a difficult decision, but a necessary one. The old stallion deserved his retirement. And now that Anne was firmly ensconced as the mistress of Barton Court, she was in a position to give it to him. The pastures on the estate were lush, the weather pleasant, and Anne could still see her former mount—to brush him, pet him, and spoil him with grain—as often as she wished.

It was but one of the many benefits she'd enjoyed since her marriage to Hart.

After a scandalously short engagement, the two of them had wed in a lavish spring ceremony at St. George's Hanover Square. Julia, Stella, and Evelyn had acted as bridesmaids, the three of them garbed in double-skirted silk gowns that complemented Anne's elegant bridal robe of lace-trimmed white satin.

It had been a grand affair, with guests traveling from near and far to see the two great houses of Hartford and Deveril joined in matrimony. The church had been packed with titled aristocrats from the furthest reaches of England, along with a smattering of rarely seen twigs from the lowliest branches of Hart's and Anne's respective family trees. Even Marcus and his sisters had been present, much to the horror of Lord Brookdale and his lady wife.

Anne hadn't regarded Brookdale's opinions. The truth was, she'd grown rather fond of Hart's half siblings in recent months. Ethel and Ermintrude were dear girls with a wealth of humor and intelligence beneath their shy exteriors. As for Marcus, good honest work had done wonders for his disposition. Returning briefly from Scotland to attend the wedding, he'd appeared well on his way to becoming the gentleman he'd always longed to be.

Anne didn't doubt that he and Mariah would be married within the year. The two of them were still besotted with each other and, as Julia had reminded them, one wedding often followed another.

"You're next," she'd whispered to Stella as they'd assisted Anne in draping her long lace veil before walking down the aisle.

"Or not," Evelyn had countered. "One needn't get married to have a happily-ever-after."

"She's right, dearest," Anne had agreed with unassailable confidence. "Your happy ending is whatever you wish it to be."

Stella had blushed and demurred, unusually silent in the face of her friends' chatter. Ever since her unfortunate encounter with Mr. Hayes at the Earl of March's Christmas party, Stella had been strangely unforthcoming on the topic of romance. If Anne didn't know better, she'd imagine her friend was keeping some kind of secret.

Anne thought of Stella now—*and* of Stella's mare, Locket. Damselfly rather resembled the flighty gray in temperament. But where Locket was fast and responsive, Damselfly was as wild and unpredictable as a firework on Guy Fawkes night.

Hart seemed to share Anne's assessment. "The moment I release her," he said, "she's going to explode across this arena like a Catherine wheel."

"Rubbish." Anne stroked a gloved hand over the mare's arching neck. "We're friends of old, aren't we, my girl?"

"Have a care, Anne," Hart said. "Your mother would never forgive me if I let you come to harm."

"My mother isn't here," Anne reminded him.

It wasn't for lack of invitation.

Upon their marriage, Hart—the dear, foolish man—had invited Anne's mother to come and live with them. Mama had refused, of course. She couldn't abide the country, not even for the six months of the year that Anne and Hart were committed to reside at Barton Court.

Instead, Mama had made good on her promise to visit Italy with

Mr. Fielding. Accompanied by several of their spiritualist friends, they had departed but a month ago and, according to Mama's last letter, were presently ensconced in a villa in Tuscany.

Anne expected to see her mother again soon, if not in Somersetshire, then in London. Anne and Hart would be returning there for the winter, both for the sake of their families and for that of the crucible company. It was to be the future pattern of their life—half the year spent in the country and half spent in town. A dream existence, to Anne's mind.

"*I'd* never forgive myself," Hart said, still holding Damselfly's bridle. "Perhaps we should wait—"

"You may let go of her," Anne told him gently. "I know what I'm doing."

Hart's jaw tensed. For a moment, it appeared he would argue.

New to the role of husband, he sometimes fell prey to bouts of overprotectiveness. Anne had often been obliged to remind him that she wasn't made of glass, liable to break at the first tumble. She was more than capable of looking after herself. Marriage hadn't changed that fact, regardless of how much Hart cherished her and wanted to keep her safe.

He knew she valued her independence. And he understood how important it was that their marriage be an equal partnership. It was how he always treated her, as his equal.

Unless, that is, his worry over her safety got the better of him.

"I wish to God I'd never mentioned you riding her," he muttered as he let go of Damselfly's bridle. "If anything happens to you—"

Anne didn't hear the rest of it. Her husband's words were lost in a whistle of wind as Damselfly took flight, bolting across the arena in a lightning flash of energy. The chestnut mare was as expressive and fiery under saddle as she was when pulling Hart's curricle with her equally volatile sister.

A lesser rider would have been toppled in the first second. Even

Anne, with all of her vast experience, was hard-pressed to maintain her seat. Years of riding Saffron had blunted her skill. She was used to the old stallion's temperament and the ease with which they'd always communicated. Communication with Damselfly was, by contrast, like learning to speak an entirely different language.

But Anne was nothing if not a quick learner.

She shortened the reins to reestablish her contact and, deepening her seat, brought the mare back under control.

Damselfly shook her head in protest, but Anne would not be moved. With her weight and her hands, she urged Damselfly into a smaller circle, focusing the mare's attention on bending to the pressure of Anne's leg.

"That's it," Hart called out from his place along the white-washed wooden rail of the arena. There was unmistakable relief in his voice. "She's listening now."

Anne's mouth tugged into a distracted smile. She continued to work with Damselfly, bending her to the right and to the left in a series of alternating circles, first at a trot and then at a canter. The mare was wonderfully responsive once one had her attention, conscious of Anne's slightest shift in weight and the faintest pressure of her hands and leg.

It was a new experience, and an exhilarating one. By the time Anne dismounted, she was grinning from ear to ear.

Hart caught her in a crushing embrace. "Are you all right?"

Anne gave a breathless laugh. "Are *you*?"

"I've aged ten years since you got on her," he said against Anne's hair. "But otherwise—"

"Foolish," she teased. "Did you doubt my riding skill? And I one of the Four Horsewomen! One of the Furies!"

"You can laugh. But there was a moment when she first galloped off—"

"I had her well in hand." Anne slipped an arm around his waist, still holding Damselfly's reins loosely in her opposite hand. "I didn't mean to worry you."

"You always worry me. But I do trust you, old thing. I'd never expect you to be anything less than what you are, even if your exploits do occasionally threaten to give me an apoplexy."

"I know that," she said, leaning into his embrace. "It's one of the reasons I love you."

Hart's expression softened. He bent his head. His mouth claimed hers in a deep, lingering kiss.

She stretched up to return it, their lips clinging sweetly until Damselfly stamped her foot with impatience. Anne broke the kiss with another laugh. "We do pick our moments."

If it wasn't the horses interrupting, it was the servants, or even Eris. Only this morning, the now fully grown black cat had jumped onto their bed, staking out her place beside Hart on his pillow, never mind that he and Anne were in the middle of a rather passionate embrace.

"We do at that." Hart gazed down at her with warm affection. His mouth tipped up at one corner. "But I can't complain."

Her heart swelled with love for him. "Nor I."

As much as they bantered—nettling each other and even, sporadically, lapsing into argument—their brief marriage had been successful by every possible measure. There was no great mystery to it. They simply enjoyed each other's company, both outside the house and inside of it.

Especially inside of it.

Hart was a romantic. Anne hadn't realized how much so until their wedding night. His love for her had no limits. But there was nothing maudlin about it. Nothing treacly or poetic. Indeed, he was as likely to tease her during their lovemaking as he was to make her melt in his arms. She loved nothing more than doing the same to him.

And *he* loved *her*, absolutely.

Anne wondered sometimes if they'd ever get enough of each other.

For now, the answer seemed to be *no.*

"Shall we return to the house?" he asked.

She smiled up at him. "With pleasure."

Author's Note

When writing *The Lily of Ludgate Hill*, I was inspired by several historical figures, places, and events from the Victorian era. I was also heavily influenced by my own experience with losing my father to congestive heart failure two days before Christmas in 2021.

Grief is a powerful emotion. And when that grief manifests as the result of losing a parent, it can alter the dynamics of a family to an extraordinary degree. The child sometimes takes on the role of caregiver while their remaining parent grieves. In such cases, the child's own grief may be suppressed for a time, never fully expressed or worked through in a healthy way because all of their energies are taken up with holding their family together.

This is what has happened in Anne's case. Her situation is doubly difficult because, before the death of Anne's father, Lady Arundell had always been a pillar of strength. Seeing her mother brought low by grief has a destabilizing effect on Anne's life. And when her mother's period of mourning goes on for years longer than mourning etiquette prescribes, Anne is forced to carve out a life for herself in the shadow of that grief or else (she fears) risk losing the one parent she has left.

For more on the Victorian inspiration for Lady Arundell's

protracted period of mourning, and for information on my other historical research for *Lily*, see my notes below.

The Widowed Queen Victoria

A Victorian-era widow was expected to mourn the death of her husband for two years' time. The first year and a half was spent wearing lusterless, unrelieved black and the final six months wearing shades of gray and lavender (known as half mourning). When her two years of mourning were finished, a widow's public display of grief was over. She could at last reemerge into society—and into color.

In 1862, when *Lily* is set, Queen Victoria had only just lost her husband, Prince Albert. No one had any reason to believe she would exceed the requisite two-year period of mourning. Indeed, anything longer than two years would have been viewed as deeply eccentric. Anne alludes to this in chapter six when she compares her mother's prolonged mourning period to the Queen's recent loss:

> Prince Albert had died six months ago, leaving the Queen, and many others in society, immobilized under a crushing weight of grief. But Anne didn't expect Queen Victoria to give way to that emotion. Her Majesty was resilient. She would surely be herself again when a year or two of formal mourning had passed.

In fact, as we now know, Queen Victoria kept to her blacks for the remainder of her life. She was, in this way, the model for Lady Arundell—a woman who, as Anne describes, "enmeshed [grief] into her very bones, casting herself and all those around her into a perpetual season of black-clothed sorrow."

As with Lady Arundell, Queen Victoria's grief made her selfish and shortsighted when it came to the needs of her children. She exercised a ruthless control over their lives, even as she dismissed their needs as individuals. The Queen's grief also made her easy prey for the spiritualist movement. Highly attached to the symbolism of mourning, and perpetually grieving for Prince Albert, she was rumored to have corresponded with spiritualists and even to have attended a séance in hopes of reaching her deceased husband.

Ludgate Hill is Life

In chapter eighteen of *Lily*, Mrs. Frazil states that "Ludgate Hill is life." This perfectly encapsulates what the street represents both in my story and in the tapestry of Victorian London. At the time, Ludgate Hill was one of the busiest and most diverse streets in the city. In his 1863 reminiscences on *London Scenes and London People*, William Harvey calls it "the greatest thoroughfare in London." He describes it as:

> A steep, narrow, inconvenient causeway, with a double row of ugly houses, tumbled or rather jammed together, with an apparent determination to make a site fit for a dozen dwellings receive twenty or thirty; the pavement disagreeably narrow, the road perpetually crowded with every conceivable form of horse-drawn vehicle—advertising vans, carts, wagons, omnibuses, imperiling each other at every turn; private carriages, cabs, and occasionally a donkey fish or vegetable stage—boards on wheels—all sorely in danger of being pounded into one shapeless mass; here and there some luckless pedestrian, sorely pressed for time, and bobbing, at the risk of life or limb, between the triple row of lumbering locomotives, in order to effect a passage from side to side.

Ludgate Hill stood in stark contrast to wealthy, rarified neighborhoods like Mayfair. For Anne and her mother to leave their house in Grosvenor Square for a ramshackle dwelling amid the chaos of

Ludgate Hill was essentially for them to choose life—to reemerge back into the world after a prolonged period of mourning.

Graphite Mining and the Plumbago Crucible Company

Hart's crucible business, the Parfit Plumbago Crucible Company, mirrors the real-life origin story of Morgan Advanced Materials, a company founded by the Morgan brothers in 1856. The five Morgan brothers had originally been importers and exporters, running a hardware and druggist business. However, in 1851, while visiting the Great Exhibition, they came across a new variety of American-made crucible that would drastically elevate their fortunes.

Composed of a mixture of clay and graphite, the American crucible promised to heat metals faster than any other crucible on the market. Foreseeing its economic potential, the Morgan brothers obtained the sole right to manufacture the crucible in the British Empire. They set up a small factory in Battersea, which they named the Patent Plumbago Crucible Company. At the start, it consisted of only a small brick kiln and a solitary horse for grinding the clay.

Within a few short years, the horse was replaced with two 35 horsepower engines. By the 1880s, the Morgans' business—now renamed the Morgan Crucible Company—was one of the largest crucible companies in the world.

Trade: A Scandalous Occupation

During the mid-Victorian era, fashionable ladies and gentlemen often exhibited a well-bred disdain for those whose fortunes arose from trade. Working for a living was viewed as vulgar. Even worse, it was common. To be a tradesman was to serve one's customers. In short, to be a servant.

A tradesman was, therefore, not viewed as a gentleman. Quite the reverse. Tradesmen and shopkeepers were often presumed to be from the lower orders of society. In Hart's case, of course, nothing could be further from the truth. But an aristocratic pedigree was no protection from the stain of the shop.

An affiliation with trade had the power to ruin a gentleman's reputation among the members of his own class. It could also taint his family by association. This is the main reason Hart keeps his crucible business a secret from his relations, and why he uses another man's surname in the company title instead of his own.

Acknowledgments

I began writing *The Lily of Ludgate Hill* one month after my father died. I was devastated, grief-stricken, and eventually a bit numb. Looking back on it, I don't know how I pushed forward. But I do know that I couldn't have made it through without the support of the wonderful people in my personal and professional life.

First and foremost, I owe a huge debt of gratitude to my mom, Vickie. Thank you for being with me, for encouraging me, and for putting up with all my anxiety about writing when we were both so anguished and exhausted after losing Dad. We've been in the Swamp of Sadness this past year. I'm still not sure if all my writing projects have been an added burden or if they've been a lifeline that kept us from going under. Either way, we're still here and I'm so grateful for you.

Tremendous thanks are also due to my fierce and fantastic agent, Kevan Lyon; to my brilliant editor, Sarah Blumenstock; and to Liz Sellers, Yazmine Hassan, Jessica Plummer, Megha Jain, Angelina Krahn, and the rest of the amazing team at Berkley/Penguin Random House, who work so hard on behalf of my Belles.

Additional thanks to Isabel, Dana, Alissa, Rel, Flora, Sarah, and Renee, for reading early drafts of this story and providing such useful feedback. And, as always, many thanks and much love to my animal family: Stella, Jet, Tavi, Bijou, and Asteria.

Lastly, I'd like to thank my dad, Eugene. You weren't here for this story, but there's so much of you in it. You are deeply missed, endlessly loved, and honored in everything I do and everything I am.

The Lily of Ludgate Hill

MIMI MATTHEWS

READERS GUIDE

Discussion Questions

1. Lady Anne Deveril has kept to her mourning blacks for years in order to show support for her mother's grief. Does this act of solidarity help or harm her mother's recovery? How does it impact Anne's own process of healing from the loss of her father?

2. Anne tolerates, and often encourages, her mother's involvement with spiritualism, believing that the spiritualist movement serves as a distraction from grief. Was spiritualism a wise diversion for Victorians who were grieving? Or did it feed into an unhealthy obsession with death?

3. Felix Hartford has been supporting his father's secret family for years, despite receiving no thanks from Mrs. Neale and her children. What might motivate him to persevere with them? Would you continue supporting friends or family members in such circumstances? Or would you leave them to their own devices, knowing they might fall into bad circumstances?

4. Hart failed Anne in the moment of her greatest need and, at the start of the story, Anne still hasn't forgiven him. Was she wrong to hold a grudge for so many years? Could you trust someone again who had hurt you or let you down in this way?

5. Riding her horse, Saffron, is one of Anne's few acts of physical independence. It allows her to be alone with her friends, fellow horsewomen Stella, Evie, and Julia. In what other period-proper ways might ladies like Anne exert their independence? How would you have dealt with the Victorian-era restrictions on women's freedom of movement?

6. When Anne believes Julia is in danger, she's willing to risk everything to come to her aid. She even swallows her pride and asks for Hart's help. How much would you risk to rescue a friend in need? Would you be willing to enlist the help of a former love?

7. As the illegitimate son of a gentleman, Marcus Neale has difficulty finding his place in the world. Does Hart make things better or worse by sending him to a good school and providing him with a comfortable life? How do you think Marcus will fare in Scotland once he's obliged to work for a living?

8. Victorians of Hart and Anne's class had great disdain for those in trade. A connection with it could not only damage a person's reputation, it could taint their family by association. Knowing this, was Hart wise to keep his crucible business secret from his relations? Or should he have shared the truth of his success, despite knowing they wouldn't approve?

9. When Anne and her mother move from Mayfair to Ludgate Hill, their world expands to include a wider and more diverse group of people. How did the teeming industry of Ludgate Hill contrast with the fashionable respectability of a wealthy neighborhood like Mayfair? How might Anne and her mother benefit from being exposed to a greater range of classes? Would this have helped or hindered their ability to move on from their grief?

10. During Anne's years of grieving her father, she is greatly comforted by her relationship with her horse, Saffron. Her world is further brightened when feral kitten Eris joins the Deveril household. What role do animals play in the story in terms of comfort, companionship, and bringers of joy? What role do animals play in your own life?

11. Friendships are important in Anne's life, especially those she's formed with her fellow horsewomen. She worries that moving to Ludgate Hill will isolate her from them. Moving to the countryside after her marriage risks isolating her even further, particularly in an era with no phone, email, or text. How might she maintain her close female friendships after marriage? How important is it to nurture these sorts of close friendships as we move through life?

12. Hart has a strict personal code of ethics when it comes to doing business. He advocates for safer working conditions and refuses to participate in the exploitation of the plumbago miners, whether in England, Scotland, or Ceylon. Does his stance ultimately make a difference in the way business is conducted?

Don't miss Stella's story in

The Muse of Maiden Lane,

coming soon from Berkley!

Hampshire, England
December 1862

Stella Hobhouse raced down the gaslit corridor, the voluminous skirts of her white silk and crepe ball gown clutched in her gloved hands, and the swelling notes of Strauss's "Lava-Ströme" waltz chasing at her heels.

She was well aware of the ironclad rules that governed the lives of ladies. Those rules were somewhat less rigid among fashionable society than they were in the suffocatingly restrictive Derbyshire village that she and her pious clergyman brother, Daniel, called home. But one rule remained as inflexible in London as it was across Britain entire: a respectable female *did not* color her hair.

Only actresses and—Stella blushed to admit to herself—prostitutes would resort to such tawdry tricks. A young lady of Stella's station would never reduce herself to purchasing a bottle of Circassian gold hair dye. Not even one procured through the post.

Great God, what had driven her to do it?

And what on earth had possessed her to copy, of all things, the exact shade of auburn hair portrayed in the Whistler painting she'd seen on display in the Berners Street Gallery? The very painting that had been recommended to her by the handsome artist she'd encountered sketching at the British Museum?

It was a question she'd been asking herself ever since she'd entered the Earl of March's grand gothic ballroom and spied that very same man—a person she'd never expected to see again in her life—seated in his wheeled chair at the edge of the polished wood floor. He'd been dressed, not in the plain suit and carelessly knotted cravat he'd worn at the museum, but in flawless black-and-white eveningwear. She'd realized, all at once, that he was a guest here. Not just an eccentric artist who loitered about museum portrait galleries, but a *gentleman*.

Mortification had rushed over her in a mighty flood, drowning out all rational thought. Her only instinct had been to flee the ballroom before he saw her. And that's precisely what Stella had done: fled.

She ducked into a dimly lit anteroom at the end of the corridor. Music drifted after her, rising and falling, a waltz she was meant to be dancing with some gentleman or other. Resting her back against one of the shadowy, silk-papered walls, she pressed a hand to her corseted midriff, willing her nerves to steady and her breath to calm.

It wasn't as though she'd committed a crime. It was only a bit of playacting. A chance to be someone else for a change. To experience the world as a young lady whose hair hadn't turned completely gray at the age of sixteen.

Aside from her best friend, Lady Anne Deveril, only Anne's mother, the Countess of Arundell, and Anne's beau, Mr. Hartford, were aware of what Stella had looked like before she'd dyed it. There was no one else in attendance at the house party who knew her. Even if there were, Stella doubted very much that they'd recognize her. As a young lady with gray hair, possessed of modest breeding and little fortune, she was often dismissed and ignored. No one ever saw her. Not really. Indeed, no one seemed to notice her at all.

But tonight, she'd drawn every eye. Anne had called her luminous. Ethereal. And for the first time in her life, Stella had felt that way.

Until she'd seen *him*.

And it *was* him, whatever his manner of dress. He had the same inky black hair. The same turn of countenance, with sharply hewn features and a mouth that curved with equally sharp humor. A *dangerous* countenance. It was the face of a gentleman who saw too much. A face from which nothing—and no one—was hidden.

Stella exhaled an uneven breath. It wouldn't do, this ridiculous surge of schoolgirlish embarrassment. She was two-and-twenty. A steady, sensible young lady, not some green girl prone to fits of the vapors.

She must compose herself and return to the ball.

It was the only practical course. Lord March's house party was a week in length. She couldn't very well hide thc cntire time. Besides, there was a good chance the gentleman wouldn't recognize her. He'd met her only once before, and then just briefly.

Perhaps she'd overacted?

But of course she had!

There was no way the gentleman would remember her. They'd been in each other's company for less than five minutes that day at the museum and had exchanged no more than a handful of words. He'd doubtless forgotten her the moment she was out of his sight.

To be sure, Stella felt a little foolish, now she thought of it rationally.

Straightening from the wall, she smoothed her skirts, steeling herself to return to the ballroom. It was then she heard it; the unmistakable rattle of wheels drawing ever closer down the length of the marble corridor. The sound came to an abrupt halt outside thc door of the anteroom where she was hiding.

A gentleman's deep voice broke through the shadows. "Good Lord," he said in cheerful amazement. "It *is* you."

Teddy Hayes rolled his wheeled chair into the dim interior of the anteroom. He wasn't about to wait for a gilt-edged invitation. Not after he'd spent the last three months excoriating himself for not discovering the mysterious young lady's name on the last occasion they'd met.

He'd been so thunderstruck by her then, so dazzled, that it hadn't even occurred to him to ask until after she'd gone. By then, it was too late. There had been no one around who could enlighten him. No fashionable acquaintances who might know her identity.

Such was the price of being new to London.

Teddy was a visitor here. A guest, not a member of polite society. Aside from the small circle of friends that his older sister, Laura, and her husband, Alex Archer, surrounded themselves with, there was no one to whom Teddy could apply for information. Love his relations as he did, he was reluctant to ask them for help in such matters. Some things were private. Especially when it came to the subject of silver-haired goddesses he'd encountered in the British Museum.

"Why did you run away?" he asked.

The young lady stood with her back to the wall. Her white pearl-and-crepe-festooned skirts bowed out in front of her in an arc of petticoats and crinoline. "I did no such thing," she said stiffly.

It was the first she'd spoken since he'd entered the room. She had a soft, even voice, with a hint of velvet at the back of it. The kind of voice that could soothe as easily as it could seduce.

Teddy's blood thrummed with an unexpected pulse of heat.

He instantly dismissed the feeling. He hadn't gone after her because he was attracted to her. Not as a man, anyway. His interest was purely artistic. "You did," he said.

The same moment he'd clapped eyes on her from across the crowded ballroom, she'd spun on her heel and disappeared out the doors in a flurry of glittering skirts. He'd been left staring after her in dismay as the orchestra struck up the opening waltz, wondering for all of fifteen seconds whether he'd been mistaken.

"I felt a little faint," she replied, a trifle defensively. "I needed air."

"And you're taking it here?" He cast a dubious glance around the anteroom as he wheeled himself to the nearest lamp. It sat upon a low inlaid walnut table beside one of the damask-upholstered settees. Striking a friction match, he lit the wick. The room was at once bathed in a soft glow of light. "You might at least have opened a window."

"It's storming outside," she replied as he turned his chair to face her. "In case you hadn't noticed."

Teddy's gaze swept over her. She looked different than she had that day at the British Museum. He should know. The memory of her had been etched into his brain for months.

It wasn't because she was the most beautiful woman he'd ever seen—though she *was* beautiful. It was because she was different. And not just an oddity in her manner, or in the style of her dress or coiffure. She was *strikingly* different.

When he'd encountered her that day in the King's Gallery, her hair had been uniformly silver—the color of fine platinum or sterling. When coupled with her silver-blue eyes and the tender gravity of her manner, it gave her the look of a shimmering, vaporous spirit newly alighted from the heavens to engage with lowly humankind.

She'd reminded him of one of the mythological Pleiades; the seven sisters the Greek god Zeus had famously transformed into stars to grace the night sky. Teddy had never in his life seen a woman that better embodied the myth. As an artist, the sight hadn't failed to make an impression on him.

"I notice everything," he said.

The young lady's throat worked on a delicate swallow. She edged toward the door. "I beg your pardon. I must return to the ballroom. My friends will be wondering—"

"I trust you're not afraid of me?"

She stilled. Her lips compressed in a vaguely affronted line. "Indeed, I am not."

"You appear so."

"If I do, it's only because I don't know you."

"We've met before," he reminded her. "It was some months ago.

You were in the King's Gallery of the British Museum admiring a Van Dyck drawing."

She stiffened. "I remember."

His mouth quirked. Naturally she did. He'd offended her then. Been too blunt. Too free with his opinions. It was a failing of his, one made worse by the virulent strain of scarlet fever he'd contracted in his youth. The illness had left his legs partially paralyzed but had done nothing to curb the sharpness of his mind. Indeed, his sister often remarked that the more Teddy felt constrained by his disability, the less of a guard he was willing to set on his tongue.

It wasn't deliberate. He didn't mean to be rude or unkind. But he knew firsthand how short life could be and how suddenly it might all come to an end. The time one had left was too precious to squander. He had no patience for mincing words.

"I recommended a painting to you," he said. "Whistler's new piece—*The Woman in White*. It was on display at the Berners Street Gallery at the time."

She blushed to the roots of her hair. Her *auburn* hair. It was now the same shade as the titian-haired lady depicted in Whistler's painting. "I could hardly forget," she said rigidly. "But it doesn't follow that I know you. We haven't been introduced. Not properly."

"That's easily remedied." He wheeled a half turn closer to her. "My name is Edward Hayes. Most everyone calls me Teddy. And you are?"

"Stella Hobhouse," she blurted out, "but that isn't the point—"

"Stella," he repeated. A pleased smile tugged at his mouth. "Like a star." Surely it was a sign? He was meant to find her again.

She drew herself up with offended dignity. "I did *not* give you permission to use my Christian name, sir."

"Why shouldn't I when it's so beautiful?" He wheeled nearer. "By the by . . . what happened to your silver hair, Stella?"

Her mouth fell open. "Why that's . . . that's none of your business!"

"You dyed it, I suppose." He frowned. "I wish you wouldn't have."

"How dare you, sir? To presume to make personal remarks about my—" She broke off. "Is this how you address ladies of your acquaintance?"

"With honesty and candor? Indeed, it *is* how I address ladies. It's the same way I address gentlemen. I see no need to insult you by dancing about with euphemisms."

"It's not an insult. It's decorum. Politeness. There are rules—"

"Yes, I've heard of them. I suppose that's how it must be in London. But we're not in London any longer. We're in Hampshire." His smile returned. "And house parties are wild places, I'm told."

She stared at him, the expression in her silvery-blue eyes both intrigued and appalled. "How is it that you come to be here? Do you know Lord March?"

"I don't," he admitted.

"Then what are you doing at his house party?"

"I'm not here by choice," he said. "My sister and brother-in-law were invited. As I traveled with them from Paris, they thought it best I accompany them."

It had been the only way to set Laura's mind at ease. He'd been in his chair for nearly five years, the first several of which she'd been his caregiver. It was a difficult role for her to relinquish. Never mind that Teddy was better now than he'd been in ages. She still worried about him to an excessive degree. The thought of him remaining alone in London, even with a manservant to assist him, had been altogether too outlandish for her to contemplate.

"They told me there would be great opportunities for sketching." He cast a grim glance at the rain beating down upon the windows. "I'm reserving judgment."

She inched toward the door. "Your relations are acquainted with Lord March?"

"Only slightly. My brother-in-law is arranging to purchase a new strain of the earl's roses for our perfumery in Grasse. Hayes's Perfumes. Perhaps you've heard of us?"

Again, she stilled, her curiosity seeming to get the better of her. "Hayes's Lavender Water?" Her face brightened with a glimmer of recognition. "Is that *you*?"

For once, Teddy was grateful for the negligible fame that his late father's perfume business brought to the family name. "It's partly me. I inherited half of the company when my father died. But it's my sister and brother-in-law who run it. My interests lie elsewhere."

"You're an artist," she said.

"Trying to be one." He paused. "May I ask you an impertinent question?"

She huffed a reluctant laugh. "Haven't you already?"

His smile broadened. "Tell me, Stella—"

Her chin dipped. She shook her head. "Please don't call me that—"

"Tell me, Miss Hobhouse," he amended. "Would you object to my painting you?"

Photo by Vickie Hahn

USA Today bestselling author **Mimi Matthews** writes both historical nonfiction and award-winning Victorian romances. Her novels have received starred reviews in *Library Journal*, *Publishers Weekly*, *Booklist*, and *Kirkus Reviews*, and her articles have been featured on the Victorian Web, the *Journal of Victorian Culture*, and in syndication at *BUST* magazine. In her other life, Mimi is an attorney. She resides in California with her family, which includes a retired Andalusian dressage horse, a Sheltie, and two Siamese cats.

VISIT MIMI MATTHEWS ONLINE

MimiMatthews.com
MimiMatthewsAuthor
MimiMatthewsEsq
MimiMatthewsEsq